Hot Cop

LAURELIN PAIGE
and
SIERRA SIMONE

GW00568947

*everafter*ROMANCE

EverAfter Romance
A Division of Diversion Publishing Corp.
443 Park Avenue South, Suite 1008
New York, New York 10016
www.EverAfterRomance.com

Cover design by Sara Eirew
Editing by Nancy Smay at Evident Ink

For more information, email info@everafterromance.com

First EverAfter Romance edition June 2017.
Print ISBN: 9781682306093

To Kiawah and an alligator named Clive

1

LIVIA

Three hundred and sixty-four days.

That's my first thought when I wake up. I haven't even opened my eyes.

There are three hundred and sixty-four days before doom and destruction come for me in the form of my thirtieth birthday.

Three hundred and sixty-four measly days.

It's not nearly long enough. I'm practically already on my deathbed. I can feel my skin drying out and wrinkling as I lie here. My bones are getting brittle. If I slipped and fell, I'd likely snap a femur. Gone are the days of being carded at nightclubs and bars. Everyone can see I'm a stone's throw away from the grave.

I moan and pull the covers over my head.

I'm twenty-nine, and I've accomplished nothing in my life. The end is looming. I'm almost thirty.

I might as well keep my eyes closed.

Before I can give in to slumber, my phone rings. Curiosity drives me to pick it up. There are only two people who ever call me—my mom and my brother—and neither would ever dare to call so early in the day.

I look at the name on the screen and sigh. If I ignore it, Megan will just call back.

After pushing accept, I put the phone to my ear. "Really? A

phone call? Is your keyboard broken or something?" Because seriously. Who calls instead of texts?

"What?" she asks, confused by my greeting.

Perhaps she hasn't known me long enough to find my fussiness endearing. "Nothing. What's up?"

"Not much. I'm not working with you today, and I wanted to check up on you." It's only been two months since I transferred to Corinth Library, and yet it's been long enough for the extremely nurturing (and extremely extroverted) children's information specialist, Megan Carter, to have taken me under her wing. Though at times she teeters on overbearing, I find I'm quite fond of her. "You seemed a bit down when you left the bar last night. Everything okay?"

"Except for the quickly approaching occasion of my death, I'm great!"

"Oh brother. Drama queen much?"

I throw the covers off and climb out of bed. "Am I, though? Or am I a realist? Facing my inevitable annihilation head on?"

"It doesn't sound like you're facing anything. You're lamenting. Dramatically lamenting. Everyone gets older. Everyone turns thirty. You still have a year before you do. Welcome to life, sister."

I shuffle toward my kitchen as she talks, heading for the Keurig I bought myself as a birthday present. It's been one day, and I'm already in love forever.

"Don't you mean 'welcome to death'?" I put in a pod of southern pecan, push start, and wait for happiness to pour into my *I Am Figuratively Dying for a Cuppa* mug. Seemed to go with the topic of my mortality.

Megan doesn't think the joke is funny. "This is really bothering you, isn't it? Why do you think that is?"

Oh God. I didn't really want to talk about my feelings.

I sigh, a favorite pastime of mine. "I don't know. I'm just missing something. There has to be more than this." From the kitchen, I look around at the two-bedroom condo. I was able to afford the down payment by using the last of my inheritance from Grams, the rest of it having gone to pay for my Humanities and Western Civilization degree at The University of Kansas. My personal book collection is already close to outgrowing the space, but it's been all I've ever needed. Exactly what I've always wanted.

Why does it feel so empty?

"You need a man," Megan says decidedly.

"I don't. That is not what I need." I mean it, too. But I do need *something*.

I run my finger down the edge of the pamphlet that's been hanging on my fridge behind the Rainbow China delivery menu since I visited the fertility clinic last month.

Is this what I need?

The cost for artificial insemination isn't as much as I'd expected. I could swing it if I really tried, even on a librarian's salary. But a nameless father... My mother would go ballistic.

Still. I'm mulling it over.

Now that death is fast approaching, I should probably mull faster.

"You don't even miss sex?" It seems like an innocent question, but from Megan, I'm certain this line of questioning is the kind that will lead to a blind date if I'm not careful.

"My vibrator works just fine," I tell her. "And isn't cocky or conceited and doesn't leave."

"No, it just runs out of batteries."

"I have the rechargeable kind."

"That's not the same. Listen, Livia, I'm going to give you some hard words." But I don't hear what she has to say because a series of beeps covers her speech, indicating I've received a text. Several texts.

I pull the phone away from my face to read the messages.

So I think I'm in trouble.

Like big trouble.

Like really really big trouble & now the cops R here and U might need 2 bring bail cuz my mom's doing a surgery and

dad's delivering a baby & they can't come help me but I did something.

LIVIA.

REMEMBER ME WHEN I WASTE AWAY IN JAIL.

WHAT IF I MISS THE NEXT SEASON OF SKAM?

They're from Ryan, a teen I work with a lot at the library. Now *she's* a legit drama queen.

I put the phone back to my ear. "Hang on a sec, Megan." Then I type Ryan a quick message.

What's going on? BE BRIEF.

She responds with a panoramic picture of what looks to be the parking lot of her high school. I can't make out much of what's going on except there are lots of cars lined up behind her, there's a policeman, and it appears Ryan has chained herself between two trees and has therefore created a barricade across the school driveway.

Today the drama seems to be warranted.

After quickly saying goodbye to Megan, I shoot another text to Ryan.

Be right there.

I throw on some leggings and an oversized T-shirt that maybe should have been in the laundry instead of on the chair in my bedroom. Then I throw my hair into a messy bun and check Ryan's response.

U R the best! Pick up an iced caramel macchiato on your way? Kthnx.

• • •

I don't stop for the iced caramel macchiato.

Traffic seems to be flowing okay when I arrive at Shawnee Mission East, Ryan's high school. I pull my car up to the parking space closest to the commotion and survey the situation before getting out.

As the picture suggested, Ryan's blockade must have been

preventing cars from rounding the circle drive for morning drop off. The chains are gone, but traffic has been diverted to another entrance because she's still standing in the middle of the driveway. She's wearing a gold and purple cheerleading uniform and holding a sign with letters so bold I can read them from here: **Your Impure Thoughts are Not My Problem.**

I'm starting to understand.

Ryan's only fourteen, but she's already a social activist. She rarely misses an opportunity to protest when she feels a person or a group has been wronged. One day she marched outside the library fighting for mothers' rights to breastfeed in public. Another day she joined her church youth group at Civic Hall to protest the taxation of groceries. Once she handed out pamphlets at Crown Center about the plight of the sperm whales. Maybe it's because Kansas City is landlocked, but it turns out people in the Midwest don't care so much about the emotions of large sea creatures.

Maybe that's just me.

But I do care a lot about the emotions of this fiercely passionate girl. She's well-meaning and big-hearted. Whatever trouble she's gotten herself into, I hope I can help her out of it.

I chug the last of my southern pecan coffee—I'm so glad I thought to bring it with me (I'm going to need the caffeine)—and step out of my car. Immediately I hear Ryan.

"Do I give you impure thoughts?" she shouts to a group of tardy students as they hurry toward the school. "Do I?"

Oh dear.

Though class has surely started, there is a small crowd gathered near her. Several adult women are there—probably administrators—a couple of teenage girls, and a police officer.

I head toward them.

The cop is talking with one of the adults as I approach, his back to me.

"You're strong enough to pick her up," the woman tells him. "I can tell you work out." She's flirting so hard I can hear it from yards away.

"CrossFit," the cop says with a shrug. "Five days a week."

God, he's one of those. Cocky. Conceited. Cop-like. I know the type. I brace myself for our upcoming interaction.

"It's completely obvious," the flirter continues. "Why don't you just move her yourself? Carry her fireman style." She's good at this. She has black hair, pasty white skin that is so unnatural it had to have been applied, and red, red lips. I have a feeling seduction is her primary hobby, if not a part-time job.

"I can't touch a female minor—it's against department policy. We'll have to wait for the woman officer dispatch is sending over. But I appreciate the use of the bolt cutters."

Bolt cutters. So that's how they dealt with the chains. Now that I look, I can actually see a pool of silver links by the tree on this side of the road.

Ryan, Ryan, Ryan. What did you do?

Patiently, I stand behind the cop waiting for a good time to interrupt.

"I'm not a minor," one of the teenagers says, twirling a long piece of dirty blond hair between her fingers. "I'm eighteen. You could touch me, Officer Kelly."

…and this seems to be the moment.

"Pardon me," I say in my librarian (aka friendly but assertive) voice. "What's going on?"

When she hears me, Ryan spins in my direction. "Livia!" She almost runs to me then seems to remember she's not budging on purpose. "Hey, where's my Starbucks?"

I throw a stern glance at her then shift my eyes back just as the cop turns around.

And then I understand what all the fuss is about.

He's hot.

Like, I-forgot-what-I-was-going-to-say hot.

I-should-have-shaved-my-legs hot.

Here's-my-panties-sorry-they're-so-wet hot.

I'm not even sure exactly what it is about him. His body? His closely trimmed beard? His sober expression?

The oversexed Snow White wasn't exaggerating when she said he obviously works out. His thick arms fill out his sleeves, and even with all his gear on, I can tell his shoulders are broad and his waist is trim. He's not just fit—he's mega fit. He's, like, can-I-touch-your-guns fit, and I've never thought in my life I'd use the word guns to refer to a guy's muscles, but it's appropriate.

And yet, as hot as his bod is, it's his face that has my heart stuttering. His cheeks and jaw are chiseled, the jut of his chin almost hidden by his beard. His nose is straight and strong, and, then, damn. The pièce de résistance are his aviator sunglasses, which make him look like sex in a blue uniform.

It's possible I need to go lie down.

"And you are?" Officer Too-Hot-To-Remember-The-Name-I-Just-Heard-Him-Called asks.

"I'm…here," I say because I can't seem to find the answer to his question when he's staring at me, and I can *feel* that he is, even behind those metallic lenses.

"Yes. You are." He almost smiles, and I have a feeling that isn't something he does on the job all too often. He's much too solemn. Too professional. Too all about the facts and nothing but the facts, and holy Jesus I'm happy to provide him with whatever facts he wants.

Just as soon as I remember what facts are.

"That's Livia," Ryan chirps behind us, reminding me of that specific fact. "She's here for me!"

Bolstered by this bit of information that I can give with confidence, I proudly say, "That's right. I'm Livia. Livia Ward."

With both hands on his duty belt, the cop looks from me to Ryan and back to me again. "Are you her…mother?"

"No!" I gasp, completely horrified. "Oh my God, do I look old enough to be her mother?" I *knew* I should have started using wrinkle cream at twenty-five. "She's fourteen! I'm not old enough to have a fourteen-year-old daughter."

"Her mother's been called," one of the women says from behind him. "And her father. Both were unavailable."

I purse my lips as though I've proved some kind of point.

The cop, who hasn't taken his focus off of me, simply says, "It's my job to ask, ma'am."

I cringe. "Don't call me ma'am." As an afterthought, I add, "Please."

There's no response from Officer Solemn.

Silently, I continue to fume.

The one fortunate side effect of the humiliating reminder that I'm aging (and apparently not so gracefully) is that it's knocked me out of the this-cop's-too-hot-to-think stupor. "I'm her friend," I tell him. "I work with her at the library. She texted me when she thought she might be in trouble."

The cop—Officer Kelly I remember now—looks at me sternly, his expression giving nothing away. "Do you have some identification on you?"

"Does it look like I have identification on me?" I don't have any pockets, and I'm not carrying a purse. In fact, I think I might have left so fast that I didn't even throw it in the car. *Shit.* Just what I need. A ticket for driving without a license. "Do I need my ID?"

He looks me over from head to toe. I wish I could see his eyes so I could have an idea of what he's thinking. "No, I suppose not."

"Good." I relax enough to get in a decent breath. "Then we can deal with the matter at hand. What exactly is happening?"

"Well, as you can see, the minor—"

"Ryan Alley. She has a name." I can already tell Ryan's going to be in trouble. Officer Kelly doesn't seem like the kind of guy to let something slide. Maybe if he sees her as a person instead of just "the minor," he'll give her a break.

"The minor," he continues as if I didn't say a word, "chained herself in between these two trees on either side of the school's driveway, thereby causing a traffic jam at this morning's drop off. We've cut the chains with bolt cutters procured from the school office by the attendance secretary—"

"That's me! I found them!"

Great. Oversexed Snow White's a hero.

He turns toward the woman and nods appreciatively with just enough smile to send a blush crawling up her face.

His smile is actually killer. I almost wish I'd brought bolt cutters just so he'd give it to me.

Officer Kelly returns his attention to me. "But the minor has refused to move. We're waiting for backup to proceed."

I shoot another look at Ryan. *Refused to move? Are you kidding me?*

Of course she can't read my mind, but she gets the gist and she shrugs.

"How much trouble is she going to be in?" I ask the cop, softer now that I realize I have nothing to bargain with.

"We can talk about that once we resolve our situation here."

I rock my weight to one hip, talking as I think. "If I can talk her out of this…get her back into the school before anyone else gets here…would that make a difference?"

"It's not just up to me." He turns to look at the group behind him.

As if he's beckoned her, one of the women walks over to us—not the flirty attendance secretary, but the one who called Ryan's parents. "Hi, I'm Sharie Holden, the principal here. Thank you for coming. We'd love to be able to work this out with as little excitement as possible." She whispers the last part of her sentence, as though that will automatically minimize the drama of the situation.

At least she seems like an easier pushover than Officer No Nonsense. "Will there be any consequences if I make that happen?" I ask.

"I can't let her actions go completely unpunished. Half of the school saw what she did here today. I can't let that slide."

"You're right," I say with a tone that says I clearly disagree. "In fact, how about I call Channel Nine and have them cover the protest so far? Make sure no one misses it when they drag her away in handcuffs later too? Ryan can even make a statement. Sound good, Ryan?"

"Yes! Statement!" She bounces on the balls of her feet. "I already have one prepared!"

The color drains from Sharie Holden's face. "On second thought, I think we could probably get away with just a warning. If you can get her back in class without any press finding out, that is."

"Okay, okay." I feel good about this. Ryan and I have a bond. She might not listen to reason, but she'll listen to me. "What is she protesting?"

Ryan pipes up in answer. "This stupid school has banned cheer uniforms on game days. Cheer uniforms! Because some boy complained it made him think impure thoughts. As if women are to blame for what men think. It's ridiculously unfair. I cry rape culture! I cry injustice!"

"Why does she even care?" the blond teen says.

"Right?" her friend replies. "She's not even a cheerleader."

"I'm a cheerleader, Officer Kelly," the first one calls to him.

"Of course you are," he mutters under his breath, and I almost feel sorry for him.

Almost.

"It's only during the school day, Ryan," Principal Holden says. "They can still wear their uniforms at the games."

"That's not even the point!" Ryan groans.

I have to stop myself from groaning with her. "You really banned the cheerleaders from wearing their uniforms because a boy complained of impure thoughts?" I ask incredulously. "I hate to tell you this, but teenage boys are going to have impure thoughts no matter what girls are wearing."

"She's not wrong there," Officer Kelly admits.

"Certainly." Her smile is tight. Fake. The kind of smile that accompanies a lecture. "But we believe in respectful behavior at our school, Ms. Ward. We surely aren't going to encourage objectification of women."

Irritation starts to bubble in my chest.

Don't do it, Liv. Don't do it.

But I do it anyway. I argue. "Objectification is a whole other topic. Right now you are putting the blame of what men think—and by extension, what men do—on what women wear. This is old rhetoric, Ms. Holden. Aren't we past this?"

The fake smile is gone. She's barely even pretending to be nice now. "I appreciate your opinion, but since you don't have children enrolled in our school, it doesn't really count for anything."

That does it. I'm past irritation. Now I'm outraged.

"Actually, since I'm a taxpayer and this is a public school, my opinion does count. And because this is America where there's still freedom of speech—" And since actions speak louder than words, I end my rant abruptly and march over to Ryan.

Taking her sign, I hold it up proudly.

Ryan breaks into a grin and resumes her protest. "Do I give you impure thoughts?" she shouts to someone walking his dog along the school grounds.

"Oh, come on," Principal Holden complains loudly.

Officer Kelly sighs and saunters toward us.

"Do I give you impure thoughts?" Ryan yells in his direction.

He ignores her, unfazed.

When he's near me, *really* near me, so close I can feel the heat radiating off his body, he stops and says in a low voice that I'm sure only I can hear, "Now if *you* were wearing that outfit, the answer would be a definite yes."

My head twists toward him. "What did you say?"

"You aren't helping things," he says louder.

"That's not what you said," I say, quieter. Because I want to hear the other thing he said again. Want to feel the shiver down my spine at the thought of him thinking those things—*impure* things—about me.

He doesn't repeat it. Doesn't acknowledge it. He holds his palm out toward me instead. "Hand me the sign."

My grip tightens on the handle. "I'm helping *her*."

"Are you? It's my impression that you want this whole thing resolved with the least amount of damage to her record. Am I right?"

Oh, God. His smirk is incredible. I can't look directly at it.

"Keep talking," I say, but he's already said enough. I know what I need to do. I just like the way his voice sounds, the way it rumbles in his chest when he lowers it so that Ryan won't hear what we're saying.

"Get her to class, and I'll make sure there aren't any consequences for obstructing traffic."

This isn't like him. I know it's not. He's not the type to let charges go. He's about order. He's about the law. So why's he doing it? I'm wary.

But I can't take my eyes off him. I'm transfixed, under his spell.

I hand him the sign.

He gives another hint of a real smile, this time it's all for me, and my knees practically buckle beneath me.

If I look at him a moment longer I might actually, literally faint.

I spin and grab Ryan's arm for support, pretending I meant to simply get her attention.

"Ryan—" I say.

"You're going to tell me to stop this, aren't you?" She pulls away, and I just manage to catch my balance. "Well, I won't. I won't stop fighting for women. I won't stop fighting against injustice."

I cross around to face her. "Of course I'm not going to tell you to stop fighting. I'd never tell you that. Haven't I always encouraged you to speak your mind whether it be through words or action?"

She narrows her eyes, unsure whether or not to trust me. "Maybe."

"I'm encouraging the same thing now. Just, there are sometimes better ways to be heard. Look." I gesture to the few people standing around her. "This is a very small crowd. You'd have much better reach if you took the matter to the next school board meeting where you could actually effect change. Don't you think?"

She twists her lips as she considers.

"Those aren't even our uniforms," the cheerleader shouts randomly from the side of the driveway.

I lean in toward Ryan and whisper, "Also, it doesn't seem like the women you're fighting for are very appreciative of your efforts."

She puts an arm around my shoulder. "They just haven't been woken yet, Liv."

"I don't think this is what's going to wake them."

She throws her head back in frustration and groans. Then, suddenly, as if she hadn't been completely ready to march to Washington on behalf of the cause, she shrugs and says, "Okay. I should get to second hour anyway. American history. We're watching a documentary about suffragettes."

She removes the remains of the chains that I notice now are still on each of her arms and hands them to me. Then she strolls toward the school building.

"Where's she going?" Principal Holden asks me anxiously.

"To class!" I announce smugly.

"Not dressed like that! There're no cheerleading uniforms in school!" She marches after Ryan, urging the rest of the administration to follow as well.

"She has a change of clothes," I tell no one in particular. "I hope." Man, being someone's mentor is a tough job. It might require more caffeine than one K-cup pod.

"Officer Kelly, I'm only sixteen," the cheerleader's friend calls over to him, "but that's the age of consent in Kansas."

"I'm frightened that you know that," I say.

"Go to class before I fine you both for truancy," Officer Kelly says, but not before I hear him let out a soft chuckle at my comment.

"What's truancy?" the two girls ask in unison.

"Oh my God," I roar, "you need to go to school."

They scurry off, and though I'd like to take credit, it's probably more likely because the bell has just rung.

And now everyone's gone but me. And the cop.

The very hot cop.

It suddenly feels harder to get air in my lungs than it did just a second before.

"Nice job with her," the cop says, nodding his head in praise. "Maybe you can help keep her out of trouble in the future."

I bristle. "Just because she's passionate doesn't mean she's going to get in trouble in the future." It's really his compliment that's bothering me. I'm bothered by how it made me feel. How it made me feel good.

"Right," he says, and I swear he's thinking things about me that would make me die a thousand deaths if I were to find them out.

I frown, feeling awkward. "Well. Anyway."

I should thank him, but he speaks first. "Have dinner with me."

"What? Dinner? Why?" That wasn't at all the kind of thoughts I hoped he was thinking about me. Not at all the kind of thoughts I want him to be thinking about me, yet my stomach flutters anyway, like it's a good thing. Stupid stomach.

"Because in the evening I get hungry, and I find that eating a meal tends to make that hunger go away." He's completely straight-faced, and it's so sexy I'm not sure I can stand it.

I look down, away from his fuck-hot jaw and his fuck-hot lips. "You don't need me for that."

"Eating alone is lonely."

But I can't escape that fuck-hot voice. My skin is on fire even in the cool spring wind. "I'm sure what's-her-name from attendance would be glad to join you for dinner."

"I'm not asking her. I'm asking you."

I look up at him, and my heart trips. Even behind those glasses, I can tell he can't take his gaze off me. Goose bumps skim down my arms.

Dinner. I eat dinner. I could eat dinner with him. What would be wrong with that?

If I could see his eyes, I'm sure I'd have said yes by now.

I might say yes anyway.

"Heya, Officer Kelly." Apparently the attendance secretary didn't go inside after all. He turns toward the vampire—I swear, she hasn't seen the sun in a decade. "I left a sticky with my number on your motorcycle. Call me sometime."

Officer Kelly makes a non-committal noise. But then adds, "Thank you again for the bolt cutters."

Vampire secretary simpers at him. "It was no trouble, really."

I don't listen closely to the rest of their exchange because without his attention on me, I can think again, and I suddenly remember what would be wrong with dinner and why I absolutely do not want to go out with Officer-I've-already-stolen-your-panties-Kelly.

Because he's a man.

And men leave.

Especially this type of man—the type with the confident smile and the tight-fitting uniform. (Seriously, the way his ass fills out those pants...)

There's always a woman waiting in the wings for a hot cop like him. A flock of them, even. In a place like Kansas, he's the closest thing we have to a rock star. He could have anyone he wants. He doesn't need to try to bang the hippy librarian driving the Prius with a Black Lives Matter bumper sticker and NPR playing on her radio. We're oil and water. He's the type who has a reputation. I'm the type who'd show up with a sign and protest it.

Without giving him a response or even a goodbye, I take off. I bet I'm already at my car before he even notices I slipped away.

2

CHASE

"Every year, I think I won't have to come up here and tell you this, but then every year, here I am."

The sound of the HR director's tired voice echoes through the large meeting room at our city hall. There's a cough, the sound of someone behind me discreetly trying to eat something crunchy out of a plastic bag, the whir of a ceiling fan overhead.

The HR director sighs heavily, his shoulders slumping, and gestures to the PowerPoint slide behind him. The slide reads:

Don't have sex on duty.

"That's it," the director says, a touch mournfully. "That's all there is to it. Don't have sex in your police car. Don't have sex in uniform. Don't pretend to do a business check at Arby's and then have sex in the Arby's bathroom. Just don't do it. Because then I have to fire you, and it's so much paperwork for me, and then I have to climb back up here *next* year and beg you not to do it again. Please don't make me."

There are a few awkward laughs, a few sly shoulder nudges. Everyone remembers last Christmas, when Captain Knust caught Zach Simmons doling out a little extra Christmas cheer in the backseat of his patrol car. To the Captain's college-aged daughter.

Or the year before that, when Mike Fox and his wife wanted to act out some role play and Fox's mic button got stuck, which meant everyone on duty heard him say, "Now that's the long arm of the law!" right as he came.

Who would be dumb enough to do that shit? I think to myself. Aside from the fact that the backseats of most patrol cars are cramped vinyl shells that have been puked on, pissed on and worse—it's against the rules, and I don't break rules.

Rules are good. Rules are there for a reason. It's my job to protect those rules and make sure everyone else follows them. That satisfies something deep down inside me—not like a hunger for power or anything—but it's the same feeling I get when all the weights are in order at the gym or when my house is clean and my lawn is mowed. Clean and neat, everything in its place.

I do law so that there can be order.

I think of that kid today, though, definitely *out* of order and creating massive snarls of traffic trying to get out of the parking lot during the morning drop off. There were three fender-benders, one verbal altercation between a dad and a vice principal, and Officer LaTasha Palmer had to issue a property damage citation because one impatient mom had driven up over the curb and crashed into the school fence.

It was pure chaos—*unnecessary* chaos—and then the most exquisite woman I've ever seen marched right up to me in skintight leggings and flip-flops and started creating *more* chaos. Normally I wouldn't have welcomed yet another upset adult demanding answers and action while I tried to sort out the mess, but the thing was, I kind of felt for the kid. She reminded me of my sister—in fact, I couldn't be sure Megan *hadn't* chained herself to school property at one point—and it was almost a relief when Livia appeared and started defending her. Because I didn't want the teen to get into trouble...I just had to make sure the parking lot exit was cleared so cars would stop crashing into each other.

So I was glad the teen had someone there for her. And it didn't hurt that Livia wore those tight, tight leggings, which showed off every curve of her sweet thighs and scrumptious ass. Even the

T-shirt she wore had been accidentally sexy, the thin fabric revealing a cute pink bra when she stood directly under the spring sun...

My dick stirs in my pants thinking about it, just as it did this morning when I looked at her. God, I'd wanted to pull her hair out of that adorably sloppy knot and twine my fingers in it, wanted to bend her over the hood of my car and run my greedy hands all over her body. I wanted her in the kind of hungry, urgent way I haven't wanted a woman in a long time.

I have to find her again.

She never gave me a real answer about dinner, after all.

The dispirited voice of the HR director brings me back to the present, and I listen as he describes more ways we can't have sex on duty. Although now I'm wondering less *who would do that* and more if *I* would do it, given the right woman. Like, say, a brown-eyed spitfire with leggings and the kind of face they model Disney princesses after.

The HR director wraps up his speech and leaves the room with the defeated air of a man who knows he'll be back to give the same speech again next year. The chief takes the low stage at the front of the room, giving us all a quick smile as he adjusts the microphone.

"Thank you for that policy refresher, Eric," he says to the director's retreating back. "And even though I know it's not normally how we do things, I thought I'd take the opportunity to open the floor to any questions you might have for me. No chain of command, no formality—just ask and I'll answer."

A ripple of interest goes through the room of bored officers. Our new chief has been pretty invisible for the most part, hiding out in meetings or in his office, and so having the chance to talk to him directly is unexpected.

But not unwelcome...

I shoot a glance over at my sergeant, Theresa Gutierrez, who is already raising her eyebrow in a *well, are you going to do it or am I?* look.

I stick my hand in the hair.

The chief smiles and points at me, the two quick blinks before saying, "Officer?" telling me that he doesn't know my name.

"Hi, yeah," I say, suddenly aware that all the eyes in the room are on me. I think of Livia this morning, all bravery and determination in her flip-flops and messy bun. I think she'd approve of me right now, and for some reason that sends a little glow through my chest. "I was the head of the body camera committee last year, and we submitted a recommendation for the department to purchase the cameras for every officer working the field as soon as possible. I was wondering where we were on that?"

There's a sudden tension in the air. Not only had I coupled the committee's recommendation with a detailed budget analysis and cost breakdown by manufacturer, but I'd also done a department-wide poll and found that over seventy percent of the field officers *wanted* body cameras. But even though I'd done all the research legwork, even though most the cops here want the upgrade, the administration keeps stonewalling us.

The chief's smile has frozen into something that can only be described as irritated politeness. "I believe there was a memo sent out last month that addressed this very concern."

"With all due respect, sir, it didn't address anything. It just said that the department was still considering all their options. But we," I gestured around the room, "think that this issue is important enough that we need to have it resolved now."

There are nods and murmurs of agreement around me. The chief lets the forced smile slip a bit. "With all due respect back to you, Officer, this decision is a bit above your pay grade. And while I appreciate your passion for it, I ask that you appreciate the complicated budgetary nature of such a purchase, not to mention the statements made by many citizens concerned with privacy. It's not a decision to be made in haste."

"It's been over a year since the recommendation, sir. I don't think you have to worry about haste anymore."

I shouldn't have said it, I know that the moment the words leave my mouth. It's easily insubordination, something I could be written up for, and by the way the chief's eyes narrow, I wonder if he is really considering it.

"I'm sure what Officer Kelly means," Sergeant Gutierrez cuts in smoothly, "is that most of the other agencies in the Kansas City metro already have body cameras built into their budgets in the coming years. If we're not careful, our city could be the only one still using outdated policing standards."

"I just want to make sure we're serving and protecting our citizens to the best of our ability," I add to my supervisor's remarks.

The chief smiles again, a mechanical smile. We've got him trapped and he knows it, because in a room full of street officers, the chief can't admit he cares more about preserving admin salary perks than spending money on citizen and officer safety.

"Duly noted," he says after a minute. "I'll make sure to check on the status of the cameras today and send out another depart-ment-wide memo."

"Thank you, sir," I say. It's not what I wanted, but it's not a total loss either. Like Livia and her teen friend, I live to fight another day.

· · ·

"Son, you've got to cut that out."

I look over from the couch I'm sprawled on to Pop's chair, where Pop is drinking his third—or maybe seventh—cup of coffee for the day and searching for the volume on the remote so he can turn up the sound on the HGTV show he's watching. Pop has two passions in his twilight years: shows about buying houses and bad coffee. The first means that he's always fussing around outside in the quest for maximum curb appeal, even though he has no plans to sell the place, and the second means that our house always smells like the inside of a diner.

Yes, *our* house. I live with my grandpa.

It's a long story.

"What do I have to cut out?" I ask with a sigh.

"That. That right there—all this sighing. I can't hear these idiots arguing about which tiny house to buy over all your mooning."

"I'm not...*moon*ing, whatever that means."

Okay, well maybe I have been mooning a little. I'm not normally the type to flop around on the couch on my day off—not when there are baristas to flirt with and some pavement to pound on my daily run. But I've already pounded seven miles of pavement *and* hit the gym, and I still haven't shaken off this funk. It's partly the meeting from yesterday—this body camera issue giving me the itchy feeling of work left unfinished, which I hate—but it's partly something else.

Someone else.

The someone else being the reason I didn't flirt with any baristas this morning or answer the texts I got last night from my latest crop of badge bunnies.

Livia Ward.

I couldn't take my eyes off her, and now, a full twenty-four hours later, it's like she's still in front of me, blocking my vision of everything else.

I have to have her. Dinner, drinks, handcuffs—the Kelly Trio—and I need it all, the whole works, probably at least two or three times. Maybe then I can start thinking like a normal human being again.

Pop takes a sip of coffee and puts it next to his iPad mini, which is only used for mah jong and some game called Ant Smasher. Then he folds his knobbled hands over his belly and levels a *cut-the-bullshit* stare at me. I call it the Vietnam look. It's a look that says, *I was in a fucking war...you think you can pull one over on me?*

"Son," Pop says, still giving me the Vietnam look. "You've been sighing all morning. You sighed before the gym. You came back and sighed after the gym. Now you're even sighing at the tiny houses, which don't deserve any guff from you. Is it a woman? Did you meet a woman?"

"I meet lots of women, Pop."

"I'm not talking about the women you pick up going quail hunting."

"Quail hunting?"

Pop rolls his eyes. "Hunting for chicks! Finding a bird! I thought your generation was supposed to be smart!"

I blink at him.

"My point is, you don't sigh over those women, ever. So this woman must be special."

Special.

I think back to Livia's thick hair, the color of coffee after a dash of cream; I think back to her skin, smooth and clear and the color of very light amber. I think of the way she faced down the swarms of teachers and me to protect her friend. And I think of those leggings, so tight and so flimsy—flimsy enough I could rip them apart with my bare hands to get to that perfect ass underneath...

Yeah, Livia is something special all right.

"Chase, my boy, you're mooning again."

"Okay, okay," I admit. "There was a woman yesterday on a call. And she was beautiful and feisty and—" I search for the right word. "Fragile?"

Pop shakes his head at me. "Now, don't you go saving some damsel just because you think she's in distress. She probably doesn't need saving, especially from the likes of you."

The doorbell rings once, then four more times in rapid succession, as if someone is really excited about the opportunity to ring a doorbell. And I know exactly who that somebody is.

I swing my legs off the couch and stand as I ask Pop, "From the likes of me? I'm a police officer. Saving damsels is in the job description."

"I don't mean as a police officer. I mean as a man who likes to go quail hunting."

I open the front door as I mumble, "I still don't get what quail hunting means."

My brother-in-law, Phil, stands in front of me holding one

26

very sleepy toddler and the hand of one very bouncy four-year-old, who is almost certainly the manic doorbell ringer.

"Ah, 'quail hunting,'" Phil says, dragging his sons over the threshold. "A beatnik slang term for dating, or more specifically, searching for women to date."

"See? You're the only one who doesn't know what it means, Chase," says Pop from the living room. My oldest nephew, Keon, runs right up to his chair and clambers on top of Pop's belly. He immediately grabs for Pop's iPad.

"Ant Smasher," he demands seriously.

At the mention of Ant Smasher, my other nephew, Josiah, lifts up his head from his father's shoulder. He squirms down silently, his binky firmly in his mouth and his stuffed cow in his fist, and he also makes his way over to Pop's chair. Soon the two boys are arranged happily with the iPad balanced on Pop's belly between them, and Pop is even happier snuggling with his great-grandsons and cradling their curly heads in his spotted and gnarled hands.

I turn back to Phil, holding my hand out for Josiah's diaper bag. "Nice one with the quail hunting," I tease.

He grins. "It's cheating a bit, since both my sections this semester are on mid-century American lit. I've been reading nothing but beat poets for the last three weeks."

Phil teaches American Lit at the University of Missouri at Kansas City, and Thursdays are the days that both he and my sister work evenings, which means Thursdays are my days to watch my nephews. Those boys are everything to me, feisty, dimpled, squirmy balls of everything, and I would do anything for them. Which doesn't just mean being the best Uncle Chase I can be, but also the best Officer Kelly.

You see, Phil is black. Which means my nephews are black. Which means this has been an occasionally uncomfortable few years for our family, with me also being a police officer.

But I'm working on it, on learning and listening. Phil helped me write up my body camera proposal for the department, and I've gone out to his classes to talk about the nuts and bolts of policing. There've been hard parts, hard conversations, and there's still so much I don't know, but as a family, we keep trying. For Megan—my sister and Phil's wife. For Keon and Josiah, who are currently squealing over the dead ants on the iPad and making Pop chuckle as they wrestle to smash the virtual bugs.

Phil gives Pop a handshake and then gives me a quick inventory of the diaper bag as we walk back to the door. "JoJo only wants grapes today, but if Megan asks, he had veggies and protein too. She's on a food pyramid thing lately."

"Got it. And if she catches me lying, I'm blaming it on you."

Phil shakes his head. "Grown man's afraid of his baby sister."

"Have you met her? Of course I'm afraid of her."

After a pause, Phil admits with a smile, "I'm afraid of her too."

After my brother-in-law leaves, I stand for a minute in the doorway, thinking about my sister again. When Phil said her name, a little bubble of a thought had emerged…a bubble with dark eyes and leggings…

Livia said her teen was someone she worked with at the library—did that mean she worked *at* the library? Surely not—Megan has been working there for years, there's no way I wouldn't have noticed Livia before.

So maybe she's actually a tutor? I know lots of local tutors met up with their students at the library. Or maybe a volunteer?

Megan will know, I decide. Megan knows every coworker, volunteer, and patron that enters her domain. And especially someone like Livia, all fired up and ready to fight with the police and the school and anyone else she has to.

I grin to myself, remembering her waving that sign in the air. I wonder if she'll be that fired up in my bed—and there's no doubt in my mind that she *will* be in my bed. I'm Chase Kelly, man. I always get the women I want…and I get them fast and easy. It's time to shake off my funk about this body camera drama at the department and get my head back into the game.

My favorite game.

I grab my wallet and phone, glance in the mirror at my jeans and Captain America T-shirt, and then, like the sexy badass I am, shoulder the diaper bag and drag the Red Flyer wagon out of the garage. I walk back inside to my nephews, prepared to bribe them with promises of grapes and as many picture books as they can carry.

"Who wants to walk down to see Mommy at work?"

3

LIVIA

"It happened again?" Megan half asks, half exclaims.

"Yep," I stage whisper. The children's section of the library is quiet tonight, but this is the kind of conversation that would be particularly bad if an overprotective parent overheard. "Watching a Logan O'Toole video. This time I caught the guy in the act."

"You mean, he was actually—?" She holds up her hand to make sure no patrons can see her and makes a motion as though she's jerking off.

I nod. It's the third time in a month I've caught someone using the library computers for VPU—Very Personal Use—and though I should be used to it by now, I still continue to be astonished every time.

"What did you say?" Megan's eyes are wide. So far this has been the only bit of excitement on an otherwise slow night. As the children's specialist, she doesn't generally have to deal with the VPUs anyway, which makes the tale extra enthralling. She did, however, once have a flasher—an old man in a trench coat, stocking cap, and white knee socks who loosened his belt in the middle of a story time reading of *Brown Bear, Brown Bear, What Do You See?*

"Trust me," Megan says every time she recounts the story, "Brown Bear didn't see much."

Though I've seen many VPUs in my day, tonight has been

the first time I've actually caught a man with his Personal Item in hand. I'm still a bit stunned, but I think I did well in the moment. "I told him, 'Sir, these computers are for public use and the viewing of pornography is strictly prohibited. Please kindly log off and leave the library.' Then I handed him a box of Kleenex and walked away."

Megan laughs, clapping her hand over her mouth when she realizes she's been a tad too loud. "Lysol that computer down. Then spray it with bleach. And tell me which one it is so I can make sure to never use it myself."

"It doesn't matter if I tell you which one it is. They've all been used for that purpose at some point, I'm sure! Men are disgusting!"

I lean across her desk and prop my chin up with my hand. I'm still getting to know her, but I've already learned a few things about her. I've met her husband and two boys a couple of times, and I've heard her mention her only sibling is a brother. "You're surrounded by them. How do you manage with all that testosterone?"

She shrugs as she goes back to cutting out shapes from colored paper for an upcoming children's program. "I grew up with just my Pop and my brother. Guys are all I know." She cocks her head and looks at me. "Do you really hate men that much?"

I stand up, affronted. "I don't hate men at all! I don't hate kangaroos either, but I'd probably have better luck at getting one to stick around."

"That's a stupid analogy. Where the hell are you going to find a kangaroo in Kansas? You just haven't found the right guy yet. The right guy will stick around. Look at Phil."

She's missing the point, which is that it would be just as hard to find a decent man as it would be to find a kangaroo. It's why I've stopped looking.

It's a hard point to explain without sounding like a quitter. Or asexual.

But I like Megan, so I try anyway. "You didn't know Phil was the right guy until you gave him a chance to be the wrong guy, did you?"

She pauses her cutting, and for a moment I worry she's going to tell me she knew it was love at first sight. After a beat, she says, "I guess not. No."

"Right," I say, as though I've just gotten a Bingo. "And I don't want to do that. I don't want to not know. I don't want the uncertainty part. I'm done giving chances."

She opens her mouth, and I sense a rebuttal coming, but I don't need to hear it. I've made up my mind on this. So I jump in before she gets the chance. "Look. I've had three serious boyfriends. Not as many as some, but enough to learn that relationships are like playing roulette—odds are, the ball isn't going to land on your number. You got lucky with Phil. But how many times did the ball land somewhere else before Phil landed on you?"

She doesn't bother to hide her smirk. "I don't know. Phil landed on me pretty quickly."

I run two fingers over my forehead and sigh. "I didn't mean…"

"I know what you meant," she huffs. "That's how life works, Liv. You don't get anything good without risk."

I can tell by her tone that she's annoyed with me, and I hate it when people are annoyed with me. So much that, if I hadn't *just* turned twenty-nine, I'd tell her she was right (even though she clearly isn't, in my case.)

But since I am now on the path to death, I feel bolder about the things I believe in and this point is one I believe in particularly strongly. "I prefer living without that heartache, thank you very much. I like the safety zone. Maybe the returns aren't as exciting, but I know what I'm getting."

Megan's jaw tightens into a frown. "Let me guess—you don't like going to Vegas either."

"Ew. No." I shudder.

She shakes her head, unable to solve the mystery that is me. "Well, if you're happy in your career, happy in your home, and you don't want a man, I don't know what you're missing. Maybe you need a dog."

Her eyes light up, and I turn to follow her line of vision and see Keon, Megan's oldest son running toward us. Behind him, Josiah, her youngest, toddles after his brother. He barely manages to cross the distance without tripping over his feet, his stuffed cow flapping at his side as he waves his arms for balance, and my chest fills and tightens with the overwhelming cuteness. Is this what they mean by ovaries exploding?

"Yeah, something like that," I reply, with no intention of getting a dog. But something. For sure.

Josiah coos behind his binky as he nears his mom, and I'm grinning ear-to-ear when my eyes casually drift to meet those of the man who is following behind the boys. I'd expected it to be Phil, and so I'm surprised when it's not.

Then I'm shocked when I realize who it is instead.

Officer Panty-Thief Kelly.

Officer I'm-Sexy-in-Blue-Jeans-Too Kelly.

Officer I'm-Not-Wearing-My-Sunglasses-and-Now-You-Must-Drown-in-My-Eyes Kelly. His blue, blue eyes. They're pools of cobalt, and I forget to blink when I look into them. Forget how to breathe. Forget how to look away.

Now *this* is what they mean by ovaries exploding. Mine are exploding. They've exploded. *Kaboom.* His manly aura has sent signals to my baby-makers and caused instant combustion. That's how hot this man is. And he's not even in his uniform.

Imagine him not in anything at all...

Bad idea, bad idea. My knees buckle, and I have to grip the counter. I will him into his clothes again in my mind, but not before imagining the washboard abs he's barely hiding under that tight T-shirt.

Oh God. I'm woozy. Too woozy to even question why he's here.

Thank god for Megan.

"Let me guess," she says, gesturing with her scissors toward the diaper bag that I now notice is slung over Officer Kelly's shoulder. "Phil forgot to pack something." However impossible, she seems completely unaffected by the cop's magic manliness and super-blue death pools.

Also, she's familiar with him. Which is a good thing since it seems he's the one who brought her kids.

I'm not usually this slow. It's just. That body. That beard. Those eyes.

Speaking of those eyes...they dart over in my direction, sending sparks shooting like fireworks throughout my body, then return to Megan. "No, everything's there. Kids wanted to pick out a book." He picks up Josiah who goes easily into the cop's arms. "Didn't we, buddy?"

Josiah grins and makes an *mmm* sound behind his binky, kicking excitedly.

"Unca Chase pulled us in the wagon," Keon says, tip-toeing so he can see over the edge of the reference desk. "He said we can fill it with all the books!"

"Only five each!" Megan says in a rush. "Which is plenty!"

"Aw, that's hardly any," Officer Kelly says, triggering another elated burst from Josiah.

Keon mimics the man. "That's hardly any."

Megan seems about to argue but then glances down at her little boy's anticipating face. "Yeah, well if any of them get lost, it's on you," she says threateningly to the cop.

And all I can think is how insane it is that a woman can *talk* to such a gorgeous man—let alone *threaten* him—when I can barely stand in his presence, especially now that he's cuddling and cooing at these kids like he's shooting one of those charity calendars where the hot cops model with adorable children and he's *so freaking hot*, and ah, fuck. There go my ovaries again.

I'd thought about him several times in the day since I'd seen him. Not that I'd *meant* to think about him, but he'd been attractive, and sometimes attractive things can get stuck in the brain the same way a catchy tune can. At least that's what I'd been telling myself.

Problem was, I hadn't been remembering him properly. I'd remembered him hot, but not *this* hot. I hadn't known about the blue eyes and the broad forehead he hid under his cap. I hadn't realized his pecs were this toned underneath his protective vest. I hadn't remembered his perfectly sculpted chestnut hair or the black ink that peeked out under the sleeve of his T-shirt.

"How about we compromise? How high can you count, Keon?" the gorgeous man asks.

"Ten!" Keon says, immediately demonstrating his counting skills by rushing through the numbers at high speed.

"Great. Then pick out ten for you and ten for Josiah. Got it?"

Keon is already running off toward the picture books. The cop puts Josiah on the ground, and my lips break automatically into another smile as I watch him wobble happily after his brother.

When I move my attention away from the kids, I find the cop's eyes waiting for me. My heart skips a beat. Or ten. I'd have Keon count if he hadn't just run off.

"Officer Kelly," I say in greeting. Because I don't know what else to say. Because I have to say *something*. I can't just stand here, combusting under his gaze.

He scans the length of me, slowly, burning every inch of my skin before returning to my eyes. "Ma'am."

"Don't call me ma'am!" I snap, as much upset about the way he makes my belly tighten and my thighs clench as I am about the way he continues to address me. "I'm twenty-nine. I am not a ma'am yet."

"Though Livia believes that thirty is death," Megan snickers, "so you can probably call her ma'am after that."

I press my lips together and pretend I'm not scratching her eyes out in my head.

Suddenly her brows shoot up. "I didn't realize you two knew each other."

"We don't," I say quickly, eager for her to know that I most certainly do not know this very fine-looking man.

She studies me, then Officer Kelly. "Right." She drags the word out, and I'm not sure what she's thinking, but whatever it is, it's not good.

"Ms. Ward was a witness at an incident yesterday," Officer Kelly explains, his eyes never moving from mine.

"Ah, so you haven't been properly introduced." With scissors still in hand, she points first to me while looking at the cop. "This is Livia. She works upstairs with the grown-ups and the teens, and she's cool, so don't be a dick." Sternly, she adds, "You know what I mean."

Then she points to the cop and turns her attention to me. "Chase is my big brother. His nobleness comes off as stern and overprotective sometimes, but he's really a teddy bear."

He scowls. "I'm not. I'm a warrior."

"You wish." She rolls her eyes and returns to cutting out the star that has been dangling from her paper for the past several minutes.

Chase—even his name is sexy—glances toward his nephews, checking up on them, then returns his heated gaze to me.

And I'm just standing here. And no one's saying anything. So there's awkward silence.

At least I consider it awkward because, as far as I'm concerned, any silence between strangers is awkward. Especially when the stranger is six feet of pure sex and it's oozing off of him like a contagion that I'm afraid I'm about to catch—if I haven't gotten it already— and when I do, there's every chance I'll jump on top of the counter behind me, spread my legs, and beg him to come on in.

So obviously I can't let the silence continue.

I put on a smile that exudes more confidence than I feel and turn to my friend. "Megan, you never told me your brother was a hot." *Oh my God. I didn't just say that.*

But I totally did. My face is heated with embarrassment. "A cop! I meant a cop."

I can't look directly at him, but I catch him out of the corner of my eye, grinning like he won the lottery.

Jesus, his grin is like a superpower. I'm instantly wet.

Okay, I was wet before. I have to be honest.

"I guess it hasn't come up in conversation," Megan says, as though she didn't notice my blunder. She sets down her scissors and stares at me point blank. "And of course he's hot. He's related to me."

I didn't think my blush could deepen, but apparently it can because now I feel it down to my toes.

And that's my cue to leave.

"Well, look at that," I squint at the clock on her computer. "My break is over. I have to get back upstairs. Nice meeting you. Again. Officer Kelly. Chase." It's strange saying his name and yet I want to say it over and over. I want to scream it.

I want him to give me a reason to scream it.

What am I thinking? What am I thinking? I meant all those things I said to Megan.

But, God, look at him...

He cranes his neck to check up on the boys who are hidden in between the stacks, and my uterus aches. He's so damn good with them. He's just so damn...good.

I sigh and, with his attention elsewhere, slip around the children's reference desk, and make a quick escape toward the elevator.

I'm inside the car and the doors are closing when a large hand reaches in and stops them. A large sexy hand that can belong to no one other than Chase Kelly. Two seconds later, he's in the car with me.

The elevator is small, and it feels like he takes up all the room. I push the button for the top floor and then step as far to the side as I can. I swear he only spreads out wider. His body grazes mine and goose bumps break out all over my skin. I huff in irritation. Where is he even going? Wasn't he watching the kids?

He doesn't offer an explanation, and I refuse to ask.

Fortunately, the ride is short, and I have work to do. As soon as the doors open, I rush to the cart I'd loaded earlier and start pushing it toward the fiction section. It's slow enough that I'm not needed on the floor where Chase might feel obliged to try to talk and disarm me with his cobalt deathrays. So yeah, I'm planning on hiding in the stacks.

It's a good plan. Problem is, as soon as I start pushing, Chase starts following.

Perhaps it's a coincidence. He could have been heading for fiction. Maybe that's why he came up here—to grab the latest Scandinavian murder book, or no. That's not what he'd read. He'd read epic fantasy, Le Guin or Rothfuss maybe. Or maybe something more in the Neil Gaiman or Terry Pratchett vein. He struck me as the kind of guy who liked his books smart and a little fun.

So I stop and pretend to look at a book on the cart, giving Officer Kelly a chance to pass me by.

Except he stops too.

Goddammit.

Of course he stops.

He probably isn't even a reader because a subscription to *Playboy* online does not count as reading.

With my jaw set, I take a deep breath and force a smile. "Can I help you with something?" I have no idea why my voice sounds as high as it does. Or why my heart is beating as fast as it is. Or how his cheekbones can be as perfect as they are.

"You can, actually," he says, his eyes twinkling.

Aw, Christ on a cupcake, he knows how to twinkle. I let out a string of curse words in my head, including a bunch that I've made up on the spot that are specifically related to how amazingly Chase Kelly fills a pair of jeans.

I'm hopeless. This is hopeless. "Is this library related?" I ask him. "Because if it isn't—"

"I can tag along while you shelve."

"Fine," I say through gritted teeth. I shove the cart harder than I need to, hoping it will alleviate some of my irritation, but if it does, I don't notice. Chase and I are walking side by side now toward the fiction section, and all I'm aware of is the wall of heat between us. It beckons me closer, makes me wonder what it would be like to press up next to him. Makes me wonder what the scratch of his beard would feel like against my cheek.

I push the cart up to the P's, pick up a handful of books, and start looking for their places on the shelf. We're silent at first, and it's killing me, but after what happened downstairs, I'm not saying a word until he does.

He leans back against the bookshelf and crosses his arms over his chest, which causes his biceps to flex, and until now, I had not been aware that arm porn was actually a thing, but apparently it is. In this position I can see his tattoo better. The silhouette of a ram's head is at the bottom and, above that, concentric circles like the bottom half of a bulls-eye, maybe. The rest disappears under his sleeve, leaving me to guess and wonder what it looks like.

I pretend not to notice he's watching me too. It's not like I like it or anything.

Okay, I like it. Hot guy checking me out? How could I not like it?

"So, I'm vetted now," he says eventually.

"Vetted?" I reach for another book, avoiding looking at him directly. "What do you mean?"

Out of the corner of my eye, I see him shrug. "I'm Megan's brother. It means you can go out on a date with me. I'm not some random stranger."

Oh God. The date he'd asked me on. I'd hoped he'd given up on that.

"Being Megan's brother doesn't automatically vet you. You can still be a giant douchebag and share DNA with a good person." Another handful of books and this time I bend down to search for their placement.

"But I'm not a giant douchebag." Is it my imagination, or is he suddenly closer?

I peer up at him. "How do you know for sure? It's hard to be objective when you're both the one doing the judging and the one being judged."

He crouches down beside me, and my heart practically leaps

into my throat. "How about you go on a date with me, and you can tell me if I'm a giant douchebag?"

I mean to let out a mocking laugh, but it comes out sounding more like a giggle. "I'd rather not."

He moves to meet my eyes. "Why would you rather not? You said I was hot."

"I said—" I stare at him, open mouthed, shocked that he'd bring that up. I'm so humiliated. Again. "That was a slip of the tongue." I return to shelving, refusing to look at him. Ever again. Ever, ever again.

Fine, I sneak one more peek at him, but this is definitely the last one.

"So you're saying you don't think I'm hot?"

Oh my God, he's so hot.

"Aren't you supposed to be watching your nephews?" Yes, I'm changing the subject.

"Megan's taking her dinner break; it's been ten minutes. Tell me, Livia. Are you absolutely not attracted to me?"

I study him for several seconds before my eyes flicker involuntarily to his lips.

What the hell am I thinking?

I shoot up to my feet. "This feels like a trap."

Chase follows me up, caging me between the bookcase, the cart, and his body. His hard, hard body.

"It's totally a trap," he says, his voice low and husky. "I'm trying to trap you into dinner with me."

I swallow, but I can't get the lump out of my throat. He's close enough I can breathe him in. He smells like musk and sporty body wash and, faintly, of baby bottle, which somehow makes him even sexier. My eyes wander back to his lips, and I can't help wondering what it would feel like to be kissed by him. I bet he kisses hard. And deep. I bet his kisses bruise and burn.

His head tilts toward mine. "For the record, the feeling's mutual."

"What feel—" It takes me a second to remember he's referring to me accidentally calling him hot. And another second to realize he's now calling *me* hot. "Oh my God." I turn away, my skin so flushed I'm sure it's warm to the touch.

Even with my back to him, I can feel him grinning. I'm so glad I amuse him. Is that his interest in me? Comic relief?

I'll never know because I'm never speaking to him or looking at him or thinking about him ever again.

But when I reach for another pile of books, he says, "Hand me a stack. I'll help."

And so I turn and hand him a stack as big as I can hold. He grips it easily in his large hand, and when the tips of my fingers brush his and my body starts to hum in response, I decide that maybe this is how it's going to be when I'm around Officer Chase Kelly, and maybe I should just accept it.

Accepting it doesn't mean I'm going on a date with him. But he can certainly help me shelve a few books.

We settle quickly into a routine, reaching around each other for a new stack, Chase placing the higher books while I shelve the lower ones, chatting while we work.

"How come I haven't seen you around here before?" he asks.

"I transferred a couple of months ago from Central."

"Ooh. Central. Sorry." He looks around like he's about to tell me a secret. "You got a downgrade."

"I don't know," I say a bit whimsically. "Corinth has charm."

"If by charm you mean underfunded and falling apart, okay, yeah. I feel you." He's not completely off base—Central is where the administration offices are and somehow the majority of the budget and programming attention gets allocated there.

"But Central is corporate," I explain. "It's top of the line. It's buzz buzz and hullabaloo. It's always having to learn new stuff in the Maker Space and experiment with systems and come up with trendy branding and watch out for the big boss. And only sometimes does it feel like it's actually about reference or matching people with good books."

"You like that, don't you? Playing matchmaker."

"I do," I say proudly. Because not only do I like it, but I'm also good at it. I'm good at listening to someone tell me which books they've enjoyed, which they haven't, what they think they're in the mood for and then finding just the right book for them to read now.

"Okay then," he says, his tone challenging. "Go ahead. Match me."

We're standing next to each other, barely a foot separates us, and somehow I think he's not asking me to find him a book, which is good because I couldn't begin to think of a book to recommend right now.

"Okay," I say, anyway. Then nothing else. My breath quickens as he searches my face, his eyes landing on my lips before skimming down to my breasts. I'm sure he can see how they're peaked through the thin fabric of my blouse. He has to know it's because of him.

"Livia?" His voice is ragged, and fuck. It's so sexy, I can hardly stay standing. It's been so long since I've been attracted to a guy. I mean, really attracted. To the point where I'm sure that my vibrator can't compare with even what I just imagine about his fingers.

I meant what I'd said earlier—I'm not interested in men or dates or anything involving emotions. But the stairwell's fairly quiet and Megan still has time on her break...

"There you are!" Ryan pops out from around the bookshelf, and I jump away from Chase as far and as fast as I can.

"Nothing. It was nothing. We were nothing. Shelving." I smile tightly, brushing back an imaginary hair behind my ear. "Hi, Ryan. What's up?"

"Just looking for you." She looks at me suspiciously. Then eyes Chase. "Heya, Officer Kelly. Livia's not in trouble, is she? Liv, you should have texted! I would have been here for you! Paybacks and all!"

"Nope. Not in trouble," I say hurriedly. I'm blushing, and I know Chase is grinning his cocky grin, even though I refuse to look at him to be sure. "What do you need?" I ask again, desperate to get the attention off of us. Off of me.

"Cool. Well. I have a paper due tomorrow. I know. I procrastinated until the last minute, but that's a long story, and I don't think that you'd really consider it my fault if you heard all the details because I'm not the one who—"

"Ryan," I interrupt. "Get to the point."

"Oh. Right. American History. I have to do a paper on a woman who has shaped American History and everyone else is already doing Susan B. Anthony and Betsy Ross and Hillary Clinton. I want to do someone cool and unheard of, but I don't know who that would be. But I knew you'd know."

"Um. Okay." Normally this would be an easy one. But my head is not in the game. I'm still thinking about Chase and his lips. And his eyes. And his...everything.

"Frances Elizabeth Willard," he says. "Do a report on her."

"Who's that?" Ryan asks.

"You don't know her?" He feigns shock. "She's your soul sister. A protester and suffragette."

"My kind of woman!"

Chase goes on to highlight Frances Elizabeth Willard's contributions to society, but I'm no longer listening. He's good with Ryan. Like he was good with his nephews. Is that something a man's either born with or not? As much a part of his DNA as his thick hair and strong jaw?

I think about Chase's good genetics. I think about the constant ache in my heart. I think about the newer ache between my legs, and an old idea starts to re-form and become something new.

"Now stop talking about it, and get started," Chase says, interrupting a Ryan-length monologue. "Library closes in two hours, and you're going to need all that time. Better hustle."

"Aye aye, captain." She salutes, and miracle of miracles, she actually goes off to work without further pushing.

He's good. He's real good.

"Well?" Chase says when he turns back to face me, and I'm

sure it's because we were in the middle of something, but that was a bad idea. I have a better idea now, so I maintain a three-foot distance between us and avoid gazing directly into his eyes.

"I do admit that I might have misjudged you," I concede, leaning against the bookshelf, my hands tucked behind my back.

He raises a brow. "Because I'm a guy, and I know who Frances Elizabeth Willard is?"

"Because you're a guy who supports your local library." I can't help myself—I meet his eyes. His goddamn twinkling eyes.

He grins, slowly, and I know that he knows he's got me.

He leans against the opposite shelf. "Dinner tomorrow. Six o'clock."

"Seven." He's got me, but he doesn't have me that easily. "I work before that."

"Tell me where to pick you up."

"Tell me where to meet you. I'll drive myself." No way am I going out with him without an escape plan.

He considers. "I haven't decided yet. I'll text you."

"I haven't given you my number."

"Then give me your number."

There's no way for me to have the last word on this one and win. There's either I give it or I don't, and if I don't, this is done.

And I don't want it to be done.

I give him my number.

Because maybe there's something to what Megan said earlier after all—you don't get anything good without risk.

Well, I've decided there's something that I want. Something I'm willing to take a risk for after all.

And if I get it, I have a feeling it's going to be real good.

4

CHASE

When I settle into my patrol car the next morning, I decide that nothing can touch my good mood. Nope. Nothing, because tonight Officer Kelly has a date with the sexy librarian. And if I thought those leggings would give me carpal tunnel from all the stroking off they inspired, then I'm going to have something much worse than carpal tunnel after seeing her in that pencil skirt and tight no-nonsense bun yesterday. How do teenage boys even handle her being their librarian? I'd be terrified to shine a black light in the men's restroom at the Corinth Branch.

Note to self, see if Livia is willing to play Sexy Librarian after we play Find the Nightstick.

So the normal rounds of criminals, liars, and people who yell at me for giving them tickets don't bring me down.

The dirt bag who tries to lie about slashing his ex-girlfriend's tires the night before doesn't bring me down.

The irate doctor who accuses me of discriminating against people who drive nice cars in order to boost ticket revenues doesn't bring me down.

Even the white lady who yells at me after I write her a ticket for causing an accident doesn't upset me.

"*Failure to avoid collision?*" she reads off the ticket. "How *the fuck* am I supposed to avoid a collision when the car in front of me stops without warning?"

"They were stopping for a red light. In general we would consider the red light a warning that cars ahead of you will be stopping," I say, aware that I'm being snarky, but keeping my voice bland and pleasant. It's easy to stay pleasant when I know I'll be pressed against Livia later tonight. "I also have three independent eyewitnesses saying you were tailgating that car and visibly texting on your phone. If you'd been following at a safe distance, you wouldn't have hit them."

"You can't know I wouldn't have hit them," she hisses wildly.

"Actually," I say cheerfully, "I can know that. Given the incredibly short skidmarks and given that the coefficient of friction for dry asphalt is generally between a .7 and .9, I'd say you would have only needed an extra six or seven feet between you to have avoided the accident. Less than a single car length."

She blinks at me.

I flip over her accident report form and start writing out the formula for her. "So the mass of the vehicle is irrelevant here, and without a drag tire I don't know the *exact* coefficient of friction, but we'll be generous and say it's .7, and so if f equals force…"

She's now staring at me incredulously.

"It's physics?" I offer.

"Fuck physics," she snaps. "You'll be hearing a complaint from me, Officer Kelly. You've been nothing but unprofessional. And those eyewitnesses are bullshit—no one can prove I was texting!"

"That's why I didn't write you a ticket for texting, I wrote you a ticket for crashing into the back of another car."

She practically snarls, snatches her ticket out of my hand, and leaves. I finish the physics formula by myself for fun, get the answer I knew I would, and then finish up my report.

Good mood undented, I spend the next hour running speed along one of our busiest roads, my phone wedged between my cheek and my ear as I hold the LIDAR gun steady and track cars as they drive by.

"Do you think she prefers it if a guy dresses up or if he's more casual?" I ask Megan. I called her to not-so-subtly investigate Livia before our date tonight; I am very, very invested in it going well. My dick is too.

"Let me guess," Megan says, "it'll be the Kelly trio? Dinner, drinks—"

"—handcuffs," I finish for her. "And don't knock the Kelly trio. It's *very* popular in certain circles."

"You mean the circles of women aged twenty-three to twenty-seven who live within walking distance of a bar?"

"Oh, come on."

"Face it, Chase, you have a type."

"Beautiful women?"

We're miles apart, but I can practically hear her eyes roll. "*Shallow* women. Badge bunnies. The kind that get off on playing 'License and Insurance' and then afterwards are more than happy to hop on to the next officer. Livia's not like that, Chase. She's not impressed by your badge or those dumb sunglasses—"

"Hey!" I protest. "My sunglasses are not dumb!"

"—and she's definitely not shallow. She's smart. And passionate. And determined. And she's sworn off men, so I don't know how you convinced her or hexed her into agreeing to a date with you, but it's probably not because you've dazzled the panties off of her."

I think about that a minute, my good mood threatening to deflate the tiniest amount. Not because Megan told me Livia had sworn off men, since I'm pretty sure once I get her to myself she'll decide to *un*swear off men…for at least two hours. Four if she has a hot tub.

No, my good mood is wavering because my own sister is clearly wary of me dating her friend. "Megan, you know that I'm not like a *total* asshole right? I'm not planning on fucking it and trucking it. I'll be a gentleman."

"Hmm."

"Don't *hmm* at me," I say indignantly. "Maybe I didn't dazzle the panties off her, but she must have seen something in me she likes. Even if it's just the promise of a fun night."

"Don't you ever get tired of being just a fun night? Being just Officer Good Times?"

The answer is so obvious that for a moment I think I misheard the question. "No, I don't, baby sis. No, I don't."

Again, I can hear her eyes roll. "I don't believe you, dude."

I make a scoffing noise as I adjust the phone and aim my LIDAR at a Lexus barreling down the far lane. "You don't have to believe me. But I will tell you, I definitely wouldn't mind if I had more than one fun night with Livia. A few would be ideal. And do you think she'd wear those leggings if I asked her? I can't stop thinking about what it would be like to tear them apart with my hands and—"

"*Oh my God.* I'm hanging up."

"Fine. I have to pull over this car anyway. If the date goes badly, I'm blaming it on your poor intel."

Megan makes her own scoffing noise and then hangs up, and I drop the phone in the seat next to me and reach for my lights and sirens. But as I do, as I pull over the SUV and have yet another doctor accuse me of profiling expensive-looking cars, I wonder about what Megan said.

Am I sick of being Officer Good Times?

I mean, of course not.

Right?

But for the first time, I'm not sure if I believe myself either.

• • •

I'm at the steakhouse fifteen minutes early, which is *on time* in Chase Kelly's book. I've never been late for work or a date a single time in my life; in fact, I've always been early, which is a point of pride for me. And Livia walks in at seven on the dot, something that endears me to her immensely, although the moment I register that I, Officer Kelly, am charmed, my mind goes blank.

Just blank.

There is nothing but her.

She walks in on heels that make her legs a mile long, her long hair down in a tumult of soft waves. The maître d' helps her take off her checkered wool coat, and then I.

Am.

Speechless.

My heart hammers up in my throat as the blood pools deep in my groin. She's wearing a bright red dress—so fucking short that I'd be able to finger her easily if we were in a booth, which we tragically aren't. The red sets off the warm undertones of her bronze skin, highlights the deep brown of her eyes. The lines of it hug the delectable curves of her tits, which are just small enough that she can get away without wearing a bra.

My cock thickens as she begins walking toward me, and I can verify that she is definitely *not* wearing a bra. Oh God, what if she's not wearing panties either?

I bite back a groan and push back my chair to greet her as she comes to our table, tugging the hem of my sweater down in one smooth move as I unfold myself to help disguise the effect her presence has on me.

As I step forward to greet her, I notice the color high in her cheeks and the way her teeth dig into the soft coral of her bottom lip.

She looks nervous.

That gives me pause. I don't mind a woman meeting me cold or shy or overly eager, I don't even mind a case of the first date jitters—since first dates are pretty much all I go on, I see a lot of those.

But nervous—truly nervous—that bothers me a little. Do I make her feel unsafe? Is it my size? My job?

In a split second, I change gears. I can be patient when it comes to the Kelly Trio, and I find that the idea of wooing my nervous little librarian on date after date doesn't sound tiresome at all…it sounds delightful, actually. A challenge. A test to see if I'm worthy enough to remove all traces of trepidation from her face and fill her expression with eagerness and surrender instead.

And get more time with this fierce, sweet bookworm all to myself.

I lean in to kiss her cheek, careful to angle our bodies so that I don't press against her with six feet, two hundred pounds of hungry cop. Instead, I anchor her with a firm hand at her elbow, pleased to feel the goose bumps that spread underneath my touch. And then I brush my lips against her cheek, making sure she can feel them, making sure she gets just the tiniest brush of my scruff as I accidentally-on-purpose slide my jaw against hers as I pull away.

She shivers.

I look down into her eyes as I straighten up, and I'm suddenly aware that I'm supporting a lot of weight in my hand, as if her knees are weak from my kiss.

Well done, Officer Good Times!

Her eyes are wide, the pupils so blown and her irises so dark that her eyes are just huge liquid wells of want, and I feel a familiar tug in my groin knowing that I put that look there.

"I forget how big you are," she murmurs, her head tilted up to look into my face.

I give her my biggest grin and open my mouth, but she cuts me off before I can say it, shaking her head. "I know, I know. I walked right into that one."

But the ghost of a smile flits across her lips as I help her into her seat and push in her chair.

When I sit across from her and we start looking at our menus, I notice the smile has vanished and the nervous look is back, along with a determined set to her shoulders. The combination of uneasiness and backbone intrigues and worries me at the same time.

"I don't know what Megan told you," I say, "but I don't bite."

She looks up from the menu, her teeth back to digging into the plump flesh of her bottom lip.

"Well," I amend, staring at her mouth, "sometimes I do bite. But only when I really, really want to."

The color high in her cheeks intensifies, and she angles her menu to hide her face from me. "You're one cocky cop, I'll give you that much."

I reach over and pluck the menu out of her hands so I can see her face. The blush still darkens her cheeks and—oh fuck *me*—her nipples have drawn into tight little furls underneath her dress. There's a sharp pull of heat deep in my groin, my dick stirring to life as I think about what the ripe tips of her breasts would feel like on my tongue, how much they'd harden if I sucked them.

Livia clearly has something else on her mind though. "I was looking at that!"

I tap both menus on the table until they are lined up evenly and then put them on the edge of the table. "You're not a vegetarian, right?"

She looks confused. "Right."

"Are you from the Kansas City area originally? Raised eating Kansas City food?"

"Yes."

"Then you're set. This is a steakhouse, Livia. Order a steak."

She narrows her eyes at me. "You're trying to boss me around."

"You were trying to hide from me."

She sputters. "I don't *hide*. I'm not a hider. I'm very confident and outspoken, and I'm never shy—"

Her cheeks keep reddening as she talks, her fingers twisting in the tablecloth, and I lean back in my chair and study her.

"—and just…you flustered me, is all, and I wanted some space to think without you being so…so…you know." She gestures helplessly at me.

Uh. What does that mean?

"I'm so…what?" I ask cautiously. I'm back to being worried that she feels unsafe around me.

"Well, I can't *say* it," she whispers furiously.

I keep my posture casual and my voice calm, speaking in my easiest, most non-threatening voice. "Livia, I don't want you to feel uncomfortable or unsafe with me. I understand that it's not enough for you to know my sister or know that I'm a police officer, so I'm going to give you a promise and I hope that my words are enough. This is just dinner. If you don't like me or it, or anything, you can walk out that door and I promise I won't follow you or try to contact you again. If you do like it—and me, which I hope you will—then it can still be just dinner, and we can try it again another time. But I won't pressure you, or try to wheedle you into something you don't want to do. I want you to have a safe and fun evening, however that looks for you."

She stares at me, chewing on her lip. "And what do *you* want to have, Chase?"

What do I want to have? I want to have this librarian with her legs around my waist while I drive deep into her; I want to bury my face in her neck as I fill a condom; I want to taste her cunt and leave stubble-burn on the insides of her thighs.

But I don't know if telling her that will make her less skittish. In fact, probably not. Especially because she's now staring hard at me, as if this is some kind of test.

"I can't promise commitment," I finally say, a little reluctantly. I never have to have this talk with the badge bunnies, and I'm a little out of practice. "If that's why you're asking me. But I can promise that I'll be a perfect gentleman until you ask me not to be."

"And then what will you be?" she asks in a low voice.

I lean forward, letting my eyes burn and my voice edge into a growl. "Greedy."

Her breath catches. There's a moment when the noise around us seems to fade away, when the gentle lights of the restaurant cover us in a soft glow, and she seems to bloom open. Her eyelashes flutter and her body curves toward me.

"I think I'd like to see you greedy," she says, her tongue running along her bottom lip.

I feel her words everywhere: my bones, my skin, my throbbing erection.

"Your wish is my command, kitten." I lean forward over the table, my eyes hot on her sweet face. "Are you wearing a bra tonight?"

She licks her lips again, her breathing now quick and shallow. "No," she admits in a whisper. "The dress has a low back, and I…" She trails off, looking at me with something between helplessness and defiance. It makes my cock harder than it already is.

"Panties?"

I can see the pulse hammering in her neck now. She gives me a quick jerk of her head from side to side.

No panties.

I'm fully hard now, imagining her soft cunt exposed to the air so close to me, imagining it growing wet and needy as we sit here.

"Would you like to show me?" I ask.

There's a sharp intake of breath from her, her lips wet and parted, her large eyes blinking fast. "Show…you…?" she repeats slowly, as if she isn't sure she heard me correctly.

"Yes, Livia. Would you like to show me what your cunt looks like?"

The flush is now creeping up her neck, and she takes a small drink of water, as if to buy herself time. But when her eyes meet mine again, I can tell her hesitation isn't because she doesn't want to show me.

It's because she does.

"If I…*wanted to*…how would I show you?" she asks, the faintest quiver in her lower lip.

God, I still can't fucking breathe. She's so *much* right now, so quivery and so big-eyed and so flushed. Her nipples are still so hard—what must be achingly hard—through her dress, and she keeps smoothing this one curl over and over again around her finger. All I want to do is dive under this table and press my face between her legs, tongue her until she can't remember the difference between a filet mignon and a Kansas City Strip, between rare and well-done.

"Well," I say, once I can remember how to speak again, "you'd spread your legs under the table. I'd pretend to drop something. And then I'd duck under the tablecloth and see if you're telling me the truth about wearing panties."

Something about the word *truth* seems to trigger a surge of rebellion in her.

"I'm telling the truth," she says, with an indignant toss of that thick, silky hair. "See for yourself."

And then she spreads her legs under the table.

"So my little librarian is brave," I murmur. And then I hook my ankle around her chair underneath the table and easily yank her closer to me. "And bold."

She gasps as the chair moves underneath her, and I don't give her a chance to catch her breath before I knock both menus off the table. And then I bend down to retrieve them, my body half under the table, my hand making a pantomime of searching for the lost menus. All while I duck under the tablecloth and see for myself how she's prepared her cunt for our date.

It's dark under the table, too dark for what I want, and so I move off my chair to one knee at the side of the table. The restaurant is dim and our table is conveniently screened by enough plants and low walls that I'm not worried about being seen. As I grab for the menus with one hand, my other finds her ankle.

She startles, glancing down at me with fearful delight. "Chase?"

"I couldn't see under there," I say, my hand sweeping up the firm curve of her calf to the bend of her knee. "I needed to feel."

Her thigh trembles under my hand…and then she spreads her legs even wider. "Good girl," I whisper. "Let me feel you."

She holds her legs open for me as my whole hand slides under the hem of her dress, and then my fingertips brush against something impossibly silky and soft and—*oh fuck me*—groomed completely bare.

The bare skin has made her extra sensitive, I think, because even the light ghosting of my fingers over her mound sends shivers through her. "So you weren't lying," I murmur. "You came here with a naked pussy."

Her voice is tight and breathless when she answers. "I told you I was telling the truth."

"Did you do it for me, Livia?" My fingers brush lower, and there between her lips is the plump button of her clit.

She sucks in air as I give it a firm circle with my thumb. "I don't know," she confesses. Her voice is embarrassed, but her hips are currently rocking against my hand trying to get more pressure against her clit as I rub her.

I could do this literally all night, but I know we'll start to draw attention if I don't stand up soon. I allow myself one more caress, this time dipping a finger even lower into her folds. "Fuck, Livia," I mutter, my self-control evaporating the moment I find how wet she is. "You're so fucking wet."

"Mmm," she says. There's a flush creeping up her neck now, goose bumps everywhere, non-stop shivers. She looks like she has a fever, and the sight of her so physically undone just by this simple touch has me ready to push down my jeans and mount her right here at the table.

I don't do that, but I do peer up into her face and ask, "Can I put my fingers inside you? I want to feel. Just for a minute."

Her eyes are half hooded as she nods and licks her lips. "Yes. You can."

I do. I slide one finger inside of her, easily finding a spot that makes her arch her back, and then I add a second finger, watching her face carefully as I do it. Her eyes are completely closed now and her chest is rising and falling so fast that the fabric is pulling against her tits. God, I just want to shove this table out of the way, yank her ass to the edge of the seat and fuck her while I'm kneeling between her legs.

With a small groan, I slide my fingers out of her tight, wet box and go back to my seat, relieved that nobody seems to have noticed my little exploratory session, and also disappointed that the explorations are over.

Livia's eyes are open again when I get there, but just barely. "Holy shit," she mumbles to herself. "Holy shit."

I grin at her and then start licking my fingers, like a contented cat. She tastes good, sweet and primal, so good that I know I need to taste her again. Soon.

Her eyes widen as she watches me lick her taste off my fingers. "I can't believe we just did that. I can't believe I *let* you."

My grin gets bigger. "And we haven't even ordered our food yet."

She shakes her head. "We haven't even *kissed* yet," she says, with some wonder in her voice.

"*Yet?*" I tease. "So does that mean we will kiss?"

That draws a smile to her face, along with a fresh flush. "I didn't mean it like that," she protests. "I meant—" She goes to cross her legs and then she gives me another one of those soft inhales.

"Are you pressing your thighs together right now?" I ask in a husky voice.

"I—yes."

"Can you squeeze your clit like that? Can you feel how wet you are?"

"Yes," she whispers. "How are you doing this to me?"

I hold up both my hands. "I'm not doing anything right now, if you haven't noticed. You're doing it to yourself."

She looks down at her lap, taking a deliberately deep breath.

"I think...I think I'm doing this wrong," she says worriedly.

I don't like that, because from my vantage, everything is going utterly and completely right. "Doing what wrong?"

She gestures between the two of us, still looking down at her lap. "This."

I'm confused. "The date?"

She closes her eyes for a moment, and then opens them, pinning their dark depths onto me. "Kind of," she says slowly. "But I meant for this to go differently. More...um...businesslike. More transactional."

Now I'm really confused. *Transactional?* Like we would just eat food, have sex and then leave like strangers? I've had plenty of transactional hookups in my time—I mean, I've basically taken out stock in Durex at this point—but I didn't think that was what

Livia wanted from our date. I assumed she'd want fun—easy and intimate, yes, but fun all the same.

Thankfully the waiter shows up then, and I can gather my thoughts. After we order—steak and beer for me, steak and wine for her—I give her my full attention.

"I don't mind being a transaction, Livia, as long as we're both having fun at the same time. But I'm curious…does this have anything to do with you swearing off men?"

Livia sighs. "So Megan told you that, huh?"

"She did. And I know it's not my business, but if there's a story there, I want to make sure I don't do anything to repeat parts of that story. I don't want to scare you or hurt you or trigger you."

To my surprise, that seems to utterly disarm her, even though all I did was pledge not to be a dick. "That's really thoughtful of you," she says softly. Then after a minute, she adds, "There's not a story like the way you're thinking. I just have had my heart broken enough to know that I can't count on a man to be trustworthy and faithful. So I stopped trying."

That pulls on something in my chest, something I didn't even know was there until just now. It makes me want to protect her, makes me want to find any man who broke her heart and drive my fist into his nose.

I shake off the feeling. It's not mine to have in the first place, and in the second place, it should be no concern of mine that she's stopped trying to have relationships. I'm Officer Good Times! I don't do relationships either.

But still. There's something so forlorn about the way she looks right now, and I want to help. Somehow.

My mind flashes to Sergeant Gutierrez and her wife. "Is it just men you don't trust? Have you ever tried dating women?"

A smile tugs on the corners of her mouth, pulls on that weird, new spot in my chest. "You mean, have I explored being bisexual?"

"Yeah."

She lifts a slender shoulder, still smiling. "Yes, I explored that. A few times."

"Ah. Say no more." But then the meaning of her words becomes clear in my mind, and I lean forward and put my chin in my hand, giving her my biggest grin. "Actually, say more."

She giggles, a real little laugh with a real little smile and real little twinkles in her dark brown eyes. The waiter comes by with our drinks and a basket of rolls, which I immediately start destroying. It's while I'm buttering a roll that Livia switches gears from giggles to Serious Business.

"Chase, I wanted to talk to you tonight, and I know we got a little off topic earlier…"

I take a bite of roll, raising my eyebrows. "Is 'off topic' what we're calling it when I stroke your pussy in public?"

She ignores me, forging ahead with what she wants to say, that nervous but determined look back. It makes me nervous enough myself that I stop eating my roll.

"I'm done with relationships," she says, meeting my gaze with an expression that brooks no argument. Not that I *would* argue, even though every time she says she doesn't want a relationship, it twists somewhere in my chest.

I shake off the twisting feeling. "You're preaching to the choir, sweetheart."

"I know," she says with a nod. "That's why we're here tonight. See, wouldn't you agree that just because you don't imagine yourself being married, that it doesn't mean you don't have plans for your life? We're still allowed to want things, right?"

I'm starting to feel like I have no idea where this is going. "Yes?" I agree tentatively.

She nods again. "I don't need a man or a relationship, but I still need a future. I still want a future. And I know exactly what it is I want for that future."

I take a swig of my beer and settle back into my chair. "Okay, I'll bite. What is it that you want for your future, Livia?"

"I want a baby," she answers calmly. "And I want you to be the one to give a baby to me."

5

LIVIA

Chase nearly chokes on his beer.

"Excuse me, a *what*?"

I see sweat gathering on his forehead. It's the first time I've seen him be anything but calm, cool, and collected, which probably says a lot about how he's taking my announcement.

To be fair, I did spring this on him suddenly, though I didn't come up with the idea on a whim. I've been looking into artificial insemination and even adoption for several months now. Actually, for more like a year—since my last birthday when I turned twenty-eight and realized how close that was to twenty-nine which is practically thirty and how the hell could I be not even thirty and have my life be complete? Because it didn't feel complete.

It doesn't feel complete.

But what else was there that I wanted to accomplish? I had the degree I wanted. I loved my job. I owned my condo. I didn't want to get married. As Megan put it, what was there left to want?

A child. That's what.

I've always wanted a child. It was the one thing I always imagined for my future. Even after I decided I was done with men, I still wanted a kid. I want one more now, actually. Maybe it's because I'm lonely and think a child will fill some emotional hole. Maybe it's because I have a lot of ideas and thoughts I'd like to pass on. Maybe it's because I want someone to love, someone that I know is going to love me back. Someone I know isn't going to run away when things get hard.

Maybe that makes me selfish.

But are those really such bad reasons to want to procreate?

I'll be a good mother.

I'll be attentive.

I'll be adoring and protective but not *too* protective.

I'll be *there*. Isn't that what matters most?

I know I can parent alone, that doesn't worry me, but I've seen the way Josiah keeps Megan running around. I want to be young enough to keep up with a toddler. Young enough to still remember puberty when my child hits that phase. And can women even have babies after thirty? I mean, I know they can. But surely the sooner the better, right?

So it seemed if I was going to have a baby, I should have one before the angel of death arrived in the form of my thirtieth birthday. I did my research. I'd been considering my options. It just hadn't occurred to me to go about it the old-fashioned way. There haven't been any men in my life to choose from, really. No one I wanted to procreate with and definitely no one I wanted to sleep with.

Then Chase came along.

This man…

Not only do I want to rub every part of my body against his exquisite genetic makeup, but also it would be a crime if he didn't pass that shit on. I can already picture his eyes on a miniature face with my features and his perfect smile.

Unf.

Thinking about it makes my womb ache.

So I'm absolutely serious when I repeat my request. "Your baby. I want your baby."

He swallows. "That's." He nods. "No." He shakes his head. "I." He fidgets in his chair, looking around the restaurant. "Waiter!" he calls to the server walking by who is most definitely not our waiter.

"Can I get you something, sir?"

"I'm going to need another drink." Chase holds up his beer. "Another two drinks."

"I'll tell your server," the waiter says and slips away.

I open my mouth but Chase says, "I'm going to need a minute." I start to speak anyway, and he puts a finger up to silence me.

I sigh. I knew I was going about this wrong. I should have blown him first. Or I shouldn't have approached this from the sex angle at all. Should never have let him think it was a date. Should definitely not have let him touch me like I did.

God, though. I can still feel his fingers. Feel how they brushed across my pussy. Feel how they stroked inside me.

I shiver at the memory.

He was right—I didn't just come here tonight without panties because I didn't want panty lines. The truth is I'd been prepared to use any means necessary to get what I wanted, including the old razzle dazzle. Problem was he razzled me first.

I should have been straightforward from the beginning. Hopefully this isn't too botched to salvage.

I glance at Chase who is studying me, eyes squinted. He hasn't indicated that he's ready for me to speak, but fuck that. I have things to say.

Leaning forward, I rest my elbows on the table. "Look. I'm not a crazy cop stalker, if that's what you're thinking. Or someone who's trying to trap you into a marriage or a relationship or even child support."

His expression doesn't change. "You have no idea what I'm thinking."

"Then what *are* you thinking?"

The twinkle is back in his eyes, which is a relief. "That you're a crazy cop stalker who's trying to trap me into a marriage or a relationship or child support."

I stifle a laugh. "I'm not. I promise. I don't want anything from you. Other than the baby, I mean." *And really hot sex. Repeated hot sex.*

"You don't want anything from me," he repeats, somewhat skeptical.

I clarify. "I want a baby. But no marriage. No relationship. No child support. No parental claim at all."

He finishes the last of his beer and leans back in his chair. "I still don't understand."

He's a smart guy. So either he's playing dumb on purpose or he's caught up on some part of the details.

I decide to make it as simple as possible. Speak the language he speaks best. "It's easy, Chase. You want to have sex with me." I feel sensual and strong with my bold statement.

But suddenly I'm afraid I've jumped to conclusions and my confidence falters. "You do want to have sex with me, don't you?"

It's his turn to look at me as though I'm playing crazy. "Yes, Livia," he says with wide emphatic eyes. "Yes." He pauses only a second before adding, "Do I need to make myself clearer? Because I can, but it wouldn't be appropriate in a public venue."

I bite my lip, pressing my thighs closer together to ease the newest wave of agony. "I think we've already pushed the limits of public decency. But you're the cop. You'd know better than I would."

His lip curls up on one side, and I know he's considering. Damn, what I'd give to have a peek at the naughty imaginings going on inside his mind, because I know they're naughty from the gleam in his eye. Very naughty.

"Chase..." I warn.

"You're right, you're right. Already pushed the limits. Go on." But the gleam in his eye remains, and I'm giddy knowing that I'm prey, and he's a predator just biding his time.

"Okay," I say, my voice barely steady. "So, when you have sex, there are these microscopic things called sperm that come out of a man's body when he ejaculates."

"Liv, I know about sperm. But go on ahead and tell me about ejaculation. I'd like to hear what you have to say about that."

His gaze never leaves mine and I flush picturing his cum in

unproductive places—places that won't make a baby—on my belly, on my breasts, spilling down my throat.

No, inside me. That's where I want it most.

I lick my lips. "I'm saying you want to put it in me. I'm just asking to keep it afterward."

His grin is slow but magnificent. "I do want to put it in you. We're on the same page there."

My breath hitches. I take a sip of my wine, trying to hide behind my glass, and nearly choke, which only makes him grin wider. He sees everything. There's nothing I can do to escape his eyes, and the thing is, I don't really want to.

Which is good. It's good to be attracted to the person you're planning to jump into bed with. That doesn't mean anything's changed about my future. There are still no men in the picture in the long run. This is just a brief pit stop.

Chase plays with his empty bottle, tipping it back and forth between his fingers. "You really want to raise a baby by yourself?"

I shrug like it doesn't prickle me that he's asked. Does he think I can't do it? "Women do it all the time," I say. "What do you care?"

So maybe lots of people do this parenting thing in twos, but I've never known my father, and as far as I'm concerned, it hasn't hurt me in the least. My mother is a strong woman. She might have had it tough, but she didn't complain. If she could do it, I can do it.

"Good point. What do I care?" He rubs his palms on his thighs, his expression unreadable. After a beat, he shakes his head. "I'm crazy for even considering this."

"But *why* is it crazy?" I ask, eager to push his consideration in the right direction. I run through rational reasons he might be against my plan. "You don't have an STD or something, do you?"

"God, no!" He shudders as he scans the restaurant, as if he's afraid someone might have heard me. "Would you keep it down?"

"Something else that would make it irresponsible for you to procreate?"

"Shhh." He pats the air with both hands in a quieting motion.

"No one else needs to hear us talking procreation," he stage whispers. "Babies are actually not a very sexy concept."

Uh, tell that to my exploded ovaries.

I don't have to respond, though, because the waiter comes then with our dinner and Chase's next beer, promising to bring him another when he finishes the first.

"You can cancel that," he says, side-eyeing me. "This one will be enough."

I chuckle, placing my napkin on my lap before cutting into my steak as the server has asked to test the center.

"Perfectly pink and tender," Chase comments, looking at my plate. He makes even steak sound like porn, and I know my cheeks are equally pink when I say, "It looks good. Thank you."

We eat for a few minutes in silence, the air between us just as charged as ever. But now it's also thick and tense while I start to consider what I'll do if he tells me no. Will I still sleep with him without the excuse? What excuse do I have not to?

He's cleared half his plate when he wipes his mouth with his napkin. "You might not get pregnant right away. It could take a few months."

He's thinking the same things I am right now, I realize. Thinking less about the product and more about the production.

Thinking about a lot of production.

I clear my throat. "I know." I haven't been on birth control so I don't have to worry about getting that out of my system. Still, statistics say that only twenty percent of women get pregnant in the first month. "And we should probably, um, *do it* several times over the course of the week that I ovulate each cycle for the best chance."

He smirks when I say "do it" but he doesn't push me on my choice of terms. "I mean, it's not likely it will take long. I'm sure I have super sperm."

I laugh and play along. "I'm sure you do. How could you not?"

His smile fades as he grows serious. "But, do you think you

can handle that? It seems like quite a commitment for someone who's sworn off men."

"I've sworn off men because I don't want emotional entanglements, not because I don't like sex. I figured you wouldn't have a problem with an arrangement that left out feelings." The words are out before I really think about them. "Ouch." I cringe. "That sounded less shitty in my head. Sorry."

"I'm not at all offended." He heads right to the part of what I said that interested him. "So you like sex then."

I bite back another laugh and shrug, not wanting to give too much of myself away. "It's not exactly terrible."

"You *do* like sex. My little librarian's a sex kitten. Admit it. You're naughty."

I can't admit that I like sex because I'm not really sure if I do. I haven't had a lot of good sex to know. I do, however, like orgasms. And I like fantasizing about good sex while I give myself good orgasms. If sex with Chase is even half as good as he makes it seem like it might be…

"I'm not admitting anything," I say looking anywhere but at him as my body heats from the thoughts that have just entered my mind.

"You will," he taunts. "I'll show you just how naughty you are."

My gaze crashes back into his, drawn there by the fascination of his filthy words. The way he looks at me makes me crazy. Turns me into someone I've never been. My belly tightens and my pussy clenches and the sudden ache I have for the fingers he'd had inside me so briefly is sharp and intense.

I have to have him.

I have to have this, too. This baby. This meaning for my life that will extend past this moment. Past this year. Past my death.

But, right now, I have to have *him*.

"Then you'll do it?" I'm on pins and needles. I'm on the very edge of the edge.

"I might already have kids," he says more to himself than to me. "What's another one? That I know about."

"That you have no contact with," I say, reminding him of the terms, but I'm relieved because I know he's agreeing.

"Right."

I'm beaming now, almost unable to contain my giddiness. "You're going to do it."

"I'm going to do you, yes." When I scowl, he shrugs, "It's part of it. I stand by my words."

I'm not going to correct him. Fuck yes, he's going to do me. I'm elated. I'm over the goddamn moon.

With my appetite gone, I push away my half-eaten food as well as the centerpiece, making room on the table. Chase furrows his brow as I dig into my purse and pull out the papers I printed up earlier at the library.

I set them in the space between us, facing him and explain. "I used a legal forms database to pull together this contract. It's a bunch of mumbo jumbo legalese but basically it states that you agree to participate in conceiving a child and will give up any parental rights. I've already signed. There're two copies there. One for me, one for you."

He scans his eyes over the contract and his mouth quirks in— is that amusement? Is he hiding a smile? But his eyes are kind when he looks back up to me, so I dismiss it.

I turn back to my purse for a pen. "I couldn't add that you were doing this in exchange for sex—if that is why you are doing this—because that would make the whole thing null and void." I did my homework. "Sex isn't a legal means of trade," I add a bit proudly. "Prostitution laws and all."

I look up and realize he's trying not to laugh. And failing.

"What? Did I do something—" Oh. Realization dawns on me. "You're a cop. Of course you already know that. You don't need to laugh at me."

"No, I think I do." He's still very amused.

I don't mind a bit of teasing, but this is serious. I worked hard on this contract. And this is a big deal to me.

I stare blankly until he's pulled himself together.

"Sorry, sorry." He holds his hand out. "Where's the pen? I'll sign."

"Thank you." My elation returns quickly as he signs his name in fine block letters. "Underneath the two copies is a printout of my most recent health check. STD free, as you can see." He flips through the pages and glances at the one I'm talking about. "I'll need one from you too, please. Before. You know."

He hands my pen back. "Not a problem. I'll get you my records." He folds the top contract into perfectly even quarters and puts it in his back pocket before handing me the rest of the papers.

And it's done.

He's agreed.

Chase Kelly is officially going to bang me and put a baby inside me.

I'm nervous and excited all at once.

There's just one last thing. "You can't sleep with anyone else until I conceive," I say as I tuck the newly signed contract into my purse.

"That's cute."

His face suddenly falls. "You're serious."

"I need to be sure your STD screening stays current."

"I always use protection."

I ignore the way my chest pinches at the idea of Chase sleeping with someone else and concentrate on the very real, very logical reason why I'm dying on this cross. "But *we* won't be using protection, and I need to feel safe about this. It's a non-negotiable."

He taps his thumb on the table rapidly while he thinks, but for the life of me I can't tell what he's thinking. Is routine sex really that big of a deal for him? So much so that he can't miss a couple of weeks a month?

My head says it's ridiculous that he can't keep it in his pants. But my body says there's nothing ridiculous about it at all. My body likes how primal and base his urges seem. My body wants in on that.

I can't believe I'm about to say what I'm about to say. "If sex during the week I'm ovulating isn't enough…" I swallow. "Well. I suppose we can discuss some other arrangements between the two of us."

I haven't even slept with him once, and I already don't know what I'm doing.

It works though.

"Okay," Chase says, suddenly amiable. "You make a valid point. You need to know you're safe. From now on, I'm only fucking you."

I cross my legs tighter. "Until I'm pregnant."

"Until you're pregnant."

Pregnant. I'm going to be pregnant. If all goes well, I'll be having my baby before I'm thirty. I need to double-check my maternity leave.

On the topic of work… "We can't tell Megan."

"No," he agrees immediately. "Megan must never know."

"She'll try to make us into a couple," I say at the same time Chase says, "She'll try to tell you awful things about me."

I tilt my head, curious. "Awful things?"

"I meant she'll try to make us a couple." But he can't look at me.

"What awful things, Chase?" It's my turn to try to hunt his eyes down. My turn to wish he wasn't hiding from me.

"Nothing. Pretend I didn't say anything."

"You're going to be the biological father of my child. I think I should know in case there's anything that might be passed genetically." I'm teasing him. I know what kind of awful things he's alluding to. I have a brother myself.

"She'll try to tell you about a toy I had. When I was a kid." He shakes his head, his mind changed. "It's stupid. I'm not telling you."

"Officer Kelly. Tell me right this minute." When he doesn't give me anything but another one of his cocky grins I pull out the big gun. "Fine. I'll just ask Megan next time I see her, you know."

"Noooo." He drags out the word like he's really adamant. "Do not ask Megan."

"Then tell me."

"You're going to laugh."

"I won't. I promise." Which isn't a fair promise. I *might* laugh.

"Okay, but if you do, I'm going to have to spank you later." His eyes darken. "Or I can spank you anyway."

"Chase!" Now I'm imagining his hand on my ass. Imagining how the slap of his palm would sound on my skin. How he'd massage the sting away after.

It's a good thing I'll be walking out of the restaurant with a coat on because I'm so wet, I'm pretty sure the back of my dress is damp.

He sighs, resigned. Then, with no trace of humor, he says, "She'll tell you that I had a baby doll until I was seven."

I can't help it—I laugh.

Not because I think it's funny that he had a baby doll, but because I think it's funny that his manhood is so threatened by telling me.

I have to tease him about it. Forever and ever. Starting now. "Chase Kelly played with dolls!"

"Doll. Singular. One doll. Lucy. I cannot believe I told you this." He's mortified, and it's payback for all the times he's mortified me. "I had a baby sister. I saw my mother taking care of her all the time. It was natural to pretend—" He cuts himself off. "Don't look at me like that."

"I'm not looking at you like anything." I've managed to contain my laughter, but I'm grinning. He's a good guy. He's got good genes. He's going to make a good kid. I try not to wonder whether he'd make a good dad too.

Because, at least as far as my kid-to-be is concerned, Chase won't be one.

• • •

When we've finished dinner, Chase helps me with my coat and walks me to my car, his hand pressed at the small of my back.

Strangely, I don't have to direct him to my car. He already knows which one's mine.

"There are certain advantages to being a cop," he says when I confront him about it. "It would be unwise of me not to use our databases to check out my date beforehand. What if you were a serial killer or a vegetarian?"

I roll my eyes. "Your police database did not tell you that I wasn't a vegetarian."

"No, the Megan Kelly Carter database was useful for that one."

I lean with my back against my Prius door and lick my lips before I realize what I'm doing. I mean, I want him to kiss me, but I don't want to be obvious about it. And I shouldn't want him to kiss me as badly as I want him to kiss me, but I do, and my eyes keep darting to his lips, begging him with my body when I refuse to do it with words.

"I'll, um." His eyes are so blue, even in the dim of the street-light. It's distracting. "I'll text you to work out the details about…" I trail off. It's real now. The foreplay is done, so to speak. Now onto what's next.

Oh God.

He steps toward me, putting his hands on my hips inside my coat, which is unbuttoned. "About where we're going to fuck first?"

My heart beats double time. "Yeah. About that."

"It's okay to like it when I say that, Livia. Do you?" He towers over me, his six feet so much taller than my five foot four frame. Five foot six in these heels.

I have no chance against him.

"Do I what?" I say, my voice barely a whisper.

"Do you like it when I talk about fucking you?"

I blink then tilt my head up toward him. "I don't know."

"You do know. Do you want me to tell you about how I'm going to fuck you?" His mouth dances around mine.

"I don't." I can't breathe. "Know."

"How about this—do you think about me fucking you? I know you do."

I shake my head, but it's the slightest movement. Because I do. I so do. But I'm not ready to admit it to him. I haven't really even admitted it to myself.

But he's determined. "I know you do or you would have worn panties tonight."

I can't deny it. I can't do anything but fall into his eyes.

"I want you to admit it before I let you go."

"I can't."

"Yes, you can." He steps in closer, our pelvises so near to touching. His lips just above mine. "Admit you think about me fucking you. Admit you're going to go home tonight and think about me inside you. Can you do that for me?"

It's one word. *Yes.* That's all I have to say, but I shake my head again, refusing for no good reason except that I'm not ready for him to leave.

"What if I make you admit it?"

"You can't." He's so close his exhale is warm against my skin.

"Yes. I can."

"No, you—"

He cuts me off, his mouth crushing against mine, and everything, everything stands still and speeds up all at once. Like the world around us has suddenly gone into slow motion, but we're moving fast and frantic, unable to kiss and taste and discover each other as quickly as we need to.

He feasts on me, and I feast on him. His lips devour every sweep of my tongue. His teeth are playful and nip at my jaw. His beard is rough and coarse and will leave burn marks with swollen lips, but I don't care. I want it all. I'll take it all.

I throw my arms around his neck, pulling him closer, letting him know I consent. He takes my cue and his hands move from my hips to my behind. And then they're under my dress, grabbing my ass, touching me skin-to-skin. One finger moves lower, sliding past my rear hole and dips inside my pussy. I wrap my leg around him, and he lifts me up against the car, not much, just high enough that my pelvis presses against his, and I can feel the stone ridge of his erection at my core.

Jesus, he's hard.

So fucking hard that I've lost all sense for anything but him.

I'm ready to go home with him tonight. Forget about the fact that I'm not ovulating for a few more days. I'm primed now. Besides, didn't he mention super sperm? Surely they can last a few days. Or even if they can't, call this a warm-up round. Call this figuring things out before the real thing. Call this Mama needs a night out before baby comes along.

I shift and suddenly Chase's cock is knocking at just the right spot. *There. There. There.* With this and his finger in my cunt, I'm about to explode. I dig into the fabric of his sweater and start to make a sound I don't recognize from myself. A sound between a whimper and a moan, and I decide right then and there that I can never complain about VPUs at the library now that I've been Very Personally Used in a public parking lot with absolutely no regrets.

Chase grinds harder against me. "You're sure you aren't going to be thinking about this?" he asks against my open mouth. "Tell me you're going to imagine me fucking you when you go to bed tonight. Tell me, kitten."

I'm never going to stop thinking about this. I'm going to replay it over and over. Thinking of this night, thinking of Chase, will be what gets me off for the rest of my natural life.

"Yes." *I'm so close.* "Yes. I'll think about you," I gasp.

Instantly his hands are off me, and my feet are back on the ground.

I blink several times, confused. Dazed. My clit is throbbing so hard I'm in pain.

Chase straightens his sweater, his breathing heavy. "I knew I could make you admit it," he says, his cocky grin lighting up his perfect face.

"But—" Oh my fucking God, I'm going to murder him.

Murder him.

After I calm down anyway, which will require several cold showers.

"Don't pout, kitten." He pulls my coat together and buttons it while he talks. "We're going to be naked together the next time we see each other. I want you thinking about me until then."

I'm too mad to talk. Too horny to talk. Too dazed by his kiss and my hormones, and his stupid twinkling blue eyes.

After finding my keys in my coat pocket, he clicks my car unlocked, opens the door, and helps me inside. He bends down so he can pull my seatbelt across my body and fasten it.

"So we can be safe," he says. I immediately recognize it as a line from *Dora the Explorer* from library story time, and I know he's got to have learned it from having nephews.

And seeing him with his nephews was the whole reason I decided to pick him to be the father of my baby. Which is the reason I agreed to the date tonight. Which is the reason I'm about to drive home with the most painful arousal I've ever felt.

"Don't even be cute right now," I grumble, finally finding my voice.

"There's my kitten," Chase says. He brushes his lips against mine once more. "And Liv, I'll be thinking about fucking you too."

He shuts my door and backs up a few feet but makes no move to go to his car. I know him well enough already to guess he's going to stay there until he knows my car starts and he sees me drive off safely.

His waiting is the only reason I don't stay in the parking lot and rub one out before leaving.

As I drive off, I steal one last look at him. He's pulled his sweater down, but he can't hide the tent he's sporting. It's a minor consolation knowing that I'm leaving him in similar agony.

And as he said, the next time I see him, we're going to be naked together.

I end up smiling all the way home.

6

CHASE

Of course I said yes. It was a simple question, and I'm a simple kind of man, just like Mama says to be in the Lynyrd Skynyrd song. A hot librarian wants me to fuck her without a condom, empty myself inside of her, and then walk away from all the consequences.

I mean, it couldn't have been a better present had it been wrapped in Paper Source paper and tied up with a goddamn bow. And like I said at dinner, I couldn't entirely write off the possibility that there were already little Chase Kellys in the world. What's one more?

Also, there was that damn kiss by her car...I could still feel how wet her pussy was against my fingertips, could feel how eagerly she rocked against my dick, how easily she surrendered to my mouth...

Oh yes. Fucking my little librarian is going to be a fucking delight.

So...it's all pretty simple, right?

The problem is that there's a small part of me that doesn't feel so simple about it. And it's that same unfamiliar part that lives in my chest and twists at the strangest thoughts. Like the thought of Livia being broken-hearted by other men. The thought of her wanting a baby this fiercely. The memory of the way she looked at JoJo kicking happily in my arms.

I try to poke at this twisty place in my chest while I'm jumping rope, while I'm running, while I'm doing pull-ups on the rings. I poke at it while I'm at work, while I do welfare checks on the elderly and while I beg Gutierrez to let me do a body camera presentation to the city council. I poke at it while I watch TV with Pop, while we drink coffee and later while we trim the hedges outside.

After two days, I give up. This weird pull in my chest won't go away and it doesn't make sense. It's not ordered, logical, or even *wanted*—it's just there. Unasked for and confusing. Not lining up with any of the things I know to be true about myself.

Well, except for one thing.

I want to fuck Livia. I like her and I want to fuck her, and Jesus, it's messed up, but the idea of going inside her bare, of actually trying to plant a baby in her, to *breed* her…well, it gets me hard in a way I've never felt before. Urgently hard. Throbbing hard. My-balls-feel-fucking-heavy-and-full hard. I'm masturbating like a teenage boy morning and night, and still I can't take the edge off this itch for her, the edge off this need to get her pregnant. To mate with her, like I'm a fucking caveman.

So there it is. She wants me to get her pregnant, the idea of getting her pregnant turns me the fuck on, so I'm all systems go for this insane, ridiculous plan. I'm just going to ignore the distracting pull in my chest when I think about her and focus only on the logical.

Tab Chase goes into Slot Livia; lather, rinse, repeat until baby.

Which means I'm in the right frame of mind when I get a text from her three days after our first date.

My ovulation test says my luteinizing hormone is surging today, and I have salivary ferning. Tonight, at the Nite's Inn, 8 p.m., please.

It's polite and straightforward and all business, which appeals to the Spock-like part of me, although the horny part of me is pretty insistent that we take a few dirty detours tonight as well. If I want this librarian out of my system by the time I knock her up, then I'm going to need to take full and long advantage of our nights together. She agreed to include non-fertile times as part of our arrangement, and I'm already planning on exploiting that condition as much as possible. Besides, I read online that the man should ejaculate often to improve sperm motility or something like that. So me fucking her throughout the month is good for conceiving the baby too.

However, something about her text bothers me. Well, actually two somethings.

Something Number One—salivary ferning? What the fuck is that?

I tell dispatch I'm going on a lunch break, but instead of going into the break room, I go out to my Audi TT—the perfect marriage of muscle and clean, precise German engineering—and climb inside. There on the passenger seat are a bunch of books from the library about babies and pregnancy. (I checked them out from the Central Resource Library, to avoid the risk of seeing Megan and having to explain why her playboy brother is researching babies.)

And as I start flipping through them looking for any information on *ferning*, I pull out my phone and make a call about Something Number Two, the Nite's Inn. It sounds familiar somehow, but I can't remember why, except I know it's in Overland Park, the next suburb over.

While the place I live and work, Prairie Village, is a well-off residential community of upper middle class families and old people, Overland Park suffers from a lot of the issues that plague bigger, older suburbs. Empty retail spaces, seedy areas, crumbling apartment complexes filled with cockroaches tucked behind Targets and movie theaters, that kind of thing. In fact, Prairie Village during the midnight shift is so boring that when I worked midnights myself, I used to creep across the city line to see if anything more interesting was happening in Overland Park. And the answer was always, invariably, yes.

More often than not, the guy handling the more interesting things was a taciturn academy buddy of mine named Taylor, and since he's now a detective with a suit and tie and a stack of case folders taller than I am, I know he's got nothing better to do than pick up the phone.

He picks up the phone.

"Taylor here."

"Hey, it's Kelly from Prairie Village."

A sigh. "Do I need to chase you out of my city again?"

I smile, still flipping through the baby book. "Those were the days. When we were just out of academy, working midnights."

"Ah. When we were young men."

I laugh. "Speak for yourself. I'm only thirty-three."

"I hate to break it to you, Kelly, but we're old now. We're past thirty. We might as well be dead."

"Why is everyone saying that lately?" I mumble-ask, groping for another baby book when the one I'm holding comes up empty of answers.

"Because it's true. Did you really call me just to talk about mortality?"

"No," I say, giving up on this baby book too when the glossary yields no entry under the word *ferning* or *salivary.* "Do you know the Nite's Inn?"

"You mean, do I know it from all the prostitution? Or do I know it from all the murder?"

"Oh. Oh man."

"Why?" Taylor asks. "You got a lead from there you need to follow?"

"Not a lead exactly," I say slowly, glancing out of my windshield. Three blocks from here is the Corinth Branch, where right now Livia might be working on programs or sitting through a committee meeting on senior outreach or something. "I've, uh. I've got a date I'm meeting there."

I have to hold the phone all the way out to the side when Taylor laughs.

And laughs.

And laughs.

"Oh my God," he wheezes. "Oh my God. A date. At the Nite's Inn."

"She picked it," I say defensively.

"I bet she did. And did you meet her through an ad on Craigslist? Or on a street corner? Did you finally fuck your way through an entire county's worth of non-hookers?"

"No, no, no. This woman's a *librarian*." And I'm about to add, *and I've agreed to get her pregnant, so we're meeting on neutral ground*, but then I decide that Taylor wouldn't think that was any less weird, so instead I just say, "And it's a totally normal date. Super normal. We are two normal people who are going to meet and have normal non-procreative sex."

Taylor starts laughing again, wheezing and coughing. "That's what all the johns say," he squeezes in between laugh-coughs. "I hope you enjoy your normal, non-procreative sex, Kelly."

"You suck."

More laughter. "Oh man, wait until I tell everyone about this. Kelly has a date at the Nite's Inn. At the place where you pay by the hour. At the No-Tell Motel. *At the Nite's—*"

I hang up the phone and drop it into the cup-holder. Fucking Taylor. Fucking Nite's Inn. Fucking salivary ferning.

Except, wait—there it is!

"Salivary ferning," I read to myself, running my finger along the words. "When a woman is close to ovulation, changes in her body chemistry give the saliva a fern-like appearance as it dries, as opposed to a speckled appearance."

Huh. The more you know.

I close the book and text Livia back.

Okay, Fern Woman. I'll meet you at 8. Then I add, **Are you super sure about the Nite's Inn?**

She responds right away. **I'll see you then, and I'm very sure. I'm doing this on a public servant's budget! And it's close to a Steak'n Shake, so you know it's in a good neighborhood.**

…Liv. Kitten. They found a body in that Steak'n Shake's dumpster last year.

One body and all of a sudden it's a 'bad' place. You are so judgey! I, for one, won't be scared away by that one tiny thing. I like to see the best in places.

My radio goes off in my ear—a senior is causing a disturbance at a nursing home and they need all available units to respond. With a rueful smile to myself at my idealistic little librarian, I send her a final message and then climb out of my car.

See you tonight, Livvy-girl. Don't get thrown into a dumpster before I get there.

. . .

Even though I was mostly joking about the Murder Steak'n Shake, I get to the Nite's Inn half an hour early so that I can be extra sure she's not in the parking lot alone. It's not that Overland Park is a bad place—for the most part, it's an extremely safe suburb—but I dug around some more at work today and found out that the Nite's Inn is extremely popular with truckers and construction workers, due to its proximity to the highway, low rates, and plethora of prostitutes.

I tell myself that it's my normal cop instinct that wants to keep Livia safe from rough, violent men in the parking lot—I want to keep all civilians safe, because it's what I've taken an oath to do. It's the right thing to do.

I mean, I certainly would do this for any person I was meeting at an hourly motel to impregnate.

Still, I can't entirely explain away the spike of excitement I feel when I see her climb out of her bright blue Prius C. It's lust, yes, but it's also lust for more than her body—for her laugh, for her attention, for her little gasps of breath when I touch her or surprise her. I lean against the back of my Audi as she approaches, not making a secret of the way my eyes trace her body, not bothering to hide the thickening ridge in my jeans at the sight of her.

The night is warm for March, and a pleasant breeze ruffles her blouse, a white buttoned affair with dainty gathered sleeves that probably have a special name. The blouse is paired with slim black pants and little ballet flats. Elegant, classy, somehow all the sexier for how casually restrained it is. Her hair is back in one of those maddening librarian buns, and I have a brief vision of cupping that head, bun and all, as she kneels in front of me and works on my belt.

"Hey," she says as she reaches me, not quite meeting my eyes.

"Hey," I reply, watching her mouth. There's the faintest glimmer of lip gloss on her lips, as if she swiped it on quickly while she was driving. The idea makes me smile…and it makes me want to kiss the gloss right off her mouth.

She looks up at me, her eyes huge and liquid in the dark. And then her gaze falls to my mouth too. I wonder if she's remembering the kiss from our first date, the feel of my hard cock pressing into her, a hard, hot ridge grinding against her clit.

And then her gaze drops from my mouth to my belt, where I know she can see that I'm hard for her. Color floods her cheeks, and she struggles to pull her eyes back up to my face.

I have to kiss her right *now*.

I reach for her, catching her by the waist with both hands and swinging her around so I've got her caged against the car. "I'm hungry for your mouth," I tell her, dropping my lips to hers. "So hungry."

She breathes against my mouth, her entire body trembling. "Chase…" she says, sounding dazed. "We shouldn't…"

"Why not?" I say, nibbling at the corners of her mouth, at the bowed curve of her lower lip. Her lips taste like berries, sweet and ripe.

"Because…*oh*…"

I've moved to her jaw now, kissing my way to her neck, where I bite and suck as much as I please, still keeping her caged against the car.

"Why, Liv?" I ask, my lips tickling the shell of her ear. "Because *why*?"

She is squirming against me now, not in the struggling way,

but in the way where she's trying to get her pelvis closer to mine, seeking out any source of friction she can find. I give her my thigh, and she makes this little grunt of satisfaction that drives me absolutely *crazy*, squirming down onto the hard muscle of my leg as if her life depended on it. Her fingers are digging into my biceps, and the heat of her on my leg is insane, even through our clothes.

"You like that, kitten?" I whisper in her ear. "You can ride any part of me as long as you please, so long as you let me kiss you too."

"I…we shouldn't kiss," she says hazily. When I pull back to look into her face, her eyes are glassy and her cheeks are flushed.

"But I think you'd like it," I say, pushing my thigh a little harder against her pussy.

Her eyes flutter. "I would, I did…but it's not smart." Her words come out breathless and stilted. "Because we should just focus on the…you know…"

"On the fucking?"

The word from my lips seems to focus her attention. Like laser focus. I can feel her trembling against me. "Right. The fucking."

"So you don't consider kissing a part of the fucking?" I'm genuinely interested in this. I've never met a girl who didn't want to have the breath kissed right out of her by me. And anyway, *I* really want to kiss Livia. Like really, really, really want to. Want to feel those plush lips give in to mine, want to taste them, want to flick my tongue against hers. I've probably beat off two or three times a day thinking about the kiss after our first date, and the urge to have another dirty, *dirty* kiss like that with her is unbearable.

But if she genuinely doesn't want to, then I'll abide by her wishes.

After all, I'm a pretty creative guy, for a cop. I can come up with a thousand other dirty things I can do with her that will scratch my librarian-shaped itch.

"I just don't want to feel, ummmm…" she trails off as I rock my thigh from side to side, her hands moving from my biceps to fist in my leather jacket. "…confused. It's too intimate."

"Kissing is too intimate, but trying to get you pregnant isn't?" I ask.

"People get pregnant in doctors' offices. With syringes. It doesn't have to be intimate, not like kissing."

She tilts her chin up, a little show of defiance, but she's still pressing herself hard against me. I tilt my head quizzically. "Are you calling my dick a syringe?"

A small giggle escapes her, and I lean closer to run my fingers along her ribs to tickle her. She laughs harder.

"No. Well, maybe."

"Kitten, they don't make syringes like what I'm packing. If they did, the doctor's office would be the most popular place in town."

"I didn't say it was a *bad* thing. I'm excited to use your syringe." Then she flushes even deeper, as if she can't believe she just said that out loud.

I laugh too. She's so fucking adorable. I should stop bothering her about this kissing thing, but I can't help but ask, my voice laced with hope and caution:

"Is it something I can earn?"

She blinks at me, her body going still against mine. "What do you mean?"

"I mean I want to earn it. If I prove myself to you, if I can prove myself a good man. Can I earn it? Earn kissing you?"

She's trembling again, biting her lip, still clutching my jacket. She finally meets my eyes and gives me a single nod.

Sweet.

And in the meantime...

"So for now you want to keep our insemination appointments strictly about the insemination?" I ask, already dreaming up some schemes.

"Yes," she replies, sounding relieved and disappointed all at once. "Just keep it about the insemination."

"Well, I'm here for whatever you need, kitten. But I've been doing some reading online—" I drop down to one knee and then the other in front of her, my hands easily working open the clasp to the front of her pants "—and I read that you need lubricant for insemination. For *syringes*." I wink up at her; she looks shocked.

"Chase, what are you doing?"

I wiggle the fly of her dress pants open, revealing a very cute pair of black panties. There's lace and ribbons and shit. Fucking awesome.

The rough concrete of the old parking lot digs into my knees, but I don't care. I tug Livia's pants down to the middle of her thighs and then press my mouth against that spot between her legs, kissing her right through the lace of her panties before I tug them out of the way.

"Oh," Livia whimpers. She slumps against my Audi. "*Oh.*"

Panties pulled to the side, I press my lips against the top of her folds, my nose pushing into the firm skin of her mound. She smells like some kind of feminine body wash, the kind that has pictures of fruit and vanilla sticks on the label, and her panties smell like clean laundry. And under all that I can smell *her*, the smell of damp arousal. Vividly, the sense memory of her smell and taste from our first date hits me, the sharp, sweet taste of her on my fingers as I licked it off.

Fuck, I'm hard. I'm so hard that I can feel my pulse in my dick. So hard that I can feel pearls of pre-cum beading at my tip. I didn't wear boxers tonight, and I can feel the denim rubbing against my need.

"Chase," Livia protests weakly. "You can't…"

I look up at her, my lips still pressed to her panties.

"We can't," she repeats.

I pull away slightly with a grin. "This is part of the insemination, doll."

"Someone will see us."

"I already checked before you got here. There're no cameras on this side of the lot, and we're in the shadows. No one from the road or the hotel can see us. Plus, people are on their knees in this parking lot all the time."

"Oh," she says, as if she feels like she should protest more, but can't remember what she needs to protest about.

"Do you want me to stop because you don't want my tongue against your clit? Or is it because you're worried about getting caught?"

"I, um, I do want that. The first thing you said. I want it. The thing about your tongue—*fuck.*"

The moment she concedes she wants it, I hook her panties farther to the side so I can access her clit, her folds. With her legs together like this, I can't tongue her deep, I can't lap up every bit of her taste like I want to, but I can stroke her clit. I can flick the tip of my tongue against it, I can take it between my teeth and suck, I can cover her in nibble-marks and beard-burn.

And even as shallow and light as it is, I feel her begin to tense and thrash against the Audi. She makes that little noise again—half grunt, half whimper—and without thinking, my hand drops to my belt, working it open so I can give my cock a few rough yanks as I continue eating her. I love being on my knees like this for her, dirty and fast, my cock throbbing, her losing all that reserve and distance and sliding her hands against my head, not to make me work her harder or faster, but simply to feel the tickle of my hair against her palms.

And right as she nears the edge, right as her thighs begin to tighten, I pull away and get to my feet, wiping my mouth and giving her my biggest grin as I loosely belt myself up. My dick whines at me.

"What are you doing?" she asks dazedly. "*Why* are you doing it?"

"I'm keeping it all about the insemination, like we agreed. Just getting you ready for…"

"…don't even say it…"

"My syringe."

Livia lets out a groan and her head falls back. "I regret saying that now. I regret letting you unbutton my pants. I regret everything."

In response, I tug her pants back up her hips and button them, giving her pussy a gentle squeeze as I do. "I guarantee you won't be saying that tomorrow morning. Now, are you ready for me to put a baby inside you?"

"God, yes."

7

CHASE

Ten minutes later, we're standing in possibly the most disgusting room I've ever been in. And having been on multiple dead body calls and multiple elderly hoarder calls, that's saying something.

"I think," Livia pronounces, bravely stepping deeper into the hotel room, "that it has a certain charm."

She hits the lights—only two bulbs buzz on and then one of them promptly buzzes back off. There's a dusting of dead bugs inside the light dish and several fluttering alive insects right underneath it.

"You can't just say that shitty things have charm, and make it be so," I tell her, exasperated. To prove my point, I flip back the covers on the bed. Something dark and beetle-like scuttles out of sight. I tug a miniature black light out of my back pocket (I lifted one from my duty bag after my talk with Taylor) and shine it on the sheets. In the dim light of the dying, bug-covered bulb, we can see well enough that the sheets are covered in stains. Stains that glow neon bright, like a sign flashing: **DON'T SLEEP ON ME.**

"This is worse than I thought," I mumble, backing away from the bed. Out of curiosity, I shine the black light on the walls.

"Oh God," Livia gasps in horror, both hands coming up to cover her mouth. "Was a pig slaughtered in here?"

I step closer to the wall and squint at the stains, holding

the black light up higher. "Either that or someone had a *very* good night."

I click the black light off and turn to face my soon-to-be baby mama.

"Well," she says, squaring her shoulders and starting to unbutton her blouse. "Babies have been conceived in worse."

"*What?*"

She gives me a very librarian look. "I mean, historically and globally speaking. It's only our modern, Western sense of sterile hygiene that makes this seem gross—"

"Babe," I cut her off. "If you get in that bed naked, I guarantee you'll get pregnant. But it might not be mine."

She looks back at the bed, considering.

"In fact, it definitely won't be mine because *I* am not getting in that bed naked with you."

Her face seems to fall the slightest bit. "I just…I can't really afford something nicer, and it didn't feel right to suggest my place, and…" She trails off and shrugs, not making eye contact with me.

I soften. Well, my heart softens. My dick is still raring to go, especially since I can still smell her on my skin.

"Look, Liv. I'll tell you what. There's about—" I check my watch and instantly consult my mental baseball schedule "—forty minutes left in the Royals game. What do you say we go grab some wings and some beer, watch the game, and I'll take care of the rest."

She sighs. "Dinner? Drinks? That's not keeping it just about the insemination, Chase."

God I love it when she says my name. Even with a sigh.

I walk over to her and pull her into me, and to my surprise, she lets me, folding perfectly against my chest and burying her face there.

I find my sweetest, softest voice and say, "I really want wings right now."

She snorts against my chest.

"And I want you to have your baby, kitten, I really do."

"But?" she says morosely, still pressed into my chest.

I find her chin and tilt her face up to me. "But you deserve better than this room. So does your baby. I know you think that every part of this has to be hard, and maybe lots of it will be. But this—this room—this is something I can make easier, okay? Let me help."

She bites her lip and I smooth my thumb over it, loving how soft it is against my skin. "Why would you help me? I'm basically forcing you into this, anyway."

I'm a little confused by the question. "Because I like you? Too much for you to get bedbugs? Also I don't want the bedbugs?"

She squints at me a second, as if it can't actually be that simple. It makes my chest squeeze and something in my blood heat, thinking about the men before me who've made her so suspicious of the most of basic of human kindnesses.

"Okay," she relents. "Take me to wings and beer."

I drop a kiss onto her forehead. And then I take her to wings and beer.

. . .

"I never pictured you as an Audi guy," Livia admits, reaching for my ranch dressing since she's destroyed hers already. She's so fucking cute covered in barbeque sauce that I don't even smack her hand away, even though ranch theft is a crime that brought about many fights between Megan and me as teenagers. We're at the wing place, the post-game analysis blaring in the background, two spent beer glasses between us, along with the empty wings baskets. Sad celery stalks languish, wilted and pale. Livia's chewing on one now.

I pretend to be offended. "What does that even mean? An *Audi guy?*"

She shrugs with an embarrassed smile. "I guess I just figured since you were a macho cop, you'd have a macho car. A truck or a Mustang or something."

I narrow my macho eyes into very macho slits. "Are you saying an Audi isn't macho?"

She giggles at my mock-anger and then steals my napkin to wipe at her fingers. "It's very masculine," she says sweetly. "If you're into that *imported* sort of thing."

Since our check is paid already, I stand up and offer her my arm, which she takes after only a short moment of hesitation. Slowly but surely, I'm drawing her out of the protective shell she's built for herself.

"If by 'this sort of thing,' you mean meticulous engineering and unbeatable reliability, then I guess you're right. Give me your phone."

She chews on her lip for a second but hands it over. I plug in an address and hand it back to her. "Meet you there in fifteen minutes. And I'm taking care of it, okay?"

"Okay," she says slowly, looking down at her phone. I see the moment she realizes where the address is, what hotel it is. "Holy shit, Chase. No, you can't do this."

"I look forward to arguing with you once we get there. But let's do it while I've got my face buried in your cunt."

She flushes and mumbles something.

I give her bottom a little swat. "Now, into your car, little kitten. I can't leave until you're safely on your way."

She shoots me a look that borders on indignant, but poutily so. And then she gets into her Prius, buckles up and drives away. I follow her in the macho Audi, the low burn of excitement that I'd banked earlier in the Nite's Inn parking lot starting to flare back into a fire. It's really going to happen, finally, having Livia underneath me as I sink into her. As I rut into her.

Bare.

The mere word sends a shiver through me as I pull into the parking garage of the Raphael Hotel. I haven't fucked bare since I was in high school with my first girlfriend. There was a broken condom once in college and a round of just-the-tip with a woman in my academy class that ended in some 'friendly fire'—the places in my life where I can't entirely dismiss the possibility that I've contributed to the world's population of Kellys. But other than that, I've basically been a saint. Chase Kelly, patron saint of responsible ejaculation.

But not tonight. Tonight, I get to be selfish.

Tonight, I get to be responsibly irresponsible.

I've sent Liv my latest gamut of tests—all fresh from last month—and I've signed a "contract" and I've had my fingers and mouth on her enough times to be confident that she's not going to back out when it comes to the real deal. I can already imagine how tight and hot the real deal is going to be squeezing my cock, can already imagine how delicious *selfish* is going to feel when I empty myself inside my girl.

When I stroll into the lobby, Livia is already there and ready to argue some more. The hotel's too nice, she protests, I'm too nice, nobody should be nice to her because it makes her feel guilty, and so on. I just keep nodding as I check in at the desk and as we take the elevator up to the room, injecting the occasional noise so that she thinks I'm listening.

I'm not though. Instead, I'm watching her argue that I'm being too nice by insisting on fucking her in a place without bedbugs. (It also has HBO. And free breakfast. And an oversized bathtub. *And* a Keurig. I mean, I have a Keurig at the station, but for some reason it feels fancier in a hotel.) And I wonder how Livia got to the place where accepting any act of kindness—even if it also benefits the giver of said kindness too—pains her this much. Is it guilt? Is it fear of owing someone kindness in return? Is it some sort of rigid Jane Eyre-like independence that refuses to compromise for anything?

And then I wonder if that's one of the reasons she wants a child of her own so much, if a parent-child relationship is the only kind of connection where she can imagine being completely unconditional. Completely free of the fears that seem to bother her now.

The elevator doors open and we're walking down the hall, Liv still arguing, and finally, I just cage her against the wall right there in the hallway, and nuzzle my nose into her neck since she won't let me kiss her.

"I thought we were going to save this argument for when my face was between your legs," I murmur, still nuzzling.

She shivers, tilting her head to grant me access to more of her neck. "I just don't like feeling like I owe you," she mumbles, eyes fluttering closed as I ghost my nose and mouth over her earlobe.

"You made me sign a contract saying that we don't owe each other anything, right?"

"Right."

"And I hope you don't think I'm cruel enough to want something in return for a nicer hotel room."

She bites her lip. "No…I don't think that. I mean, I don't think it would be cruel for you to want something in return, but I also think you wouldn't ask it because you're already going to have sex with me anyway."

She's pressing up against me, breathing fast, and I pull my head back to study her face with narrowed eyes. If I didn't know better, I'd think this librarian *wants* to owe me something. Not with the better part of her brain, certainly, but all this talk of owing and cruelty has her awfully worked up.

And that has *me* worked up.

"I could be cruel though," I say carefully, studying her face. "I could decide that you owed me."

"And how would you make me pay you back?" she whispers, pupils dilated wide and dark. Yeah, she's into it.

Good, 'cause so am I.

"You've already promised me your pussy," I say. "But there are other ways…" I run the pads of two fingers along her lips and then slide the fingers into her mouth. She sucks without me telling her, and I almost come in my pants.

"Come on," I growl, removing my fingers and grabbing her hand. I practically yank her the rest of the way to our room, not letting go even as I dig for the keycard and tap it against the lock.

Once we're in the room, I don't waste any time noticing how

much nicer it is than the one at the Nite's Inn, I only notice her, only pay attention to her. To the high spots of color in her cheeks and the pulse thudding in her throat.

"I need to see you," I say, shrugging off my leather jacket and pulling off my T-shirt. "Let me see you, kitten."

Her eyes flare at the sight of my naked chest and torso, and then, unexpectedly, she seems to falter, to grow shy.

"I, um…" she moves her purse from her shoulder and opens it up. "I need to get dressed first."

My brow wrinkles. "Dressed? That's moving in the wrong direction, sweetheart." Then I have a thought. "Is this like a coy way of saying you need to go brush your teeth or something?"

She swallows and shakes her head. "I need to *change*," she elaborates.

"Change into what?"

She sets her shoulders back, lifting her chin with that proud look I adore so much. "If you must know, I bought a thing. A sexy thing. Lingerie."

Mmm, lingerie. Now that's the L word every man wants to hear. I definitely will require her to wear that for me soon. Very soon.

But not now. Now, I need to fuck her before my dick explodes.

I'm trying to think of a non-caveman way to express this when she admits, in a voice that manages to be defiant and faltering all at once, "I wanted to make sure you were in the mood when the time came."

I have no response to this. Does she think me groping her in the parking lot and again in the hallway means I'm not in the mood?

"Kitten. Livia. Come here for a second."

She hesitates, thinking, but then she takes a step toward me. And another. And I find her hand with mine and press it flat against my thick erection. "You don't need to wear lingerie for me. You can if you want to, but this is how you have me in slacks and a blouse that buttons up to your neck. You could be wearing one of those giant padded suits we use to train the police dogs, and I'd still want to take you to bed."

I let go of her hand but she doesn't move it from my cock. Fuck, it feels good.

"I just..." she swallows. "It's been a little while for me, and I'm worried that I've forgotten how it all works. How to make it fun for both of us."

I lean forward, enough so that I can circle my nose around hers. She breathes in a jagged breath as I do, tilting her mouth up, but I'm careful not to kiss her. "How long has it been, kitten? How long is 'a little while'?"

"Um, just some time."

I give her jaw a little nip, not hard, just enough to send a shudder through her. "How long?" I repeat.

"Two," she whispers.

"Two weeks?"

"No."

I frown, pulling away. "Two months?"

She draws herself up and meets my eyes with an expression I can't read. "It's been two years."

My mind goes blank; her words don't make any sense to me, don't compute. Two years without sex? Seven hundred and thirty days? Seven hundred and thirty *and a half* days, scientifically speaking?

"How?" I ask. Her hand is still on my dick, and I am finding it impossible to actually process this information.

"Well," she explains, "the last time I had sex was two years ago. That's how."

"You're fucking gorgeous," I say, still confused. "I wanted to tackle you and fuck you right there in that school parking lot the first day I met you. Surely even if you didn't want a relationship, you would have had no trouble finding a man who would—"

"It just never felt right," she says. "After my last boyfriend dumped me, I tried hooking up with a guy I met at a bar, and it was fine, but it still felt like being vulnerable. It still felt like opening up to someone, even though it was supposed to be casual. I don't want to open up, and I don't need to. I can take care of those needs on my own. I have a fantastic vibrator."

But masturbating is not the same, I want to argue. Part of sex is the sweat and the sighs, the give of another person's flesh, the smell of their hair, the taste of their lips. But then something else occurs to me, and it wipes all other thoughts out of my mind.

"Does this mean I'll be the first man inside you in two years?"

She nods, a shy smile on her face. I want to nibble that smile, I want to gobble her up, I want to bite and possess her. And for the first time in three days, the twisting part of my chest and the rational part of my brain are in full agreement. My cock agrees too: we have to make this good for her. It's a huge honor to be the man she's chosen not only to father her child, but to make love to her after so long—she deserves for this to be good. Better than good. Perfect.

Also, my cock reminds me, there's something very exciting in the idea of being the first man inside that pussy in so long. Almost as if it were saved for me. As if it were mine to possess.

"I've been thinking about it all week," she confesses. "What it will feel like. If it will feel tight and big and full. If you'll stretch me."

I groan. "You're killing me, Liv."

Another shy smile. "I can't wait to see you."

"Naughty kitten," I breathe. "If I could kiss you, I'd kiss you until you came in my arms. But since I can't…"

I reach for her blouse and she lets me, moving her hand from my cock—*boo*—up to my exposed chest, which does feel pretty good. As I unbutton her shirt, she runs wandering fingers all over my chest and abs and shoulders and arms, her eyes wide and her lips parted.

"I like you touching me like that," I rumble. And I so fucking do, it's like having my ego and my body petted at the same time.

"You're so strong," she marvels. Then she squeezes my biceps so tightly I feel her fingernails dig into my skin.

I hiss, but it's a good hiss, and her voice is low and needy when she says, "Hurry, Chase."

She doesn't have to tell me twice. I finish with the buttons and slide the silky fabric from her shoulders, where it flutters to the ground.

"Fuck me," I mumble, drinking in the sight of her golden skin, the smoothness of her belly, the delicious weight of her breasts in her black lace bra. Her navel is a sweet little divot on that perfect stomach, a stomach mostly firm, mostly flat, but with some softness, some curve. I have to put my mouth on it.

I drop to my knees and kiss her belly button, running my lips and then my tongue around the indent of it. My touch seems to surprise her; she jolts the second my tongue touches her skin. But her hands thread through my hair, keeping my mouth against her skin, making it clear she wants more.

I give her more. I kiss and lick along the lines of her stomach, I nibble until it tickles and she's giggling breathlessly, and then once I think I've got her relaxed and comfortable with me again, I slowly work her pants open, looking up at her from my knees as I do. "Is it okay if I finish what I started earlier?"

"Yes," she murmurs. "I would like that."

Once I have her pants unfastened, I lean back onto my heels and bring her foot onto my thigh, where I gently ease off her ballet flat. Then again on the other side. I run a finger along the arch of her foot before I set it down, not to tickle but just to enjoy the feeling of her skin, to enjoy the way every touch of mine seems to light her on fire.

Then I pull her pants down her legs and help her step out of them, so she's standing in front of me in her matching bra-and-panty set. Keeping eye contact, I slide my hands up the outside of her thighs to her hips, taking a moment to squeeze and grope her ass, and then I hook my fingers in her panties and drag them down, exposing that bare pussy completely.

My cock aches the moment I see it, and I can't resist the urge to lean in and give it a kiss. I can smell her, can see that she's already so fucking wet, and it makes me just want to shove my face in there and make her figure out trivial details like balance and keeping herself spread for me while I eat her.

But no, she deserves better. Which is why I stand up after dropping a light kiss on her clit and reach around her with one hand and easily unfasten her bra.

"You're really good at that," she says.

Normally I would say something like *of course I am* or *I've had lots of practice, baby*, but it doesn't feel right at the moment. Not like I'm ashamed of being Officer Good Times, just that I want to be more than Officer Good Times right now, I want to be the guy who made her first fuck in two years feel amazing. And I don't think reminding her of all the women I've fucked before tonight will help that. I'll ease back on the handcuffs tonight too—there'll be plenty of time to see her cuffed and naked in front of me.

So instead I help her pull the bra off, and then I stand back and look at her. Just look at her. Completely naked for me.

How did I get so lucky?

"You're beautiful," I tell her in a husky voice. "Fucking gorgeous."

Her tits are perfect teardrops with dark tips just begging to be sucked, and they're already puckered into tight buds for me. "I'm going to suck on those," I inform her. "Just so you know."

"Okay," she breathes.

"A lot."

"Okay."

"It will be good practice for when the baby comes."

"It's for the baby," she repeats, dazed. "Right."

"But right now, I have to finish something else. Get on the bed for me, kitten, and on your back, please."

She obeys, climbing on the bed, looking more like a kitten than ever. And then she slowly stretches out on her back while I work open my belt. Her eyes darken at the sight, goose bumps cropping up on her skin as she hears the leather slide against my jeans as I pull the belt free. I drop it on the ground and pop open the buttons of my jeans to give my straining cock some relief.

I crawl up on the bed in between her legs, coming to rest on my stomach with her cunt mere inches from my face. I use my thumbs to trace along the place where her thighs meet her sex; I stroke her outside folds until she squirms. And then I use those thumbs to spread her completely open for me, exposing the soft wet of her inner petals and the small opening to her sweetest secret. I finally get to see and smell and taste what I couldn't in the parking lot, this wet well, this deep-rose pink of her that has been waiting for another person's touch for two years.

"Oh, Liv," I say, because I don't know what else to say. I might come just from looking at her, come right in my jeans, because this is the sweetest cunt I've ever seen and I don't even know how I'm going to last more than a minute while I'm fucking it.

"Please," she begs.

"I like you saying please," I say, leaning in close so I can give her a long lick from her hole to her clit. "It's very polite."

"I'm always polite," she gasps. I've licked her pussy again, this time straight into her entrance, circling and thrusting my tongue as she squirms. I have to wrap my arms around her thighs to keep her still enough for me to eat her the way I want.

"You are so polite," I croon in between kisses and sucks. "You let me feel your pussy when I wanted it so badly at dinner the other night. You let me suckle your clit tonight when I wanted to. And in just a few minutes, you're going to politely spread your legs and let me take what I need. Going to let me come so hard inside you."

She moans, throwing her forearm over her eyes. "Chase…"

Two years since she's had an orgasm given to her, and I can tell. Her thighs are tight, her belly tighter, a flush creeping up her chest. I add a finger to my efforts, then a second finger, easing her open, making her soft and swollen and ready for me. She's thrashing now, trying to close her legs, like the feeling is too much.

"I can't," she pants, twisting and writhing. "Oh God, it's too much, I can't, I can't."

"You will," I growl, sucking and licking and moving my fingers in the slow, curling way she seems to like. Underneath, my cock is throbbing and aching so badly that I can't help but rock my hips against the mattress as I bring Liv closer and closer to orgasm. I can't wait to empty inside of her, can't wait to drain myself of every last drop deep in her cunt, can't wait to feel her wet heat surrounding my naked skin. Consumed by that idea, I flick my tongue over the swollen pearl of her clit faster and faster, pressing against the sensitive spot on her front walls with my fingers. I want her wet and wrung out and wanting more by the time I'm ready to push these jeans down and start pumping inside her.

Livia still chants *I can't, it's too much, I can't* above me, and then her body betrays her words, tightening around my mouth and fingers, tightening like ribbons around a maypole, and then finally, with a cry so low and long that it makes me groan in response, she unwinds and releases. Her body trembles and quakes, and she's got one hand clutching my hair and her other covering her eyes, as if she can't handle having the power of sight on top of all the other sensory information flooding her body. As if my hair in her fist and the pulsing in her womb are her only anchors in this world.

I almost can't stand it, the feeling of her coming this hard, the sight of it, the sound of it, and the minute her flutters slow and her hips stop squirming, I rise up to my knees and suck on the fingers that were just inside of her. She watches me with dark eyes, her body limp and sated beneath me.

I open my jeans the rest of the way. "My turn," I say, crawling over her with a wicked grin.

8

LIVIA

I can't take my eyes off of him. He's a god. Adonis. The way he looks. The way he moves. The way I know he's going to fuck. But it's more than what *he* is that makes him divine. Because, yeah, he's beautiful, but also he makes *me* feel beautiful.

It's been a long time since someone's made me feel like that. Like sexy beautiful. Maybe I've missed it more than I realized.

He wriggles out of his jeans as he climbs up over me, and he's good at it. Good at undressing quickly in awkward positions without getting caught in his clothes the way I would if I tried something similar.

It's a testament to how experienced he is. I should feel put off by that, but in this moment, I feel just the opposite. It's part of how he makes me feel beautiful. Because I feel special. I feel lucky. Chase can have anyone. A man with his resume doesn't need a contract to guarantee his bed won't be empty. Yet he wants me. Enough to agree to forego other sexual relationships for what might be several months.

And if I didn't believe it when he signed, I surely believe it now that his cock is naked and stone in front of me.

He tugs on his erection. Once, twice. My eyes widen. I sense his hunger growing, and—is it even possible?—his dick thickens before me.

I want it. I want it so bad. I've just come, and I'm ready for more. I'm desperate for more. The reason I'm here, the reason I'm lying beneath him, suddenly isn't foremost on my mind. I still want a baby, but right now the only thing I want is his cock inside me. Stretching me. Filling me.

Is it so wrong to want to fuck him as much as I do?

It's biology. It's hormones. That's what I'll tell myself later. If our bodies didn't want sex, we wouldn't want to procreate. Desire is part of the process, and giving into that desire is the step I'm on now.

"I've been waiting for this," Chase half mumbles, half growls as he settles between my legs and bends to swirl his tongue around my peaked nipple.

I tilt my hips up to meet him and feel a delicious jolt of pleasure as his crown grazes along my hole. But then he slides his length along my slit, knocking his tip against my clit. At the same time, he sucks my nipple into his mouth, sending another electric shock to my lower regions.

It's amazing and hot as hell but not where I want him. Not where I *need* him.

"Chase…" I beg, bucking my pelvis against him.

"Gotta be patient, kitten," he says, his mouth full of my tit. He squeezes my other breast with his hand, and I moan. He's enjoying tormenting me. I don't know how he can stand it. I can feel how hard he is as he rubs again along my pussy. How big he is. It has to hurt.

I'm certainly hurting. I can already feel another climax brewing. Slowly. Achingly.

"Chase!" I wriggle, trying to maneuver so I can get his tip inside me. "Please!"

He surrenders my breast and presses his forehead to mine. "There it is." His lips are so close, hovering just above my mouth. For a second I think he might try to kiss me. Or, that I might try to kiss him. I had reasons for not kissing—good reasons. Important reasons. Crucial-to-this-whole-arrangement reasons.

I'm just struggling to remember them when he says, "I was waiting for the magic word."

He reaches down between us and positions his cock at my entrance, and then, instead of thinking about his lips or wondering about kissing or not kissing, I'm gasping as he pushes inside me.

"Oh my God," I pant, my eyes shut tight. He's bigger than I realized, and while it's not painful, I feel every inch of him as he slides in farther. He's hot and solid and nothing like the silicone MegaMan 2000 that's hidden in my underwear drawer. "Oh my God oh my God oh my God."

"You feel good too, babe," he rumbles before pulling out. "Open your eyes."

But I can't open my eyes. I can't look at him. It's too much to see on top of everything he's making me feel.

He thrusts inside me, hitting a sensitive spot, and I jerk and cry out in surprise, because it sends me clenching in a sudden climax.

"Jesus, Liv, you're so tight when you come."

I'm dizzy and dazed from this latest orgasm, but I'm aware enough to feel that he has to fight so that I don't push him out. He wraps his arms around me and pulls me with him as he shifts onto his knees so that now I'm sitting on his lap.

I open my eyes, and there he is, right in front of me. Something in my chest tightens, and the air is suddenly missing from my lungs.

Chase grins, rocking in and out of me at a leisurely pace. "That's better."

But this is not better. Not for me. This isn't just biological desire anymore, this is… I don't know what this is, exactly. It feels too intimate. It feels too much like connection. It feels too *good*.

I don't like it, and I shift, trying to get off Chase's lap.

"Hold on. I'll fix it," he says, and however he's interpreted my restlessness, he does fix it by gripping my waist and driving into me with such force I have to clutch onto him. I bury my head in his shoulder, and even though my torso is pressed against his, the lack of eye contact allows me to relax. Chase quickly finds an earnest rhythm, and once again I can believe this is just about sex. Just about feeling good for him. Just about getting to his climax for both of us.

Soon, a fine sheen of sweat covers our bodies. His muscles tense underneath my thighs, and I can tell he's close. This is one of the things that's different from getting off by myself—someone else's orgasm is as important as my own. I'd let myself remember sex with a partner as somewhat of a chore for exactly this reason.

But Chase's climax feels like anything but work, and not just because I'm after his sperm. For one, he's exerting all the effort. But also I want him to come because I'm into it. I'm into *him*. He turns me on and gets me hot like no one has in a long time, and part of what's so sexy about him is how turned on he seems to be by *me*.

That's not something I get from the MegaMan 2000.

I pull back so I can watch him. His tempo increases, and his face starts to screw up, and I'm fascinated. Enthralled. That I can turn this man into this beast, that I can do this to him—it feels like a superpower. Is this how he feels when he's making me writhe and moan under his tongue? Like he's in command? Like he's in control? No wonder he moves like a god—this ability feels very almighty.

But just when I think he's on the brink, when I'm sure he's about to release, he surprises me by pushing me to the bed and flipping me to my stomach. His dick slides out of me, and I'm missing it.

"I'm not ready to be done," he says as he pushes my knees underneath me.

"Chase. The goal is releasing." The resistance in my tone is not matched by my body. My body is pliable, bending to how he wants me, because I'm not ready to be done either.

He kneels behind me and pulls my hips up so I'm at the right height. Then, with his cock in his hand, he rubs his crown along the slit of my swollen, soaked pussy. "I'll release. But first I'm going to enjoy you."

"This isn't about enjoyment," I moan. With enjoyment. "This is about making a baby."

He rubs his palm over my ass as he gently bucks his tip inside my hole. "For you, it's about a baby." He pulls out and immediately pushes just the tip in again. "For me it's about getting to be inside your tight little cunt for as long as possible. But if you want me to stop—"

He withdraws again, and this time he doesn't press in again right away.

"No, no!" I protest, thrusting my hips back toward him in an attempt to capture the prize. I sound desperate and needy, and I am, even though I know he's only teasing me, because he's going to go until he comes no matter what.

He chuckles behind me, amused by my obvious anguish.

It's too late, but I try to cover. I throw my head over my shoulder to look at him. "I mean. You're right. My reward is a baby. Your reward is the sex. So. Take your time."

"I plan to." There's that cocky grin again. The one that disintegrates my panties every time I see it.

Guess it's a good thing I'm not wearing panties.

Oddly, I find myself giving him a grin of my own.

But then, without warning, he shoves all the way inside me and my smile's wiped off my face with a pleasure-filled grunt.

"Fuckkkkk, Liv." He grinds into me, slow enough that I know he's paying attention to every sensation, just like I am. Consciously noting every point of contact. Taking the time to feel how his cock rubs me here and then here and, holy mother of holies, here.

I wriggle and twist, both trying to get away and feel more of him at once. Sounds come out of my mouth. Phrases that don't make sense. Words I barely recognize. *Please enough more. Yes. Ung. So good so good so good it's good I can't so good.*

I want him to go faster, want him to drive the ache from my body. I reach down between my legs and rub at my clit, needing some sort of relief, but my touch is like fire. I'm nearly ready to explode just at the graze of my fingertips, and as much as I want it, I don't think I can take it. So I drop my hand and curl my fists around the bedspread, pressing my forehead into the pillows.

"Can't. Wait," Chase pants, and, finally, he abandons his sweet agonizing torture, and picks up the tempo, pounding into me with a fervent frenzy. My belly tightens and the tightness spreads outward, through my hips. Down my thighs. My vision blurs. My body tingles, everywhere.

I'm going to come, and Chase, I can tell, is right there with me. And as much as I'd wanted to watch him when he does, I'm glad that my face is turned away from him now. Because in the beautiful chaos of this heightened state of sensations, I remember more than just what it's like to feel beautiful. More than what it's like to watch a man come. I also remember that, once upon a time, I wanted all of this, all the time. Once upon a time I wasn't done with men. Once upon a time I believed that being with someone like this could be something that lasts.

I know the memory is etched on my face when the wave of pleasure washes over me and pulls me under. I'm glad Chase can't see this because then he'd know I have doubts. And no one can know I have doubts. That's a secret I keep even from myself.

I'm still navigating my way through my own orgasm when Chase stills behind me. With his fingernails gripping my hips, he lets out a long, low grunt and presses his pelvis tight against my hips as he comes inside me. Then he collapses on the bed next to me with a contented sigh.

I turn my head to the side so that I can't see him and give myself a few minutes to catch my breath and gather my strength. My limbs feel loose and weak, and I'm exhausted. My brain feels like mush, but I force myself to think clearly. This was good—

this was *amazing*—I'll give myself that.

But now it's over. I can't let myself get comfortable.

I'm about to get up when he stirs. "You're fun," he says, nudging my back with his elbow.

I half laugh, half choke. "I'm fairly certain that any fun that was had was because of you."

"And you."

I glance back at him and find he's grinning with as much lust in his gaze as ever. "I assure you," I tell him in my very serious, very librarian voice, "I am not fun."

He laughs. "Whatever you say, kitten."

Then I laugh too because this *has* been fun. Which means maybe I *am* fun. When I'm with him, anyway.

Which is very temporary.

In fact, we aren't even *with* each other. Not really. Which is exactly the reason I need to get out of here.

I start to roll out of the bed when Chase stops me.

"Where are you going?" he asks with a note of alarm.

His reaction startles me, and I'm suddenly unsure. "To... clean up?"

"No, no, no," he admonishes. He's up now and coming around to my side of the bed with a pillow in his hands. "You're not supposed to get up right away. On your back. Put this under your hips." He guides me back down and slips the pillow underneath me. "You should sit like that for at least fifteen minutes. We should say twenty to be sure. I'll set a timer." He rustles through our discarded clothes, presumably looking for his phone.

"Uh. Okay. Thank you." I'm not sure how else to respond. I'd been in such haste to get out of the room before things started to feel too intimate, I'd completely forgotten one of the best practices for conceiving is keeping the hips elevated after sex.

More stunning is that this is something Chase knows. I'm impressed.

And touched that he cares enough to remind me.

He's probably just concerned about his obligation to knock me up. He signed a contract and all. The sooner it happens, the sooner he's back to banging a different woman every night.

I dismiss the jealous jolt that thought sends through me. I only feel that way right now because this was the first time we've been together, and the sex was so good. By the time I'm pregnant, I'll surely be over it.

But while I'm still not over it…

I shamelessly ogle Chase's bare ass while he bends to grab a beer out of the mini-fridge.

"You want something?" he asks when he catches me looking.

Despite everything we've just done together, I feel my face flush. "Water, I guess. Thanks."

He brings me a bottle of water and tosses his phone on the nightstand, facing it so I can see the timer. Next he picks up the television remote, and after flipping through most of the channels too fast to see what's on, he finally settles on ESPN. Then he stretches out on the bed by me, one hand cradling his head, the other holding his beer.

He's still naked.

And he seems to have no intention of changing that anytime soon.

I gape, but he doesn't notice.

I mean, what the actual fuck is he doing? I'm obviously stuck in my position for the next twenty minutes, but he's not. He should be getting ready to leave or, at the very least, getting dressed. Anything to get this situation back to some normalcy.

I rub my eyes and take a deep breath. Maybe I'm being too rigid. It's twenty minutes. He should be allowed that time to enjoy his beer.

I look over at him again. He's animated as he watches the recap of tonight's major games. It's so stereotypically male and surprisingly sexy. He's so relaxed, and I can't help but wonder if he needs this in his life. I have no idea what kinds of things he sees on a daily basis as a cop, but I once witnessed a terrible accident involving a semi truck and a biker. The images of the mangled aluminum frame of the bike wrapped around the rider's body will never leave my mind.

I'm sure Chase sees far worse. Watching sports and chasing skirts are maybe necessary distractions to keep the bad stuff from getting the best of him.

My insides feel gooey at the thought. I force myself to ignore it and concentrate instead on the quarter-sleeve tattoo that occupies the landscape of his bicep. I haven't had a chance to really look at it, so I study it now. At his shoulder, there's a series of numbers on top of a shield made of concentric circles. To the side are a couple of Minions, characters from a popular animated movie. Then, at the base, is a ram's head. The design puts all the pieces together as if they belong, but I can't figure out the rhyme or reason.

I twist my torso to look at it closer. "What does your tattoo mean?"

He glances at me. "Which part?"

"Any of it. What is it?"

"Well…" He hits mute on the TV remote. Then he turns his bicep so he can see his ink, and with his left hand, he points at the base of his tat. "This is a ram. And this is the shield from—"

Laughing, I grab his finger and cut him off. "I know that's a ram. I can tell what each of the individual parts are. But what is it all together? Why did you get it?"

His lip lifts in a slight smile, and his eyes drift down to where I'm still holding his finger. I blink awkwardly and let it go. Then I fold my arms over my chest, tucking my hands away in case I'm tempted to touch him again. There's no reason for touching now. There isn't any reason for getting personal at all, but I'm stuck here for the moment so I decide this probably falls under the category of polite conversation.

Chase makes a *hmm* sound, as though trying to decide where to start. "I got the individual parts little by little, because they each meant something different. All together, it's me, I guess." He moves his arm closer so that I don't have to crane my neck or disturb the elevation of my hips. "The ram is for my mother. She died when I was fifteen, and I wanted something to remember her by. Something that wasn't one of those tacky Mom tattoos with the roses. That wouldn't have fit her at all."

I wrinkle my face in polite confusion. "And a ram…does?"

He chuckles lightly, making the bed shake and this arm graze against mine. "It's her astrology symbol. April third."

"Aries." I'm not huge into astrology, but I know a little bit about everything. I'm a librarian, after all.

"Yeah. She was a true Aries too. Not that I believe in that stuff. But if I did." His brow furrows as if he's trying to figure out what he wants to say before he says it. "She seemed to fit all the character traits associated with the sign. She was energetic and courageous. Impatient. Spontaneous. Generous. A leader. Optimistic to a fault. Even after she got sick."

His voice is softer when he talks about his mother. It's tender. Reverent, almost, and it makes me want to know more, even when I shouldn't care.

"What did she have?" I ask, against my better judgment.

"Ovarian cancer. It had already spread through her pelvis before we caught it. She never had a shot. But she fought anyway. Just like a stubborn ram."

I trace my fingers along his inked skin. "That had to be hard."

"It was. Megan had to get through puberty with Gran as her guide."

I catch his eye. "It had to be hard for you too."

He shrugs, and I can tell that saying any more will threaten his manliness, so I change the subject and point to the numbers at the top of the shield. "Eight-nine-eight. What's that? Some superhero code I'm not nerdy enough to know?"

"It's my badge number," he says proudly.

"Ah. It *is* a superhero code." I am nerdy enough to recognize the concentric circles underneath. The star in the middle gives it away. "Obviously that's why you got the Captain America shield. Because you think of yourself as a cop superhero and all. Then what are the Minions supposed to—"

"Hold on." He sits up and shifts so he's facing me. "No. It's not like that."

"What?"

"I do not think of myself as a superhero," he says emphatically.

I stare at him, skeptical. "Really? You don't?"

"No!"

"Not even a little? With your superhero badge and your superhero gun and your superhero nightstick."

He waggles his brows. "Well, yes with the superhero nightstick." Then he immediately returns to defensive mode. "But no! What kind of a douchecanoe do you think I am?"

"With your Captain America tattoo. And your choice in careers." I'm teasing him now. It's too easy. And too fun.

"I'm a cop because I want to stand up to injustice. Fight for the good guys. Like Captain America. That's all." He scowls, and it's sexy and adorable and funny all at once.

I bite back a giggle. "Superhero Kelly," I taunt. He's so childlike in his honesty. I can easily imagine him as a little boy, running around in a makeshift cape, pretending to defeat the villains. "What about the Minions? Do you want to fight injustice like cute single-celled yellow organisms too?"

"Stop it," he warns, but it's the kind of warning that makes my skin tingle. The kind of warning I'm tempted to push against. "The Minions are for my nephews."

I hadn't been expecting that. "That's really sweet. That you're so close to them."

He jerks his head slightly like it's no big deal. "They're like my kids. I probably won't have any of my own. I'm already thirty-three. It's not like I'm settling down anytime soon. Or ever. So they're the closest thing I've got. That means something to me."

Our gazes lock.

"Or, you know," he says carefully. "I probably won't have any besides yours. And that one won't actually be mine. So."

The air suddenly feels heavy. Tense.

What if my baby-to-be is Chase's only kid? What if he never has any others? This man who would obviously make such a good father... Does that change things? Does that mean something to *me*?

"Liv..." he begins, but whatever he's going to say is cut off by the buzz of the timer sounding from his phone.

"I need to go," I say, bolting up from the bed. I have to get out of here. I have to be somewhere that he's not. Somewhere where his presence and his life story won't tempt me to care about him or his future or whether or not he'll ever be a dad. It's not my place to care. I refuse to let myself.

"Go where? It's late. We have the room all night." He seems truly surprised by my sudden desire to leave.

I pause while gathering my clothes and stare at him incredulously. "We can't stay here together, Chase."

"Sure we can."

"No. We can't." How did he not think that spending the night together would cross the line from baby insemination to way too intimate? This was supposed to be detached. Sex and nothing more. I should never have allowed the wings or the fancy hotel or so many orgasms. Somewhere I lost control, and I have to get hold of the reins and not let things happen like this again.

Okay, maybe the orgasms can stay. But the rest has to go.

A beat passes, and for a second I'm afraid he's going to continue to argue.

But then he says, "Okay. Right. Of course." Though he doesn't appear happy with my proclamation, he seems to get why I'm proclaiming it. "But you should stay. I'll go." He stands and grabs his jeans from the floor.

"No, I couldn't do that."

"Yes, you can." He's already got his pants half on.

And now I feel like scum. "That's not fair. You paid for the room, a room you shouldn't have paid for in the first place." I run a hand through my hair, considering what to do. "Maybe if we check out now they'll give you your money back. We haven't been here that long."

"This isn't the kind of place they rent by the hour, sweetheart. One of us is staying, and it should be you." I start to protest again, but he cuts me off. "I have to be at work at six a.m. tomorrow, which means I'll miss out on the courtesy breakfast, which is the best part of staying here."

"But—"

He puts his hands on my upper arms and bends to meet my eyes. "They have crème brûlée French toast, Liv."

"That's—"

"Crème brûlée. French toast." He says the words slowly. Prayerfully. "Someone has to eat that, kitten. We can't both miss out."

A thousand arguments flash through my mind in the space of a mere second, and I know in my gut that he has a comeback for every single one.

I don't have the will to fight him. He's too sexy standing there with his jeans still unbuttoned and his shirt still off. And crème brûlée French toast does sound pretty amazing.

"Fine," I harrumph.

"Fine," I say again though I'm feeling anything but fine about it. It's another thing I'll owe him, and I hate owing people anything. I especially don't want to owe *him*. Once I get pregnant, I'm already going to owe him so much.

"But I don't have to be happy about it," I huff dramatically, dropping my clothes to the floor in a dramatic flourish. Now I'm naked and have nothing to hide behind, which is kind of awkward when just the sight of Chase moving around half undressed makes my nipples hard. I slip off to the closet and find a courtesy robe inside. I wrap it around myself and when I turn back to him, he's nearly fully clothed.

I tell myself I'm not disappointed. We're going to have to do this whole banging thing again. I'll still have more naked Chase time. Just not tonight. And not so personal next time.

He looks at me gravely as he threads his belt through his pant loops. "Turn the deadbolt after I leave, okay?"

"Okay," I say half-heartedly.

"This hotel has a good reputation, but I won't be able to sleep if I don't know you're safe."

"I'll lock it."

"I'm serious," he says, fastening his buckle. He starts for the door. "I won't leave until I hear it latch."

He's making me feel worse. He's too sweet. Too *good*.

"I'm right behind you. You'll hear it lock." I follow after him, wishing I didn't want to invite him to stay. Wishing it were easier to watch him go.

He opens the door and pauses. "Text me."

"With the next meet-up? Or to let you know I locked the deadbolt?"

He narrows his eyes at me with the same warning that made my skin tingle earlier. Now it makes my thighs tremble. I know if he stayed there'd be another round of fucking, and I almost convince myself that it's a good idea, for conception prospects, of course.

Except I want him to stay too much. Which is precisely why it's not a good idea at all.

His eyes flicker to my lips then back to my eyes. "You can just text. Anytime. No reason. Send pics if you want."

I roll my eyes. "I'm not sending you dirty pics!"

"I was thinking more like pics of that French toast."

Grinning despite myself, I push him into the hallway and hold the door open with my shoulder. "Shut up and go," I tell him, wondering if he can see how much I really want him to stay.

"Shut the door and lock it," he retorts.

I shut the door and wait a beat before locking it, savoring the knowledge that he's still there, on the other side, until he hears the click.

9

CHASE

"Earth to Kelly."

I squint up at Sergeant Gutierrez, who is standing outside my patrol car with her arms folded across her chest. One perfectly sculpted eyebrow is raised above the line of her sunglasses.

I've been on a tear this morning, scrubbing down every inch of my patrol car, wiping down every nook and cranny with possibly more vigor and attention than is strictly necessary, but the city is quiet this morning and I need to keep myself occupied. If I don't, there's real danger that I could end up thinking too hard about last night. About the wide-eyed way Liv looked at me as she came, about the catch in her voice when she thanked me for putting that pillow under her hips.

About the way she asked me to leave.

Which I feel great about, by the way. That's how I normally roll, that's what I normally like. Nailing it and bailing it. Officer Good Times.

I feel so great about it that I've almost worn the vinyl off the dash from scrubbing. I feel so great about it that I've been checking my phone non-stop all morning, itchy to text her, even itchier to get a text from her.

I set my rag down and force myself to pay attention to my supervisor. "Hey, Sarge. What's up?"

"I've been trying to talk to you for a couple minutes now. You okay?"

I'm glad I have my own sunglasses on and she can't see my face. "Totally okay. Just a long night is all."

The eyebrow above her glasses goes higher. "I know what kind of long nights you have."

I push the itchy feeling down and give Gutierrez a big grin. "Yeah, you do."

She punches me in the arm—hard.

"Ouch!"

"You wish, Kelly. And for the record, my nights with my wife are always longer." She gives me a grin even bigger than my own. "And better."

"I have no comment on that."

"Good boy. And the chief wants to see you. Now."

I stare up at her for a moment, confused. "He wants to see *me*?"

"Yep. Apparently he hasn't forgotten our conversation about body cameras at the meeting last week, and he just called me to tell me to send you his way."

"Ah, fuck."

"Yep," Gutierrez agrees.

I grab my things and climb out of the car, steeling myself for whatever will happen. I've made the body cameras my mountain to die on, and honestly, I think it should be me who raises hell about it. As Megan has pointed out, as a man in a department where most of the administration is made up of men, I have the least to lose professionally by being a squeaky wheel.

"Good luck," Gutierrez says as I lock up the car. I give her a fake salute, and then I stride across the parking lot and into the station, stopping in the bathroom to make sure my brass is straight and my teeth are clean. Then I go to meet my doom.

• • •

"Kelly," the chief says as I walk into his office, not looking up from his computer screen. "Sit. Please."

I sit.

The chief is not an old man, but he's not a young man either. He's got the kind of muted brown hair that comes out of a Just For Men box, designer eyeglasses from the middle rack at a middle-rate optician's, and the kind of mostly symmetrical face that manages not to be remarkable in any way. He's the human equivalent of toothpaste—

serviceable, not *un*pleasant, but entirely forgettable once the experience is over.

Except this is one experience I probably won't forget. Especially if I get fired at the end of it.

"Chief Dinger," I start, not sure what he wants me to say, but he holds up a finger to quiet me and finishes whatever he was doing on the computer. Then he swivels his chair so he's facing me head on.

"Contrary to what you might think of me," he says after a moment, "I didn't come to this city to stonewall progress."

This doesn't feel like the kind of thing I should respond to, so I don't. Even though I have a thousand responses ready and waiting.

Chief Dinger sighs and looks out the window at the rows of parked patrol cars. "I don't want that reputation. Not with the officers. Not with the public."

"Sir—"

He stands up and I bite my tongue, which is *so* hard because I have so many things ready to say to him. Cajoling things, arguing things, angry things. Things I've practiced every day in my mind since I turned in the body camera committee's recommendation and got no official response.

Dinger comes around and leans against the front of his desk. "You've got two things to battle here, Kelly. There's the budget of course, but there's also this." He taps a finger on a small stack of papers next to him. "This is a petition from a local chapter of a group called Citizens Against the Theft and Negation of Individual Privacy."

He gives me a meaningful look, as if I'm supposed to know what that means.

"That's a pretty long name for a group," I offer.

He gives me a long look. I try for more.

"And their abbreviation is C.A.T.N.I.P.?"

"Son, this isn't a joke. I've got almost five hundred signatures here, along with personal essays from most of these folks, telling me they don't want videos of themselves winding up in the hands of strangers. I just got to this city last year, and I don't have any way to explain myself to the city council if this department gets taken to task for not properly vetting policies and our approach to new equipment."

I'm shifting in my chair. "Sir, with all due respect, we have studies and data from all over the country saying that both citizens and officers are safer with this upgrade—"

Dinger interrupts. "Are you saying privacy isn't important? First Amendment rights? In Kansas, anyone can file a Freedom of Information Act for any record—is it so boggling that people don't want footage of themselves being requested and then splashed all over the internet?"

I'm a pretty laid-back kind of guy, so this doesn't rile me much on a personal level. But on a logical level, on an *I Passed College Logic with a 118%* level, I'm riled. "Sir, putting aside how extraordinarily rare such a thing might be, I think that these concerns are purely policy issues. I understand that they are important, but they shouldn't stop us from moving forward. It just means that we have to develop policies and procedures to deal with these concerns, not that we should avoid doing it all together."

"There's too much scrutiny on police departments right now for us to charge into this without addressing citizen concerns."

"*Some* citizen concerns," I supplement quickly. "Because there are just as many citizens, if not more, who would support us moving to the body cameras."

Dinger nods after a minute. "Well said, Kelly. And though it may surprise you, I agree. There's a way we might be able to get around this, and I want you to be the one to help me."

I sit forward in my chair; this is the closest I've come in a year and a half to actually getting somewhere with this change. "Whatever you need, sir."

The chief hands me the C.A.T.N.I.P. petition. "Get me more than five hundred signatures. Get me a petition bigger than this, demonstrable proof that this city wants body cameras, and then I have a leg to stand on when it comes to the city council and the media. The headline can *not* be 'Local Police Rob Citizens of Privacy.' Got it?"

"Got it, sir."

"Good. Don't let me down, Kelly. Help me do this the right way."

I have no idea how I'm going to pull this off, but I'm grinning as I stand.

"Yes, sir."

• • •

I'm feeling so good after my meeting with the chief—I'm not fired! I might be able to make this thing happen!—that I pull out my phone as I walk out of the chief's office. I can't wait another moment to talk to Liv, and I have a good excuse, and after the way things ended last night, I need…something. To fuck her or talk to her or just to be around her. I don't understand it, but I need it.

Hey kitten. We talked about meeting up more than once during your fertile window—would tonight work?

There. Businesslike, friendly, all about the baby.

But I can't help but add, **I still haven't forgotten that you owe me ;)** and I press send before I can think too much about whether it's a dick thing to say or not. But hey, she seemed into it last night, and I am still very into the idea of sliding into her sweet, wet mouth.

My phone buzzes a second later. **Yes. We should meet again tonight…and maybe it will be more efficient if we meet at my place? I've decided you probably aren't a serial killer.**

I smile to myself as I walk out of the station, typing to her as I walk. Maybe we can move past the wall she threw up between us last night after all. **Definitely not a serial killer. Promise.**

Sounds like something a serial killer would say.

How can I convince you? Other than being a police officer, related to one of your closest friends, and the potential father to your child, I mean.

Bring delivery food with you. I'll be just getting off work, and the food you choose will tell me whether you're a killer or not.

10-4, kitten.

I'm full-on grinning as I walk out to my car now. Tonight might actually be the perfect night for the Kelly Trio. Dinner, drinks, handcuffs. And she's trusting me enough to let me see her in her house. That sends a warmth blooming through my chest that I don't examine too closely.

Once I get to my patrol car, I stop. No, it's too nice a day for the car. The sun is out, the breeze is ruffling faint and cool through the new spring leaves, the pavement is dry.

I head for my police motorcycle instead. As I do, my phone vibrates with Liv's address, and then with a second message.

I haven't forgotten about owing you either…can't wait to pay you back. And then there's a lipstick kiss emoji next to an eggplant emoji.

I might have some trouble straddling my bike at this rate.

• • •

After my shift is over, I park my motorcycle in the station garage, change out of my uniform, and drive my Audi from the station to Livia's place. She's got a condo squeezed into a cluster of pale brick buildings and edged by a little park. The whole affair is ringed with tired sidewalks and those trees that drop too many spiky brown balls.

It's on a busy street, and when I park my car and glance at the street and then at the buildings in front of me, my mental rolodex of police history spins and flutters on its own. It's one of the best and worst things about knowing a city so well; I know exactly how safe a place is, I know the character of the people who live around there, I know how quiet or noisy it is. Which I like, because I like knowing things.

But the worst part is staring at the street and remembering the messy fatality I worked there last year. Or the teen who was struck and killed by a drunk driver as she crossed the street on the way home from band practice five years back. Or the old woman across the street who would insist on shoveling her own driveway every time it snowed…the third time I saw her out doing it, I made a point to stop by anytime the white stuff fell and do it for her. She gave me hot cocoa and store-bought cookies for my trouble.

She died two years ago. She was dead for a week before a neighbor thought to check on her.

With a sigh, I turn back to Livia's place. I was in a good mood on the way over here, and as a cop, you get pretty good at compartmentalizing the things you deal with on a daily basis, but every now and again, it sneaks up on me. Going to autopsies for toddlers, calling in the Child Sex crimes detective for hollow-eyed children, walking into a heroin addict's house…I can't carry the full weight of that shit on my shoulders all the time. I try to keep it in another part of my brain, like there's a locker in my mind that I can shove all these things into at the same time I'm shoving my uniform into my locker at the station.

But it doesn't always work that way.

Sometimes I think all the ugliness and death I've seen has ruined me for having a real life of my own. It's one of the reasons I've never changed my stance about marrying and having a family. A family deserves a man who doesn't know what burning flesh smells like, who doesn't have to worry about transmissible diseases when he's breaking up fights or rendering first aid or walking into a drug den. How am I supposed to have a normal life when that's what a regular day looks like for me?

I knock, and Liv answers the door still in her work clothes—a pleated skirt paired with thick black tights and round-toe heels, a thin blouse and another fucking bun. She looks like a librarian wet dream. My mood picks up immediately.

"Hey, gorgeous," I say, flipping up my sunglasses. It's getting too dark for them anyway, and I want to drink in this view. Her, in her doorway, inviting me inside her house. Her smile as her fingers play with the side of the open door. "Hi, Chase," she says softly. "Come in."

She lets me in and slides past me to lead the way.

"What kind of food did you bring?" she asks, looking back. She catches me staring at her ass moving under her skirt and rolls her eyes. "Seriously?"

I grin at her.

We walk past the entryway and into the combined kitchen and living space. Even though these are probably the cheapest condos in the city, it's a fairly nice city, and so this is still a pretty nice place. Wood floors, updated kitchen, big windows. Liv's got IKEA furniture and a good eye for color and space, and so the whole condo feels clean and fresh.

Except.

Except.

I drop my bag of food on the kitchen counter and turn to face Livia. "Got enough books in here, princess?"

She blushes and mumbles something as I go to inspect the bookshelves that are double and triple stacked with books, the shelves so heavy that they sag in the middle. There are books on her mantel, stacked next to her coffee table, stacked on her kitchen chairs in dangerously leaning piles.

"There's a system," she says a bit defensively. "And I keep the library books in my bedroom so they won't get mixed in."

"You have *library* books too?" I ask. "Have you even read all of the ones you own?"

She crosses her arms and juts her chin up in a gesture that's becoming very familiar to me. It makes me smile. "Well, not all of them, but I will someday and it's my job to keep up on what's popular with the patrons."

"Uh-huh."

She sticks out her tongue at me, pink and wet, and she's the opposite of everything that weighed on my memories in the parking lot. She's playful and healthy and vibrant and alive. And I can't help it, I grab her and pull her into me, moving my mouth down at the last moment so that I'm kissing her neck instead of her lips. Her knees slump, and she sags in my arms.

"Chase," she murmurs. "The food."

"Fuck the food," I growl, swinging her up into my arms. "Where's your bedroom?"

"The door is by the couch," she says, lacing her arms around my neck. All of my depressing thoughts from earlier melt away, all my everything melts away with the feeling of her in my arms, with her giant brown eyes gazing at me as I walk us to her bed.

"I'm going to fuck you at least twice tonight," I say, tossing her onto the mattress and unbuckling my belt. "Fucking, then food, then more fucking."

"Okay," she agrees breathlessly.

"Once isn't going to be enough," I say, freeing my cock and giving it a few quick pumps as my knees hit the edge of the bed.

"No, it won't," she whispers, staring at my dick, which is now thick and hard in my hand. Her hand is under her blouse, pulling and rolling her own nipple.

I groan. She's too fucking much sometimes. The pleated skirt and that bun, and then with that dirty hand tugging on her own nipple like she can't wait for me to get to it myself. She's what every teenage boy beat off imagining; she's what every teenage boy wished their librarian would be.

She reaches up then, taking my erection in her hands and

squeezing, stroking up and down. I take one of her hands and move it down to cup my balls. She holds them with the perfect amount of pressure, her palm the perfect kind of warmth, her fingertips grazing the sensitive spot just behind them. I have a moment when I wonder just how dirty Livia might get, but I push the thought aside for now. The only thing that matters is getting my dick inside her and releasing the pressure building at the base of my spine. We can play games later.

"Enough," I grunt, pushing her hands away from me before I go off all over her fingers. "I need your cunt."

"Yes," she agrees, nodding fast. "God, yes." She reaches for the buttons at the side of her skirt, but I'm too fucking impatient for that either.

"How much did these tights cost?" I demand.

"I, uh, I can't remember," she says. Her eyes are on my cock again, her expression hungry. "Maybe a few dollars?"

"You can invoice me for expenses," I tell her and then flip up her skirt and spread her legs. With my finger, I tear a small hole in the crotch of her tights and rip them wide open, thigh to thigh, just like I wanted to do with her leggings on the day I met her. Soon, her cunt is wide open to me, covered by nothing but a flimsy scrap of lace. I tear that off too, and she squirms.

"Oh God," she murmurs. Her hand is back to playing under her shirt. "Oh God, oh God."

"You can call me Chase," I say as I put a knee on the bed.

She giggles at the old joke, and she's so fucking hot, so fucking fun, and a small window opens up in my hard, aching urgency. A window to something else, another version of us. I lean down and brush my lips across her cheeks, her nose, her hair, kissing all the places I'm allowed to kiss.

"I want to earn your mouth, Liv," I murmur, my lips on her face. "It's all I think about, kissing you."

She sighs under my words, and I want to kiss her sigh. I readjust my knee to move over her and slide into her cunt, but I keep my mouth hovering over her skin, keep my eyes burning my need into hers.

"Chase, wait," she suddenly says, sitting up, her eyes slowly kindling with something that can only be described as panic. "Wait!"

I freeze, half on the bed, cock throbbing. "What?"

"This is too—it's too—" Her expression is pleading, as if she expects me to understand what she means even when she can't find the words for it. "You're making it feel too—"

"Too what, kitten?" I try to keep my voice open and receptive. When a woman says *wait*, you wait, but oh God. I can see the welcoming split between her legs, see that it's already wet for me. I can smell her.

"It feels too real," she admits finally, worrying her bottom lip between her teeth. "Or too fast. Or too easy or something."

"It's supposed to be easy, and I'll go slow next time, promise." I start leaning forward on the bed again, and she holds up her hand.

"Too *intimate*," she says. "That's what I mean. It feels too intimate. You just waltzing in here and making me want you and sweeping me off to my room…"

But I thought that's what girls wanted before fucking? The wanting and the sweeping off? Jesus, no wonder I've never had a successful relationship.

"I just needed to remind us—or myself—that it's to get pregnant. Only for that."

"So we're back to syringe-dick now?"

She closes her eyes. "I didn't mean it like that. But yes, I'd feel better if it was more…impersonal."

I don't know why this bothers me, just like I don't know why her kicking me out last night bothers me. It just *does*.

But you know what? Fine. Officer Good Times doesn't mind impersonal at all.

"Whatever you want, Livia," I say, sliding my knee off the bed.

Her eyes are still closed. "Thank you."

But then her eyes fly open as I grab her hips and haul her to the edge of the bed so that her ass is nearly off the mattress, and then I take her knees in my hands and spread her legs wide enough for me to stand between them.

"You want to make this clinical?" I ask, and I can't help the coldness in my voice—or maybe I can—but I'm too angry to help it. And I'm angry at myself for being angry. Why do I care how she wants me to fuck her? I'm just here for the fucking, however it happens.

She turns her head away from me. "Clinical is good," she says, and in her voice I hear resignation and regret and determination. Livia Ward, always so determined to have it her way.

"Then we'll make it clinical," I say, letting go of one of her knees so I can fist my erection and bring it to her opening. "Just pretend you're doing this the right way, kitten. Just pretend you're at the doctor's, waiting for some anonymous hands to give you some anonymous man's baby." I tease her entrance with the dark and swollen head of my cock. She's so fucking wet, it'll take nothing to sink inside her.

"Chase," she says but says nothing else. I can't tell if she likes what I'm saying or she hates it. Or both.

"You're just lying back and letting it go inside you," I say, and then I mirror my words, pushing the wide crown of my dick into her folds, which part for me. "You're just waiting for it to be over. Because all you want is the baby."

I push in deeper, all the way to the root, and her back arches, her mouth parting in a silent cry. It's so tight in there I could die. "You don't care how you get pregnant. You don't care what it feels like."

I drop my thumb to her clit, rubbing in the tight circles I've learned she likes. "It's just a transaction, right? Just an impersonal transaction?"

I tilt my hips up ever so slightly as I pull out, making sure to drag the flared edge of my tip against her sensitive front walls. She gasps, her back arching again. I pull out almost all the way, and then I push back in. Hard. She cries out, her hands flying out behind her to grasp at her comforter.

"It's just a procedure, Liv. Just biology." I rub those circles and stroke in and out of her, so fucking worked up. I'm fucking her through a hole in her tights and her tits are bouncing under her blouse and her fingers are twisting helplessly against her blankets. And she's so wet and swollen, so supple and so goddamn tight, all of it squeezing my cock in a wet embrace. And her hips can't help but move under my touch, with my thumb working the firm bundle of nerves at the top of her pussy, with my penis thick and rocking inside of her, both my touch and my dick hitting all the right notes.

And yet it's not enough. Her perfect pussy, her perfect reaction to my fucking her, it's all not enough, and I don't fucking know why.

Until I do.

"Look at me," I say. A command and a plea all at once. "Look at me."

She does, turning those warm brown eyes onto mine.

"Good girl," I mutter, staring down at her as I stroke in and out of her cunt. "That's it. I want to watch your face as you come. Because it doesn't matter how impersonal I make it, Liv, you're still going to come for me. Aren't you?"

Her hands are still grabbing at her comforter. "Yes," she breathes. "I'm going to come."

I go deeper, faster, rubbing and thrusting and breathing hard. "Even if it's not intimate, even if it's not easy or real, you just can't help but come when I'm inside you, when I'm rubbing that sweet little cunt, can you?"

She moans, shaking her head.

"I can't hear you," I growl. I can feel the sweat on my face, I see the flushed heat in her cheeks.

"I can't help it," she confesses in another moan.

"Can't help what, kitten?"

Her eyes are fluttering now, her body squirming in gorgeous, taut lines. "Can't help…coming." Her heels are digging in the small of my back, her throat arched in a display of pained pleasure. "You make me come."

"Fuck yeah, I do," I breathe, thrusting in to the root. I feel the moment she trembles at the edge, like a leaf caught by the wind, and then she blows over with a sweet cry, back bowing off the bed, toes curling, her thighs clenching hard. And her pussy quivering around my cock in the most delicious caress a man can feel.

And then I let go. I grab her hips and I rut into her, all sorts of depraved images running through my mind, sinful urges, lusts that go down to the very root of life itself. To mate. To breed. To fuck until I plant my seed inside her.

She's still panting and clenching when I let loose and pour into her, filling her up as deep and full as biology demands, as my crude fantasy of her spread on a doctor's table demands. I feel the cum pumping out of me fast and hard, and I hold her hips tight, keeping her pussy speared on my cock as I finish emptying into her.

Her eyes are on me the entire time.

I give one last pulse and then slowly pull out, loving the spill of white cum that follows. My cum. Inside her, outside her, messy and claiming.

Mine.

All mine.

The moment the words enter my thoughts, I try to banish them. Livia's not mine. Her body isn't mine, and this baby won't be mine except in the loosest sense. I don't get to claim her, in fantasy or otherwise.

To hide my discomfort, I move away and grab a pillow from the top of her bed.

"Chase," she says.

I ignore her, handing her the pillow and then helping her orient herself on the bed so she can elevate her hips. I pull up my jeans, and I'm about to leave her on the bed when she grabs my hand.

"Chase," she says again.

"I need to go figure out the food," I mumble.

"Fuck the food," she says seriously.

"Liv—"

"I want you to stay in here with me," she interrupts. "Please."

I pause and let myself look down at her. She looks beautiful and open and vulnerable right now, her hair coming loose from her bun and her clothes torn and rumpled. And God help me, I like the way her hand feels holding mine. I like the way her voice sounds making such a naked and honest request.

I sit down next to her, but she doesn't let go of my hand. Instead, she tugs me so that I'm turned and she's able to see my face.

"I'm sorry," she says. "I shouldn't have said those things. Not while we were about to have sex."

"Don't say sorry," I tell her. "I don't mind. Promise."

I'm lying. And I don't know why.

She sighs and lets go of my hand so that she can move the pillow under her hips. "I mind, though. It wasn't fair to you. And I shouldn't make my neuroses your problem."

"It's really fine, kitten. You got off, I got off inside you—which was the whole point—everything happened the way it should."

"No," she says, shaking her head. When she does, her bun loosens even more. "No, it didn't. I mean, it was amazing, but I treated you like a sperm donor instead of a person."

"But I am a sperm donor to you." And why does that make me feel so bitter all of a sudden?

"Well, yes, that, but you're more too." She shifts so she can look at my face more easily. "You're a man I really like. A man I respect."

This mollifies me a little.

"You're also the best lover I've ever had. You make me feel so good."

Okay, I'm a lot mollified now.

"But I'm not used to this, Chase. I know you are, I know that your M.O. is having fun with women you plan on never seeing again. But I've never done that, and in my mind, this kind of arrangement was only going to work if we treated it like a transaction. I didn't expect it—or you—to be so easy to enjoy. It scared me a little."

I brush a strand of hair off her forehead. "You don't have to be scared of enjoying yourself."

She smiles. "I'm not, as a rule. But I didn't expect to enjoy this, and while I'm good at adapting to things I don't expect, I need time to process it. Sometimes that means I resist or shut down while I'm processing, and I'm sorry I did that to you. But I think I'm okay now."

I study her. "Okay with enjoying this?"

"Okay with enjoying this," she confirms. "And still not getting attached."

Attached. It's one of those words that I associate with bad things—pleading texts and late night phone calls and possessiveness. A toxic word. And yet, I find I don't mind the idea of Liv getting attached at all. In fact, the idea of her being possessive of me is rather pleasing. Especially because I'm starting to feel rather possessive of her.

Dial it back, Good Times.

"You're a careful woman, kitten," I tell her. I brush another strand of hair away from her face. "I know you won't get attached. You're too guarded for that."

She blinks up at me, like she has a response but she's already forgetting it. Which is good, because I don't know if I believe my own words. She *is* guarded, she is careful—she's fierce and strong and almost ferociously independent—and yet behind those walls, I see loneliness. I see sadness.

Before I can say something else about it though, she asks, "Was everything okay tonight?"

At first I think she means the sex, but then she adds, "When I opened the door, you seemed a little off. Like maybe you'd had a bad day at work or something."

"Oh. That." I consider how much to tell her. Most civilians don't want to know about their neighbors who died alone or the blood that's stained the pavement just outside their house. I don't want to poison Liv's feelings about her home just because I can't unpoison my own memories.

"Work stuff," I say, opting for a vague, harmless version of the truth.

"Like a bad case?" she asks. She looks so innocent right now, even with the ragged hole in her tights, and I know Megan would kill me for thinking it because of gender constructs and stuff, but she looks so *pure*. And I don't mean sexually, I mean it in the way that I can't bear to make her imagine dead bodies and senseless carnage and drunk assholes that get away with murder because they had the right lawyer. I mean that there's something so appealing about her not knowing that stuff, living free of it, that I can't bear to change it.

So I just say, "Yeah. Like a bad case."

She nods. "I'm sorry. But I am a little relieved, I admit. I was worried it was because of me, because of last night."

I search her face. "Did you kick me out because of the whole not wanting to enjoy our sex thing?"

She glances away, and when she looks back, I get the sense that it's her turn to hold the entire truth back. "Something like that."

I don't push her—our new understanding feels too fragile for that—so instead I just tease. "That's why I told you in advance that there would be food and more fucking. So you wouldn't kick me out into the cold."

She sniff-laughs. "It's not cold tonight."

My stomach rumbles loudly, as if to argue with the both of us. "Well, about that food," I say.

"Yeah," she responds. "Go. I'll be out in a few minutes."

I squeeze her thigh and then leave her bedroom for the kitchen, not sure how to feel about anything that just happened. The only thing I'm sure of is that a part of me—a big part of me—doesn't want to leave her alone on that bed. I want to go back in there and settle next to her, have her head nestled in the crook of my arm while I run my fingers along the lines of her belly and thighs.

I almost turn around and do it. Screw being hungry—I'm hungry for *her*. But then I think of her honesty, her admission that she needs time to process, and I think maybe I ought to give her space? This is confusing. Fuck.

But in the end, I default to food.

I am a cop, after all.

• • •

"I have to admit, this isn't what I was expecting," Livia says, perched on a bar stool and examining the plate I just set in front of her on the counter. She's changed into a T-shirt and sweatpants, and fuck me if it isn't somehow more adorable than her librarian get-up. I want to tackle her to the ground and tickle her until she's squirming and red-cheeked underneath me. I want to turn on a movie and pull her into my lap and finger her so slowly that she forgets how to speak.

"You weren't expecting me to cook?"

"You know, I am pretty sure I said delivery."

"But you also said that you wanted to make sure I wasn't a serial killer. I thought maybe making you Grandma Kelly's Irish breakfast for dinner would prove to you that I have a good, non-murdery heart."

Livia smiles down at her plate. Eggs and sausage and tomatoes and bacon. "I suppose a serial killer wouldn't make these raspberry scones from scratch."

"Or make sure you had real clotted cream to go with them," I say, delivering said cream to her in a small bowl. "And the scones are stupidly easy, for the record. Made them this morning before work before I knew I'd see you tonight. Plus I made Pop help." Grandma had him make those scones so many times back when she was alive, he could probably do it in his sleep.

"Pop?"

"My grandpa." Then I add, because she will need to know if we ever use my house as a space for impregnation, "And also my roommate."

She puts her hands together. "That's adorable."

"Sure," I say, bringing over a French press full of fresh coffee. It's a little late for caffeine, but I plan on keeping her up and sweating 'til past midnight at least, so it'll be fine. And I can tell by the way her eyes light up when she sees me pour her a mug that she's a coffee fiend.

"You're good in the kitchen," she says, curling her hands around the mug as I hand it to her.

I shrug and start shuffling the dishes off the counter and into the sink. "After Mom died, I kind of had to be. And Pop insists that a man should know how to make at least three different meals: one for a woman, one for family meals, and one for a church funeral potluck."

"Good philosophy. And stop with the dishes. I don't like it when people clean my house in front of me. It makes me feel guilty."

I ignore her, load the dishes from the food prep into the dishwasher and wipe off the counter. With the kitchen clean, I finally turn to my own plate of food, standing at the counter so I'm facing Livia as we eat. It's as I'm eating that I catch a glimpse of a library programming sheet for all the county libraries; Liv has highlighted an event with local legislators. I stare at it for a moment, letting it sink in that the library is hosting something like this.

And I have an idea.

I put my fork down and look at her. "Do you think the library could host an event where we could get five hundred signatures on a petition?"

"Oh, certainly," Liv says, brightening up. "It's tricky to do at Corinth because of how small it is, but you could host an all-day event at Central maybe, and you know, they're just now putting together the winter calendar—"

I shake my head. "It needs to be soon and it has to be in Prairie Village."

Her face falls a little. "Oh. What is it for?"

"It's for the Chief to grow a pair." At her blank look, I elaborate. "I need to demonstrate citizen support for body cameras for the police department. With signatures."

"Body cameras," she repeats, and now she's looking at me like she's never seen me before or like she's seeing me in a new light. "I had no idea you were so political."

Political. When did that word become such a kiss of death? I find I'm wincing at it, and I don't even know why.

"Citizens are safer in departments that have upgraded to them, and statistically speaking, the cops in those departments are also safer," I say. "And safety shouldn't be political."

She's nodding along.

"And more than that: cameras can prove when a cop commits a crime, but they can also prove when a cop didn't. Good cops should *want* body cameras."

"Of course," she says. "I don't understand why this isn't a given. Every department should have them!"

I can tell she's getting fired up about this. Which is validating…but also premature, because it's the kind of issue that has valid arguments on both sides. Just because I feel like the end goal is worthy doesn't mean I can dismiss any and all other objections.

She pushes her plate away and straightens up. "It's ridiculous that there needs to be signatures and petitions involved. The Chief should just do the right thing because *it's the right thing to do.* Not because he's worried about his image."

I sigh. "Well, yeah. But it is more than just image. The budget is a problem. But there's also some group now—I forget the whole name, something about citizens against the theft of privacy—"

Her eyes widen. "The C.A.T.N.I.P. people?"

I'm surprised. "You know them?"

"They rent a meeting room at the library every month," she says. "And they use our coffee pot, even though they're not supposed to," she adds darkly.

"Well, they filed a petition with five hundred signatures. They're worried about privacy and First Amendment rights, mostly."

She snorts. "It sounds so petty compared to ideas like citizen safety and holding police officers accountable."

I tilt my head, conceding her point. "Yes. But privacy isn't petty for rape victims. Or victims of domestic violence. Or citizens who might have undocumented relatives and friends. It's crucial for them."

Her face grows more serious. "That's true. But isn't this something that can be navigated? Lots of departments already are using them!"

"Exactly. It can be figured out. I just need to convince the Chief that it's worth the effort to figure it out."

"The signatures," she says, realizing. And then she brightens up again, and I get to see the way she lights up when she's having ideas, when she's passionate. "Okay. It may take some convincing, but I think I might be able to get my manager to let me host something."

"Really?"

She nods, getting more and more excited. "We could do a big civic event, right when it's getting warm. We could use the parking lot, bring in local businesses to donate food and drinks, and invite the other agencies—fire and EMT. We can structure the event around the community, and you can give a presentation about body cameras there. We'll have the petitions circulating the whole time. People will come for the free ice cream and for their kids to play on the fire trucks, and then we'll present them with this chance to make Prairie Village a better, safer city for everyone." She stops and beams at me. "What do you think?"

I think she's the sexiest, smartest woman I've ever known. I come around the counter and pull her into my arms, loving the way she wraps her legs around my waist as if it's the most natural thing in the world.

"I think you're too fucking perfect to go another moment without my face between your legs."

She flushes under my praise and laughs. "I thought I owed *you* my mouth tonight, remember?"

I'm already carrying her to the bedroom, my cock hardening like steel in my jeans.

"Don't worry, kitten. There's always tomorrow night."

10

LIVIA

I can still smell Chase on my sheets when I wake up the next morning. Still feel his presence. I keep my eyes closed and savor his scent, remembering the way he cooked me dinner and cleaned my kitchen. Remembering the tickle of his beard along my skin when his mouth was between my legs. Remembering all the dirty things he did before coming inside me for a second time last night.

The wonderful, amazing, dirty things.

I've come to terms with enjoying the sex, but that's only while we're having it. When he's gone, I shouldn't be thinking of him like this, but I can't help it. He's so vivid in my memory. So clear. His energy so warm and strong. It's almost like he never left. Almost like…

Wait.

I open my eyes and sure enough, Chase is laying next to me, fully dressed, watching me sleep.

My heart trips a beat, but any thrill I feel is immediately wiped away with a rush of anxiety.

"Did you break in?" I ask as calmly as I can. Maybe he's not a serial killer, but I hadn't considered he might be a stalker.

His lip curls up in amusement. "No. I never left."

"That's worse," I groan, flinging my arm over my eyes. If I can't see him, maybe he'll disappear. Maybe I'm still dreaming.

Maybe I'll wake up alone. As I should be. As any woman who has contracted a man to impregnate her should be.

But it's not a dream. He really spent the night. In my bed.

Ah, fuck me with crème brûlée French toast.

"It was an accident," he says, as though he can read my mind. "You wore me out. I fell asleep."

I sneak a glance in his direction. "But you obviously already got up. You're dressed. You could have snuck out, and I would never have known." I throw my arm down and stare at him point blank. "Why didn't you do that? Why are you still here?"

"Because folic acid is important for women when they're trying to get pregnant," he says, as though that clears everything up.

"And?"

"And I noticed you didn't have any orange juice in your fridge. So I wanted to be sure you got your folic acid."

I scowl. But I can't hold it for very long because he seems to really care about my folic acid intake, and that's kind of sweet. And he looks so sexy doing it. And because my thighs still ache from all the action they got the night before, so maybe I'm letting my hormones get the best of me, but I *am* ovulating.

"That sounds dirty when you say it," I say, resigned. Resigned to him being here and being hot and me being hornier than I want to admit.

"Everything sounds dirty when I say it. Come on." He pulls the sheet off of me and swats my behind. "Get up. Get dressed."

"Why?" I groan again. As long as he's here, we could get in another round of baby-making, but not if I'm supposed to be getting dressed.

"Because you can't leave the house naked," he says, standing up. "I personally wouldn't have a problem with it, but I'd have to arrest you for public indecency, and though I want to see you in my cuffs, it's not going to be any fun if you're behind bars."

Goose bumps erupt along my skin at the mention of his cuffs, but I hug myself, pretending it's because I'm cold. "We're leaving the house together?" I sigh and resign myself to this now as well. "Where are we going?"

He rolls his eyes in exaggerated annoyance. "To get some folic acid. Haven't you been paying attention to anything I've said?"

With a shake of my head, I climb out of bed and shoo him out of my room so I can get ready. I put my hair up in a messy bun and take a quick shower then throw on a green cap-sleeve knit dress patterned with chemistry formulas.

When I come out of the bedroom I smell coffee, and before I can ask, Chase hands me a travel mug with room for milk at the top.

"I didn't know how you took it," he says.

I thank him, and he watches as I doctor it up with the right amount of milk and sugar. Then I grab my purse and hesitate, my hand hovering over the hook by the door where I keep my car keys.

I look at him, questioning.

"Do you trust me driving you someplace?" he asks. "If you'd rather take your car and follow… But we aren't going far and that's kind of a drag."

I drop my hand. "You can drive me. I trust you. Ish."

"Ish?"

"I trust-ish you. Ish. Just." This is stupid. I trust him. I do. It's myself I don't trust. I might be able to manage sex without attachment—and I'm only barely sure I can manage that—but I'm not at all sure I can handle spending real time together.

But I'm already crossing all the lines of precaution, venturing into territory that makes our every interaction more complicated and our lives more intertwined. I can stop. I know I can. The truth is I don't know if I want to.

At least I don't want to before breakfast.

With another sigh, I nudge him toward the door. "Take me wherever you're taking me. This better be some damn good folic acid."

• • •

Less than ten minutes later, we're pulling into the driveway of a two-story house with yellow vinyl siding and an American flag mounted by the front door. The yard is landscaped simply but earnestly, and even though it's early spring, the lawn has been attended to. It's cute. Not too small. Exactly the kind of house I'd love to raise my kid in but could never afford on my current salary. Not in Prairie Village, anyway.

The problem is, I can't think of any good reason that Chase would bring me to someone's residence. Unless it's *his* house.

He already has his door open, but I don't move. "Your house, Chase? Seriously?"

God, I hope I've guessed wrong.

But I haven't. "Where did you think I was taking you?"

"I don't know. First Watch? IHOP? Starbucks?" Someplace a hundred times less personal, and oh my God, he lives this close to me? I shouldn't know this. I so wish I didn't know this.

"My house is better than all of the above combined." He tugs on the sleeve of my dress. "Come on. I'll make you the best lemon brown sugar blueberry pancakes you've ever tasted. And, if you're good, I might even let you have some of my sausage."

"I sure hope that's not a euphemism because I'm not happy, and also, now I want sausage." I set my empty travel mug in his cup holder though and reluctantly get out of the car.

"What's so terrible about coming to my house?" he asks as I come around his Audi and meet him on the front stoop.

Chase unlocks the door and holds it open for me.

I rant while I walk inside. "We're not dating. We're not supposed to be 'hanging out.' We're not supposed to be getting to know each other or spending time together. We're supposed to be banging and that's it."

It's then that I notice we aren't alone. There's an elderly man sitting with a laptop at the dining room table, which is clearly visible from the front door in the open-concept living space.

"Uh, hi," I say, wishing I was invisible. Or at least not so loud. "Sorry."

"Didn't hear a thing." He gives us a sidelong glance and then turns back to his screen. "I'm just *banging* away on this stupid computer here, trying to figure out how the damn thing works."

His choice of words isn't an accident. He obviously heard me.

I exchange looks with Chase. I'm sure I'm beet red. I want to die.

"I want to die," I mouth to Chase.

Laughing, he beckons me to the dining room. "Pop this is Livia. She works at the library with Megan. We're..." He looks at me, searching.

I don't say a thing. But I think several things in his direction. Things like, *Are you serious? You're the one who brought me here. You should have thought about what you were going to say before that you...you...hot cop.*

"Friends," he finishes after a beat.

I shoot daggers with my eyes. We are *not* friends. Though I'm not sure what else he could have said. Even if he wasn't contractually obligated to keep our deal a secret, *I'm her sperm donor* probably isn't the best way to introduce a woman to your grandfather.

"Livia, this is my grandpa, Dennis, but I promise he won't answer to anything other than Pop."

"Hi," I say, grinning awkwardly and too widely. "Again."

"Nice to meet you, Livia." Pop studies me, and I study him. He's leathery and wrinkled, but it's obvious he was very handsome when he was younger. He's still handsome now. His bone structure is exceptional and the deep creases by his mouth and eyes are the kind earned from a good-humored person.

It's obvious Chase comes from good genes. That he'll age well. Which I'm glad to know.

For the baby, naturally.

Though it doesn't matter what his opinion is, I can't help but wonder what Pop sees looking at me.

"Chase doesn't usually bring his women home," he says after a moment. "You must be special."

"I'm not his woman," I say definitively.

"He doesn't bring friends either." His eyes twinkle in the same way that Chase's do, and my chest tightens at the old man's words.

Is Pop right? Am I special to Chase?

I glance over at the sexy man who is now wearing an apron that says *Kiss the Chef If You Can Handle the Heat* and is currently gathering the items he needs for his pancake concoction.

"I'm making Livia breakfast," he says, pulling a carton of eggs and a carton of orange juice from the fridge. He sets the eggs on the counter then pours some juice into a glass before bringing it to me. "Behave yourself, Pop, and I'll make some pancakes for you too."

"Yeah, yeah," the old man grumbles and turns back to his computer.

I take the folate-rich orange juice and thank him. I don't want to know if I'm special to him, I decide. It will only complicate things. But he's giving me things. He's giving me some fun and some folic acid, and most importantly, he's going to give me a baby. So I let myself start to get comfortable with the idea that he's always going to be special to me.

• • •

An hour later, I'm finishing my third glass of orange juice and my second plate of pancakes. Between last night and today, Chase has proven he's a really good cook. Too many meals with him, and I'll have to double my twice-weekly Jazzercize class attendance.

Pop sits next to me, his laptop turned so we can both see the screen. "Now that I've saved the picture, how can I find it again?" he asks.

I wipe my fingers so they aren't sticky. "Since you remembered to save it in the photos folder this time like I showed you, all you have to do is pull up your folders list, like this." I demonstrate for him. "And there it is. Double click on the thumbnail to open it."

Though I'd tried to help prepare breakfast, it only took Chase two minutes to discover I wasn't any good in a kitchen, and he quickly banished me to the dining room table with his grandfather. Wanting to feel useful somewhere, I've ended up helping Pop figure out a few things on his new computer. He's slow on the uptick, but not any less guidable than the teens I work with at the library.

"Hey," Chase says, taking my empty plate from me. "You're good with him. You should teach him how to use it for real. Give him some regular lessons."

I throw him a glare. Normally, this kind of volunteer project would be right up my alley. But this man will be the great grandfather to my baby-to-be. I can't be spending time with him.

"I'm sure I don't know anything more about computers than you do," I say, not wanting to hurt the old man's feelings with a simple *no*.

Chase doesn't seem to pick up on the reasons for my hesitation. "Yeah, but I have no patience for the man." He stacks his grandfather's plate on top of the others in his hand and takes them to the sink.

"Correction, son," Pop interjects. "I have no patience for *you*."

I cough and cover my mouth to hide my laugh.

"Yeah, yeah, yeah," Chase says rinsing the plates when the doorbell rings. Then rings again. And again. Then several more times.

"Shit!" Chase turns off the water and turns to face me. His face is pale and his eyes wide.

"What is it?" I ask.

"I knew nothing about this. I swear." He's apologetic and concerned.

I stand up, my alarm growing. "Knew nothing about what?"

Before he can answer, the front door opens, and Megan walks in with a tote bag over her shoulder, Josiah asleep on her hip, and Keon in tow behind.

And now I understand the reason for the panic.

There's no time to move though. No time to react. No time to do anything but stand there and wait for the disaster that's about to happen.

"The doorbell is not a toy," she says to Keon. "You ring it once only. And we don't even have to ring the bell here because I have a key." She blazes through the living room toward us like she's on a mission. "Good morning, Pop! I have a ton of errands I'm running today and you're on the way to the dry cleaners so I brought some more Icy Hot patches for your knee and some of that Calms Forte you like to help you sleep better. It shouldn't make you too drowsy the next day. Chase can help you with the bottle if your arthritis is bothering you. Nice to see you, brother of mine, and. Oh."

She finally takes a breath. Finally sees me in the room. "Liv." She looks from me to Chase then back to me again. "Good morning."

"Uh, hi." I wave like an idiot.

Keon runs to Pop and pulls at his leg. "Ant Smasher. Ant Smasher."

The old man lifts the little boy up to his lap, and my heart melts imagining this exact thing but with Chase's child. "Nope, kid. Not on this machine. What we got on this beast? Solitaire, I think. Let's find out."

Pop pushes some buttons and whatever he manages to find, it seems to entertain the both of them.

With their attention occupied, Megan resumes darting her eyes back and forth between me and my sperm donor.

"So," she says after several seconds pass in silence. "Is someone going to fill me in?"

"There's nothing to fill," I say, then blush because I'm a bad liar and because Chase has been filling me quite well.

Apparently, he's also turned me into a pervert.

Megan narrows her eyes. "Are the two of you…?"

"No!" Chase and I say at once. Like that's not obvious.

"I'm helping Pop with his computer," I say in a rush, eager to make this situation seem anything other than what it is. Though, at this point, I'm not sure *what* it is. This morning's activities have had nothing at all to do with our contractual agreement.

"Ah. I see." Megan doesn't seem convinced, but she turns to her grandfather anyway, and says, "I told you Phil would help you with that, Pop."

"She's nicer than Phil," Pop says, nodding in my direction. "She's prettier than him, too." He winks as though he knows he's part of a cover-up.

And because I've completely fallen for this old man, I wink back.

Chase returns to loading the dishwasher. "Want some pancakes, Sis? I still have some batter left."

Yeah, that's good. Change the subject. Divert her attention from us with delicious food.

Megan doesn't fall for it. "I had a Slimfast. Thanks. Liv, can I see you in the other room for a moment?" She turns and walks out of the dining room, not waiting to see if I'll follow.

I give a final look to Chase who mouths, "*Good luck*," before I proceed after his sister.

Megan hasn't gone far, only to the other side of the living room. But it's far enough that I'm sure her brother can't hear her when she says quietly, "I haven't seen you since you and Chase went out together, and he's refused to tell me anything."

"That's…gentlemanly of him." It's nice to know he's kept his side of the bargain and not said anything.

Josiah murmurs in his sleep as Megan shifts him to her other hip. "Then did something happen?"

She wants details. And she's my friend, so details would be fair, if I were into Chase for real.

But, I'm not.

So I tell her the truth. Sort of. "Nothing happened on our date. I've sworn off men. Remember?"

"But you're here at our house for breakfast." She blinks and corrects herself. "His house." She corrects herself again. "Pop's house."

"I am." I know exactly how it looks. It looks intimate. This was why I was against coming here in the first place.

I take a breath and attempt to paint a better picture. "It's no big deal. Chase offered me breakfast while I got to know your grandpa. To see if I thought I could help him."

"With his computer."

"Right." I sigh. "I know it seems weird, but this isn't anything. Really. One date with your brother didn't change my life plans." And that *is* the truth. I still want my baby. I'm still on track for that and nothing else.

"I'm sure he's dismayed about that."

"Well." I think I have her convinced but I take it further to be sure. "Yes. He is. Poor guy. I think he really has a thing for me. I felt bad. It's why I said I'd help out your Pop."

Megan shakes her head. "You and your bleeding heart. It's going to get you in a mess one day, Liv."

"Probably sooner than later," I mumble more to myself than her.

"Oh, while I have you…" She puts her hand on my upper arm. "I'm supposed to go to a wet lab at the police academy Friday after next, but Phil has a department dinner that we need to go to. Want to take my place?"

"What's a wet lab?"

She drops her arm so she can hold her toddler with both arms. "It's this thing where the academy pays for volunteers to get drunk so that the recruits can practice field sobriety tests on actual drunk people. I've been doing it since Chase was in the academy himself. Anyway, it's fun. Free booze!"

I hesitate because that's two weeks away, and I could be pregnant by then. "I don't know…"

"Come on," she says. "How can you turn down free alcohol?"

"I'm sort of going easy on the drinking."

"Why? You pregnant or something?" she laughs.

I nearly choke, and I don't even have anything in my mouth but my own saliva. "What?"

"I'm kidding. I just couldn't think of any other reason to be sober on a Friday when I didn't have to deal with my kids."

"Oh. Haha." But it's too close to the truth. "Email me the

information. I'll go." If I have my period by then, I'll go. If not, I can just play sick. No big deal.

"Everything good out here?" Chase asks, coming into the living room.

"Yep!" Megan says with her extroverted gusto. "But I've got to be going. We have a to-do list a million miles long. Keon, put Pop's cane back where you found it. It's not a light saber."

I say goodbye to my friend, and then while she's herding her son out the door, I slip off down the hallway in search of a bathroom. The house is small, and I find what I'm looking for on the first try.

When I'm finished, the house is quieter. Megan must be gone, and I plan to tell Chase to take me home now too.

But something catches my eye in the room across the hall—the edge of a black and white poster that goes almost from floor to ceiling.

I'm curious, and the door is already half open so I take the liberty of pushing it open all the way.

The thing that had caught my eye? It's a giant poster of Jessica Alba in a stripper's outfit from the movie *Sin City.*

"Oh my God." I say it to myself, but it's out loud.

"Don't go in there!" Chase shouts in a panic running toward me.

But it's too late. I've already seen what he doesn't want me to see. I scan my eyes around the room, taking it all in. There's a poster for the movie *Gladiator* and another for the original *X-Men.* The bookshelf has a shelf dedicated to Avengers comic book memorabilia. Next to it is a student desk—the kind you buy from Target and put together yourself—and above that is a corkboard with photographs and concert tickets hung up with pushpins. There are also more pictures of scantily clad women, though nothing as in-your-face as Jessica, who seems to be the focal point.

This is a teenager's room. A teenage *boy's* room.

"It's not what it looks like," Chase says, now at my side.

"This is your room, isn't it?" I ask, laughing. I don't need him to answer. I know it's his room. It's him as much as the tattoo he wears on his arm.

Still giggling, I walk inside so I can see things better. It's just so amazing. From the graphic novels and yearbooks on his bookshelf to the collection of DVDs in the case next to the bed, there is so much to look at. So much to *learn.*

"Look," Chase says. "Be fair. I was a kid when I put most of this stuff up."

I raise a brow. "Most?"

"All," he corrects hastily. "All of this stuff."

"And you're thirty-three and just haven't gotten around to taking any of it down yet?" I already know I'm never going to let him live this down.

He throws his head back in frustration. "It's been like this since I moved out for college. Okay? Pop wasn't concerned about redecorating, and I didn't have any reason to come back and do it, so it's been a sort of museum of my teenage years. I only moved back in about a month ago when Pop had his knee surgery, and no, I haven't gotten around to taking any of it down yet. But I'm planning to. Soon."

"Right," I say skeptically. I cross to his bookshelf and skim a few of the titles. There's some Alastair Reynolds and Stephen King and Ray Bradbury. I wrinkle my nose at a Beastie Boy auto-biography, but the beat-up copy of *American Gods* makes me feel remorseful for assuming he only read *Playboy.*

Honestly, I'm grateful to be wrong.

"I actually tried to convince Pop to take my room so he wouldn't have to deal with the stairs, but he's too proud and stubborn."

I lift a shoulder nonchalantly. "Or maybe he likes his bedroom. Maybe it has memories for him just like yours has for you."

I can feel his eyes on me as I wander over to the corkboard. The photographs pinned here seem to be from various occasions in his life. In some he's a teenager. He's thinner and beardless, but still attractive. Still as cocky, if I'm interpreting his expressions correctly.

In others, he's younger, and I wouldn't recognize him if it weren't for his nose and eyes.

Then there are pictures of family.

"Is this is your mother?" I ask, pointing to a woman with a round face who looks like a cross between Megan and Pop.

Chase moves up next to me, presumably to see what I'm looking at. "Yeah. That was not too long before she died."

"And after she died you moved in here?"

He nods. "Dad was killed in a car accident when Megan was just a baby. I don't even remember him. So when Mom died, Gran and Pop took us in."

"When did your Gran pass?"

"A few years ago. That's her with Keon." He points to a photo of an elderly lady with Chase's chin holding a newborn baby. There's something so sweet about it, something so honest, it makes my chest pinch, and I have to look away.

I find a picture where teenage Chase has his arm around a blonde with her hair in retro cinnamon buns, Gwen Stefani style circa 2001. "Is this your high school girlfriend?"

"One of them. You jealous?"

"No!" I'm a little bit jealous. Which is stupid.

But I remember being that age. I still believed in relationships back then. Still believed in happily ever afters. What would it have been like for us if I'd met him back then?

Butterflies stir in my stomach, the kind that have less to do with lust than they do with infatuation. They haven't stirred in so long I barely recognize the feeling.

"Did you ever bring girls back here?" I ask, broaching dangerous territory. I'm thinking dangerous thoughts. Having dangerous fantasies. Wanting dangerous things.

"Never," he says earnestly.

"Yeah, I don't believe you." I cross over to his DVD case by the door, pretending to be curious about what he liked to watch when he was a teenager—and I am—but really, I just need to have some space from him before I let this crazy twitterpated feeling get the best of me.

But Chase follows me. "I'm dead serious. Pop has a shotgun. He was always threatening to shoot my dick off if I knocked a girl up. Scared the shit out of me."

I laugh nervously, keeping my eyes on the movies. "And here you are trying to knock a girl up now. You must have gotten over your fear."

"Pop has arthritis. He'd have too much trouble loading the gun." There's a soft thud of a door closing, and I look up to see that he has shut us in. "And I have always regretted the lack of action this room has seen."

My heart rate picks up, and immediately, my panties are soaked. I'm already half fantasizing about what it would have been like to be his teenage girlfriend. Sneaking around, fumbling and fucking behind my mother's back, convinced that he and I are meant to be forever.

But all this is wrong. The fantasy, the location. The motivation. "Chase." I shake my head, insistently. "No. We can't."

"We can. We should." His eyes darken and he starts for me.

Facing him, I back away. "Your grandfather's just in the other room!"

"He's taking his morning nap."

My backside meets the desk behind me. I'm trapped. I have nowhere to go. A thrill runs through my body.

With a wicked grin, Chase moves in until he's nearly pressed against me.

"What if we wake him up?" I ask, already breathless.

"He has his hearing aids out. He can't hear shit." Chase pushes up my dress and rolls his thumbs over my clit through my panties.

I gasp. "I mean. I guess this is still within the window of ovulation."

"Exactly why we should," he agrees.

But, really, I'm barely thinking about my fertility cycle. It's just an excuse to play out this fantasy of mine. A fantasy that's for me alone. I'm not willing to share it, not even with Chase.

I bite my lower lip when I notice the outline of his cock, pushing thick and large against his jeans.

He follows my gaze. "See how hard I am for you, kitten?"

"Uh-huh." I shudder as he presses harder against my nub.

He bends down so his mouth is near my ear and whispers, "There might be a baby in there right now, just waiting to be made. All it needs is your tight. Warm. Pussy."

Fuck. I'm done for.

Fingers shaking with anticipation, I start working the button of his jeans.

"Turn around," he commands, urgently, before I've gotten his pants unzipped.

I turn and gather my dress around my waist and hold it in place with my elbows. Then I lay my palms flat on the desk, bracing myself for what I know is coming.

Like I imagine he does with the people he arrests, Chase kicks my feet apart, spreading me as much as he needs. Then he moves in closer behind me. He's so frantic, he doesn't even pull my panties down. He just pulls them to the side to make room for his cock.

I'm so wet, he slides right in.

"If I'd have known you when I was a teen, I'd have beat myself raw," he says, pumping into me with vigor. "I'd have imagined fucking you just like this."

"Keep talking," I pant.

"Oh, you like that, do you? I knew my librarian was a naughty girl." He slows down ever so slightly so he can snake an arm around me and up my dress. He tugs the cup of my bra down and releases my tit from captivity and squeezes. "Teenage Chase would've had to have you. He'd have done all sorts of nasty things to you in the back seat of his Acura Legend."

Even as I'm gasping from pleasure, I giggle at the image of Chase in what was likely his first car. Damn, I would have loved to have done that too. Sneaking around without my mother knowing. Getting fingered in his car when we're supposed to be at the library or the school play or the game.

"For you, I would have found a way to bring you back to my room instead," he says. God, he's so there with me, putting all my naughty thoughts into words. "Fuck Pop and his gun. I would have told him that I was helping you with your physics homework. And then I would have fucked you against this very desk."

I close my eyes and moan, picturing our open textbooks falling to the floor as he pounded into me from behind. My belly starts to tighten and pull. I'm so turned on, I'm already feeling the crest of my climax approaching.

"But Teenage Chase wasn't the Sex God he is now. I'd have to ask you what you wanted. You'd have to tell me how to touch you." Pinching my nipple, he brings his other hand to brush along the skin of my pussy lips. "Right here, kitten? Like this?"

"Yes," I whimper. "More. There." I can't talk in multi-syllabic words.

"Show me, baby."

Without thinking about it too hard—if I do, I'll get too timid—I take one hand off the desk and bring it over his so I can lead his finger between my folds to find my clit. Then, directing his pressure, we rub me to orgasm.

As soon as I explode, he focuses on pursuit of his own climax, squeezing my breast and rutting into me wildly as he praises and adores me. "Jesus, Liv. You're so sexy. So tight. So gorgeous. Right there. Right there. I'm gonna come, kitten. I'm gonna come."

He stills, bursting inside me, and I wonder as he grunts and relaxes behind me, if we were both young and stupid, would I have hoped he'd be filling me with a baby then, too? The way that teens in lust-that-they-think-is-love often do? Not to trap him, but to solidify what we had. To hold onto it for as long as possible.

I almost wish we really were that age, just so I could feel that way about him and not worry about the things I know now about love and relationships and men who don't stick around.

"I'll say it again, Liv," Chase says, kissing the back of my neck before pulling out. "You're fun."

I don't argue this time. I simply smile and put my dress back in order while I scan the photographs in front of me a final time. "It's kind of a shame all of this is going to come down. It gives a pretty vivid picture of your youth." I've committed as much as I can to memory, though. Recording what might be useful when I'm raising his offspring—no other reason.

Chase buttons his jeans and glances around the room. "Well. Not all of it's coming down. Jessica will stay."

"Oh right," I chuckle. "Of course."

Silly as it is, I find myself wishing I was Jessica Alba. Wishing that I too could stay.

11

LIVIA

Stairwell at Corinth.

I hit SAVE on the entry I've just added to yesterday's date in my Google Calendar. Then, after thinking about it a second, I click the entry again and hit "edit." In the notes section I add one word: **Twice.**

I hit SAVE one more time and then click on VIEW so I can see the entire month at once.

I quickly count the dates that have entries. There are eleven in total.

Holy shit.

That's eleven times that Chase and I have had sex in the last two weeks! That's a fuck lot of fucking. And that isn't counting extra for the entries that have notes like yesterday's stairwell incident.

Mmm. The stairwell.

My toes curl just thinking about the way I had to clutch onto the railing so that I wouldn't collapse from the punishing sequence of orgasms he delivered.

Yeah. The stairwell was nice.

It's really probably not an entry I should include on the calendar. I'm well past my fertile period, and my "meetings" with Chase are now primarily about keeping him satisfied—the man has a voracious appetite. But I included a couple of the times right after I was ovulating, in case I have my dates wrong. Once I decided to include those, I didn't know where to draw the line, so I've continued recording them all.

I figure it's better to have more data than not. That way I'll be able to accurately quantify the sacrifices I made in order to get pregnant.

I chuckle at the thought. As if having sex with Chase could ever be considered a sacrifice.

My humor quickly fades as I realize something else from looking at my calendar—my thirtieth birthday is even closer than it was a month ago.

Funny how that happens.

The familiar dread and death thoughts settle over me, making me feel antsy and anxious. I'm old. My body is old. My legs ache. My back aches. My breasts ache. Death is near.

Maybe I'm just fussy because I'm pregnant.

Or it's PMS.

And if it's PMS, why the fuck am I not pregnant yet? After eleven times with Chase's so-called super sperm, surely I should be knocked up by now. Is it me that's the problem? Can I not get pregnant the natural way? Will I need infertility treatments to get my baby?

I'll have to get a second job for that. A third job.

Which wouldn't leave any time for the actual banging.

Of course, if I *am* pregnant, there won't be any purpose for banging.

I throw my head back and groan. I want a baby, and the sooner the better. But the idea of no more sex with Chase is so horrible, it makes me want to puke.

Wait.

Do I actually *need* to puke? I sit back upright and concentrate on the way my body feels. Am I nauseated? Is this morning…er—I look at the time—*early evening* sickness?

Maybe I should take another test. Yes, I've taken five already this week (one just this morning), and all of them have been negative. But my period isn't actually due until tomorrow so maybe it was still too early. And twelve hours could make a big difference in hormone production. Probably.

Before I've made up my mind about whether I want to use—and possibly waste—another pregnancy test, the phone rings.

"Who the hell calls!" I shout to the empty room. But my annoyance dissipates when I see Chase's name on my screen. Well, not his name, exactly. He's listed as "Hot Cop" in my phone. Naturally.

"I was just thinking about you," I say, in lieu of hello.

It hasn't slipped my attention that Chase is the only person in my life that I don't harass about calling me. He doesn't do it that often. Most of our communication is via text, as all communication with decent people should be. But sometimes, when he's driving or working out or he needs a quick answer to something, he rings me up instead.

And I've decided that's fine. It's a temporary relationship, anyway, and the calling thing has been…useful.

"No wonder you sound so happy." His voice alone gets my body reacting. My heart races and the blood starts flowing to my lower regions.

Not that I'd ever admit it.

I curl my feet underneath me and shrug even though he can't see me. "Actually, I'm moody today. And my breasts are tender to the touch. It's either PMS or I'm pregnant. No period yet, but the symptoms, it turns out, are pretty much the same as being knocked up. How the hell am I supposed to know the difference? How did anyone ever stand the waiting in the old days?"

"I'm sorry. You said something about touching your breasts, and I missed everything you said after that. Did you say you're *not* having your period?"

Normally this would elicit a laugh, but like I said, I'm moody. "No. I'm not. Jerk."

"Good. I need you."

"You *need* me?" I know what he means. I just can't believe he *needs* me again so soon.

"I'm outside your door in three, two…"

My doorbell rings. Shaking my head, I click END on the phone call and jump up to let him in. After a couple of steps, I turn back to shut my laptop. Chase doesn't need to see my tracking notes. Then I run to answer the door.

"You need me again already?" I say, when I see him face to face. Looking him over, it appears he's just come from the gym. He's carrying a duffle bag, dressed in sweatpants and a poly-blend shirt that appears to be the type designed to stay dry. His body's drenched from his workout, and it reminds me so much of the times I'm lying underneath him that my stomach clenches in automatic response.

I stand back to let him past me.

"Hello to you too, sexypants."

He waggles his brows as his eyes wander to my chest, and after I shut the door I confront him. "You're checking out my boobs, aren't you?" It comes out irritated, and maybe I am. I don't know. I'm not irritated with him, exactly. Just irritated in general.

Chase shrugs. "You said they were tender. I was just trying to decide if they looked bigger."

Bigger could mean pregnant. My enthusiasm kindled, I thrust my bosom out for his inspection. "Well?"

He studies me more overtly, hovering his hands above my tits as though trying to compare size. "I think I need more input," he says. "I need to feel them a bit. Caress them. Maybe see how they fit in my mouth."

I press my back against the closed door and heave out a dramatic sigh. "We just banged yesterday."

I don't know why I'm whining about it. I liked the banging yesterday. Loved it, even. I'll love the banging today, too. Like I always do.

Chase closes in on me, resting his hands on my hips. "We totally did. When your boss walked out, and I had to put my hand over your mouth and pull you behind the stairs so she wouldn't catch us?"

"Yeah?" I ask, slightly breathy from the memory.

"That was really hot."

"It was." *So hot.* I'm wet now, thinking about it. "I thought it would hold you over for a while. You are quite insatiable."

"Are you complaining?"

"I'm simply stating an observation." But my tone sounds a little like I'm complaining, even to my own ears.

Chase pulls back as though he might leave. "I can go find someone else to take care of me if you're willing to amend the arrangement."

My chest twists unexpectedly.

"Really?" I can't tell if he's serious or teasing.

He shrugs non-committedly. "If that's what you want."

I frown. "It's not." It's not what I want at all. That's why I told him upfront that he had to remain monogamous. That's why it's in the contract. "I'm not amending the arrangement. And I'm not complaining."

"That's what I thought." He grins and moves in again.

Until I halt him with my palms. "But you're all sweaty and gross. Take a shower first."

I say this last part at the same time as he says, "I'll hit the shower first."

"Yeah, good idea."

He picks up the duffle he brought in and slips off to my bedroom to use the en suite shower. I watch him leave because he has a nice backside. Even nicer in those sweats.

Once he's out of sight, I throw my head back and knock it three times against the door. Then, rubbing my head, I move to my kitchen island. I lean my elbows on the faux granite counter and let out a frustrated groan.

What the hell is wrong with me?

I'm glad Chase is here. I really, really am. I was excited the minute I saw his name on my caller display, and despite my fussing, I'm horny for him too. I actually always get hornier when I'm premenstrual, so maybe I *am* about to bleed.

Of course I've read that can be a symptom of pregnancy too.

But as happy as I am that he's here, the anxiety I was feeling before his arrival has tightened into a thick knot in my chest. First, there's his *needs*. While I agreed willingly to be there for him, even outside of my fertility window, there is a part of me that is bothered by the amount of sex we've had that hasn't been for the explicit goal of procreating. Or, more accurately, it bothers me how much it doesn't actually bother me.

What does it mean that I want to jump him as much as I do, simply for the sake of jumping him?

I don't have an answer, but it feels complicated. It feels like I'm connecting with Chase on levels I never meant to. Like he's connecting with me.

Except now he's mentioned finding another woman.

This isn't the first time we've had sex outside my fertile period, but it's the first time he's mentioned going elsewhere for release. Does he *want* someone else?

Of course he doesn't. I was giving him a hard time so he responded in kind.

Except, maybe that's not true. Maybe I'm just telling myself that so I'll feel better. But I don't feel better, because I'm not sure what's true anymore.

I'm not worried that he'll cheat on me. Is cheating the right term? I'm not worried that he'll cheat on our arrangement. I know he's dedicated to the terms. But I hadn't considered that he might be thinking of other women. That he might be *wanting* other women. Other women that he could get into his bed at the drop of his badge.

And that sucks balls if he does because I want him to only want me.

The revelation hits me like a ton of bricks. It isn't a good one. In fact, it's a terrible one. It's selfish. I know it is. He's already giving me more than I'm giving him. I shouldn't covet all of his desire on top of that. It's not fair and it's exactly what we're *not* supposed to be about.

But I want it all the same. I want it, and it means bad things. The worst things. It means I like him. It means I care. It means I want to feel like, in some way, he cares about me.

Even if it's only sexually.

Especially if it's only sexually, because that's the only way it will ever be okay to care about him. And it's the only way it will ever be okay to let him care about me.

With that realization, I'm suddenly desperate to be with him.

I run to the bathroom where he's still showering. He's left the door open so the steam hasn't fogged up the room, and I can see him distinctly through the clear glass wall of my walk-in shower. He must hear me because he turns toward me when I come in.

"Almost done here, babe," he says, soap lathered on his chest and torso.

But I didn't come in to rush him. I came to join him.

His eyes are still watching me as I pull my *When in Doubt, Go to the Library* T-shirt over my head and let it fall to the ground. I took off my bra when I got home from work and changed into loungewear so my breasts are now exposed and Chase's eyes widen greedily at the sight. His hand moves down to tug on his cock, which is quickly hardening in front of me.

I consider making the rest of my strip routine more of a tease, but I'm too eager to be with him. Too eager to touch him. Hurriedly, I pull down my leggings and panties together and kick them aside. Then I walk around the wall and into the shower to join him.

"Liv, you've just made me a very happy man," he says, turning his back to the spray so he can face me. He pulls again on his erection, which is now rock hard, and my mouth waters. I plan to take care of that. Soon.

But first...

Besides the texts setting up locations and meet-up times, I haven't ever been the one to initiate sex, and honestly, I'm not sure what I'm doing. I've let Chase do all the guiding.

Fortunately, my confidence doesn't let me down. I know what I want, and that's what I go after.

I walk to him, throw my arms around his neck, and kiss him.

For half a second, Chase seems stunned. I move my mouth against his, and he's frozen, his body still as though he's afraid if he moves, the moment will be broken.

Then suddenly he wakes up. He enfolds me in his arms, pulling me against his slick body. Our lips tangle and our tongues explore, and it's not unlike our first kiss where we were frenzied and urgent.

But this is also entirely new. It's bold and brave and sure.

It's familiar, too. And personal. And exactly all the things I'd feared kissing could be with him, and why I hadn't wanted to ever kiss him again. My chest tingles and expands. I feel dizzy, and closer to Chase than I've ever felt before.

And that terrifies me. In all the best and worst ways.

But it doesn't matter anymore that kissing feels too intimate or too scary. The fear of intimacy was that it would lead to growing attached. And dammit, I'm already attached. I realize that now. This is already going to sting when it's over. There's no stopping that. So I might as well enjoy it while it lasts.

I might as well enjoy *him* while it lasts.

The water continues to fall down his backside. Rivulets escape down his front, and I leave his mouth to follow one with my tongue as it weaves down his torso. The journey brings me to my knees, face-to-face with the "other Officer Kelly." We've become good friends the last two weeks, his cock and I.

Furtively, I peek up at Chase. He'd been reluctant to let me break our kiss, but now his eyes are dark as he watches my lips hover above his crown.

"I want to see you put it in your mouth, like a good girl," he tells me. "Can you do that for me, kitten?"

I nod, but all I do is lick the waterdrops off the circumference of his head, like it's an ice cream cone that I don't want to drip. I glance back up at him.

"That's not going to cut it, babe," he tells me, bucking his hips toward me.

Giggling, I suck the tiniest bit of the tip into my mouth, enjoying the way his legs shake and his belly trembles with his groan.

"Fuck. Liv." His hands tangle in my hair, and I can tell he's trying to resist directing me, and maybe I should be glad about that, but the thing is, as much as I wanted to put my mouth on him—as much as this was my idea—I don't know what I'm doing. Not only has it been several years since I've given a blow job, but I've maybe never given a fabulous blow job. And just like teenage Chase who didn't know how to touch a woman, I don't know how to suck this grown man.

I want him to show me what to do, but I don't want to ask outright. I wrap my hands around his thighs, take his head into my mouth then let it fall out again before I stare up at him coyly. "Like this?"

"Take it all the way, honey. You can do it." He's encouraging me, but I hear the impatience under his words.

I want him impatient. I want him restless and eager so that he'll abandon his manners and let his instincts lead the way.

So I take him in as instructed, but it's a half-hearted attempt to please him. I draw my lips over him too slowly. I don't take him deep enough.

Again, he bucks, driving his cock in farther.

"Mmm." My lips vibrate over his length, and he groans in response.

"More of that, Livvy." He threads his fingers tighter against my scalp and I relax my neck muscles, hoping he'll take over. My stomach twists in anticipation. "More," he says again, rocking his pelvis back and forth in a gentle rhythm. "Flatten your tongue."

I flatten my tongue, looking up to find his eyes are closed and, from his expression, I'd guess his restraint is threadbare. I pull my head back and take him in, once more too slowly.

He pushes my head this time, forcing me to take more of him. I press my lips tighter around him, rewarding his dominant behavior. It seems to work, because he grunts and pulls my head back before pushing me down on him again.

I dig my nails into his thighs. We're working at his tempo now, Chase fucking my mouth at the depth and speed he likes best. I'm taking notes. Remembering exactly how far he likes to be sucked in and how he likes my tongue and how he likes it when I moan against him. It's so fucking hot. If I weren't so mesmerized by watching him, I'd reach down and rub myself, but this is about him. I want it to be about him. Because I don't know how much longer I'll have him.

Chase's leg muscles harden and his balls start to draw up. He's close, and I ready myself to take all he has to give. All the times he's emptied himself into me for my benefit, I'm happy to swallow it all now for him.

But just as I think he's going to come, he pushes me off of him and pulls me to my feet.

"What are you doing? I would have—"

He doesn't let me finish telling me what I would have done because he captures my mouth with his in a deep searing kiss. He turns me and presses my back against the wall. "I don't want to come in your mouth," he says. "I'd rather have my tongue in your mouth while I'm coming in your cunt."

I don't argue because that does sound nice. Besides, he's kissing me again and my mouth is preoccupied with better things than talking. He lifts me up so I'm at the right height and I wrap my legs around him, inviting him in.

He buries himself inside me, with one plunging thrust. Then he doesn't move, he just stays nestled in my pussy, as though he's anchored himself to shore, while he kisses me and kisses me. In all the ways I imagine that he's always wanted to kiss me. In all the ways I've always wanted to be kissed by him.

When he starts to stir, he moves leisurely at first, until neither of us can take it and we're both arching and bucking, trying to get deeper and deeper, trying to get "there" and everywhere and then we're coming, both of us together. Quaking like we're two rocks compressing against each other on a fault line under the surface of the earth.

We make small talk while we dry off. Decide what we'll have for dinner. Talk about the size of my breasts, which we decide are probably about the same size as always. We don't talk about the rest. About the kissing or that I initiated, or that this time, more than any other time, was less about contracts or babies or getting off than ever before, because I don't know if there are words for what it really was. It was more than just sex, and I can't pretend it was only for Chase.

The truth is, I don't know what this was. But I do know that things are different now. Because now I know that I actually care. About him.

I also know that the longer this goes on, the more it's going to hurt when he's met his contractual obligation and moves on.

But I'll have a baby on the way then to soften the blow. I can focus on attaching to my child instead. Hopefully, that will happen sooner rather than later.

And yes, I'll miss this. I'll miss the touching and the teasing and the orgasms.

God...the orgasms...

My libido wouldn't mind if this month ends up with no viable bun in the oven. Denying it is pointless.

But I'm praying that the kisses we shared tonight were the last. I'm not sure my heart can take much more time together than it already has.

12

CHASE

"If you don't stop checking that thing, I'm going to throw it out the window," Sergeant Gutierrez threatens.

I put the phone away with an exaggerated sigh and then turn to smile at her, my big dimpled smile that sometimes gets me out of trouble. We're driving in her car, and she doesn't take her eyes off the road to scowl at me, so she just scowls at the highway instead, but it looks like she's fighting off a smile too.

"Can't you conduct your one-man dating service when you're off duty?"

I watch the concrete walls flit by on the highway as she pulls into the right lane. "I feel like 'duty' is a strong word for this afternoon, Sarge."

Now she's really grinning. "Well, yeah."

With our captain's permission, we are heading down to the regional police academy for an hour or two, both to watch a wet lab in progress and to talk to the administrators to hammer out the logistics for hosting one. Even though our city is fairly quiet and mostly residential, a few trendy new restaurants in the heart of town have meant an uptick in drunk driving, and our captain thinks most of the officers could use a refresher course in sobriety testing.

So we're looking into the possibility of hosting a wet lab of our own, yes, but also it means an afternoon of watching rookie cops and drunk people—two of the funniest groups to watch on the planet. It'll be a nice break from the calls about nursing home escapes and rich teens shoplifting.

We take the exit toward the community college, where the police academy is located, and I surreptitiously pull out my phone to check it again. Livia hasn't texted me today, and normally I wouldn't be shy about texting or calling her myself, except it seemed really important that I let her text first today...for some reason. The problem is that I told myself to give her space before she stepped into the shower with me, and now all I can remember is kissing her.

Fuck, that kiss. *That kiss.* Her mouth so eager and soft under my own, the warm spray of the water at my back, and the steam curling around our ankles...

The damp hair clinging to her temples as I wrapped her legs around my waist and fucked her against the wall....

Her soft cry as she came, echoing off the bathroom tile and sending bolts of possessive lust straight down to my groin...

I shift in my seat, my cock pushing against my pants. I'd said that thing yesterday about finding another woman to take care of me mostly to tease her, but partly out of embarrassment at my own need to fuck her *all the time.* I've never needed to fuck someone like this—insatiably, constantly. It's driving me crazy.

Why hasn't she texted me yet? I check my phone again.

"Kelly!" Gutierrez barks. "Stop with the phone! How many different women do you need to talk to in a day anyway?"

"It's actually just one. The same one for almost a month actually."

Gutierrez parks the car and then slowly swivels her head to stare at me, her mouth literally hanging open, which maybe I'm a little offended by?

And I don't know why I said it, because it's not like everybody at the department doesn't know I'm a giant manwhore. And I've never minded people thinking that, been a little proud of it, actually. Officer Good Times and all. But maybe it's that I want someone to *know*. Not necessarily about the baby stuff, but just about everything else. Her apartment full of sagging bookshelves. How it felt to have her in my room, teasing me about all my nerdy shit. Watching her banter back and forth with my crotchety old grandpa.

This tug and twist whenever I think about her, like a knot behind my ribs that can't be undone. Even when I'm with her, inside her, even when I'm giving her the deepest, most biologically essential parts of me as I ejaculate inside her—even then, the knot is pulling tighter and tighter, like no matter how close I get to her, it'll never be close enough.

I don't know how to feel about it, and I don't like things I don't know, so mostly I'm just trying to ignore it. Compartmentalize. I'm good at that shit.

But I still kind of want to talk about it, and both Pop and Megan are out of the question, so I find myself telling Gutierrez more as I absent-mindedly click my phone screen on again. It's starting to worry me, this silence from Liv.

"It's a librarian, down at Corinth," I tell my supervisor, clicking my phone off again. "She works with my sister."

"A librarian," Gutierrez repeats, as if I just told her I've been sleeping with an alien. "You…and a librarian?"

I give her my best frown, even popping up my sunglasses so she can see my mock-hurt eyes. "What's that supposed to mean?"

"Nothing," she says, grabbing her keys and climbing out of the car. I get out of the car too, and we walk toward the front door of the academy. "Just that normally you seemed to go for the women more like you."

"More like me?"

"Do you really want me to elaborate?"

I open the door for her and then follow her inside the depressingly bland building. "Is it going to be mean?"

"Kelly, face it. You're the stereotype of a bachelor cop, and the women you sleep with are the stereotypes of women who like bachelor cops. I just don't want you to wreak havoc on some poor woman's life because you're bored or you're dying—"

"I'm not dying!" I protest.

She flips her sunglasses up to the top of her head and squints at me. "You're over thirty, aren't you?"

"If one more person says that—"

"Just don't be a dick, okay? Especially to some sweet librarian. They deserve better than that. Now if you want to go ruin the life of someone down at the post office, be my guest. You know the last time I had to mail a blood kit up to Topeka, they actually *refused* to—"

But I never did hear what the post office refused my sergeant because we turn a corner into the room they're using for the lab, and I see a flash of coffee-brown hair and hear the lilting alto of a familiar laugh and stop. Right in my tracks.

Gutierrez doesn't notice this, walking straight over to one of the academy instructors to talk, which is good. Because I can't move. Can't think. Can't breathe.

Livia is here.

Livia is not supposed to be here, and I have no idea why she is, but she is indisputably here at this wet lab, in this room, with me and twelve drunk civilians.

Here, playing Aggravation with a couple of middle-aged volunteers with a plastic cup of something clear and bubbly next to her. Here, looking gorgeous in tight jeans and an over-sized Hamilton sweatshirt with the neck cut out, so that it exposes the bright blue line of her bra and the elegant, edible curves of her shoulder. Her hair's up in a sloppy knot, with tendrils wisping down over her neck and temples, and fuck, even dressed down and casual, she's still the sexiest thing I've ever seen. It's effortless how she does it. Something about her skin maybe, so clear and soft, or maybe it's her giant brown eyes. Maybe it's the delicate bones of her face, the high cheeks and the sweet point of her chin. Or maybe it's something about the way she holds herself, her shoulders curving in slightly but her head high, as if she's trying to protect herself but is too proud to admit it.

I want to protect her.

I want to watch those shoulders uncurl, that mouth smile without reservation, and I feel a surge of pride for her as I remember how she was last night with me. Brave and fearless and bold. Taking something she wanted. Trusting me. Trusting me to accept her gift and cherish her for offering it.

I'd finally earned her mouth, the kiss I'd been dreaming of, and I have to admit, I'm a little proud of *me* for doing that.

She's here, even though I have no idea why, but now it's okay that she hasn't texted. Just seeing her makes my chest feel light, and so it's with nothing but happy anticipation that I walk up to her and give the knot on her head a gentle tug.

"You come to this bar often?" I joke.

She turns at the sound of my voice and the feel of my hand in her hair, and stands up. And for a minute, I think she's going to give me another kiss, and I wouldn't mind one bit. Technically, it probably would be against some policy or another, but the wet lab volunteers are almost always former cops or family and friends of cops, and so there's usually some informality going on.

I grin down at her, and then she growls at me. Like... actually *growls*.

I can't decide whether I want to tackle her and kiss the growl right out of her mouth or if I want to run and take cover, but I don't get a chance to do either.

She takes a step forward and sticks a finger in my face. I catch a strong whiff of alcohol. "*You.* You are the last person I want to see."

I blink. That was not the greeting I'd hoped for. The light and airy thing in my chest sinks, and I'm filled with a nagging itch of worry.

"Did I…miss something?" I rack my brain, trying to think of anything that could have gone wrong between yesterday and today, because the last time we were together, she was limp and boneless with sweaty, wet ecstasy.

Well, not entirely *bone*less, if you know what I mean.

She narrows her eyes at me. "You did miss something, Chase, but I didn't."

"I..." I got nothing. I have no idea what's going on.

I look past her to her table, where her board game friends are valiantly trying to pretend they're not watching our exchange. In fact, I have a feeling the rest of the room is doing the same, even though everyone is still going about their business of chattering and playing cards and drinking. They still haven't brought in the recruits to test the volunteers, so our audience is mostly just drunk people for now. Which is good, because I have to get to the bottom of this. I can't have my kitten mad at me; the thought of her being angry with me, of her not wanting to be around me, actually hurts.

That's normal, right? I mean, I'd probably feel that way about any woman I was trying to impregnate.

"Hey!" Livia says, jabbing a finger into my chest and breaking me out of my thoughts. "Pay attention to me!"

And then she pokes my chest again with a frowny pout, a puzzled little line between her eyebrows. She pokes harder, her finger pressing into the stiff wall of the Kevlar I wear under my uniform. "Why are you so hard?" she complains.

I refrain from making the obvious joke and answer as seriously as I can. "It's body armor, babe. It's supposed to be hard."

"I want you to be soft," she whines.

"Well," I say, "tough shit."

Cue an epic pout from her, all soft lips and long eyelashes.

I lean in and add, "Nothing's soft around you, doll."

Suddenly another finger in my chest. "*No*," she says angrily. "You don't get to be all flirty with me, not today. Not after what you did."

What I did? I scan her face, currently aglow with indignation, and that itchy worry grows itchier.

But I force myself to stay cool, stay light and fun, because if she sees how much she twists me up inside, I'm afraid I'll scare off my shy girl. This girl who made me sign a contract explicitly promising not to care too much about her.

Okay, Chase. Light and fun. Act like you don't care.

"What did I do?" I ask. Lightly and funly.

"You *lied*, Mr. Officer Blue Eyes. You *lied to me.*"

"Mr. Officer Blue Eyes," I repeat with a smile. Her cheeks are flushed with heat and her eyes are sparkling with hot irritation. If I fucked her right now, she'd scratch and bite, and suddenly that's all I can think about.

Except—sigh—I probably shouldn't fuck her right now. Her anger aside… "How many drinks have you had today, Livia?"

She shakes her head. "Nuh-uh. This is not about me being a tiny, miniscule amount of tipsy." Her normally precise voice stumbles over the word *miniscule.* "This is about you *lying* about your super sperm!"

Well. Everyone is certainly staring at us now.

I take Liv's elbow and guide her into a corner of the room, deciding that sober Liv probably wouldn't want to rant about sperm in front of a room of strangers.

Once we get into the corner, Liv yanks her elbow out of my grasp with the unflappable dignity of the drunk. "You said you had super sperm," she continues in a whispered hiss. "And you *don't.* You have the opposite of super sperm! You have *un*super sperm, you have microsperm, you have…"

Her eyes glance around as she tries to think of something especially cutting. They land on my arm, where my tattoo peeks out from under my sleeve. "You have *Hydra* sperm. Captain America would hate your sperm."

Whoa.

"Now, let's not say things we're going to regret in the heat of the moment."

She growls again.

"And baby, you barely know my body at all if you think my sperm is unsuper, micro, Hydra sperm."

"I do know your body, and I know about your giant, awesome cock—"

"Okay, well maybe you know my body a little bit—"

"—and you were supposed to get me pregnant and you didn't." Her eyes get glossy and her chin has the faintest tremble in it. And for some reason, seeing her chin quiver is like being punched in the chest. I can't stand it.

I'm already pulling her into my arms when she manages in a teary whisper, "I got my period this morning. I'm not pregnant."

"Oh, Liv," I say, cradling her tight to my chest. "Oh, kitten."

And I'm a fucking asshole. Because *this* was the reason Yesterday Chase wanted Today Chase to give Livia some room, wanted to let her take the lead today instead of me barging into her life and demanding sex, like I basically have been the last two weeks. She told me yesterday that she was nervous about getting her period today, and like the horny asshole I am, I forgot about it the moment I got my dick inside her.

Way to go, idiot. It's not like this is the most important thing in her life or anything.

"I'm so sorry," I tell her. "I'm so, so, so fucking sorry."

And I am. I'm sorry I forgot, but more than that, I'm disappointed and sad for her, because I know how much she wants this.

And maybe I'm a little disappointed for me too. I don't even know why. Maybe just a natural male instinct to want to make a woman pregnant? Maybe I really wanted to believe I had super sperm?

It's definitely not because I've already caught myself imagining what Liv's stomach would look like all curved and heavy with my baby. Definitely not because I've wondered if the baby would have brown eyes or blue, and how they would look blinking up at Livia as she nursed. And it's extra definitely not because I can still remember the coos and chirps my nephews made as sleepy, chubby newborns, the way they felt dozing on my chest while I watched HGTV with Pop. Or because I miss it, and the idea of it being my own little boy or girl to snuggle makes my chest glow with warmth—

It's definitely not because of any of those things. I'm sure of it.

It wouldn't even really be your *baby, asshole. Livia doesn't want you around after you knock her up.*

Livia keeps her face buried in my chest, her hands sliding up to press flat against the Kevlar, her shoulders trembling as she sniffles into my uniform. "I knew it would take time," she says, her voice muffled. "I knew it would. I just…I hoped it would be fast. That I wouldn't have to get my hopes up and then be disappointed. I don't know if I can go through this again and again—I want to be pregnant now. I want this to end."

But I *don't* want this to end.

The realization lands with the force of a two-ton bomb. I don't want this to end at all. I don't want to stop fucking Livia. I don't want to stop seeing her. And that's *now*—how the fuck will I manage it when she's pregnant with my child?

I make a comforting noise and stroke her neck, but I'm anything but calm on the inside. My mind is racing, trying to process this new information.

I don't want this to end.

I don't want this to end.

Livia pulls back with another sniffle, wiping at her face with the sleeve of her sweatshirt. "I'm okay," she mumbles. "I'm done crying about it. Maybe they have more vodka…these cramps are killing me."

I look down at her, her eyes and nose red from her tears, her messy bun even messier now, her sweatshirt too big and her shoulders hunched in, as if trying to guard her heart. And I remind myself that Livia *does* want this to end. She asked me to help her in one very specific way, and she made it clear she didn't want commitment or a boyfriend or even casual sex simply for the sake of casual sex.

I'm a means to an end for her. An eight-inch syringe attached to an admittedly great body. She just wants me to be Officer

Good Times, Mr. Officer Blue Eyes, not the kind of guy who gets attached. Not the guy who can't stop wanting her.

Except.

There is a way she lets me want her. That I think she even likes me wanting her.

And if it's the way I get to keep her wanting *me*, then it's the way I'll go. Because I'm not ready at all to say goodbye.

So I take a breath, swallow down all this stuff I don't understand, and go back to being the kind of guy who can make Livia happy, however temporarily.

"I know another way to help those cramps, darling," I say, leaning in close. "You let the nice policeman help you release some tension, hmm?"

She bites her lip, staring at my mouth. "But it's…you know. All sorts of stuff going on down there."

The hungry look in her eyes has me heating up. We're already in a corner, and so it only takes a couple steps to get her backed against a wall, my hands braced on either side of her so she can't move. "I'm not scared of all sorts of stuff," I say in a low voice. "Just let me get two fingers inside your panties, and I guarantee I can make you feel much, much better…"

Liv's breathing fast now, her pupils growing wide and color rising to her cheeks. I have a brief moment to congratulate myself on distracting her from her sadness, and then the door opens and the rookies shuffle into the room with all the nervous, hesitant energy rookies have.

I step back from Liv right as the lead instructor tells the recruits to circulate through the room to practice the field sobriety tests on the various volunteers. I try to look casual and cop-like and not like I was just telling a hot girl that I wanted to finger her.

"Ready?" I ask Liv.

She glances down at my hand—no, my *fingers*—and blushes even deeper.

"For the sobriety tests," I clarify, with a grin.

And then I beckon a few of the recruits over. "Here's a good one," I announce, as they shyly come forward. I look at the awkward cluster of them, too tight ponytails on the women, acne still on the faces of some of the men. They're all holding tiny notebooks and pens and they're practically shaking at the prospect of having to do actual policework on actual people. God, it's like they get younger and younger every year.

"Now, this lady is pretty drunk," I begin.

"I am not!" Livia protests from behind me.

I ignore her. "And she's getting belligerent. You'll get those from time to time. The secret to handling a drunk is: *ask, tell, make*. Let me demonstrate." I turn to Liv, who currently has her arms folded tightly over her chest and her body leaned against the wall. "Ma'am, I'm going to run you through our field sobriety tests. Will you step away from the wall, please?"

Livia glances warily from me to the recruits, and I can tell she's weighing her options. After all, she came here to act as the drunk guinea pig for the rookies…but she didn't come here to get teased by me. "You come over to me," she says finally. "I'm not moving."

"Ah, see?" I tell the recruits. "Now we will make a demand. Ma'am, step away from the wall."

This fires Livia right back up. "I don't have to do anything you say," she pronounces with great poise. "Because of the Fourth Amendment."

"Many drunks are also amateur constitutional scholars," I say as I take a step towards Liv. "Unfortunately for our drunk tonight, I can verify certain physical cues—

like the smell of spilled vodka—that give me legal cause to detain her while I investigate criminal activity. And also we can't do the sobriety tests while she's against a wall."

Liv sidles to the side as I approach. "So I suppose you're going to try to make me now?" she says, trying for haughty decorum and failing.

"Yep," I say. And then in a lower voice, I say, "It's all pretend, kitten. I wouldn't do what I'm about to do next in real life."

She seems relieved for about half a second, then her eyes widen. "Wait, what—"

But I already have her hoisted over my shoulder in a fireman's carry, her pert jean-clad ass up in the air and her scrumptious thighs clasped tight under my arm.

She starts hammering my back with her small fists. "Put me down!"

The rookies are giggling quietly as I drop her onto a nearby table and step back. She sways, closing her eyes, like she's dizzy.

"Now, in real life, you probably wouldn't physically carry a drunk somewhere, and you might also want to give them more chances to comply. But it's my experience that drunks are a lot like toddlers—life's going to be easier for everyone involved if you don't expect them to think and behave like rational adults."

I face Livia again and ask, "How much have you had to drink today, ma'am?"

She still looks a little off-balance from her trip. "Um. Three or four in the last two hours?"

I pull out my penlight and shine it in her eyes. She blinks, and then sticks out her tongue at me.

"See?" I say, shaking my head. "Belligerent."

One by one, I have the recruits come up to see Livia's pupils and how slow they are to react to light changes. I demonstrate how to test for nystagmus—tiny, uncontrollable eye trembles—and we make Livia do the walk and turn test. We also make her stand on one leg and recite the alphabet backwards. By the end of the hour, all of the rookies have had a chance to run tests on all of the volunteers, and Livia looks ready for another drink.

"Excuse me," she mumbles and pushes out of the room. I check to make sure Gutierrez is still occupied, and then I follow Livia out, turning the corner where I see her going to the water fountain.

It's my turn to lean against the wall. With both hands on my belt, I watch as Livia bends at the waist to get a drink of water. God, that ass. I need to have it in my hands.

She straightens up and catches sight of me. "Officer."

"Drunk lady."

She gives me an appraising look up and down—it's equal parts hunger and something else. Respect, maybe. "You know a lot of things about your job," she concedes as I un-lean myself and walk towards her.

"I'm glad you think so, kitten."

She sighs. "And about next month…"

A tiny bell of panic begins tolling in my mind. Is she about to tell me that she doesn't want to continue our arrangement? I can't have her bail on me—I just can't—and I decide right here and now exactly how I'm going to convince her otherwise.

I step in close to her and she takes a step back. "Before you get started about next month," I murmur, taking another step and pushing her against the bathroom door. "I believe I was going to help you with something."

"You were?"

I reach around her and twist the knob of the bathroom door, pushing her inside and turning her body all in one smooth motion, so that by the time the automatic lights kick on, I've got her front pressed against the cinderblock wall and my hands on her wrists, moving them high above her head.

"Chase…" she breathes.

Yes. Yes, this is what I wanted. To have her melt for me, to have her addicted to me.

"Do you want to play pretend again?" I ask in her ear. Without waiting for a response, I kick her legs apart, which sends her ass back into my groin. She gasps at the contact, then moans as my hand slides down from her wrist to her waist and reaches under her shirt.

"What are we pretending?" she manages.

"How about you're a tipsy librarian and I'm the bad police officer who's going to detain you with two fingers."

"What do you mean *with two fing*—oh, holy shit." Her head drops back against my shoulder as I unzip her jeans and stroke the rise of her pubic bone through her silk panties. "Chase, you shouldn't…" She doesn't sound like I shouldn't though. She sounds very much like I should.

"You can invoke your Fourth Amendment rights any time, princess," I whisper, finding the plump button of her clit and then skating my middle finger over it.

She shivers and shakes her head. "I won't," she promises.

"Good girl," I murmur, pressing down and beginning to circle her clit in earnest. My other hand reaches for her other wrist so that I have both her wrists gathered in my hand, and I keep her that way for me—stretched and spread while I do my work. Pinned and at my mercy. She lets out a long moan as I slow down my rhythm to a get the right amount of pressure for her. "That's it. Let me make you feel good."

My cock aches and throbs with her like this, and I'm on fire with the need to fuck her, but this is more important. Making her come. Making her want this.

I drop my hand to get under her shirt and palm her tits, squeezing and fondling and kneading as I continue to rub her through her panties. Impatient with the silk, I slide under the panties altogether and resume my work, this time with my fingertips directly against her swollen flesh.

"You shouldn't," she moans again.

"I told you I don't mind this stuff," I say, nipping at her earlobe. And I really don't, but I don't go lower than her clit because I don't want to push her boundaries, at least not now. Not when I need to convince her to give me and my super sperm another chance. So I just focus on making her come, on making her feel the full height and strength of my body as I press against her.

"As soon as you're ready," I promise, "I'm going to fuck you until you're pregnant. I'm going to rut inside you until you're growing my baby. Got it?"

"Got it," she whimpers, squirming under my touch. She's close, so close, and so am I, even trapped in my uniform pants. I rub a little faster, a little meaner, almost like I am the bad cop who's taking advantage of her, like this is all for me and not for her.

It seems to turn her on, my fake-meaness, and she is panting and writhing and her hands are scrabbling at the wall.

Then I feel the first shudder of her orgasm as she trembles against me. She gasps my name as she falls over the edge, a sharp exhale like she's been struck. "*Chase.*"

It almost does me in, hearing that, seeing her writhe and squirm with my hand down her panties and her arms up on the wall. God, she's so fucking hot like this. Quivering and wild. I press her completely against the wall as she continues to pant out her orgasm, kissing the back of her neck. And then when she's finally still and quiet, her eyes closed and her breathing more even, I step back.

"This month," I growl. "I'm knocking you up."

She turns and faces me, her expression a little dazed. She nods. "Yes, this month. We're going to try harder." And then her gaze drops to my pants, where I'm sure she can see the hard length of my cock pushing unhappily at the fabric. She steps forward with a small smile, and then her hand is on me, squeezing and palming me through my pants.

I groan.

"But if we're going to try this again, we have to do it right," Livia says seriously, as if we're at a library meeting and not like she's stroking me through my pants. "I want to make sure I'm giving this the best possible chance."

Her grip is fucking perfect, a little hard and palming the full length of me, and it's making it difficult to think. "Sure, baby. Me too."

"Which is why this month you're going to save all of your orgasms for me."

Her other hand is now cupping my balls, and I have to lean a hand against the door or I'm going to fall over.

"I already am," I say. "I haven't been with anyone else since the day I met you."

She smiles and squeezes my tip. My eyes roll into the back of my head.

"I know you haven't, Chase. I'm not talking about that."

I open my eyes and stare at her. "Um. Then what are you talking about?"

And then her words really sink in. *All* my orgasms. She can't possibly mean...

"No more jerking off while I look at my Jessica Alba poster?"

"No jerking off looking at the poster," she confirms. "Or in the shower. Or anywhere. You save it all for me."

"You sure you want that, kitten? Feeding my full appetite?"

She nods, squeezing me again. God, it's so hard to argue with her like this. She's got me by the balls...and the dick. "I know I won't be fertile the whole month, but I don't want to take the chance in case I have the dates wrong or something."

She drops her hand, wearing a smug little smile. I groan at her denial. "Shit, you're mean."

"I'll be off my period in five days. Then you can fuck my brains out. But until then, you save it for me. All month long, all your orgasms. All for me."

But as she gives me a cute little wink and I give her a semi-playful, semi-I-hate-you-so-much-right-now spank on the ass, I wonder if she even realizes the truth beyond my sperm and beyond my body.

It's already all for her.

13

LIVIA

"That's my mom," Ryan says, nodding at the car approaching on the opposite side of the road.

It's a quarter after eight and since I didn't feel comfortable letting the young teen wait for her ride alone after the library closed, I'm out here with her. I squint, but in the spring twilight, I can't make out the driver. "Are you sure that's her?"

"I know my own car," she says, looking both ways before skipping across the street. We're nowhere near the crosswalk, but it's late and the roads are quiet. No one will mind her jaywalking.

I watch as she opens the back door to the BMW and climbs inside. Satisfied that she's gotten in okay, I start to turn when the front passenger window rolls down and Ryan's mother leans across the empty seat to shout over to me.

I feel stupid yelling across the street, so I glance down both sides of the road then trot over and bend down at the open window. "Hey, Dr. Alley, how are you doing?" I've met her before, briefly, but I still feel awkward. I'm much better with teens than adults.

"Busy, busy. You know how it is." She's a surgeon with a doctor husband and a teenage daughter. I have a feeling that I don't have any idea at all how busy her life is, but I nod in agreement anyway. "Thank you for asking. And it's Diane. Please."

"Sure. Diane," I say, hoping it sounds natural. Then I wait, certain she called me over for more than just a greeting, but if she doesn't fill the silence soon, I'll have to do it myself and I'm bound to sound like an idiot when I do.

Thankfully, she goes on. "I just wanted to thank you for always being there for Ryan. I know she spends a lot of time at the library, and she's really relied on you to guide her. She talks about you all the time. You've been a great support to her this year in her schoolwork and both John and I are very appreciative of it."

"Oh, that's sweet of you, but no thank you is necessary." I stop myself from saying it's my job because I don't want Ryan thinking that I only think of her as a line item on an employee task list. She's much more than that. It is kids like her that make me enjoy the job as much as I do, but I also know that saying that could embarrass her.

"Ryan has been a great support to me too," I say, settling on an angle of the truth I think she'll be happy to hear. "She keeps me socially conscious and constantly pushes me to challenge my comfort zone. Thank you for sharing her with me. You've raised a fine teen."

Diane glances back at her daughter. "I certainly think so. Thank you for noticing."

Ryan's eye roll is so obvious I can practically hear it. "Okay, Mom. Stop trying to steal my friends. It's not cool. She's way too young for you."

"You might not like hearing this," I say, directing this to Ryan, "but I'm actually closer to your mother's age than yours."

"But you don't act it. And that's what counts."

The comment is coming from a fourteen-year-old, but it feels like a balm to a sensitive spot. I'm practically dying—I know this. I've seen the calendar. I feel it in my bones. But at least this kid thinks I'm still young.

Dr. Alley—Diane—shakes her head. "Hey, just remember I'm your ride. Treat me like a bae!"

"Ohmygosh, Mom!" Ryan slaps a palm over her face. "Don't try to be cool. Please. I'm begging you. That is not a word you should ever say again. I'm so embarrassed."

"You don't have kids of your own, do you?" Diane asks. "Enjoy your JOMO right now."

Actually, I'm feeling just the opposite. This is exactly what I want. This banter. This tight-knit relationship. I can't wait to have this for myself. It reminds me what I'm trying for.

Ryan, on the other hand, looks like she wants to die. "That's not even how you use that term! You can't say 'enjoy' your joy of missing out. Enjoy your joy? It doesn't even make any sense! Just. Can we go now?"

She's so put out, I vow then and there to be an actual cool mom who never tries to use the "in" lingo with my kid.

But then Diane whispers loudly, "I do this just to humiliate her. It's the best thing ever. Remember it if you have kids of your own. You'll need any source of humor you can get." And then I make a mental note to keep it as an option.

Chuckling, I step back from the window. "Looks like you two should probably be going. I'll see you soon, Ryan." I wave as they drive off, then jog back across the street.

As soon as my feet hit the opposite sidewalk, red and blue lights flash and a siren blares.

"Ah, shit," I mutter to myself.

I wait as the patrol car pulls over to the curb and the officer gets out. I'm already preparing to drop Chase's name when the cop comes around the front of the vehicle, and I can make out his face clearly.

Relief sweeps through me when I realize who it is. "Oh, it's you! You scared me, Chase. I thought I was really in trouble."

"Who says you aren't?" He looks me over and, with those aviators with the reflective lenses, he's just the way I remember him from our first meeting. Complete with the hot cop uniform and the hot cop attitude.

Unconsciously, I take a step backward. Just because he's *so* hot, it's almost hard to be near him. "Don't tease me," I say, nervously. Not nervous because I think I'm actually in trouble but nervous because of how swoony he is right now. I almost wish I *was* in trouble. "I didn't think that was you because you were in a car. I've only ever seen you on your bike. Where is your bike, anyway?"

He ignores my question and takes another step toward me. "No teasing, ma'am. Do you know why I stopped you?"

"Oh for pete's sake." I wring my hands together in front of me. "How many times do I have to tell you not to call me ma'am?"

"Do you have any identification on you?"

I roll my eyes. Apparently he's going to play this by the book. "I don't. I have my car key. My purse is locked in my car. Which is in the parking lot over there."

"And you know why I stopped you?" He tilts his head, studying me. Studying the anxious way I'm playing with my hands.

I drop them immediately. He's a cop and somehow that triggers something automatic in me. Who doesn't get worked up when approached by a police officer after having just broken the law, even a minor law?

But then he lifts up his glasses for just a second and gives me a wink, coupled with that painfully sexy grin. "It's just a game, Liv. I'll stop if you want me to."

That would be bananas though. Because I don't want him to stop. Because I know this cop. Intimately.

"Don't stop," I say, a little too eagerly, which earns me another grin as he slides his sunglasses into his chest pocket.

But his smile fades into a stern expression as he repeats his question from earlier. "Do you know why I stopped you?"

"I'm going to guess it was because I was in the middle of the street. Or because you're horny. It's been a couple of days, and since I'm not due to ovulate for another day or two I'm sure you're going to want to get something in before that." I unbutton the top button of my blouse in case that's the direction he wants to take this.

His gaze flick briefly to my cleavage then back to my eyes. "Jaywalking is considered an ordinance violation."

I let out a huff. I'm not sure how he wants me to respond, and I'm ready for this game to move to the next level. Does he just want me to admit my guilt? Why isn't he pouncing all over me like usual?

I stick out my chin defiantly. "You know what else is considered a violation? Chase Kelly wasting his sperm. You haven't been doing that, have you? Is that why you aren't jumping all over this right now?" I motion a hand up and down, gesturing to my body—the body he is decidedly not jumping all over.

Chase blinks, unmoved by my antics. "As I was driving up, I clearly saw you crossing the street in an area that is not designated for pedestrian crossing."

I try a new tactic. "Are you going to give me a ticket, Officer?" I peer up at him through my lashes, but I can't keep it up without laughing. "Is this where the women bat their eyes and flirt to try to get out of getting in trouble? Or do they cry? I want to get it right."

Chase arches an eyebrow. "Are you asking how you might bribe a police officer out of getting a ticket?"

I cozy up to him, tugging on his shirt. "Not just any police officer. I'm asking how the women try to bribe *you*." I wink, and it is a game, but also I really want to know. I want to know what he comes face to face with everyday. What women offer him. What his temptations are.

But the minute I touch him, Chase is on the defensive. "Stand back, ma'am."

I don't have to move since he's already stepped away. "Now turn please and place your palms on the vehicle."

"Are you…arresting me?" A tremor of excitement runs through me. This game suddenly got fun. "On what grounds?" I turn around and put my palms on the car like he's asked, pretending I'm put out.

"Attempting to bribe an officer of the law." He comes up behind me, so close I can feel the heat of his body and smell the familiar musk of his scent.

"But I hadn't even gotten to the bribing part yet!"

"It counts." He pats me down, and I'm pretty sure it's nothing like how officers really pat people down, or there would be a lot more people talking about it on *The View*. His hands feel along the sides and under my breasts but then he cups them and squeezes them together before moving lower down my body. When he kicks my legs apart, his hands explore up the entire length of my thighs and his fingers rub along the crotch of my panties.

"I have nothing to hide," I say breathlessly as he swipes inside my panties this time. "I promise."

He stands back up and twists my arms so my hands are gathered at my lower back. "I beg to differ," he says low at my ear. "It seems you have quite a prize down there. I bet a lot of people would want that very much if you didn't keep it hidden."

He punctuates his statement with the click of his cold metal handcuffs as he slips them on my wrists. "You have the right to remain sexy," he says. "Anything you say can and will be used to get you in my bed."

I bite back a giggle at his twist on the Miranda rights, but Chase's delivery is completely solemn, which makes my breath ragged and goose bumps rise on my skin.

"You have the right to use my body to give yourself a delirious, life-changing orgasm." He bends in close to my ear and whispers. "If you have trouble...don't worry, I'm a bit of an expert in that department."

Yes. Yes, he is.

He straightens and resumes his regular tone. "And trust me, I know how to put these handcuffs to good use."

And now I'm so wet I'm dripping.

I've never been so lucky to be pulled over in all my life.

Chase opens the door to the back seat of the police car but suddenly he pauses. "Are you expected anywhere right now?"

"Uh. No." I try to guess exactly what he's getting at. "If you're asking if I'm still okay with playing Get Arrested by the Neighborhood Hot Cop, I'm cool. This is completely consensual."

I must have guessed correctly because he nods slightly then says, "You can argue about it more at the station," and pushes my head down with one hand so I don't bump it as he puts me inside.

He closes the door and then gets in the front seat and starts the car.

I'm grinning as he drives us off the street into a dimly lit corner of the Corinth parking lot, which thanks to our lack of infrastructure updates is *really* dimly lit. Next, he picks up his radio. "Dispatch, this is 898 going on e-call," he says.

I want to ask him what he just did and what *e-call* means, but I already know he won't tell me. Not right now, anyway. I make a note to ask him later.

He hangs up his radio and shifts to face me. "Now. What are we going to do with you?"

He's so good at the role playing—well, yes, maybe because he actually *is* a cop—

but he's so good at pretending that all of this is real, that I'm really just a stranger who he's caught breaking the law, that he's really arresting me.

He's so good, I decide he deserves for me to try to give him my best character in return. I try to imagine what I'd really be feeling if I'd just been arrested and were afraid for my reputation, but it only takes me three seconds to realize that real-life emotions are not appropriate in this situation. In real life, if I were cuffed in the back of a police car, I'd probably be guilty of something big, and not daydreaming about how I was about to bang the arresting officer. In real life, if the arresting officer was touching me the way Chase was—the way I hope Chase will later too—it would be sexual assault.

So instead, I abandon reality and play the scene I think would be fun.

"Please don't do this, officer," I beg. "Do you really have to take me into the station? I can't have an arrest on my record. I just can't!" I sound pretty authentic, if I do say so myself. My voice cracks and my lip trembles. I can't fake tears, but I wrinkle my face so it looks like I'm on the edge of crying.

His rubs his scruff as his stare turns greedy. "It sounds pretty important to you to avoid this arrest."

"Oh, it is. It is. I'll do anything."

That's all it takes to get him in the back seat with me.

I scoot away from him, intent on acting shy despite my offer. Chase won't let me forget. "You'll do anything?" he asks, scooting after me until I'm backed into the corner. He slides his hand up my bare leg not stopping when it meets the hem of my skirt.

"Anything, Officer Kelly." I lick my lips and widen my eyes. "My hands though... Maybe you could undo the cuffs?"

He laughs with a hint of fake meanness in his tone. "I think I like the way you look wearing my cuffs. And I'm pretty sure that anything you could do to get yourself out of this could be done just as easily without your hands."

"Oh," I gasp as though I'm way too innocent for what he's suggesting. "But if that's the only thing that will get me out of this situation, then I guess..."

"It's the only thing, sweetheart." He's already opening his pants for me. Already stroking the length of his hard cock. "Unless you'd rather I take you on down to the station."

"No, no! Please. I'll do it." This sure as hell better not be a game he plays with other women, because this is our game, dammit. I've decided.

I watch him as his hand pumps up and down his erection once more, and I wonder for a minute how difficult it's been for him to keep his hands off himself. I've made myself available to him every time he's asked, but still. He's had to be tempted.

It's an extra turn on to me right now, knowing that he's saved himself. Knowing that everything inside his cock has been waiting for me. It's got me hot and wet and eager. Though my character's pretending that this is terrible, real life Livia Ward has never been so eager to put a cock in her mouth.

I pull my knees up underneath me on the back seat, then I bend and suck him off.

He doesn't take control this time, and I don't wait for him to, either. I know what he likes. I know the way he wants my tongue and how deep he wants me to take him in. I give it to him exactly like I know he loves, until his thighs are tensing and his breathing has grown shallow.

He lays a hand on my head then, petting the loose tendrils of my hair. "Would you swallow for me?" he asks above me, and I'm not sure if he's asking as arresting Officer Kelly or as the guy who's saving all his sperm for me. "Would you take all my cum down your throat if I asked you to?"

I'm still trying to decide how to answer, or if I even need to. My mouth is otherwise occupied, after all, and speaking isn't at the top of my priority list. But if those weren't factors, and if this weren't a game?

I'd told him we had to do this right. That we had to save all his sperm for babymaking alone, and I meant it. Right now though, I wish I didn't mean it. I wish that there was a Chase and Livia that existed somewhere else, in another dimension, where the goal wasn't a baby and our time together didn't have obligations attached to it. Because then I would. I'd do whatever he wanted me to. I'd drink his cum. I'd wear it all over my body. I'd beg for pearl necklaces and wrist icicles and maybe sometimes I'd be with him without thinking about his cum at all.

Maybe.

But there isn't another dimension.

And I don't have to answer for real because he cups his hand around my neck and gently pulls me off his cock and presses his face up near mine, as though he means to terrorize me.

"Wasn't it good enough?" I ask, forcing my voice to tremble. "I can do better! I can swallow!"

"Good girl." He nips at my ear, and it tickles and makes my toes curl. I'm helpless because my hands are bound, and that makes this even hotter. "I knew you'd swallow. But I don't want you to. I want my cum inside your cunt."

I gasp dramatically. "Does it really have to be that, Officer? Can't it be something else?"

"No. It has to be this. You said you'd do anything and this is what I want." He pushes my thighs apart and kneads at my clit through my panties. "You're soaked. You want it too, baby. See?" He sticks his finger inside my crotch and scoops up some of my wetness to show me.

"That doesn't mean anything," I protest.

"It does. It means you want me. Taste how much you want me." He puts the tip of his finger to my mouth and pushes until I open up and suck my wetness off his finger. "Good, right? That's how much you want my cock inside you."

God, I really do. I'm antsy with how much my pussy aches for him.

"But." I give him a final objection. "I'm not on birth control, and I could get pregnant."

He laughs. "Sounds like a personal problem."

I have to bite my cheek so that I don't laugh too, though, for some reason it doesn't really seem as funny as it once might have.

I don't have time to ponder on that because Chase is moving on with our scene. After pushing me back against the door, he pulls my legs out from underneath me. "You're going to sit back and be a good girl while I take off your panties," he says. "Next you're going to get on my lap, and you're going to ride me until I come. Then, and only then, if I come good and I come hard, then I'll take those cuffs off your pretty little wrists, and I'll forget I ever saw you crossing that street tonight. Got it, sweet thing?"

I press my lips into a pout and nod. I pretend to struggle as he pulls my panties down my legs and pockets them, and he pretends to reprimand me, telling me the harder I make this for him, the worse trouble I'll be in when this is over.

Finally, I'm bare and my skirt is hitched up to my waist. Chase sits back and pulls me onto his lap where I sink down easily onto his cock. I'm so used to him now—his size, his fit—I adjust quickly, but I whimper as though the invasion is painful. As though it's the worst thing in the world to be sitting on him, my breasts bouncing even in my bra as he helps lift me up and down over him.

And in a way, it is the worst thing in the world. Because in this moment, while we're sweating and moaning and he's hitting that one spot and my cunt is tightening around him, I realize how alive I feel. How young. How far from thirty and death and the graveyard. Not only do I feel it right now while I'm playing this naughty game with Chase, but I felt it at the wet lab and in his bedroom and the hotel room the first night we were together. I felt it in the restaurant on our first date and in the library when he helped me shelve books. I feel it whenever I'm with him. Not just when we're naked and fucking, but when we're teasing and talking and just being together.

And that is the worst thing in the world to realize.

Because we're temporary, he and I. And this isn't going to last.

I'm still thinking about that when I climax and the pleasure that pulses through me has an edge of sadness. He follows quickly with his own orgasm. I slump on his shoulder, panting, trying hard to blink away the tears that are gathering in my eyes.

When Chase has recovered, he lifts me off of him and tucks himself away before pulling out his key and unlocking the cuffs. Taking one hand, he rubs my wrist where it's gone red from the metal.

"That. Was. Fun." He grins widely at me. "See? You're fun."

I start to deliver the same old protest I always deliver when it occurs to me—

maybe all of this youth and aliveness isn't just because of Chase. Maybe I'm those things all on my own. He might have brought it out in me, but it doesn't mean I can't hold onto it. Even Ryan sees it in me. I'm young. I'm fun. I don't have to be afraid of turning thirty. If I were really at death's door, would I be fucking sexy policemen in the back of their cars or having a baby on my own?

No. I wouldn't.

So I genuinely grin back at him. "You're right. I am fun. And guess what else. I'm not dying."

"Uh. That's great?"

"Yeah. It's pretty great." Then, because I'm fun and young and alive I lean forward and kiss him. Kiss him really good. Like I mean it. Like I mean other things too. Things that aren't actually possible between us—like how nice it would be to visit that other dimension and thank him for showing me this other side of me. Things that are maybe too nice to say to just a guy who I've contracted to impregnate me, but it's okay to say it like this. As long as I *only* say it like this, in a kiss.

His eyes are shining when I pull away, and he can't seem to stop looking at me.

"Where's your bike, anyway?" I ask, trying to get the attention off of me.

"In for maintenance." He hasn't let go of my hand. I notice that now.

"And what's e-call mean?"

"I was signing out for emergency only calls. Basically I was taking a dinner break." He's still staring at me, still studying me like he doesn't want to stop.

I push a strand a hair behind my ear, suddenly nervous from this strange new tension between us. "Is that what you call this? Dinner?"

He shakes his head slowly, as though not quite sure of himself. "I don't know what to call this. I've never done this before."

My heart speeds up for no apparent reason. "Which part?"

"Never had sex in a patrol car. Never fucked someone I was pretending to arrest while on duty. Never fucked anyone at all while on duty." His lip curls guiltily. "Now I have used handcuffs. I can't deny that."

I giggle. "How could you not have used them? They're your main prop."

"Exactly." The humor dissipates and the air between us feels stretched and thin. It's not uncomfortable. Just fragile.

Then Chase says, "But I've never done anything quite like this. There's never been anyone like you, Liv. There will never be anyone like you."

And now I can't breathe. Because those are words that Other

Dimension Chase might say to Other Dimension Liv and they might be beautiful and they might mean everything.

But in this dimension, Livia Ward knows that beautiful words never mean everything. They're only a prelude to a packed suitcase and a lonely bed.

And whatever I'm thinking is crazysauce. We've been roleplaying all night, and my head's a mess. That's all. He didn't mean it how it sounds.

I clarify to be sure. "Of course there's no one like me. Because I'm the only woman you've ever been contracted to impregnate. Right?" I throw in a laugh to make sure the mood is light, like it's supposed to be.

"Right," he says smiling in return. "Because you're the only woman I've ever been contracted to impregnate. Of course."

It's dark, though, and it might mean nothing, but I'd swear his smile doesn't reach his eyes.

14

CHASE

"Are you touching yourself?"

There's a breath, a pause, and another breath. "Yes," Liv finally whispers. "I am."

We're on the phone—she's at her house and I'm in my car on my way from the station. The past four days have been a mess—I got called in for a fatal car accident that's needed a lot of follow-up and Liv's been working a few extra shifts while one of her coworkers is away *and* I had double babysitting duty this week—and so it's been the better part of a week since I've been inside her. Since I've come at all. And I am about to *explode.* This morning I got hard pouring a cup of coffee because it reminded me of the long silken tresses of Liv's hair. Yesterday it was from eating a scone, remembering the quick pink dart of Liv's tongue as she licked scone crumbs off her lips.

And don't even get me started on the backseat of my car—every time I see it, I'm hit with the full fucking force of what we did there two weeks ago. She's my first policy violation, the first time I've ever broken the rules as a cop, and I should feel guilty, but goddamn. Every fucking second of that night was worth any of the trouble it could rain down on my head.

And now my already-hard arousal is painfully hard, just remembering her moving over me with her hands cuffed behind her back. The rub of my jeans against my dick as I shift gears in the Audi is almost too much. I have to unload inside her before my body revolts and I come in my pants like a teenager.

"Keep touching yourself," I tell her over the phone. "I need you ready when I walk through that door, baby, because I'm not going to be able to wait."

"Okay," she says, in that breathless, absentminded way that lets me know she's starting to touch herself in earnest now. I thump an impatient hand against the steering wheel. *Fuck.* I want to be there *now*, want to see the glide of her fingers over her slick pussy. Except in this state I'd be too impatient to watch for long; I'd push her fingers out of the way and make her use my cock to masturbate with instead.

The drive is only a few minutes, but I'm a wild man by the time I get to her place. I'm still listening to her whimper and pant over the phone as I pound on the door, my cock thick and hard in my jeans, my balls full and aching.

I don't even let Liv get the door open all the way before I'm on her, pinning her to the wall in her foyer and kicking the door shut with my foot as I find her mouth with my own. She's wearing nothing but a sundress right now, barefoot and flushed from playing with herself, and when I reach for her hand, I find that her fingers are wet. I suck on them, licking them clean, fluttering my tongue against the pads of her fingers until she's moaning and rocking her hips against me.

"I'm so full and ready for you, kitten," I murmur as I pull her fingers from my mouth. I move her hands down to my belt, which she fumbles excitedly with. Once my fly is open, she tugs my cock free and gently palms my balls.

I buck in her hand, moaning. It almost hurts, being this full. I haven't gone this long without ejaculating in…well, since I started having sex, actually. I am going to die if I'm not inside this woman's pussy within the next heartbeat.

"I'm sorry," I say, grabbing her ass and carrying her over to her little dining table with her legs wrapped around my waist. My bare cock rubs against her wet pussy as we walk, and I nearly have a stroke. "I can't wait another second."

"Me neither," she whispers as I set her on the edge of the table.

"I've been waiting for this all day," I grunt, jamming my hips between her thighs and grabbing myself by the root to line up with her entrance. Her narrow slit is glistening and opened, like the petals of a flower.

My hands are shaking, and we both inhale the moment my blunt tip presses against her pussy. "God, I fucking need it."

"It's yours," she breathes. "Take it."

I do as the good woman says, sliding my hand over her thigh to cup her ass as I shove my cock inside her. She cries out, but I don't give her time to adjust, time to stretch to my girth, I just shove in deeper, all the way to the hilt. And then I groan. She's so fucking wet that I can hear our bodies move together and apart as I begin pumping inside of her, and she's so hot and tight that my shaft is being squeezed from root to crown.

"I'm sorry," I mutter, grabbing her hips and changing the pace so that I'm pounding into her. The table shakes; her tits bounce under her dress.

"Don't be," she gasps in between thrusts. "Feels—so—good."

I grunt in response, my eyes as hungry and Livia-starved as my cock, taking in every detail of this. Her wild tits, her parted mouth, the slick and easy slide of my dick in and out of her pussy. I try and try to take my fill of her, the sight and sound and feel of her, but I can't, I can't get enough.

And it's now, embarrassingly soon, that I feel the twisting heat at the base of my spine and the tug of my heavy balls as they draw up, and with the table pounding against the wall, I unleash a series of brutal, fast, deep thrusts that leave me bottomed out in her cunt and leave her gasping and clutching desperately at my shirt.

"Gonna come," I mumble. "Gonna come so hard."

"Give it to me," she demands breathlessly. "Give it all to me."

"Shit yes. I'm gonna. I'm gonna."

And I do, the first wave of release like getting my guts torn out, it's so sharp and so strong. I practically roar, and then I sink my teeth into her shoulder as my shaft pulses and pumps cum into the deepest parts of her. Pulse and pump, pulse and pump, over and over again, and I've never come like this, so much and so fast and so hard, and it takes forever to unload inside her pussy. It feels like minutes and hours, keeping her pinned with my teeth and speared with my cock as I empty myself. Until finally, finally my body tenses one last time—one final spurt of my seed—and then stills.

The hurricane of need is finally sated.

Balls drained, mind slowly clearing, I can finally think, finally feel something other than the soul-deep need to fuck. I stop biting Liv's shoulder, giving the shallow teeth marks a soothing lick and kiss, and then straighten up and look down.

"Look, baby," I say. "Look how much I gave you."

She follows my gaze down to where we are joined, her eyes going dark at the sight of my seed spilling out around us, and I swipe a little with my thumb and use it to start rubbing her clit. She hasn't come yet, something I'm acutely aware of and little embarrassed about, to be totally honest. Another first for me—I've never been so desperate to come that I haven't made sure my partner comes first.

I rectify that sin now, rubbing her in the firm circles she likes while I'm still hard inside her. And it's while she's staring down at the messy, dirty biology of us that she tenses and climaxes with a low, sweet moan, her head falling back as she grabs at my shoulders. I can see the fluttering muscles in her thighs and feel the gentle squeezes around my sensitive cock as she orgasms, but it's her face I really watch, open and vulnerable and *happy*.

She's happy with me inside her. She trusts me and opens to me, and that means more to me than I can even really explain to myself. I remember the stupid contract, I remember her words—so unintentionally cutting coming from her mouth, even though I've thought them myself a thousand times: *Of course there's no one like me. Because I'm the only woman you've ever been contracted to impregnate.*

But I can't think about this. Not now, not ever. Liv has made her wishes known, and anyway, I'm not *that* guy. I'm not the hearts and flowers guy, I'm not the guy who's made for couples book clubs and wine of the month clubs and other mundane couple shit. Even though I know with Livia it would never feel mundane. Ever.

Stop it, Kelly. Think of something else.

Liv is still breathing hard when I ease out of her, relishing the spill of my seed as I do. I could stare at that for ages, but instead, I do the polite thing and go get her a warm washcloth from her bathroom. It's as she's cleaning up and I'm trying to push back thoughts of trust and happiness and contracted pregnancies that I remember what day it is.

"Hey, you're due for your period soon, right?"

She looks up and a small smile spreads across her face. "You remembered."

"I downloaded some kind of period tracker app on my phone," I admit.

She laughs at that and stands up, tossing the used washcloth in the sink. "I bet now your targeted internet ads are all messed up."

"You're telling me. Every time I log into Facebook, I get ads for those period panties on the side. I used to get ads for bullets and beard grooming supplies. What are you doing to me?"

She adjusts her dress with a smirk. "Maybe it will be good for you to live outside your masculine bubble for a while."

"So have you taken a test yet?" I clean myself off with a paper towel from the kitchen and button up my jeans. "I know it's early, but how can you stand the wait?"

"I'm not actually due until tomorrow," she says, the smirk sliding off her face. It's replaced by a look I can't quite parse.

"They have those tests where you can test up to five days before your period. I saw that on the box. You could totally take a test now!" I'm starting to feel a little excited—for her, of course, all for her.

LAURELIN PAIGE & SIERRA SIMONE

"Mm." Liv makes a noncommittal noise and goes into her bedroom, returning with a fresh pair of panties.

I follow and hover, like a bearded shadow. "Don't *mmm* about this! Let's go to the drugstore and get a test now! You could take it tonight!"

Okay, maybe I'm feeling a lot excited. Which is stupid, because if she *is* pregnant, then it's that much sooner that she dumps me—if dumping is even the right word. And that possibility fills me with dread, but even with that dread, I can't help but want to know. I can't help but feel a spark of excitement at the potential spark of life inside my librarian's belly.

Liv puts on the underwear slowly, as if buying time for a response, and even though she's not trying to be sexy, I start to thicken and swell again at the sight of the thin lace moving up her legs, at the flash of her perfect ass as she lifts her dress. Finally she straightens, smoothing her dress down, and says one word. "No."

"Come on," I beg playfully. "Let's go get one."

She shakes her head firmly. "There's no point in taking one at night, it needs to be the morning because—"

"—hCG levels are highest in the morning, I know."

She narrows her eyes. "You know about hCG?"

"The pregnancy hormone? Megan's been pregnant twice, Liv. You know how unafraid she is of body talk. I picked up a thing or two." I don't mention to Livia that I've been steadily reading my way through every pregnancy book the library owns, since maybe that seems a little over-committed to the whole process.

Or creepy. You know, one or the other.

"But just because the levels are highest in the morning doesn't mean you can't test any other time, especially this close to your period."

"Fine." She gives a little huff, as if irritated that she can't smack me down with her superior knowledge of human pregnancy. "Maybe I could. But I told myself I wasn't going to test until tomorrow and I don't like changing plans when I've already attached emotional processes to them."

I blink at her.

A sigh. "What I mean is, I don't want to get my hopes up and then be disappointed, like what happened last month. But if I do it the way I planned, it's like I can protect myself a little. Because I've emotionally rehearsed what it will feel like doing it on the day I'm supposed to get my period."

"Look, kitten. I don't emotionally rehearse shit, and I'm still okay. Look at us—

at this—" I gesture between our bodies. "I'm so glad I didn't emotionally rehearse our first date. I'm glad you blindsided me with this whole baby madness."

She bites her lip. "You are?"

"Yeah," I say, almost as surprised as she is to hear the genuine truth of it in my voice. "And it was spontaneous and crazy and I didn't know how to feel about it at first, but that's part of the fun, doll. That's part of being alive. If you plan to avoid every bad feeling, eventually there's not going to be room for the good feelings either."

She stares at me, still chewing her lip. I see my words turn over in her mind, sinking down and attaching to something deep inside her. She gives a little nod, more to herself than me, but her forehead is still slightly creased with defensive worry.

She protests in the faint tone of someone who's already given up, "But the tests I ordered from Amazon haven't come in yet and I don't want any local people seeing me at the pharmacy."

I grin, fishing my keys out of my pocket. "Now that is a problem I can fix."

• • •

Bisceglia Pharmacy is a tiny, dusty relic tucked into a dying strip mall on the other side of the Kansas-Missouri state line. I see Liv's doubt as we pull up to the pharmacy and there's a dog chained up out front gnawing industriously on an old shoe.

"Uh," she says, stepping over the dog, who doesn't stop his chewing to look up, "is this like…a *licensed* pharmacy?"

"We're in Missouri now, princess. This is what shit looks like here."

Liv shoots me a look as we walk through the door—which is propped open with a rabbit-eared television set—and into the dimly lit pharmacy. "You know, it's not nice to be geographically snobby."

"I lived on the Missouri side of Kansas City until Mom died," I tell her. "So I feel a little entitled to some trash talk. Also this place was my first job. So I'm double entitled."

Liv glances around the store, paneled in fake wood, and lined with shelves of probably-expired food and packages of medicine with hand-written labels. There's also no other living being in sight, other than the German Shepherd outside. "This place had employees?"

I laugh a little as I lead her over to the corner where the condoms are kept discreetly behind a display of Dr. Scholl's shoe inserts. It's a corner I visited a lot as a younger man when I lived in the area. And I always noticed the pregnancy tests were right next to the condoms, as if in warning of a teenage boy's fate if he wasn't careful enough. Cover your stump before you hump and all that.

"I was a cashier and delivery boy," I explain as we get to the shelf of pregnancy tests. I'm relieved to see they look fairly fresh, although I make a note to check the expiration date just to be sure. "A lot of Bud's customers were getting too old to pick up their prescriptions, so he started a delivery service for them."

"Bud?"

"The pharmacist. He opened this place and still runs it, even though he's over ninety now. And see, I told you the boxes had the thing on them!" I point to one of the newer looking boxes, which has purple letters proclaiming *Five Days Sooner!* I check the date on the edge of the box to make sure the test is still good, and then I hand it to Liv. "Let's get the bathroom key, and then I'll go pay while you take the test."

Her eyes widen and she looks around the store. "Take it *here?*"

"Yeah," I say and I know I'm smiling like a kid but I can't help it. "I don't want to wait another minute to find out. Do you?"

"It's just—" She glances around and I know she's trying to find a concrete reason to say no. Trying to manifest a real obstacle out of what is an abstract feeling of fear and uncertainty.

I'm not going to let her. Not only because I'm itching to find out if she's pregnant or not, but because she hasn't had anyone to push her out of her comfort zone in so long that I think she's become stuck there. Inventing reasons not to trust excitement or happiness, inventing reasons to believe that good things can't belong to her. That she doesn't deserve them.

And while I call her *my girl*, my Liv, my librarian, I do know she's not actually mine, as much as I'm wishing she was. But maybe this is something I can give her, that I can do for her. Show her that it's okay to hope. It's okay to be excited. That it's more than okay, it's necessary and good, and the best part of being alive.

So I don't let her cut in with any excuses. I take her hand and lead her over to the small unisex bathroom by the register. Then I step behind the counter, into the pharmacy area. "Hello?"

Bud himself comes pottering around the corner, followed by another German Shepherd. A smile spreads under his bristly white mustache. "Chase Kelly!" he rumbles in happy surprise, pulling me into a hug. His bald head only comes up to my collarbone. "You rascal. What are you doing here?"

I hug him back and then pull away to throw a mock-rueful glance back at Livia, who is clutching the pregnancy test box and looking mortified. "Well, Bud, I think I got a girl pregnant."

Bud sighs. "I knew you would eventually. And you're so young!"

He's giving me a very disappointed look, so I remind him, "I'm thirty-three now."

"Oh. I guess that's not so young." He scratches his mustache. "Thirty is when you stop producing human growth hormone, you know. And your DNA telomeres start degrading. It's when the body starts dying."

"Exactly!" Livia says from behind me.

"I'm not dying!" I protest for the millionth time in the last two months. "And neither are you, Liv."

"We're kind of dying, though," she says.

In front of me, Bud nods in agreement.

"Take your vitamins," he adds, with a touch of sternness, "and then you won't die so fast."

I have something like a Vietnam flashback to all the vitamins Bud's fed me over the years. And they weren't the fun Flintstones ones either. "I'll be sure to do that. Anyway, is there any chance we can get the bathroom key so she can take the test now?"

"Oh, that lock has been broken since the Bush Administration," the old pharmacist says. "Just go on in."

"Oh no—" Liv objects. "We can just buy the test here and then take it at home, and—"

"Young lady," Bud says, all sorts of sternness back in his voice. "If you are pregnant, you need to know *as soon as possible*. And you are not leaving my store without all the vitamins and folic acid I can give you."

Livia opens her mouth to argue more, but Bud bustles toward her with flapping hands and semi-grouchy rumbles about young people who don't listen and does she think he has all day to convince her about the importance of early folic acid intake and to just be a dear and listen, and then before she can muster a defense, she's in the bathroom with the test and the door closed behind her.

"Nice work," I tell Bud, pulling out my wallet.

He waves my money away. "It's on the house. I'm happy to see you settling down and starting a family. When you were younger, I was worried you'd be one of those young men who never built a life because they were too busy chasing skirts."

"Quail hunting," I say, thinking of Pop.

"Now that's a term I haven't heard since *I* was young," Bud says. He pats my shoulder. "She's a good girl. I can tell these things. Now, are you going to give that baby your name? Marry the girl?"

I open my mouth to tell him no, that I'm not actually settling down, that I'm not done chasing skirts. That this is just a skirt that wanted me for my sperm and nothing else. Except I don't want to tell him that. Because I don't want it to be true. For just a moment, I want to pretend that Liv really is my girlfriend, that I'm really on the precipice of fatherhood, that I've got a ring stashed away in my house somewhere, just waiting for the right moment.

"Yes," I pretend. "I'm going to make her mine. We're going to be a family."

The words sound so good, they feel so good to say. A weird heat prickles in my eyes, balls into a huge knot in my throat.

That earns me another pat on the shoulder. "Good boy." And then with a second pat, Bud trundles back off into the back to fill more orders, his dog following obediently after him.

As soon as he's out of sight, I squeeze my eyes shut to stop the burning there. I clear my throat. I remind myself of why I chose not to have a family, why I can't have one. I can't drag a perfect woman and an innocent child into a life of late night callouts and emotional baggage from rough calls, and the daily stress and tragedy I live. And the irony is not lost on me that while I'm trying to convince Livia that she deserves good things, I'm also reminding myself of why I can't have them.

But it's different. It's totally different.

Just—*fuck*. I wish it weren't.

I hear the toilet flush, but there's no other sound from the bathroom. I push my misery back into its proper compartment and decide to focus on what matters right now, on the potentially amazing thing happening right this very second.

I knock on the door. "Liv? Everything going okay in there?"

"I'm fine," her voices comes, muffled and a touch irritable. "I'm just doing another one."

"Another test?"

"There's three in the box, so I just...Oh."

The *oh* is strange, completely devoid of emotion but also slightly stunned, as if the lack of emotion is because whatever has just happened has surprised her so much that she doesn't know how to react yet.

I lean my head against the door with a *thump*, my heart flipping over along with my stomach. "Liv, does that *oh* mean what I think it does?"

She says faintly, so faintly I can barely hear her through the door, "There's another blue line on the first test I took. There's two lines."

And I forget everything. Every fucking thing. The contract, my reasons for not wanting a family, the fact that this means Liv is about to dump me now that she has what she wants—everything. There's only the chest-twisting joy and the renewed heat behind my eyes and a smile so fucking big my cheeks hurt.

"I'm coming in there—"

"Chase, no! I'm still on the—"

And I don't even care, because I'm charging through the door and going to my knees and pulling Livia Ward into my chest, even though she's still on the toilet, even though she's still clutching her last unused test in her hand.

"Oh my god, kitten," I breathe into her hair. I kiss her head and close my eyes. "We are having a baby."

The word *we* comes out so easy, like a breath, like a tear, natural and gentle and warm, and Liv doesn't correct me. Something I'm grateful for, because I want to pretend, want all those noisy reasons why there isn't a *we* to stay forgotten. I kiss her hair again and pull back to study her face. "You okay, doll?"

She nods, biting her lip. There's something distant in her face. Shock, maybe. The reality of getting something she wants so much. Maybe it's sitting on the toilet still and having a big cop come in and smash you into a bear hug.

"Sorry," I say, letting go. I offer a smile that she doesn't return with one of her own. "I shouldn't have come in. I'll be outside."

And I leave the bathroom even though the thought of being away from her—her and the tiny little baby bean in her belly— actually makes me ache. In my chest and even lower; it's sinking in that I got Liv pregnant, and God, that's fucking hot as shit. It makes me want to try to get her pregnant again and again and again.

I hear the toilet flush again and the water run, and then after a few minutes Liv comes out carrying the two positive tests. "I guess we should ask Bud for the extra vitamins," she says numbly. "I've already got some pre-natals that I've been taking, but I'm almost out and…" She trails off, as if she can't hold on to the thought.

I don't push her, although I'm torn between wanting to figure out what's wrong and pulling her into my arms and making love to her right here in the middle of the pharmacy. Instead, I call Bud back, who loads her up with all sorts of vitamins and ginger candies for nausea and several packages of dental floss for some reason. And then we drive back to her condo in silence with her sighing and staring out the window.

When we get back inside her living room, she's still white-knuckling those tests, holding on to them the way you might hold on to a life preserver if you were drowning.

"Hey," I say, ducking down to meet her eyes. "Look at me. What's going on?"

She blinks down at the tests in her hand. "I don't know. I don't know how to feel. What to think. I wanted this so much and now that it's happening…it's like it doesn't even feel real."

I set the bag of vitamins and floss down on the table and then come back over to her and take the hand that's not currently clutching two used pregnancy tests. "Come here, babe." I lead her over to her couch, and then I sit, pulling her down onto my lap. And then I slide my hands up her thighs to reach her stomach under her dress.

She sighs again, this time one of pleasure, and I feel her flicker back to life under my touch. I also feel my cock harden underneath her, eager to stake its claim again. I'm going to fuck her at least once more tonight, I decide. Crawl between her legs and lick all of her worry away.

I rest my fingertips well below her navel, right where her panties meet her warm, soft skin. "It's real, Liv. This is real right now."

She looks at me, finally really looks at me, and I see all the unguarded fears pressing up against the inside of her. In the dusk-lit apartment, her eyes are huge and dark and pleading. "The last two months have been like some kind of…dream," she whispers. "I don't know if I remember what real feels like."

Her words twist something inside of me. Suddenly I know I feel the same way, like this whole fantasy we've been letting ourselves act out has somehow become more real than the things we told ourselves we wanted at the very beginning.

And I don't know what that means.

Although, as I slide my hands up to stroke her waist and the taut skin above her navel, I realize that it doesn't bother me like it did before, the not knowing. The chaos of new feelings. The messy implications of how I feel about Liv and how I feel about this little life sprouting inside of her that's half me.

I can't stand it anymore. The woman who's pregnant with my child is straddling me, all soft and gorgeous and everything I want, and *I just can't stand it any more.* I withdraw a hand from her dress to reach up and thread my fingers into her silky, dark hair, and then I pull her mouth down to mine with an urgency that surprises even me. I devour her mouth, I claim it, I lick inside past her teeth and I bite at her lips and I keep her face tight to mine as she moans and kisses me back, just as fiercely, just as urgently.

"This is real," I tell her, and now I don't know if I mean the pregnancy or if I mean *this*—the chemistry, the connection, the *us* we're both too afraid to acknowledge even to ourselves. "This is fucking real."

"Yes," she pants against my mouth. Her hands are down at my belt, her fingers brushing against the ridged lines of my stomach as she fights to work it open. "This is real."

She gets my belt open and my jeans unzipped, and in a second's work, I have her panties hooked to the side and her wet pussy slowly sinking over my dick. She groans as she impales herself, and I groan too, just watching her. Watching the flush creep up her chest, the sweet points of her nipples poke through her dress. The

HOT COP

unabashed, naked pleasure on her face. She feels good, and I'm the one making her feel good.

"Is that what you needed, baby?" I ask, flexing my hips up to drive my erection in deeper. "You needed my cock?"

She nods, her hands almost frantic to push back my shirt, pull my hair, dig into my arms. "I needed it," she whispers. "I always need it."

"Yeah," I grunt, wrapping my hands around her waist and moving her over me. "Fuck yeah, you do."

She's soft and tight, and I feel so fucking hard and big inside her. She always makes me feel so big, like a porn star. Like a god.

I move her the way she needs, the way that rubs her inside and out, and I pull her down for growling, hungry kisses, and I reach up to squeeze and fondle her breasts, and I keep her speared on my dick until she's trembling and crying out my name, *Chase, Chase, Chase.*

But when I come, I only grunt her name once, *Liv,* and then pull her tight to my chest as I keep spurting my orgasm inside her cunt, murmuring in her ear, *this is real.*

This is real.

This is real.

15

LIVIA

A Danish study says that frequent sex can prevent preeclampsia.

I stare at the text I've written. Then, before I can talk myself out of it, I push SEND and set my phone on the library cart.

The ache between my legs is intense, but this text is not only an excuse to see Chase. There's legit science behind it.

It's just this is the third time legit science has been behind the sex-requesting texts I've sent him in the week since I found out I was pregnant.

The first time it was the study that showed that intercourse could lower blood pressure in pregnant women. The second time I'd read an article that orgasms were helpful for strengthening the muscles used in labor. Both times, he'd responded without delay or argument.

Both times orgasms and banging were had.

This time seems to be no different. My phone is already vibrating between the computer and the edge of the cart.

Preeclampsia is way bad. I'll be there in fifteen minutes.

No! I'm at the library, I respond.

Then, as my pussy throbs with reminding need, I send another right after. **You better make it thirty.**

It's slow today. Surely we can slip off somewhere for a quickie.

Suddenly feeling guilty, I hide my phone behind the computer and look around to see if anyone's watching me. As if anyone who saw me would know what terrible thing I'd just done.

Ugh!

I curl my hand into a fist and bang it against my forehead a couple of times. What am I doing, what am I doing, what am I doing?

And why am I doing it?

I drop my hand and stare blankly across the library. My arrangement with Chase is absolutely definitely supposed to be over.

And it absolutely definitely will be.

Soon. Super soon.

It's just that being pregnant hasn't felt the way I've thought it would. It's exciting and wonderful, but also strange and staggering, and Chase is steady. He steadies me. Keeps me solid and in place when it feels like the rest of my world has tilted. Reminds me what's real, like he did with the words he whispered in my ear the night I found out I was pregnant.

That night he was so convincing; I almost believed he meant things about us—

deeper things. Permanent things.

But of course he didn't.

With a sigh, I lean my head against the screen of the computer. Who am I fooling? I like him.

I mean, *it*! The sex. I like the sex. I want the sex. That's all. Nothing else. I want the sex. And not permanently. Just for an unknown extended time.

Oh God, I'm an addict! A sex addict! Is that really what this is?

I open up the web browser on my computer and type in *sex addict* in the search box. The first article that appears lists characteristics of addicts, and thank the Lord, none of them sound like me.

Well, except for maybe having delusional thought patterns. Does this count as a delusional thought pattern?

I groan inwardly.

Whether I'm actually a sex addict or a Chase-sex addict, there's no question that I'd be better off ending this as soon as possible. Pull the Band-Aid quick and all that.

Except.

Is there really any harm in a few extra rounds of Hide the Nightstick?

Yes. The harm is that it's even harder to quit him later on.

I groan again, this time out loud. The old man who's been camped out in the armchair all evening looks up from his book with a frown. My apologetic smile doesn't seem to make him any less grumpy.

Great. Now Chase is interfering with my job.

Wait. I think "interferes with job" was one of the characteristics on the sex addict list...

This was exactly what I'd feared about Chase's kind of sex—intimate instead of clinical and straightforward. I'd have had no problem saying goodbye if he'd fucked me like any one of the men I'd been with in the past. Chase made it too good. Chase made me into him.

It! Into it! The sex. I'm not into *him*; I'm into the *orgasms*.

They've seemed to feel even better since I've gotten pregnant. I wonder if there's something to that.

Now I type *pregnant and horny* in the search box and hit RETURN. Before I have time to scan the results, a woman approaches the cart.

I minimize the browser at lightning speed—maybe this wasn't a search I should have conducted at my workstation—and give the patron my full attention.

Rephrase: I *attempt* to give her my full attention.

Ever since the first stick showed two lines instead of one, I've found focusing has not been one of my better traits. I don't know if it's hormonal or if I'm just distracted. Probably a combination of the two. Because, seriously...the hormones.... My breasts hurt so much I can't even stand the shower pouring water on them. I'm so tired, I can barely make it through Stephen Colbert, and oh my God, the peeing. I finally had to lie and tell my manager I had a bladder infection because I'm in the bathroom at least once an hour.

But also, I'm completely distracted. There's a baby inside me. A *baby*. A baby I wanted and planned for, but now it's actually here. Growing. Living. Being. And the wait to meet him or her seems so eternally long while the wait to prepare for his or her arrival seems so ridiculously short.

It's a lot to think about, and I find that, no matter what I'm doing, there's always a part of my brain dedicated to thinking about the huge miniscule thing going on inside me.

Like now.

"The computer says it should be on the shelf," the patron says. I've already forgotten what book it is she's searching for. "But when I looked, I didn't see it there."

"Hmm," I say politely. Because nine times out of ten when the patron looked, they looked wrong. It's the Dewey Decimal System. It's not hard, but it baffles a lot of our patrons.

(Note to self: My baby will know the Dewey Decimal System as early as he/she knows his or her ABCs.)

"Let's go take a look. It was probably mis-shelved." I totally don't believe it was mis-shelved, but I do believe in the "customer is always right" philosophy, even though the customer is generally always wrong. So I'm placating.

I leave my cart to help the patron find the book, and sure enough, the book is exactly where it's supposed to be. Not only do I find it immediately, but I also find it while wondering if I should stop drinking coffee all together or if I can go ahead and drink two cups a day. I've found varying opinions on the internet, and while I definitely intend to ask my doctor when I see him, I don't have an appointment for another week. I could quit until I see him just to be safe, but I'd hate to waste a week of Keurig enjoyment.

"I swear it wasn't there when I looked before," the woman says when I hand her the copy of *The Modern Maker: Men's 17th Century Doublets*.

"It was pushed back really far," I lie. "Easy to miss. Is there anything else I can help you find?"

She kindly says no and thanks me for my help, and I head back to my cart thinking about how soon I should stop wearing heels and start wearing compression hose to avoid varicose veins, and I don't even blink when I see Megan standing at my computer.

"Hey," I say, genuinely glad to see her. "I haven't seen you in a few days. What's up?"

"Well, I'm not pregnant and horny. So I think my day isn't half as bad as yours is." She turns the monitor toward me, her brow raised in a *gotcha* expression.

I keep my features schooled even though I feel my face heating as I glance at the web page. According to the list of article titles that showed up from my earlier search (*Very Horny During Pregnancy, Help! I'm Horny and Pregnant, Horniness During the First Few Weeks, Sex Toys for the Horny Pregnant Woman*), horniness during pregnancy is definitely a common problem. That means there's a perfectly reasonable explanation for my addiction to Chase. This is good news!

That Megan has discovered this is not good news. Not good news at all.

But I don't need to panic. I know how to solve this. "I was doing a search for a patron," I say, somewhat confidently. It's false confidence, but it counts.

"Oh, really?" She clicks to a new tab, this one listing the browser history from my shift.

Ah, fuck. Megan's been standing here a while.

I scan through the list, my cheeks getting redder as I read each new line.

Pregnant and Horny
Sex Addict
Coffee and Pregnancy
Your Baby at 5 Weeks
What to Expect the First Trimester
So You've Missed Your Period

How Far Along Am I?
Do Cheetos have any nutrients?
9 Benefits to Sex During Pregnancy
Sperm and Pregnancy

Megan pins me with her stare. "Should I scroll down further?"

"The patron had a lot of questions," I say. Not quite so confidently this time.

"Uh-huh."

"I'm a very helpful librarian." I reach over and hit the link to clear the browsing history, nudging Megan out of the way so I can take back my station.

She still doesn't believe me.

But that's fine. She doesn't have to believe me. I'm not admitting anything, and if I don't admit anything, she can't *know* anything.

Unfortunately, my nudging doesn't get rid of her. She simply circles around the cart and plants herself where she can stare at me, her eyes wide and expectant.

I ignore her and focus on my monitor. There are serious things I have to be doing right now and all. Like, make a booklist. For teens. It's been a few weeks since I've made a new one and suddenly it's a crucial priority.

I open a new tab and start a page on the library website. I start typing. *Books to Read If You Liked Julie Murphy's* Dumplin'—

Megan shakes the cart, disrupting my typing.

"What?" I ask, annoyed, as though there's nothing left for us to talk about. Because there's not.

She gives me a look that calls bullshit. "You know exactly what! You're pregnant!"

"Shhh!" I glance around to make sure no one has heard her besides the old man who now looks grumpier than ever. Thankfully, I find no one.

Good thing too, because Megan is not to be silenced. "And from the looks of your Google history, I'm going to guess you're five weeks. Which means you just found out. Which means you don't really have a bladder infection. You're just knocked up."

"Megan!" I lean across the cart and hiss a warning. "Stop saying that. Someone will hear you."

"Am I wrong?" She's persistent, but quieter, at least. "Before you answer, if you tell me I'm wrong, and you end up being pregnant, I'll know you were lying in a few months when you can't hide it anymore, and I'll remember."

A stone of shame sinks through my chest.

I hate it.

"That's not fair," I say pouting. "You know guilt works on me."

My statement is as near an admission as she needs. Her face lights up with victory, an expression not unlike one I've seen many times on her brother, and I can tell she's about to prompt me for more information.

"Who's the father?" she asks.

I avert my eyes and answer with a half shrug. "There is no father."

"Come on! Tell me!" Her gossip loving soul is itching for me to spill. She's practically vibrating with excitement.

Now here's the thing—I always knew there'd be this moment, this moment where my friend asked about my baby's father, and I've always been prepared to tell a story. *One night stand, blah blah blah, keeping it, blah blah, dad's not in the picture.* This lie is already formed.

But now that I'm here standing in it, I'm surprised by how much I suddenly want to tell her a different story. How much I want to tell her the truth. How easy it would be to confess everything. Tell her she's about to be an aunt. The words sit on the tip of my tongue, ready to fall and be heard—*Chase. It's Chase's baby.*

But it doesn't matter how much this actual moment has thrown me off guard or how much it burns to not say it out loud—I can never tell her this secret of mine. Not ever.

And, anyway, this baby isn't Chase's. It's mine. Only mine.

"I don't want to talk about him," I tell her, emphatically. "Please. I'm doing this alone." Another stone drops inside me.

This one feels much too complicated to call just shame. It's also disappointment and regret. And loss.

Megan nods, slowly. She's not happy with my response. She might even be a little hurt. But she's a good friend and a decent human being. She understands limits and naming the father is clearly one of mine. She'll honor it.

That doesn't mean she's done talking about it altogether. "Does he at least know?" she asks next.

"He knows. He's not going to be involved." Simple. Clear cut.

But this ignites Megan's inner sense of justice. "That's not right, Liv. He needs to pay child support. I can help you go after him for that. I know a great lawyer who can—"

"No!" I say a little too loudly, and you know what, old man? If you're bothered, you can read your book at home. "Absolutely not," I stage whisper. "He's not going to pay child support."

"And you're okay with that?"

"I *asked* for that."

Megan really doesn't like this. Twice she starts to say something and has to bite back her response. I get it. I do. She's a happily married woman with a traditionally structured family. My choices have to seem strange to her.

After several heavy seconds, she says carefully, "If the guy is a really terrible guy, and you don't want him involved in the baby's life, I'll understand. But if you're trying to be heroic about this, you don't have to be."

"I'm not trying to be heroic." Then, because it's Chase, and I can't let her think terrible things about him even if she never knows it's Chase, I add, "And he's not a really terrible guy. Not at all."

Her face relaxes and lights. "That's terrific! Because, look." She exhales and I can tell she's getting ready to say hard words. "Having a baby is hard. Doing it on your own is...well, I know you can do it. Of course you can. But you deserve everything you can have. And so does your baby. And maybe...maybe so does this not terrible guy. So maybe you shouldn't rush into any decisions. You could find a way to have the baby *and* the guy."

I don't mean to, but for the briefest seconds, I think about it. Think about having the baby *and* the guy. The baby *and* Chase. We're already still fooling around. We get along. He's good with kids. He's good with me.

I take a breath in, imagining it, and find it aches because it feels so good to imagine.

But that's all it is—something to dream about. In reality it's a mess. It's a ridiculous notion with nowhere to go and the worst of foundations. What do we have between us besides good sex? A baby, that's what. You can't put that on a kid. You don't base relationships on pregnancies. You don't start relationships with a contract.

And I never wanted a relationship anyway.

I meet her eyes and tell her soberly, "I want the baby. I don't want the guy." My gut twists when I say this out loud, and I'm not sure my expression doesn't show it.

Quickly, I turn back to the computer, intent on picking up where I left off on my list of readalikes for *13 Reasons Why*, but my eyes are suddenly watery, and goddammit, if I cry in front of Megan, I'm going to be really fucking unhappy about it.

"Who's the father, Liv?" she asks softly.

I shake my head. My voice is a whisper. "No one."

"Do I know him?"

I stop typing, and, before I look up at her, I gather my frustration and aim it all at her. "Megan. There's nothing I want to say about him. I don't want to talk about him. Ever."

"Okay, okay. Sorry." A beat passes. Then another. Then she's coming around the cart, her arms open wide, a big smile on her face. "But what I should have said was—you're going to have a baby! Oh my God! Congratulations!"

"Thank you." I hug her, letting my watery eyes spill now. Over her shoulder, I watch the old man pack up his books and, after throwing us a cutting glare, move deeper into the library. Something about this lightens my mood, and I'm smiling when I let go of Megan, even though I'm wiping away a few tears.

"And you're happy? These are happy tears?"

"So happy." And I am. I really am. "I'm still adjusting. I only found out a week ago, and it's kind of overwhelming."

"Kind of," she repeats sarcastically. "You know those sci-fi stories about aliens taking over people's bodies and turning them into crazy creatures who go around killing everyone? I'm convinced they're based on women's first pregnancies."

"That's…terrific."

She laughs. "It is, actually. Terrific and terrible all at once." She raises a suggestive brow. "And the hormones are getting to you already."

"…yes?" They are, but I don't quite catch her drift.

"*Pregnant and Horny. Sex Addict.*"

Oh yeah. That.

I sigh. "That was just…" I trail off. It's not exactly like I can tell her I'm just addicted to sex with her brother. Who only slept with me to begin with because of a contract.

"I know exactly what it is," Megan says. "All the extra blood flow to the nether lands. Makes you extra itchy for the good stuff. There's some awesome toys I can recommend but nothing does the trick like the real thing. And now that I know you really are into men, this won't be a problem. Let me pull out my contacts. We've got to fix you up!"

Oh God. I hadn't expected this problem. "I'm not into men. I told you!"

"Obviously one was into you."

"Well. That was…" *Chase.* That was Chase. The ache returns inside.

"A one time thing? An accident? You were going to the mailbox to pick up your latest BarnesandNoble.com order and slipped and fell on a penis?" Of course she doesn't bother to lower her voice, even when speaking about male genitalia.

Thank goodness the old man moved.

I glare anyway. "I was going to say *complicated.*"

She bumps me with her shoulder. "Nothing gets you over

complicated like rebound sex. Especially if you're Pregnant and Horny, you sex addict."

Rolling my eyes, I turn back to the cart and the computer screen. "I don't need rebound sex." Especially not when I'm still having the complicated sex.

Oh shit. The complicated sex!

I glance at the clock on the computer. Chase will be here any minute!

While I check my phone to see if I'd had any texts from him, Megan continues her argument. "You should at least do a rebound date. And I know the perfect guy!"

"Of course you do," I say half listening.

One text message from ten minutes ago. **On my way. Be wet.**

Yeah, Chase will definitely be here any minute.

I glance as nonchalantly as possible toward the front doors. He's not here yet. Good. I have time. I type the word **MISSION ABORT** into my phone.

"Phil's friend Daveed is coming into town Saturday after next," Megan says. "You have to do dinner with us. He's a blast. He's an author, newly single, and I know you'd love him. It would be so much nicer to have a foursome."

I glance up from my screen. Did Megan just suggest I go out on a double date?

She totally did.

"Uh, I really don't think I want to start something with this baggage." I look down at my belly, emphasizing my specific baggage.

Megan tsks. "It's just one date. Daveed doesn't even live in town. It's not starting something. It's dinner."

"Even one date. Seems like a waste of everyone's energy." I don't want to go on a date with a random friend of Megan's. I'm not interested. At all. And somehow it feels like a betrayal, though, for the life of me, I don't know whom I'd be betraying.

I glance back and my phone to see if Chase has gotten my text and realize I never hit SEND on my message. Kicking myself, I do it now.

"If you're still hung up on your baby daddy..." Megan says casually.

And something inside jerks into reaction. "I'm not hung up on anyone," I say quickly. Because I'm not. "And anyway. That's the day we're doing the event to help Chase get signatures for his petition."

She grins, delighted. "I'm going to be here for that too so it will work out perfectly! We can leave for dinner straight from the fair."

I'm about to interject with another reason this is a bad idea or simply tell her flat out that I don't want to go when she says, "Unless you think it will bother Chase."

The hair on the back of my neck stands up. "What? Why would it bother Chase? There's nothing between me and Chase."

And then, as if drawn simply by the force of his name, Chase appears behind her at the library doors.

Fuck.

I mean, seriously *fuck!*

But he sees us. Sees my panicked look and then glances down at his phone as if he's just gotten a buzz from an incoming message. Goddamn Verizon in Prairie Village. The service coverage is always so goddamn slow.

Chase, however, doesn't seem as concerned about the situation as I am. Which is really kind of sexy, actually. The way he remains poised and together. The way he acts like a secure anchor in a rocky sea. Right now while I'm sweating buckets, he nods reassuringly in my direction and then disappears down the stairs.

Down the stairs.

Not out of the library.

Why didn't he leave?

I want to follow after him or call him but Megan's staring at me, as if waiting for an answer to something, and she might have said something while I was focused on Chase, but I can't even remember what exactly we were talking about.

Oh. Wait.

She wants to fix me up with someone.

My phone buzzes in my hand. **My cock is hard and waiting for you in the supply closet.**

My pussy clenches with desperation.

"Okay. Fine," I tell Megan. "I'll do it. I'll go on the date." Because, like she said, it's one date. And at this point, I'll do anything to get rid of her and end this uncomfortable conversation so I can get downstairs and get on Chase.

And sure, I should probably be one thousand percent not into fucking him now that Megan is super detective about who the father of my baby is, but I've already come to terms with the fact that I'm pregnant and horny and that's what's ruling my life at the moment. My pregnant womanly needs.

At least now I realize it's just a hormonal thing. *I'll order myself a new supercharged vibrator from goodvibes.com,* I think as I rush down the stairs, *and I can put an end to banging Chase for good.*

After this time, anyway.

16

LIVIA

"This is the last time," I pant.

My palms are pressed hard against the sliding glass doors in Chase's sunroom. My dress is around my waist, my knee is hitched up so it will leave an imprint on the glass, and his cock is pounding into me at just the right angle when it occurs to me that I might be in trouble.

And I'm not talking about the baby I have coming.

"The last time. Totally the last time." He braces my raised thigh with one hand and the other grips my hip. His fingernails dig in with a delicious bite that adds to the storm of pleasure gathering below.

"I'm serious." I rotate my pelvis, trying to get him in just the right spot. Or every spot.

"So fucking serious." He growls. "Jesus, you feel good, kitten."

"So good."

"But no more after today," he says, his words running together.

"No more. No more," I chant rhythmically, which soon gives way to, "Right there, right there, right there, right there. Don't move."

"I'm not moving. This is all you, babe. Look."

I glance at our reflection, and sure enough, he's standing still, and I'm the one who's pushing back onto Chase with eager ferocity. That's how desperate I am for him. How in need.

The sight takes me to the edge. I'll go over soon. One little nudge will do it.

"You look so hot like this," he says, adoringly. "In this position. So greedy. If you weren't already dressed right now, I'd shoot my cum all over your backside."

I picture it, picture myself covered with Chase. Marked by Chase.

That's all it takes.

"So hot, so hot, so, so hot," I cry, tumbling over, spilling like a rough river over the side of a cliff. Spots form in front of my eyes, stars in a daytime sky as pleasure pulses through my shuddering body.

My strength gone, my leg falls, and Chase, with both hands on my hips now, drives into me with wild strokes. "I'd mark you all up. You'd be covered with me all over your gorgeous ass." Soon he's coming too. Grunting and grinding against me as though determined to push every last drop of himself into me.

I'm spent, but I push back against him anyway, eager for every last bit he'll give.

Because this is the last of him I'll get. It *has* to be.

When I'm settled and my panties are on again and my dress straightened, I turn to scowl at Chase. "I only agreed to meet at your house today because you said Pop would be here too."

"Hey." He puts his hands up like he's innocent. "How was I supposed to know he'd want to take the kids to storytime?"

I look pointedly at him. "Uh, maybe the big red circle on the calendar hanging on your fridge with the words *Take Kids to Storytime?*"

Chase grins like he has no regrets. "I guess I didn't notice."

"You're a cop, Chase. You notice everything."

"You really think having my grandfather here would have stopped us?"

I want to argue. I want to pretend we have more restraint than that.

But we've had sex as much this last week as any week when I was trying to conceive.

I let out a reluctant sigh. "You're right. We have no self-control. It's the pregnancy hormones, for me. What's your excuse?"

"Your breasts," he says, without missing a beat.

I raise a questioning brow.

"They're so big now. They were already perfect, but now they're…just…" He's staring at my chest like he's a starved man. "I'm already getting hard again looking at them."

I spin around, horrified. "Stop looking at them!"

"And now I'm looking at your backside. And remembering how hot you were just a few minutes ago, fucking my cock. You were so crazy and determined and sexy—"

My belly clenches and I have to cut him off before we're rushing at each other again. "Stop talking! And looking." I turn around again toward him and find he's still gazing at me, his expression more amused now than lust-filled.

It doesn't help. Because any way he looks at me, he's still looking at me.

I run a hand through my hair, which came loose during our fun against the window. There's only one solution to our problem, one that was intended for this point in our contractual relationship all along. "Obviously the only thing that can stop us is to not spend time together."

Chase tugs at the neckline of his T-shirt and nods. "I suppose that is obvious," he says slowly.

I don't know if that's an agreement, but I'm taking it as one. I head toward his dining room to clean up my things. "We have the library fair this Saturday."

He trails behind me. "That's just a few days away."

"And we've figured out everything we need for it. There shouldn't be any other reason we need to meet before then." I gather the flyers and papers I'd brought to show him in preparation for his body cam presentation and stuff them in my bag.

"Exactly," he says, handing me my notebook. "So we're good. This can really be the last time if we want it to be."

I glare. "It was the last time, Chase." He's lucky that I don't chuck the notebook right back at him.

"That's totally what I meant." But he's grinning again, and I can't decide if it's because he doesn't really care one way or the other if we stop or if he just doesn't think we ever will.

Either way, it puts the responsibility of ending this on me. It's a lot of pressure. Especially when he looks as delicious as he does today. All casual and guy-like in his faded jeans and *Deadpool* T-shirt, his blue eyes doing that gleaming thing he's so good at.

"Well, anyway." I drag my gaze away from him. "I should get going." The walk toward the door feels like I have concrete blocks on my feet instead of shoes. It's. So. Hard. To. Go.

Chase escorts my slow departure. "What are you up to for the rest of the day?"

"I don't want to tell you." I'll tell him. I'm just stalling. Stalling leaving.

"Now you have to tell me."

"You'll laugh at me."

"I'll find out. I'm a cop. I have ways."

I'm pretty sure he's talking about cop ways, but something in his tone makes me think about other ways he could find out. Ways like capturing my wrists above my head, raising up my dress, and massaging my clit until I'm ready to comply with anything he asks.

I force the naughty vision from my head and casually cross my arms over my now steepled nipples. "Okay, I'll tell you. But you have to promise not to make fun."

"I can't promise that."

"I'm going to Babies R Us to register for baby stuff."

He doesn't laugh, but I think it's because he's too stunned. "Liv, you're only six weeks pregnant."

We're at the front door now, and instead of opening it, I spin back toward him. "So?"

"You have thirty-four more weeks to go."

I shrug. "I like to get things started early."

"No one registers this early. No one."

"You don't know that," I say defensively. Though, he's right. According to the baby board I've joined, it's really too early to do anything until after the first trimester. But I'm excited. And I like to plan.

Chase is chuckling now. "You haven't even seen your OB yet."

"Only because he couldn't get me in yet."

There's a beat of silence. A beat when I know I should be leaving, and he knows I should be leaving, but somehow I'm not leaving.

"Have you even had time to research everything you need?" he asks eventually.

"I've been researching since before I even got pregnant. Duh."

"Well." God, his grin. I could drown in his grin. "You'll want a feeding pillow."

"Got it on the list."

"And a decent carrier so you can wear your baby. There are a lot of different options and a lot of them are crap. I tried a bunch with Megan's kids. My advice—don't get the cheap ones."

I imagine him wearing a carrier, a sleepy newborn pressed against his chest, and suddenly I can't breathe. "Okay."

"What about car seats? What brand are you getting? Do you know which one is safest?"

He has a lot of good questions, and I'm sure I could look up reviews online, but right now all I want is the one he wants. The one he thinks is best. "Do you have one you recommend?"

"There are a few that are better than others. It really depends what options there are."

And there are a lot of options. I'm sure.

"I should probably just come with you," he says, at the same time as I say, "Maybe you should just come with me."

My belly flutters like I'm a teenager who's just been asked out on a date. I'm pathetic, and I can't even bring myself to care right now.

"Want me to drive or…?"

"I'll drive," I offer, opening the front door. "Then I can just drop you off on my way back home."

He goes to grab his house key and makes sure he has his wallet. When he comes back he hesitates. "This is spending more time together. Is that going to be okay?"

And now my entire body tingles because whatever he thinks about our odds of keeping our hands off each other, he cares about how I feel.

"We already banged, so I'm sure it's fine," I say, heading out the door, beyond glad that he's doing this with me.

"Right," Chase says, on my heels. "Because there's no way we'd end up banging twice in the same day."

Yeah. I'm totally in trouble.

• • •

Chase walks around the display crib, examining it from every angle. He even bends down to look at the legs and the base. When he stands again, he's frowning. "I don't like this one."

"Why? It's cute. I like the scalloped woodwork." I see nothing wrong with it myself. And it's the one the store says is their best-seller. That has to say something.

"You can't buy baby furniture just because it's cute, Liv." He points at the side where the mattress meets the front panel. "This is a regular-sized mattress in here and there's a gap at the side. There should be no gap at all. This isn't safe. I don't like it."

"Oh." Now I'm frowning too. "I didn't notice that."

"Cribs are responsible for more deaths than any other nursery product. You have to be really careful about them." He walks over to a less decorative crib behind the popular one. "This one has much better crafting. And it has a better standards rating on Consumer Reports. I looked it up while you were going gaga over the bedding with all the books."

He's referring to the Land of Stories bed set I'd found. "I

wasn't going gaga. It was just a cute idea." It was patterned with children's classic books like *Alice in Wonderland* and *The Wizard of Oz*. I added it to the registry, of course.

"Yeah, yeah, cute idea." He nods again to the crib. "We should get this one."

I purse my lips. "You mean *I* should get that one."

"That's what I said."

It wasn't, but I'm sure it was a slip-up. I'm grateful he caught the issue with the crib. It's something I never would have thought of. I put the one he suggested on the registry, and we move to the next department.

Chase has been great going through the store with me. We've been here for almost an hour already, and he's been patient and fully engaged, making sure we go down every aisle and look at every suggestion on the registry pamphlet the store provided us when we signed up.

Er, when *I* signed up.

"You added the feeding pillow to the list?" he asks as we turn down the nursing aisle.

"I told you I did." I look down at the iPad though to make sure I really did. (I did.)

When I look up again, he's holding up the two pumps from a double electric breast pump on display to his chest. "Please, please, please can we get these?"

I roll my eyes. "Oh my God. Are you twelve?" I don't mention his second slip of the word "we."

"This is like having a video game on your chest." He pretends to shoot the pumps in my direction.

I snatch one out of his hand. "Yeah, that's exactly what it's like."

"I'd never leave my house." He's examining the remaining pump, as if trying to figure out how he could make one of his own.

"You'd never leave the house if you had breasts, period." I grab the second one from him and return it to the shelf.

He stands over my shoulder to look at the screen of the registry iPad. "Put it on the list. Put it on. Put. It. On."

Shaking my head, I add it to the list.

The next aisle is dedicated to medicines and related baby needs. "I'm adding diaper cream, Purell, baby Tylenol and Mylicon drops," I say, putting them into the system.

"Good, good." Chase wanders ahead of me and stops at the Vaseline. "Petroleum Jelly? Put lots of that on there."

I bite back a laugh. "It's not for what you think it's for."

"It says multi-purpose, kitten." He moves farther down the aisle. "Add the Lanolin ointment too. Megan's nipples were cracked and nasty. You're going to want that."

My head pops up from the screen. "Are you telling me my nipples are going to be nasty?"

"No, not your nipples, babe. Never. But they might hurt. So put the ointment down. Gel packs too that you can stick in the freezer."

"'Kay. Got it down." We might be done with our sexual relationship, but it is nice to have someone looking out for my tits.

We split up at the travel systems, and I spend my time looking at the jogging strollers wondering if I should take up running just so I can get one of the slick carriages.

But that would actually involve running.

When I give up on that dream and return to Chase, he seems to have picked out what I need.

"This is the travel system I'd get," he says, pointing to a sleek convertible stroller with an accompanying infant car seat. "Except..." He moves some boxes around, looking to see if there's another option. "I guess you have to go with this one."

"What's wrong with it?" I'm not putting anything into the registry that isn't one hundred percent the best.

"Nothing's wrong with it. It just has two bases." He won't meet my eyes when he says it, as though it bothers him to tell me.

My forehead creases as I try to make out his point.

"For two different cars. So you can move the carrier back and forth."

"Oh." I won't need that. And that kind of bothers me too. Like, my chest feels empty and tight all at once.

Which is dumb. I shouldn't feel bad for being a single mom. I don't feel bad. "Well, maybe I'll have a babysitter or something who could use it."

"Yeah, good thinking."

We're quiet for a bit after that. I don't know what he's thinking, but a heaviness has settled on me. An awareness that this thing we're doing today isn't really ours. It was fun and I'm so appreciative of his help, but this is going to be my baby and my baby alone. It's not always going to be like this. He's not always going to be beside me.

I don't want to examine what I'm feeling too closely. I'm afraid of what I'll find inside me. But one thing I do know—I wish I didn't have as many feelings about that as I do.

"Can we get one of these in my size?"

I look over to see Chase holding up a onesie that reads *Tit Faced.*

"No. We cannot." But it makes me laugh, and I need that right now. I want to hold on to the laughter.

"Fine." He puts it back. "You definitely should put this one on the list, though." He holds up another onesie that says *I'm Proof that My Mommy Puts Out.*

I'm laughing again. "If I put that on the registry, I guarantee you, Megan will be the one to buy it."

"Ew. I do not like to think about Megan thinking about you putting out. With me." He puts the onesie back on the rack.

"But she doesn't know I put out *with you.*"

"But I do. And it's weird." He tucks an article of clothing under his arm. "We're getting this for sure."

"*I'm* not getting anything right now." I might be registering early, but there's bad luck and there's bad luck. It's bad luck to buy anything too early. I'm curious though. "What do you have?"

"*I'm* buying it, so don't you worry about it." Apparently Chase doesn't believe in the bad luck karma.

And maybe I don't really either. But I don't want him buying anything for the baby. Now that would be weird.

I grab the onesie from him, sure it's the *Captain Adorable* outfit that I already saw (and added to the registry). But it's not. It's a simple white onesie with black letters that say *My Mom is Beautiful.*

My chest knots, and I look up at Chase.

He shrugs like it's no big deal. "Someone needs to remind you when I'm not around."

Then he's thinking about that too. About how he's not going to be involved.

I let him buy it for me. For us. For his baby.

And so I'll remember when he's not around.

• • •

Chase pulls into his driveway and turns off my car. "Here are your keys, *Grandma.*"

I giggle. He's referring to how cautiously I drove when I was behind the wheel. "That's why I let you drive this time. I couldn't take you watching my every move."

"I wasn't watching your every move," he says, but he can't look at me because he knows he's lying.

"'The speed limit's forty-five here. You can move a little faster,'" I say in my best Chase impression. "You wouldn't have told me that if you hadn't known I was only going forty-three. You were totally watching the speedometer."

"I was being helpful." His grin is wide, and I know my own smile matches his.

I shift to face him, pulling my knees up under me in the passenger seat. "I knew the speed limit. Officer."

"Then why weren't you going faster?"

"Because I was afraid you'd tell me I was speeding." I giggle again. I feel like I've been laughing all day. It's noticeably nice. Like, it makes me notice how much I don't laugh in general.

He twists in his seat, as much as his large frame can against the steering wheel in my small car, anyway. "Let me tell you a secret." He lowers his voice and bends near. "I speed. All the time."

I lean in closer and lower my voice to match his. "I know. I was watching."

He chuckles softly, a light rumble against his throat. His smile fades as he reaches out to sweep a tendril of hair off my face. I slant toward him, wanting his skin against mine.

He moves with me, turning his hand so his palm can cup my face.

"Livia…" he says, letting the end sounds of my name trail off and up, like a prayer, and my chest expands because I swear I know the meaning of that prayer. I've prayed it myself in my own way, though never quite like this. Never so fully realized in its intention.

I close my eyes briefly, absorbing his touch and his warmth and his everything. When I open them again, he's looking at me in this way that isn't quite lustful or wanton but is just as intense.

I've seen it before, but it's only now I think I might understand what it is because I feel it too. This acute desire for *more*. Not more sex—though definitely more of that too—but for more of other things. More of this. More time. More life together.

I want to tell him.

The words are trapped, just inside my mouth. *I don't want this to end.*

I don't want this to end.

And I think maybe he doesn't want this to end either. And if I tell him, if I let myself be brave enough, I'm almost sure he'll say all the things I want him to say. Things I haven't even yet allowed myself to realize I want him to say. *Be mine. I'll stay. I'm your guy.*

It makes my heart race just thinking about it. It makes me happy too, and I'm suddenly bursting to tell him. "Chase?" I pause, not because I'm hesitant, but because I want his full attention before I go on. In the space, I practice the words again in my head. *I don't want this to end. Please don't let this end.*

"Yes, kitten? I'm listening," he says reassuringly, as if he knows what I'm about to say. That I'm about to change everything.

And then his phone rings.

He groans in frustration. "I'm sorry, babe. Gotta get this. It's work."

I'm used to this. He's had to answer calls before when we've been together, even had to leave two or three times to go work a serious accident. It's the life of a cop, he's told me. They always have to be prepared. Always have to be on standby. It's usually no big deal.

But this time is different. I watch him as he talks on his cell. He doesn't say much, mostly it's, "Yeah." And "Uh huh." It's not his words that give him away, but his expression. It's gone hard and cold when just a moment ago he was open and warm. The crease at his brows sharpens, and though he's not quite frowning, I can feel the edges of his lips wanting to curl down.

Then there's an "Of course," and he hangs up.

"What's wrong?" I ask, the moment before nearly completely forgotten.

His head shakes dismissively. "Nothing. Something at work." He pockets his phone, taking the opportunity to not look at me.

He's trying to bottle it up. I can see it. He's putting whatever this is behind a stony mask. Compartmentalizing. Hiding from me.

It's a punch to the gut how much that hurts. The *more* that I want includes this—

all of this. All of him. The things that bother him, the things that sting. I want to crawl into his lap, grab his shoulders and shake it out of him.

I want him to look at me.

Reaching over, I rub my hand up and down his bicep. "What is it, Chase? You can tell me."

He grips the steering wheel and pushes back, flexing his arm muscles, and I can tell he's struggling.

"Please, honey. Tell me?"

"A guy on the force got killed today." Finally, he glances over at me. His eyes are stormy. "Jason Eaker."

"Oh, baby. I'm sorry." I stroke his arm, wanting to comfort him the way he comforted me that first month when I got my period. I want to pull him into me and run my fingers through his hair, hug him to my chest and whisper that it will be okay.

But he's not opening up to me that way. He's barely here with me, barely looking at me. His body is stiff and he's talking to me about facts while the rest of him is locked somewhere else, out of my reach. I want to get inside him, where his feelings are. Where his heart is.

"How did he die?" I ask, hoping that I can coax him into leaning on me.

He swallows. "It's crazy really. Routine traffic stop."

"A routine traffic stop?" My mouth suddenly goes dry. I'd expected that his fellow officer was killed while doing something dangerous like chasing after a bank robber or making a drug bust or bringing down a sex trafficker. "Jason Eaker was a traffic cop?"

"Yeah," Chase says softly, not seeming to understand what I'm getting at. "I know him quite well." He blinks then corrects himself. "I *knew* him well. Sarge said he had pulled someone over for a busted light, and while he was giving the ticket, a drunk driver came by, hit him, and took off."

"Oh my God," I whisper, but what I'm thinking is *that could have been Chase.* "Are you okay?" I want him to turn and let me hold him, but now, just as much, I want him to hold *me.* Because I'm not sure *I'm* okay.

He remains somber though, staring out the front window at his garage door. Focused on the details and not on the pain. "This loss is going to be hard on the force. It's the second death we've had in the line of duty in the last couple of years. Jason was young too. He's leaving behind a wife and two boys. I don't even think the oldest is in school yet."

"That's awful." My voice breaks and a tear slips down my

cheek. That could have been Chase and that wife could have been me, and while he's stoically handling the very real death of his friend, I'm barely holding on over the realization that cops' jobs are dangerous. Barely holding on over the realization that Chase could die.

He hears the crack in my voice and turns toward me, alarmed. "Oh, kitten." He wipes the tear off my face. "I didn't mean to make you cry."

"It's a sad situation," I sputter, embarrassed by my tears. "And I'm hormonal. It's not your fault."

"Even so, I'm used to this shit. It's part of the job. I shouldn't be dumping all of this on you."

Except he's not dumping anything on me. He's barely sharing, and as much as I want him to tell me more, as much as I wish he'd tell me everything, I find myself pulling back now too. Back behind familiar walls where it's safe and pain free.

"I should go," he says, and I don't argue.

All the things I wanted to say before his phone call are long gone, and as I drive away I'm no longer worrying about our end; I'm worrying about Chase's end.

It's a late lesson to learn, but now that I have I can't stop focusing on it. He's a cop. And cops die.

Chase is going to die.

• • •

I'm still thinking about it at work later. Still thinking about the dead officer.

I feel terrible for the family that lost a husband and father, and can't stop thinking about how I'd feel if I were the officer's widow. I can't even begin to imagine how Chase is feeling.

A book comes to mind that I think he'll like. *Deaths and Entrances*, a collection of Dylan Thomas poems. I decide to check it out for him, hoping he'll find it comforting, even if he won't let me be his comfort directly.

In the back room, I pull up Chase's name in the database and scan the title out to him. Then, because I'm curious like that, I peruse the list of books he already has checked out.

What to Expect When You're Expecting
Mayo Clinic Guide to a Healthy Pregnancy
The Expectant Father
The Healthy Pregnancy Book
The Pregnancy Countdown Book: Nine Months of Practical Tips, Useful Advice, and Uncensored Truths
and *World War Z*

At the sight of the last title, I bring my hand up to my mouth so my laugh isn't too loud for the quiet library. A book about the zombie apocalypse seems out of place in the company of the other books he's checked out. Books about babies and gestation and women's bodies changing with the growth of life. Books he's obviously checked out because of me. Because his child is living inside of me.

It startles me to feel the tear drop slowly down my cheek, but once I recognize it, it's all I can do not to follow it with a dozen more. Thank God I'm not in the front because soon I'm crying pretty good.

I don't want Chase to die.

I don't want him to die and I don't want to lose him and I want more and I don't want things to end because *I love him.*

I'm in love with him.

I'm such a fool. Such a stupid, stupid fool. It's been there all along but I couldn't admit it. I didn't *want* to admit it.

And it's not because of the orgasms. Or his uniform. Or those sexy aviators he wears. Or his beard. Or because I'm filled with pregnancy hormones. It's not because he cares about justice and body cameras and Captain America. Or the way he takes care of his nephews and has them tattooed on his body. It's not how he handles Ryan or talks about his mother or how he moved in with Pop to look after him.

And it's not the way he makes me feel alive and fun. Or how

he makes me feel beautiful. Or how he cares about me having my baby. Or because he gave me a baby. Or even how he bothered to check out pregnancy books—from Central even, probably so his sister and I wouldn't find out.

It's not any *one* of those things. It's *all* of those things. It's all of *Chase.*

I'm not into men, but I'm *so* into Chase. I'm so in love with Chase.

And maybe, if I read the signs right, there's a possibility that he might even be into me.

I've been scared to say it because I'd have to look at my life and decide if I could be brave enough to try to fit him in. But now I can't ignore it any longer, and I have no choice but to look and see what we could be.

And it's nothing.

Because even if Chase wants to make something work between us, even if he wants to be a couple and raise our child with me, even if he is the rare unicorn of a guy who doesn't leave—and those are a lot of seemingly impossible ifs to overcome, but if he could, he'd still be a guy in a dangerous job. He'd still be a guy who has the very real potential of encountering a criminal or a drunk driver or an angry cop killer.

He could die.

And that would destroy me.

But the worst part is that I'm not the only one he'd leave behind, and that thought hurts more than I can bear. It's one thing for me to single-handedly raise a child who has never known a father, but to try to make up for the loss of a parent is an entirely different thing.

I can't stand the idea of my kid with that kind of wound.

I can't imagine the hole that Chase's absence would create if he orphaned a child while in the line of duty.

I can't handle the thought of comforting that kind of heart-ache in someone else, let alone in myself.

So the words I said this morning have to stand. We can't see each other after Saturday. We have to be done. Done having sex. Done shopping for baby things together. Done dancing around emotions we don't want to face.

Just done.

17

CHASE

The civic fair at the library comes together perfectly, of course, because Livia Ward is perfect and amazing at her job and also this little city can step pretty lively when it wants to. The Corinth parking lot has been cleared of cars and is currently hosting fire trucks, ambulances, police cars and several stalls from local businesses and restaurants, handing out coupons and ice cream and balloon animals for the kids.

I was nervous about my presentation at the beginning of the fair, even though I'm generally pretty confident when it comes to these kinds of things, but usually if I'm giving a presentation, it's at a meeting full of city employees and other cops. Not in front of real, honest to God civilians, and not in front of my sister and not in front of the woman who is pregnant with my child.

The woman I can't get enough of, no matter how hard I try. The woman who is breaking down every single fucking wall I have.

Plus, it's a high stakes issue for me, especially after Eaker's death. I have to present my case for body cameras in a compelling enough light that I get five hundred signatures out of this fair. And while there are easily more than five hundred people here, a majority of them will definitely need to sign my petition if I am going to hit my target number.

Despite my nerves and the beautiful distraction in the form of Livia Ward in a pencil skirt, the presentation itself went fairly well, with me standing on a platform in the parking lot in my uniform, the newly leafy trees providing enough shade for me to use a projector screen to exhibit data points and hammer home the salient information. And at the very end, I pulled up a picture of Jason Eaker, smiling with his family outside his son's preschool.

"This is Officer Jason Eaker. He was thirty-five, in the Army for six years before he went blue, and he has two children. I rode in his funeral escort yesterday." A sound rippled through the people in the parking lot, a collective exhale of sadness at the mention of his death. I appreciated the sadness, the real and tangible expression of it, and yet sadness on its own wasn't enough to change anything. "He was working a routine accident on 75th Street when he was struck and killed by a drunk driver. It was a hit and run, and because he was riding his police motorcycle that day, he didn't have a dashboard camera to record the events. The hit and run driver still hasn't been found—but maybe, if Jason had been wearing a body camera, we would have footage of the car. Maybe his family would have some closure."

People were nodding by this point, and I continued. "This isn't meant to supersede other reasons why getting body cameras is imperative. A police officer's life is not worth more than a civilian's. But I'm telling you about Jason to highlight the point that this upgrade benefits civilians *and* officers. And I hope you'll keep that in mind as we circulate the petition around. Thank you."

There was a healthy smattering of applause, a lot of people coming up to ask questions and talk afterward, and then my part was over. Now, all I can do is wait until the end of the fair to see how full the signature sheet is.

After I'm done talking to various citizens and media people, I feel a graze on my arm. It's Livia, a smile on her face and the near-summer breeze playing with loose tendrils of her hair. I have a bit of post-presentation adrenaline and she's so fucking beautiful and it's been three days since I've had her shamelessly panting and bucking against me, and so I slide an arm around her to yank her in for a kiss.

To my surprise, she pushes me away, casting a nervous glance around. "Chase! Megan's here!"

"I don't care," I growl, because I almost don't. In fact, I actually don't.

"I care," she protests, still looking around. "And we said—remember, we said that last time was *the last time.*"

I give her a martyred look. "I need one more last time."

She heaves a giant sigh, but a smile is pulling at her mouth. She looks like she's about to answer—and I can tell it's going to be an answer I'll like very much—but then something in her face closes up.

I turn to see Megan—who, like all the Corinth employees, has been drafted to work the fair—walking up to us. Livia makes a noise that can only be described as a squeak of panic, and then squeaks something else about checking on the children's section, and then hurries off before Megan reaches us.

Megan stares after her with narrowed eyes and then turns those narrowed eyes to me. "What did you do?"

I hold my hand over my heart. "I was a complete Boy Scout." *Except for the part where I told her I needed to fuck her again.*

Megan isn't buying it. "Uh-huh," she says slowly. "Sure."

I try to make an innocent expression, but it must not be successful because nothing about my sister's face changes.

"Well," she says, still looking as if her bullshit meter is (rightfully) beeping, "Phil has got the kids here to see the trucks and stuff. And I was wondering if you would mind taking them tonight after the fair winds down? Just for a few hours?"

"Of course," I say, already wondering if I could rope Liv in with my plans. We could go get ice cream with the boys, maybe go see the latest Disney movie and irritate Megan because we'd kept them up too late. We could feed them popcorn and hot dogs and take them home and snuggle them on the couch. And the minute I picture spending an evening with the kids and Liv, I want it. Suddenly nothing seems more attractive than playing Family with her for a night.

"Excellent," Megan pronounces. "Phil and I are going on a double date. His friend Daveed is in town, and—"

I don't really absorb the rest of what she's saying because I'm watching Liv as she approaches the double doors of the library, and she's being intercepted by Phil and the boys and a guy so handsome he looks like a fucking *GQ* cover model. Dark black skin, high cheekbones, a smile so dimpled and toothy that it even makes *my* pulse race a little and I'm pretty much the definition of straight.

And Phil is introducing Mr. Gorgeous to Liv, and Liv is blushing because who fucking wouldn't in front of this guy, and I am actually seeing red. Like scarlet bloodbursts of raw jealousy flowering behind my eyes. I want to hit something, scream into the air, grab Liv and carry her off like fucking Tarzan so everyone fucking knows she's mine. *Mine.*

Mr. Gorgeous doesn't stop at a smile either, he leans in and gives Liv a hug—like a real, *I am a man who likes your body* hug where their chests touch and his hands move gently on her shoulder blades and he drops a kiss on her cheek.

I practically bellow at this; I almost roar like an angry lion. And then I start towards them, nothing in my mind but getting between them, staking my claim. But by the time I'm halfway across the parking lot, Phil and the kids and Mr. Gorgeous are drifting over to the face-painting station, and Liv is walking back into the library. Megan is keeping pace with me, and I realize she's talking.

"Sorry, what?" I say, trying to pull the frustration out of my tone because she doesn't deserve my shitty mood, but also oh my God, watching Liv get hit on by that guy and enjoy it was like getting punched in the gut. Kicked right in the dick.

Megan lets out a noise that is both long-suffering and also *I do not suffer fools gladly.* "I was saying that Liv was talking to Daveed just then. He's her date tonight."

My legs make it two more steps before my mind absorbs the words. Then I stop. Like my feet are bolted to the asphalt.

"What did you say?"

I can tell immediately by Megan's expression that she's already explained this to me while I was in my jealousy coma. "Daveed's in town, and I thought I might try to hook him up with Livia since she needs a good man to shake her out of her 'no man' funk, and since he's a novelist and since she's a librarian, I thought they'd be a good fit. Also he's super fucking hot."

I might actually snarl at her.

She holds up her hands. "Whoa, tiger."

"Livia is going on a date tonight with Mr. GQ Cover Model tonight." I don't say it like a question. I say it the way I say things to criminals and addicts and adult children who don't check on their elderly parents. Bitingly matter-of-fact.

"Yes, she is."

"She's not fucking going on a date. Not with some other guy."

"Don't even start with me, Chase Kelly," Megan says, grabbing my arm and making us stop. She steps in front of me so that I have to look at her. "You had your chance with her, and you blew it. And besides, you aren't interested in anything more anyway, right? You give a girl the Kelly Trio and get the hell out. Why the fuck do you care what Livia does?"

Because she's mine.

Because her baby's mine.

But no, it isn't even those things, or at least it's more than them.

It's because I love her.

The thought, with that one word like a flashlight swinging in the darkness of my mind, nearly takes me out at the knees.

I love her. I am in love with Livia Ward, sexy and careful and stubborn and fragile as she is, I am so fucking crazy in love with her. I want her and I love her and no one else gets to have her.

There's something in Megan's face right now that unsettles me. Because it's almost like she's not angrily demanding answers, but that she sees all of my conflict, all of my vulnerability, and the big brother in me is both irritated and a little nostalgically grateful for it.

I finally say, "It's not important." A lie, but I don't have time to explain the truth to her, and Liv might kill me if I did anyway.

Megan folds her arms across her chest. "I care about that woman, Chase, so it is important to me. Tell me you're not going to upset her. Tell me you're not going to go in there and make things more complicated for her."

"I can't tell you that."

My sister huffs a tiny bit. "At least tell me you're not going to be a dick."

I run my hand through my hair, impatient, crawling with the need to find Liv and just hold her, touch her. Tell her that I love her and that she's fucking *mine*.

"I'm not going to be a dick."

Megan searches my face, going so far as to reach out and push my sunglasses to the top of my head so she can see my eyes.

"Megan," I say, but nothing else. I can't tell her anything else, not about the baby or the contract or that I am addicted to Livia and to the smell of her hair and to her giant, dark eyes. I just have to hope my sister loves and trusts me enough to let me go after her friend.

With a sigh, Megan steps to the side. "Don't make me regret this," she warns me. "She better be on that date with Daveed tonight."

I don't respond to that. Partly because I don't have a polite response to that at all, and partly because my legs are already moving again, taking me to my girl.

• • •

After the warm sunlight outside, the library feels unnaturally dark and cool inside, a spacious cave lined with books. And it's nearly empty—aside from a lonely sort of beeping from the shelving room behind the desk, there's no other sign of human presence. Everyone is outside enjoying the perfect weather and free ice cream.

There's a flash of a white blouse towards the rightmost opening to the stacks. I head towards the movement, not even thinking any more, just doing, just acting.

I turn the corner to see Liv disappear between two rows of shelves, a book in her hand. I stalk her steps quietly, not to sneak up on her, but because I'm making sure we're alone as I follow her, making sure there's no one else back here. And then when I'm sure we won't be interrupted, I step around the corner.

She turns and gives a little jump, sucking in her breath. "Chase, you scared me—"

But I'm already backing her into the shelf, grabbing onto the edge with both hands and trapping her between my arms. "You're going on a date tonight?"

I can see the pulse in her throat as she struggles for an answer. But I can also see her pupils dilate, the way she arches ever so slightly towards me, the hungry way her eyes drink in the tight muscles of my forearms.

"Yes," she whispers. "But..."

"But what, Livia? But you weren't going to tell me? But you were just going to let another man touch you and want you?"

"I had to get Megan to stop bothering me about it, and you know what? It doesn't matter. We said we were done."

"We might be a lot of things," I say in a low voice. "But done is not fucking one of them."

And then I bring my mouth crashing down against hers, a hard and hungry kiss that has her responding instantly, like I'd dropped a match into a puddle of kerosene. She's pressing against me, her hands snaking into vicious pulls of my hair, digging points into the muscles of my arms. I can hear her noises, the unwilling pants and sighs she makes as she practically tries to climb my body, as my hands find her ass and her tits and her inner thighs.

With a frustrated grunt, I yank the zipper of her pencil skirt down past her ass and then together we tug the damn thing up past her hips. I don't wait for it to move up any farther; I break our kiss to concentrate on getting my fingers into her pussy, where I can show her exactly how done we are.

"Let's see if you're wet for me," I breathe and she groans, trying so hard to spread her legs enough to let my fingers in. The moment I touch the soaked lace of her thong, I know.

She's fucking wet for me.

I push impatiently past the lace to her slit, to the hollow between her plump lower lips, and the minute my two fingers nudge her entrance, she's grinding down on my hand and literally fucking herself on my fingers. I don't have to move them, I don't have to say anything to her, her body simply feels me and instinctively tries to come.

It's the hottest goddamn thing in the world.

"Do that on my cock," I rasp. I use my other hand, which is shaking, to undo my belt and my dress uniform pants. I pull my boxer briefs down enough to bare my erection, which is fury-dark and thick. "Do it on my cock."

She looks up at me with hungry eyes and swollen lips. "But what if a patron…"

"I don't fucking care," I say through clenched teeth. "Put my cock inside you and fuck it."

"But someone could see…" Her protest is faint though, full of longing. I grab her waist and spin her so that I'm facing the direction someone would come from in the stacks.

"I'll keep watch, trust me. Now make me come. Show me what that pussy's good for."

"Oh God," she moans, my mean words doing her in just like I knew they would.

And I'm mean for her because it turns her on, but I'm also a little bit mean for me too. I want to say things to wound her the way I'm wounded.

Because this all hurts. I fucking love her and she has a date tonight and I'm jealous as shit and it all hurts.

Livia wriggles out of her thong and takes my dick in her hand, licking her lips as she rubs a thumb over my slit and smears the small teardrop of precum across my crown. "This is wrong," she whispers, and I don't know if she means fucking in the stacks or fucking me after we said we were done.

And it doesn't matter.

She turns so that she's facing away from me, puts one elegantly high-heeled foot up on a shelf, and then guides my tip to her swollen and needy opening. She slides herself back against my shaft, letting out a shaky breath as her foot drops off the shelf. I don't let her lean forward, instead placing an arm across her belly and curling a hand around her neck to keep her as upright as possible.

"Now move," I say into her ear and jabbing my cock in deeper to make my meaning clear. "Make me feel good."

She whimpers a little, a whimper of pure, defeated desire, and then she starts to move.

It's a tight fit; it's always a tight fit in her sweet little cunt, but this position, standing up with her legs close together and my hips pressing into her ass, it's so fucking tight that my eyes nearly roll back in my head. And she can't really push against me while I've got her trapped like this, so instead she squirms and wriggles.

She circles.

She grinds.

Here in the stacks, with her skirt around her waist and her high heels making dents in the industrial carpet, she rubs herself inside with my cock. And with my police uniform undone enough to show my cock, with my hair rumpled from her pulling it and her lip gloss still on my mouth, I make her.

"Does he know my baby's inside you?" I growl, shoving my cock in so deep that her feet nearly lift off the floor. "Does your date know that you're mine?"

"I'm not yours," she says, but her voice betrays her, breaking and uncertain. And she keeps herself speared on my cock. "We don't belong to each other."

"That's bullshit, and you know it." I let go of her, stepping back to slide out of her cunt, and she lets out a soft, unhappy noise.

"Give it back," she pleads, turning to me. "I need it."

"Oh really?" I say, coming forward and grabbing her ass to lift her up. She wraps her legs around my waist and immediately starts trying to impale herself on my cock. "You need it?"

"That doesn't mean anything," she says, still desperately trying to fill her pussy again. "It just means I'm hormonal. It just means we're sexually compatible." But she sounds like even she knows her words are lies. She's not fooling either of us.

I thrust into her, her pussy so wet that it's an easy stroke back in. Her head falls forward against my shoulder as I bottom out and I'm somewhere deep inside her belly.

"You're mine, princess. You were mine the moment you let me feel your bare pussy in that restaurant. You were mine the moment you let me kiss you so dirty outside of it. And you were definitely mine when you came around my cock and hoped I'd put a baby inside you."

Her face is in my neck. Kissing, licking, objecting. "I'm not yours," she mumbles. And then another kiss and lick and nibble. "Oh fuck, Chase, just like that, it's so deep, Jesus, so fucking deep."

"You think he'll be able to fuck you like this?" I ask. "You think another man can make you come like I do?"

Finally, honesty. She shakes her head. "No," she breathes against my neck. "Only you."

"Fucking right there's only me. And there's only you, kitten. No woman makes me as hard and big as you do. No one makes me come so fucking much, for so fucking long."

And then I go deeper, not just with my cock but with my words, with the twisting feeling in my chest. "I didn't mean for it to happen, Liv, I promise. I never meant for it to happen and I didn't think I even could, but I've fallen for you. I want to give you more than a baby, I want to give you *me*. I want to give you everything."

Her head comes up, her body going tense and rigid in my arms. "Chase, don't," she begs in a whisper, her panicked eyes looking into mine. "Don't say it. It'll just make it harder."

Something cracks open in my chest, something dark.

"You don't want to hear it?" I say, taking a step forward so that she's pinned against the shelves. "Fine. You can feel it."

Her head rolls back as I stab up into her, as I angle her hips so that each pump and stroke works her clit against my body. Her tits—so large and plump and swollen from the baby—bounce deliciously, and I want to suck on them. I want to wrap them in pretty ropes, I want to push them together and shove my slicked up cock through them.

"Go on your date, kitten," I say, fucking her now with deep, brutal thrusts. "I dare you. You go and see if he makes you feel like I make you feel. But you're going to go with my baby in your belly, and you're going to go with my cum dripping down your thigh. You're going to sit across from him sore and sticky and used. You're going to sit across from him remembering how hard you come for me and only me."

Her hands are everywhere, searching for anything to hold on to, and I feel it the moment she detonates at my words, a shuddering, gasping detonation as she trembles and quakes in my arms.

And she chants my name like it's the only thing that can save her, *oh God Chase please Chase Chase Chase*, and when she says it, I know I've got her. At least tonight, at least for one night, she's completely mine. No matter how good her dinner is, no matter how handsome and charming her date, she gave her entire self over to me to be marked and pleasured and fucked.

With that thought, I let myself go. I hammer into her with short, hard strokes, I imagine her sitting at a restaurant still sticky and damp with my cum, I imagine her getting home and fingering her still-wet pussy as she thinks of me. It's the image of *that*—of her spread on her bed, her fingers wet with my cum and eagerly fucking her pussy—that draws my balls up so tight I think I might die. And then I explode.

I can't roar out my orgasm in the middle of this quiet library, so I growl my way through it, grunting with each thick pulse of my cum, each eruption of my hot, angry release. She takes me, takes it all, every cruel thrust and every surge, still whispering my name in that prayer voice as my own orgasm keeps hers going and going and going.

It takes a long time to unload in her, my balls are so full. But eventually, finally, we are both still, both panting and dizzy and emptied out.

I set her down as gently as I can, holding on to her waist at first because she seems a little wobbly. She balances herself with a hand on a shelf and then, dazed, adjusts her skirt and searches for her thong. I find it first, tucking it in my pocket and then buttoning my own pants back up.

Livia takes a deep breath.

"I'm still not yours, Chase. And you can't be mine."

"Kitten, I—"

"Don't say it," she pleads, her eyes starting to shine. "You can't say it."

"Let me," I plead back, taking her face in my hands. "Let me."

She shakes her head, dewdrops of pain starting to form on her lashes. "You'll leave. All men do."

"No, Liv. I'm not going to leave."

"You're going to want other women."

The hurt in her voice guts me. I want to pull down trees and wrestle with lions and jump into fires—anything to prove to her that she's *it*, she's the only thing I see and smell and want. "No," I breathe, begging with my face and my hands and my voice for her to see. "It's you, baby. I choose you. There's no one else after you or beside you, there's nothing I want other than our real thing."

She swallows and blinks away, tears spilling out of her eyes now. "You're going to die."

"Everyone's going to die. That doesn't mean we stop living."

She lifts her chin, and for the first time today, I see a shadow in her face that I've never seen before. Or maybe I've seen it before, but never this dark, never this full of broken certainty. The tears track glistening streaks down this shadow, this shadow that I now realize is a wall she's built to protect herself.

"You have to go get the boys," she says, wiping her tears away with quick, vicious motions. "And I have to get ready to close the building. We can't do this."

"We have to do this," I tell her, leaning my forehead against hers and wiping more tears away with my thumbs. "Because I'm not giving up."

"You should," she says in a hollow voice, pulling away from me.

And then she walks down the aisle of books and disappears, leaving my thumbs still wet with her tears and my chest wet and sawed wide open with pain.

18

LIVIA

"I'll kill him," Megan mutters when she finds me closing up the library a few minutes later. I hid in the bathroom long enough for Chase to leave the building, so I already know what I look like. "What did he do?"

I wipe at my eyes, but it's useless. They keep leaking, an endless stream of hurt. "Nothing." I shut down the computer at the main desk. "No one. What did who do?"

She glares at me like she can see right through me. "Chase. This was Chase, wasn't it?"

"No. No." I don't know why I'm so determined to keep this a secret. Our relationship has blown up, and I'm fully aware I have no control over it anymore.

Only minutes ago, he was inside me. I can still *feel* him, my pussy aching where he pierced into me. He fucked me hard and deep, like he wanted to be all the way inside me. Like he was trying to reach my heart.

He has no idea how completely he already has.

But I'm only just beginning to process the things that he said to me. I need time to let it settle and sort before I can talk about it properly, and if I admit anything to Megan, I'll have to admit it all.

I move to the back room and make sure the door is locked before shutting it. When I look back at Megan, her arms are folded over her chest. "My ass this wasn't Chase."

Of course she's going to make this hard for me.

I let out an exasperated sigh. "Why would Chase make me cry?"

I go to turn the main lights off, not waiting for an answer. If she thinks she knows something, she can just come out and say it. I'm too exhausted to play this game.

She follows behind me. "If it's not Chase, what is it?"

"I'm pregnant, Megan. I cry at everything."

"Tell me then. What thing set it off?" She's a fiend for gossip, but I know she isn't just trying to get a scoop. She really does care, and the frustration laced in her tone is mingled with compassion and concern.

She deserves something from me.

I flick the switches then turn to her and give her a splash of truth. "Those boys," I lament in a whisper. "Those two boys."

"Officer Eaker's?"

I nod and clear my throat before going on. "They're going to grow up without a father now, just because their dad was trying to be one of the good guys."

"Oh, Liv." She pulls me into a bear hug and strokes my hair with long soothing sweeps of her hand. "But death is a risk that goes with the good guy thing. Gran never liked that part of Chase's job. I think she worried about it until the day she died. Honestly, it's probably why Chase doesn't let anyone get too close to him." She leans away to meet my eyes. "Jason's wife knew what she was getting into before she married him, if that makes you feel better. She chose him anyway."

I shake my head. It doesn't make me feel better at all. "His kids didn't get a choice. Now they're fatherless."

"That is worth crying about," she concedes. "Losing a parent while you're young is especially hard."

I hear the raw threads of experience in her tone. I didn't have a father growing up, but I never knew him. I have no memories to mourn over. No sad reminders.

"Is it as terrible as I imagine?" I ask her, slipping out of her embrace.

It's Megan, so I'm expecting a speech. But all she says is, "Yeah. It is."

That's all the validation I need. I don't want to talk about it anymore. Don't want to think about it.

I finish locking up the doors and hold the last one open so Megan can go first before I follow her out. After making sure the door has latched, I look up at her, pleadingly.

Somehow, she reads my mind. "Do you need to cancel tonight?"

"Yeah." Relief wraps around me. "I do. I'm sorry."

"No problem. I understand. I'll make an excuse for you."

"Thank you. I owe you." I look around before heading to my car, afraid Chase will pop out of nowhere. I can't take seeing him yet. I need distance and some solid time to think.

Megan notices my hesitation. "You're all clear. He took the kids as soon as he came out of the library and got out of here in a hurry."

I nod in gratitude before realizing that I've just admitted that I am, at the very least, avoiding Chase.

Sighing, I try to come up with an excuse. "It's not—" But I don't know what else to say. I'm tired of excuses. I'm tired, period.

"Don't worry about it, Liv. He's my brother. I already know."

With that, I go home to sort out what *I* already know.

• • •

The first thing I do when I walk through my door is run to the bathroom and throw up.

Nausea has been slowly creeping in, but this is the first time I've actually felt sick enough to need the toilet. After I'm done, I sit with my back against the tub and lean my face against the cool tile of the bathroom wall like I've done many a night after drinking a little too much. It seems appropriate. Being pregnant with Chase's baby feels exactly like a hangover after partying a little too hard.

Partying *a lot* too hard.

It's been a long day. A long, hard day. There's so much swimming in my brain. My head and my body have been in constant replay mode of our earlier encounter in the library. The dirty things. The sweet things. The break-down-my-walls things. *I've fallen for you. I want to give you me. I want to give you everything.*

But then, like I told Megan, I picture those two little boys without Officer Eaker, and those little faces look so much like Chase in my head and the walls around me build right back up.

The problem is I can't stay away from him.

And it seems, he can't stay away from me.

I know what I have to do. It's a bigger thing than I'd planned to do, but I was probably always naive to think there was any other way. If I can't put distance between Chase and me figuratively, I'll have to do it literally.

I let myself be miserable about it for the length of a good cry. Then I get up off the floor, brush my teeth, and go call my realtor to tell her I want to put my condo up for sale.

• • •

I awake the next morning to the sound of someone knocking on my door.

"Who the hell drops in?" I frustratingly ask the empty room. It's a worse offense than calling. Doesn't anyone just text anymore?

I consider pulling the covers over my head and ignoring my visitor, but I already have a good idea who it is.

And I should see him.

No matter how nauseated I am.

"Hold on," I shout, pulling on a pair of sweats to go with my sleep tank, and then I drag myself to the front door.

I check the peephole, and my breath catches when I see him. It's amazing how he does that to me every time I catch sight of him. He looks ragged, like he had a restless night's sleep. Still better than I look, I'm sure. I don't need a mirror to see that my eyes are puffy and red rimmed, and though I don't need to throw up, I'm probably pale from the morning sickness.

Well, this is me. No use pretending it's not.

I've barely opened the door when he's pleading with me.

"Don't shut the door. Please. I need to talk to you."

I never planned on shutting the door, but his desperation pulls at pieces of my heart that are weary from being pulled at. It makes me hesitate. Maybe meeting with him right now isn't the best idea.

Except, that's not fair. Because even though this conversation is going to be hard, he deserves to have it. He deserves to say whatever he needs to say and hear me tell him directly that I'm leaving.

"I need to say things too. Come in." I open the door wider and step aside for him to walk past.

I lead him into the living room where the curtains are open and people can see in. I know that windows and an audience are probably not deterrents to getting my panties off, but it's a nice façade. It's also unnecessary. There's no way I'll end up wrapped around him today. It's not right to lead him on, and anyway, each time we're together it's harder for me to let him go.

Though I gesture for him to take a seat on the couch, he doesn't sit so we're both standing, our bodies fidgeting awkwardly. It's a small space, and the tense emotions between us don't have any room to dissipate. They gather tightly around us making the air thick and hard to breathe. My chest aches with how much I want to run and hide from this. It's almost as strong as the desire to wrap myself in his arms and let him tell me everything can be okay.

But I know he can't tell me that. He can't know everything will be okay.

Which is why I have to move.

I start to tell him. "Chase, I'm—"

"Please," he interrupts. "Let me go first."

It would be easier if he would just let me nip this in the bud, but it's too late for that, I suppose.

"Okay." I curl up on my armchair and tuck my feet underneath me. "Go ahead."

He's quiet for a while, seeming to study the titles of my books stacked in piles at the window. Though I've never felt uncomfortable in silence with Chase, I do now. I find myself wanting to fill it with apologies and explanations, and part of me wonders if this was his plan or if he's just trying to decide what to say.

Finally he talks. "I was in patrol before I was in traffic," he starts. "Two years. It's exactly the kind of job that you think it will be. Standard 9-1-1 calls. Checks on the elderly. Domestic violence. Lots of home burglaries and car burglaries. Every time you show up at a call, you know you're going to see the worst of people."

I'm not sure why he wants me to know this about him, but I give him my full attention, imagining how hard it would be to do the kind of work he's describing.

He wanders over to the window and looks outside. "Even when you're checking on a senior, if the person's not dead when you get there—which they sometimes are—there's still a reason why the cops have been called. The house smells. The yard's neglected. It's pretty grim when a person's gotten too old or demented to care for him or herself and there's no one to step in and figure out the next step but us."

After glancing at me, he points somewhere down the street. "I used to check on a senior that lived over there. Mrs. Heisdorffer. I helped her shovel snow. And I was the one who went in and found her body when the neighbor told us they hadn't seen her in a week."

My eyes burn, and I have to blink fast. "I had no idea. I'm so sorry."

"The first time I came here, you asked me what was wrong. Do you remember that?"

I nod.

"That was who I was thinking about. Mrs. Heisdorffer."

"You should have told me," I say, wishing sincerely that he had.

"There's that kind of story everywhere, though. Every street, every corner of the city holds an imprint. I couldn't unload all of that on you."

I want to argue, but it's probably pointless now. Still, I hate the hollow ache in my chest discovering he's kept a part of himself closed off from me. "It's not good for you to carry this all by yourself all the time," I say. "Please don't think you always have to."

"I talk to Pop sometimes," he says, and while I'm glad he has that comfort, the ache inside me intensifies knowing that it should have been me he leaned on. "It does start to wear on you. It gets under your skin and in your blood. You start to think it's all you are and all you're worth—the awful things you see, the terrible things that people do."

I uncurl, animated in my protest. "That's not all you are, Chase." There's not a bone of awful in him. Not a bit of awful, and I can't stand the thought that he thinks any different.

But he puts a hand out, silencing me. "You're right. And I'm getting there. I promise."

I frown and sigh. Then fold my knees up under me again, waiting for him to go on.

"It's better in traffic, I should tell you. But you're never pulling someone over to tell them they're an excellent driver. And there's a lot of accidents, Liv." He lowers his voice, soberly. "You see a lot of death."

"I can't imagine." Except, I can imagine. And that's what scares me—that I can so clearly imagine *his* death. "This isn't—"

"I know," he says, cutting me off. "I'm rambling, but I have a point." He turns and looks at me directly. "I was only twenty-two when I got out of the academy. I wasn't thinking about families or kids. And when it came time, when other guys started settling down and getting married, I couldn't understand how they were able to do that. How they could take everything awful that the job was and is and bring it home to a spouse, let alone kids.

"I decided I could never do that. I'd never have kids. I'd never have a wife. I made sure my life didn't allow for those things to even be options."

I inhale sharply. His declaration should make things better because we're both on the same page, but for some reason it hurts to hear him say it.

Quickly, I look away, desperate to hide my anguish. "That was a smart decision."

"No, that was a stupid decision, Liv." His sharp tone draws my focus back to him. "It was the stupidest decision, because I let the job define everything I am. But like you said, I'm more than that, kitten. I have more than that to give to you and to our kid—"

"Chase—" I warn. It's not *our* kid. It can't be.

He raises his voice to speak over me. "—and I'd forgotten that until I met you. But I remember now. You make me remember that I'm a whole person, and I want to be that whole person with you." He crosses to me and sits on the ottoman at my feet so he's close now. Too close. "I love you."

"Don't say that." But it's too late. He's said it and I heard it and it fills me everywhere like a light cast into a dark cellar. It's warm, his *I love you*, and I want to hold it and claim it and never let it go. I'll never unhear it now.

Still, I protest again, as if I can erase the echo still hanging in my condo. "Don't say that."

"Why?" he asks with patient frustration. "Because it will go away if you don't hear the words? I love you, and you can't change that. I love you, and it doesn't mean I'm not afraid. It means you're worth being afraid for."

He stretches out his hand and rests it on top of mine. "Be afraid with me, baby."

I want to. There's nothing more that I want than to be afraid in his arms.

But even with his touch burning into my skin, his words from before burn deeper. The descriptions of his job. The ways he has to shield himself from what he sees. The reminder that he's surrounded by death. Those words ring louder than the *I love you*s he's given so freely.

I know he's more than his job, and I yearn to be the one he can open up and share all of himself with, just…

I bolt from the chair, jumping over him to get away. To get distance. "I can't," I say, pacing the room.

He twists to face me. "Why not?"

"You weren't part of the plan. You're just a sperm donor." I wince at the hurt flickering in his eyes. It hurts me to say it, but he has to hear it. It's the truth.

He stands, unwilling to give up. "Can you tell me that you don't love me?"

No. I can't.

I shake my head. "It doesn't matter. This isn't about just me anymore. I can't be Jason Eaker's wife, trying to explain to my child why Daddy's not coming home tonight."

He takes a step toward me. "You think that cops are the only people who die? What about my mom? What about the young couple in the accident I worked on last week? They left behind four kids, Liv. There's no assurances no matter what."

I shake my head again, unable to deal with the words he's saying.

"I get it, baby. I do." His voice is a balm, soothing and soft. "You're scared and it's okay to be scared. But you're so afraid of losing the thing you want that you won't let yourself have it in the first place."

My face crumples, and I have to really work to fight back tears. It's all happening so fast—this baby, him. Us. It's too fast and I don't know how to process all of it at this speed, like I'm in a car and the brakes have gone out. I just want to pause and think.

Chase reaches for me, and my body leans toward him like metal pulled to a magnet.

But I catch myself before falling into his arms. "Don't. Just." I spin so I'm not facing him directly. "I need a minute."

I take off for the bathroom, not because I don't think he'll follow me there, but because it's the only room that has a lock.

And I need to pee. Always. Stupid hormones.

So I click the lock and sit down to do my business. Holding my head in my hands, I let the tears fall.

It's too much. All of this. Him. These emotions. This seed of a child inside me.

I can't even really get away from him the way I need to. He's always with me now, my pregnancy a constant reminder of Chase and what he's been to me. I've been stupid to think I can ever run away from him. I'm trapped now, forever attached to him, and while a part of me thinks that being forever with Chase is all I've ever needed, there's another part of me that's stuck in this other place. This lonely, terrifying, depressing *safe* place.

I don't know how to make this choice. What if I screw up? What if I choose wrong?

My head is still whirling as I finish up. I wipe and am about to flush when something catches my eye. Something very red and very bad. I wipe again to be sure it's not just mild spotting.

It's not mild spotting. It's blood. Too much blood.

And suddenly the reasons for the panic and terror and anxiety I've been feeling seem small and ridiculous and out of place, and new panic and terror bursts out of me in a shrill scream of just one word.

"Chase!"

19

CHASE

My body responds with an electric jolt, and I'm on my feet at the bathroom door in the space of a heartbeat. "Liv?"

Her voice is choked with panic when she answers. "I'm bleeding."

My own panic thrums through my chest, metallic and whirring. I've read enough pregnancy books by this point to know that this is really, really bad. And all I want to do is rush in there and cradle her in my arms and also call 9-1-1 and also just *fix it*, because that's what I do, I show up to a scene and fix things.

That's what I do.

And then a calm settles over me—not as detached as it would be on a call, but still rational, still capable and in control. I can handle an emergency. I'm an expert at emergencies, actually, and it's never mattered more than in this moment, when my heart is on the other side of a bathroom door from my body, bleeding and scared.

"Liv, I need to come in there. May I?"

"Hurry," she says, her voice quiet, and I hear the lock slide open. I open the door.

She's on the edge of her tub across from her cabinet, which is open and spilling forth a pastel pile of wrapped pads. She has one in her fist, but she's not moving to put it in her panties.

She's not moving at all.

I recognize the look in her eyes at once. It's the same look I see on the faces of people who've just been in car accidents, their bodies and thoughts still vibrating from the unexpected collision. The same look I see on the faces of family members when I tell them a loved one has died.

It's shock. The numb incomprehension before a great pain.

I squat down and brush her hair away from her face. "We have to go to the ER, sweetheart. We have to go right now."

She doesn't respond, except the trembling in her hands increases. I cover them with my own and get all the way to my knees. "I need you to be strong for the baby right now, okay?"

And for me, I want to add. But I don't, because it's my turn to be strong for her.

"Does it hurt?" I ask.

She shakes her head. "It feels like nothing. No pain. Just blood."

I breathe out a small sigh of relief. Bleeding is bad, but bleeding without cramping is slightly better. I've already mentally mapped routes to all the nearest hospitals, and decided it will actually take less time for me to take her in the Audi than to wait for an ambulance.

She finally looks at me, her eyes starting to gloss over. "What if the baby is dead?" she whispers. "What if I only got to have it for such a short time and it died?"

"Then we hold on to the feeling that we got to love a baby, no matter how briefly." I squeeze her hands and then I stand up, helping her stand too. "But this baby's not done fighting to live, and neither are you. Which is why we're going to the hospital right now."

She moves slowly, jerkily, like a marionette with tangled strings, but my words have roused her a little. "Should we call 9-1-1?" she asks as she unwraps the pad and puts it in her panties. It should feel nice that she's doing something so private in front of me, but it worries me instead. She must be terrified if she's letting her walls fall down, especially when she seemed so determined just five minutes ago to build even more walls between us.

"It'll take them longer to get to us and get us to an ER than it would be for us to drive ourselves. And they won't be able to do much for this kind of thing anyway."

She pulls up her pants and nods slowly. "Okay then."

I pull her into a tight hug. "Do you trust me?"

She nods against my chest. "Yeah. I do."

"Then I'm going to make it okay."

I take her hand and lead her out to my car, and she lets me.

. . .

I break almost every traffic law I know of on the drive to the hospital. At a safe speed, obeying all lights and stops, it would be a ten-minute drive. But with Liv silent and bleeding next to me and my hand gripping the gearshift like it's keeping us alive, I get to the hospital in less than five minutes. This ER has valet parking, thank fuck, because there's not a snowflake's chance in hell I'm leaving Livia alone even for as long as it takes me to park a car.

I pull up to the curb and climb out of the driver's seat, and I as I do, I feel the light bite of something against my thigh. The bite of something cold and small and hard in my jeans pocket, something I had the boys help me pick out last night. Something I brought with me to Liv's house this morning, back when I hoped…

The feel of it *now*, when Livia has so thoroughly shut me out and the pregnancy is in danger, is almost too much. A dagger twisting between the ribs.

After Liv is out of the car, I give my keys to the valet in exchange for a ticket. I recognize the triage nurse when we walk in.

"Officer Kelly," she says, surprised. "Don't usually see you without the uniform." And she's right—as the closest major ER to Prairie Village, I walk through these doors pretty frequently, usually on follow-up for accidents.

"It's not a good morning," I say, with the kind of understatement that is the first language of cops and trauma nurses.

She nods, looking past me to Liv, who is pale and quiet. "Let's get you triaged and in a room then."

There is the usual process of emergency rooms—blood pressure and temperatures and dates of last menstrual cycles and Livia repeating the same information over and over again. Yes, she's bleeding. Maybe a few tablespoons, maybe more. No, there's no pain.

Then there's a urine sample to leave, a short wait in the waiting room, and then the nurse comes in to bring Liv back to a room. I hesitate when we stand up from our waiting room chairs. I want nothing more than to go back with her—the need to is cell-deep, urging me to stay by the woman I love and our baby—but I have to respect Liv's wishes. Her need for walls and privacy.

And so I'm prepared for her to insist on doing this alone, just as she always has. I'm prepared for her to reject help, to her to tell me she doesn't need me. That's Livia Ward—lonely and beautiful and determined to suffer rather than open herself up enough to ask for help. I try to put on a mask of stoic acceptance, because I'm here for *her*, to be strong for *her*, and if that's what she needs, then I'll do it, no matter how much it slashes at me.

But that's not what happens.

Liv reaches for my hand and refuses to let go. She doesn't say anything, but the nurse's gaze flicks between us, assessing, and I can tell I'm already locked into the role of "baby's father" in her mind. If Liv doesn't say anything, the staff will assume that I'm welcome back there.

"Liv?" I ask. I try to sound solid, stable, but my heart is pounding. I want to go back there. I don't want Liv out of my sight for a second.

Liv doesn't answer, but she squeezes my hand.

I squeeze back, hoping it tells her all the things I can't. That I'll be by her side as long as she wants me, that I'm here for all the ugly and scary parts. That I'm here to be strong for her.

"If you guys will just follow me," the nurse says.

Liv and I walk together back to the room, Liv leaning into me. I have to remind myself that it doesn't mean all the things I want it to mean, it just means that Liv wants someone with her right now, not that she's moved on from all the things we talked about earlier this morning.

But God, I want it to mean everything.

It's a Sunday morning, and so the ward is as quiet as I've ever seen it, but Livia still seems a little overwhelmed by the slow bustle of nurses and techs wheeling machines around and the low sound of someone moaning from a room. I've been in this ER with my hand clamped over a woman's gashed artery, I've tackled violent drunks who've attacked nurses here, I've accepted a stale donut from a nurse while we watched the other nurses forcibly catheterize a man who refused to willingly leave a urine sample after he mowed down an elderly man gardening by his sidewalk.

I'm not overwhelmed by the Sunday Morning ER.

We get into her room and the nurse asks her to change into a gown, and then whisks out through the weirdly patterned curtain all ER rooms seem to have. Liv takes a deep breath and then another one, and before she can ask, I put my hand on the curtain to leave too so she can dress in privacy.

"Stay," she says quietly. "Please."

My chest collapses inward with a pained gratitude. "Of course."

I still turn to give her space as she dresses, and then I feel a small tap on my arm.

"Will you help me with the ties in back?" she asks, and there's a note of something in her voice that adds to the collapsing-with-gratitude feeling. Like she's asking for something more than having her gown tied. Like she's admitting she doesn't want to do everything on her own any more.

Like she's admitting that she wants me.

I try to squash these thoughts down and seal them away. The only thing that matters right now is being strong for her, being whatever she needs. And right now, that's having her gown tied.

After I tie it, she arranges herself on the bed, and I step forward to unfold the blanket, which is still warm from the mysterious blanket warmer hospitals have. She looks up at me in surprise as I silently spread it over her legs, and then a look of relief and comfort passes over her face.

"Thank you," she murmurs. "Feels nice."

I squeeze her knee, but I don't answer. I don't know if I can. There's so much in the air between us right now—the painful things I admitted to her, her rejection of me, the danger the pregnancy is in. The thing in my pocket that she doesn't know about.

After a minute or two of silence, she says, "I have something for you. In my purse."

Now, it's my turn to be surprised. "A present?"

She blushes a little. "Well, no. It's a library book. I checked it out in your name."

That sends a weak chuckle through me, and the way her eyes brighten at my laugh and smile remind me of how little I've smiled today. I smile again as I stand to get her purse and I'm rewarded with a small smile of hers.

"It's the gray book," she comments as I open her purse to see that she has not one but three library books wedged inside. A glow warms my chest at the sight. Livia working in a library is like an alcoholic working in a liquor store. Except it's so fucking adorable, I can't stand it. My bookworm. My librarian.

I get the gray book and go back to my chair, flipping through it. It's a book of poems, and even though I generally don't read poems unless they're in the middle of an epic fantasy novel, there's something about these that capture my attention right away. They aren't the choppy poems about plums I had to read in college or the dense rhymey-rhymey sonnets from high school. There's a music in the words that leaps off the page, a playful melody and force of vision that capture me right away.

"It's Dylan Thomas," Liv says, as I flip through the pages.

"The 'Do Not Go Gentle' guy?" I realize that maybe I did read him in college after all, but I think I was too busy hitting on the TA to absorb much of the actual poetry.

"Yes," she says. "And also he was an alcoholic and chronically unfaithful and not a little emotionally manipulative. But his words are magic. And this last week, after Officer Eaker died, I thought of his poems. How they're sad and somehow energizing at the same time. He writes about death the way it should be written about."

I'm tracing the words of the last poem in the book as she talks. The poem is called "Fern Hill" and it's as musical and poignant as all the others, but it's the last two lines that capture me, that make me feel sad and trapped and happy and free all at once.

I read them aloud, for no other reason than I need to. "'Time held me green and dying/though I sang in my chains like the sea.'"

"That's what we are," Liv whispers. "Green and dying. All at once. Both."

I look up, feeling the words and something else coursing through my veins. "Green and dying," I echo.

"I think I've been thinking about the *dying* more than the *green*," she admits with a rueful twist of her mouth. "And maybe it's weird to feel different now, with the bleeding and everything that could go wrong, but I want to sing in my chains like the sea too. I don't want to be afraid anymore." She puts her hand low on her belly and I know she's thinking of the fear we both have right now, that our baby might not make it. That we might never get to meet the new life we created together.

"The collection is called *Deaths and Entrances*," she continues. "Somehow that feels more important than calling it *Deaths and Births*. Like maybe new things aren't just births, but new chances. New people."

My heart is thudding in my throat because I think I know what she's building herself up to saying, and I want her to say it; I need her to say it more than I've needed anything in my life.

She swallows and meets my eyes, her eyes that dark, rich liquid color I can't fucking resist. "Chase, I—"

Before she can finish, the curtain yanks sharply to the side and someone in scrubs is wheeling a sonography machine into the room. Livia closes her mouth, pressing her lips together as if whatever words she was going to say are still fighting to get out. If it weren't for my gut-deep fear about the baby, I would shove the machine and its tech outside and make her finish, because I have to know what she was going to say. I have to know how she feels, and living any longer with this uncertain agony twisting in my ribs might actually kill me.

The sono tech, oblivious to the strained silence she created, hums to herself as she sets everything up. Then she turns to me with a polite smile that is more "no-nonsense" than it is polite, really.

"Do you mind stepping out so we can have some privacy?" she asks.

I glance at Liv, who still looks caught in the moment of trying to talk to me, and then with as much grace as I can muster while my heart is tearing itself out of its chest, I stand up to go.

I'm just the sperm donor, after all.

"He can stay," Liv says softly, and I freeze. She clears her throat so she's louder. "I want him to stay."

There's a pause, and then she adds with a shy smile, "He's the father."

Her eyes meet mine, and I don't think I'm imagining the shine to her eyes, but it's kind of hard to tell because my own eyes are burning, probably just allergies or the gusty air conditioning or—

Ah, fuck it. Yes, I'm crying.

I'm the father.

The sono tech shrugs as she rolls a condom onto the sonography wand. I tearfully frown at it as I pull a chair up next to Liv's bed. "What's that for?" I ask.

Both women give me patronizing smiles. "It's for the ultrasound, dummy," Liv tells me.

I've seen people torn open on the pavement, I've seen EMTs jam giant syringes into near-comatose diabetics, I've felt someone's sternum crack as I administered CPR, but my ultrasound knowledge is extremely limited. "I thought ultrasounds happened on your stomach?"

The tech laughs and squirts a glob of clear lube onto the wand with a loud *ffffbbbbbbtttt* noise. "Not this early in the pregnancy. It's going in the same place where the baby got made."

I'm horrified. I don't remember the baby books *or* Megan mentioning anything about rapey ultrasounds, and just...*why?*

But Liv is completely nonplussed as the tech hands her the wand to guide it inside herself under the sheet. Her face screws up to one side, as if it's uncomfortable, and I feel the urge to fix it somehow, but before I can speak, the wand is inside Liv and the machine's screen comes to life with clouds of black and white static.

I have no idea what the hell I'm looking at, whether it's good or bad, but the sono tech taps on her keyboard and moves the wand and adjusts the knobs and suddenly a dark oval appears. A dark empty oval.

Liv's breath sucks in and so does mine. I know empty means vacant. Empty means bad.

I take her hand and hold it tight. I'm here with her no matter what, and no matter what, we'll make it through this. Green and dying, deaths and entrances.

Then the sonographer moves the wand just a little more, and I see it. A little bean curled up in a sea of dark, and then a *whomp-whomp-whomp* sound comes through the machine.

"There's the heartbeat," the sonographer says with a smile. "Baby is doing just fine in there."

"Oh thank God," I breathe.

Next to me, Liv bursts into tears.

The tech takes a few pictures and then adjusts some more knobs and moves the wand again. The baby bean with its strong heartbeat disappears and reappears on the screen, like a picture coming in and out of focus. But the third time it happens, there's something else on the screen too, next to our baby bean. In fact, it looks like nothing more than a second baby bean, suspended upside down in Livia's belly, thinking little, silent baby bean thoughts.

Liv and I look at each other with wide eyes and then back to the screen.

Whomp-whomp-whomp goes the machine again.

"And there's the second heartbeat," the sonographer says, as if it's the most casual thing in the world. "You're having twins."

20

LIVIA

"Twins?" The word feels wrong in my mouth, as though I've mispronounced it or said the wrong thing all together.

But I see the picture on the screen as clear as anything, and even if I didn't, the ultrasound technician confirms it. "Twins. Let me take some measurements and then I'll print some pictures for you to take with you."

I know my eyes are wide when I turn to Chase. "Twins," I say, dazed.

His knee is bouncing with nervous energy and his hand is clutching mine as tightly as mine's clutching his, but his entire face is lit with excitement. "Twins, Liv! Told you I had super sperm."

A giggle escapes through the bubble of terror that has surrounded me since I first saw the blood. "Exactly. This is your fault." I giggle again. I can't stop giggling as I return my gaze to the monitor. Back to my babies.

"What?" Chase asks, chuckling too.

"I'm just…" It's hard to talk over the fit of giggles. It's even harder to explain this incredible, overwhelming, brutally tender joy that I'm feeling. "I'm just happy," I say, finally, tears brimming at my eyes.

"Yeah," Chase says reverently. "Me too."

The tech types something into the computer. "It looks like Baby One is measuring at seven weeks two days and Baby Two is measuring at seven weeks exactly. So, based on that, we'd say you're seven weeks one day along."

I mentally pull up my calendar app in my head. "I've kept accurate records. I should be just shy of seven weeks."

"Our measurements might be off, but it's also likely that you ovulated earlier than you thought you did."

I look at Chase. "The patrol car."

"Seriously?" He lowers his voice though the room is small enough the tech can probably hear him anyway. "Neighborhood Hot Cop knocked you up?"

I giggle again at the name of the game we'd played that night. "Yep. Neighborhood Hot Cop knocked me up."

Then I have to turn away and bite my lip so I don't start crying again in earnest because, goddammit, I love this hot cop. More than I've ever wanted to admit. And today he's been perfect, in every way. I was so scared, and Chase was calm and stable and everything I needed. He was the only person I wanted beside me, and as I sit here looking at our twin baby peanuts, I can't imagine not having him beside me for all of the rest of it.

I want to tell him, and I will, but before I can figure out what to say, the sonographer is handing us a strip of black and white print-outs of our twin embryos and packing up her ultrasound machine.

"The doctor will be in soon to talk to you," she says as she leaves.

Chase looks over my shoulder as I study the grainy pictures of our babies. They're barely anything right now. Just little specks, but they have hearts and kidneys and stumps that will soon be legs and arms. And already I'm so in love with them I can barely hold all I feel inside.

"They're so beautiful." I wish I knew what he was thinking. If he still wanted me now that I was bringing two babies to the relationship. "Don't you think they're beautiful?"

"Well." He squints at the lima bean shapes.

I laugh. "They're going to look more baby-like eventually."

"They better. Or we're going to have a hell of a time telling them apart." He grows serious. "But, yes, I think they're beautiful. Like their mom. How are you feeling about two of them?"

Isn't that the question of the hour? It's overwhelming, but I already can't think of them as anything but a pair.

"I want them. I love them. It's not what I planned, that's for sure." I sigh and look up at him. "You weren't what I planned either."

He seems about to say something, but the curtains swing open and in walks a petite woman in a white lab coat, a stethoscope around her neck and a patient chart in her hand.

"Hi, I'm Dr. DeMaio," she says quickly, as though she has places to be. "You're Livia Ward?"

She confirms my identity and birth date and then says, "I've had a chance to look at your ultrasound results and everything looks fine with both babies. One of the placentas is forming rather close to the cervix, so my guess is that's why we saw some bleeding today. But that's nothing that has to be scary, and some light bleeding early in pregnancy can be normal. We'll just want to keep an eye on it, and worst-case scenario, you might find yourself on bed rest for a while. So follow up with your OB this week for regular prenatal care and also to talk to them about the low placenta, and that should take care of you. Any questions?"

I'm so grateful that the babies are okay, and still in shock that I have more than one baby inside me, that I can't really think of any questions off the top of my head. "I see my OB on Tuesday. I'm sure if I have any questions, I can ask then."

"I have a question," Chase says tentatively.

Dr DeMaio looks to me before she nods for him to go ahead.

"Is the bleeding…? Could this have been caused because…?" He can't seem to form the question the way he wants. Finally he blurts it out. "Was this from sex?"

My face goes warm, but when I look at him, I see nothing but concern, and I realize he's worried that our rough sex in the library might have harmed our babies.

"Certainly there can be light bleeding immediately after intercourse," Dr. DeMaio says without blinking. "But that's normal and nothing to be alarmed about. Intercourse during pregnancy is safe unless a doctor tells you otherwise."

Chase starts to ask something else, but the doctor guesses what it is and adds, "And I'm a doctor, and I'm not telling you otherwise."

"Got it." His shoulders relax. "Thanks, Doc."

I roll my eyes, but really I'm relieved too. Not because I was worried that sex had endangered my pregnancy—I'd known it was fine—but because Chase is asking about the future.

Which means that he's still thinking about a future. Together.

The next half hour passes in a buzz of activity. Nurses and technicians come in to unhook me from the vitals machine and go over discharge paperwork and insurance information. Finally, I'm dressed, the pics of the babies are tucked in my purse, and we're ready to leave.

When we walk out of the ER, Megan is in the waiting room. Her eyes are pinned on the doors so she sees us right away and waves us over.

"I texted her," Chase admits guiltily. From his expression, I can tell he's worried he mis-stepped. Or he's worried about us, about where we stand right now, and that's fair. I'm worried too. We have a lot to worry about.

So he doesn't need to worry about this too. "I'm glad you texted her," I tell him honestly.

She's fidgeting like it's taking all she has not to run to us. But she's tentative too, unsure what we've found out about my pregnancy, whether it's good news or bad.

I put my hand on my belly instinctively and lead the way over to her.

"Is everything going to be okay? With the baby?" Megan asks softly, as though loud words might wake our sleeping fetus.

"Yes. I'm all good," I say, and she audibly sighs in relief as she hugs me tightly. "I have to keep an eye on it, but light bleeding can be normal, according to the doctor."

"It can be totally normal. I had light bleeding with Keon and the kid got here with no other problems. In fact, I spotted through the whole entire nine months. It can be terrifying, but just wait. This is only the beginning. There's a ton of other terrifying shit that can happen. Did I tell you about what happened when I was still pregnant with—"

"Megan!" Chase exclaims. He waits for her attention before he says, "Not the time."

"Probably should save those stories for after I give birth. I kind of scare easily." I gaze up at the brave man at my side. "Or, I did."

He smiles, just a little, and the way he gazes back down at me could melt an iceberg of fear.

Megan notices our mooning, but she doesn't address it outright. "Sure, sure. Wasn't thinking. But! I brought you a present. I was saving this for your baby shower, but it seems like a good time to give it to you now. It just came yesterday. I had to special order it."

She digs through her purse and pulls out a baby onesie and holds it up so we can both read it. *I know a lot but my aunt knows everything.*

"Uh…aunt?" I'm not sure if that's what she's coined herself or if Chase has already told her.

"Yeah, Livia. *Aunt.*" She points at me. "Because I know you pretty well." Then she points at Chase. "And I sure as hell know him. And there's no way this baby isn't his. He's been moony-eyed and dazed since the minute he brought the kids to the library, out of the blue, on a weeknight to hunt down the cutie he'd met on a call. So, yes. I'm an aunt. And I know everything. Admit it."

"I'll admit you're kind of a bitch," Chase says, seemingly as irritated as I am that she's figured out our secret.

"Well, you don't know *everything*," I scowl. "And you're going to have to get a second one."

Megan's eyes dart from mine to her brother's. "I'm not following."

I nod to Chase. He should be the one to tell her. She's his sister and these are his babies.

He lights up when he says it. "We're having twins."

It sounds so good to hear him say *we*. Like it's natural. Like there couldn't be any other way, and there couldn't be. He was always meant to be their dad. From the very beginning, I picked him partly because he was so amazing with Josiah and Keon and even Ryan, and no matter how many times I told myself it was because I simply wanted those good genes in my child, the truth is, part of me always imagined him like that with our kid. Snuggling our kid against his chest, pulling our kid in a wagon, taking our kid to the library. Helping our kid with homework.

Now I just have to expand the fantasy to include two kids.

And me. If he'll still have me.

We spend the next several minutes talking about the babies and their health and what I'm supposed to do over the next few weeks, which mostly ends up being Megan telling us what she thinks I should do based on her own experiences with her pregnancies. Finally Chase suggests that we should leave the medical advice to the doctors, and she gets huffy and says she should go and check on Pop then since no one else is looking after him at the moment and at least there her advice is wanted.

"Tolerated," Chase corrects.

Her eyes narrow, but before she can explode, I bring her in for another hug. "I want your advice, Megan. All of it. Not today, maybe, but I'm coming to you for everything."

"I'm glad you were into my brother," she says when she pulls away, her eyes glossy. "Or rather, I'm glad you let my brother be into you."

"Alrighty then!" Chase pushes her not so gently toward the doors. "See ya later, sis."

"I'm glad too," I call after her. "Thank you for coming to the hospital. And for the onesie!"

"Yes. Thank you, Megan," my hot cop shouts before turning to me.

Then we're alone.

Well, not exactly alone, because there's all sorts of people buzzing around us—

other patients and nurses and doctors and a security guard and these two little peanuts wrapped snugly in my womb with heartbeats so strong I got to hear them with my own ears.

But it's alone enough to feel the weight of all the unsaid things we carried into the hospital with us this morning. Silently, we stare at each other, with these boulders of unspoken words on our backs, and it doesn't feel awkward, but it feels heavy. Like we're both carrying such a tremendous load, and both of us are so sure that there has to be a way to make it lighter. If we can just find a way to carry it together.

I'm the one who speaks first, since I think it's my turn. I throw the ball right back at him though because I'm braver than I was, but not that brave. Yet. I still need him to guide me. Still need him to help me be strong. "So what now?"

Obviously he's going to give the ticket to the valet and they'll bring his car around and that's what's now.

But that's not what I'm asking, and I think he knows it, because he doesn't answer right away. He puts his hands in his pockets and rocks back and forth on the balls of his feet. "Well," he says, stalling. "I think you get to choose your own adventure."

"Um. Okay?" I tilt my head, imploring him to go on.

"When I was a kid, I loved those books. You know, the ones where you read a few pages and then at the bottom it says, 'If you want to rescue the princess, go to page 74; if you want to stay and fight the boss, go to page 58'?"

"Yes," I say smugly. "I know those books."

"Right. You know books." He chuckles. "Anyway. Right now, you get to choose your own adventure. You can either have me drive you back to your home, and you can do this all on your own. Raise two kids with as much or as little help from me as you want. I can be there for them if you let me. None of your choosing has to be about them."

"Or." He takes a nervous step toward me. "You can let me

drive you to my house so we can tell Pop together that he's going to have to stop being stubborn and take my bedroom. And then I can move my girl and my babies in with me where they belong. There's a master and two bedrooms upstairs, Liv. It's perfect for all of us."

My breath catches and there's a ball in my throat the size of my heart. I have so much to say and don't know where to start, and I'm not even sure I can speak coherently, but I try anyway.

"The thing I wanted to tell you earlier, at my condo…" I swallow, trying to find my voice because what's coming out sounds small and shaky, not like mine at all. "I thought I needed to be as far away from you as possible. I couldn't be around you and not want you. So I called a realtor last night to put my place up for sale. I was going to move."

They have to be hard words to hear, but his gaze remains steady and hopeful. "And now?"

"I guess I'll still need the realtor. If I'm moving in with you and all."

My eyes are wet and cloudy, but I can still see Chase perfectly when, in front of everyone in the ER waiting room, he falls to his knees in front of me. Well, one knee.

"What are you doing? Get up!" But my heart is racing and I'm really crying now and there's no way I actually want him to get up because he's digging into his pocket and pulling out a diamond solitaire ring.

"Liv, marry me. Raise our babies with me. Grow old with me and watch bad movies with me and talk dead poets with me and go shopping with me and watch the KU games with me. Let me love you and make love to you and hold you when you're scared." He grabs my hand and clutches onto it. "Hold *me* when I'm scared. Be afraid with me."

I wipe tears off my face with my free hand, but it's useless. New ones replace the ones I've removed. "You're really ready to trade in the Kelly trio for a Ward trio?" I glance down at my belly in case he doesn't understand what the Ward trio refers to—

or *who*, rather.

"How do you know about the Kelly—" He realizes where I must have heard it. "Megan," he mutters, like a curse under his breath. "And yes, I'd trade anything for the Ward trio. Everything."

"Actually, I think we could keep the Kelly trio." I step in closer so I can bend and whisper at his ear. "As long as I'm the one that gets the dinner, drinks, and handcuffs."

"Only you, kitten." He lets go of my hand and wraps his arms around me.

I run my fingers through his hair. "And I'll tear up that stupid contract."

His eyes twinkle gently. "Oh Liv. That contract was never real anyway."

"What do you mean?"

"You're a fantastic librarian, but you'd make a terrible lawyer."

"But you signed it anyway?"

"I was going to honor your wishes no matter what I did or didn't sign, so it didn't matter to me and it seemed important to you," he says. His eyes twinkle more. "Also, I really, really wanted to sleep with you."

I pout—I put a lot of time into that contract—but he kisses me so I can't hold it for long. When he lets me breathe again, he meets my eyes. "So…is all that a yes?"

I'm nodding when I answer. "I choose you, Chase. I choose the adventure. I'm tired of being scared and alone and safe. I've been so afraid of dying, I've forgotten to live. I want to be alive and green with you. I love you so much."

Then he's kissing me again, and he's so happy he stands up and takes me with him. My feet dangle off the ground while he kisses me and kisses me, but then we have to stop kissing because we've drawn a crowd and no one knows yet what I've answered until Chase sets me down and shouts, "She said 'yes'!"

Our onlookers clap and cheer. A few know Chase personally and they call out specific congratulations, but it all fades into background noise as he takes my hand and slides the ring onto my finger.

"I love you, Livvy-kitten," he says, his gaze hot on my face as I stare at my new beautiful diamond. "And I love you." He bends to kiss my belly. Then he kisses it again. "And I love you."

His eyes return to mine. "I can't promise I know the future, but I can promise I'll do everything I can to protect and keep you safe. All of you."

"All of *us. You* too. Don't do any stupid cop things, okay?" I know that's his job and it's important to him, but I want him to know that his life is important to me.

"No stupid cop things. Only regular cop things." He runs his knuckles reassuringly down the side of my neck. "I'm a safe cop, Liv. The people I'm supposed to help come first, but after them, I'll do everything I can to make sure I come home to you."

"I know you will." I don't know what will happen in the future either, and it's still scary, but I trust him. And I love him. And that's worth being afraid for. Our little family is worth being afraid for.

I gaze down at my ring again and suddenly can't wait to show the rest of our family. Megan and Pop, at least, are waiting back at his house. "Let's go home now, okay?"

"'Home,'" he says, closing his eyes as he drags out the "mm." "That sounds good when you say it."

It sounds good when he says it too. Like we've chosen it together. Like we're both turning to the same page in our very own *Choose Your Own Adventure*.

And I already know it's going to be the best story I've ever lived.

EPILOGUE

CHASE

One Year Later

"Fuck, that's nice," I grunt, sliding my cock into Livia's waiting mouth. "Suck it good, baby."

My wife obeys with an eagerness that makes my balls tight, closing her lips around me and pulling me deep. I push in until I feel her throat, savor the slick and soft heat of it, and then pull back out to admire my kitten. I've got her handcuffed to the bed, flat on her back with her handcuffed wrists secured to the headboard and her ankles tied to the edges of the footboard, spreading her so she's nice and open for me. Her tits, ripe and full, jut up towards the ceiling, and her hips squirm as her cunt aches with empty agony. I've given her an orgasm with my tongue and then another one with a wand vibrator tonight, intentionally starving her of my fingers and my cock for this exact purpose. To make her insane with need.

"Chase," she breathes, blinking up at me and still squirming. "Please."

"You want to be fucked, sweetheart?"

She groans in response, throwing her head back, which only serves to push her tits up higher. Now it's my turn to groan, and I run a finger from one peaked nipple down to a quivering thigh.

278

The moment my fingertip brushes the sensitive crease between her thigh and her cunt, she cries out.

"Yeah, you need it bad," I say in a low voice. I give her inner thigh a smart smack and then move myself in between her legs. "All tied up and begging for it."

She tries to lift her hips to get closer to my cock, which is hanging like a heavy pipe as I lean over her, the head swollen and slick with pre-cum. "Don't tease me," she says in a moan, "Chase, fuck me with it, please, please, please."

The truth is that I'm the one who's really needing it bad. It's been pure torture tonight to pleasure her without coming myself. But that's okay because I'm here now, my crown kissing the wet heat of her pussy, and I'm going to hold her hips down and fuck her until we break the bed.

With a few small adjustments, I'm thrusting into her pussy, and I'm about to black out it feels so good. "Fuck," I gasp. "Your cunt is so fucking tight."

Livia's smile is half pride, half mischief. She angles her hips up, and I go so deep I hear angels sing.

"Harder," she breathes with a big, happy smile. "Go harder."

I do, fucking into her like an animal, hard and fast and deep, feeling my balls draw up tight as her belly starts to flush and her thighs start to clench—

A loud, angry wail crackles through the baby monitor on the end table. We both freeze, sweaty and high with sex hormones.

Another angry wail, now joined by a sleepier, more confused cry. Underneath me, a small drop of milk runs down the side of Livia's breast. I glance down at us, my cock still throbbing and hungry, her cunt stretched wide around it, her all mussed and sweaty and tied up with her tits now leaking milk for our babies.

And I laugh. My balls ache, yes, but we're ridiculous and sweaty and milky and hornier than teenagers because between two needy twins—and a grandfather who's only just moved into a senior living apartment in the last week—real, unfettered fucking has been hard to come by. Most nights we're lucky if we can sneak in a quickie in the shower. But tonight, by some miracle, the twins had fallen asleep early and we thought maybe we could make up for some lost time…

Rookie mistake.

But I wouldn't trade this life for anything, not the crying or the cock-blocking babies or the days so busy and packed with laundry and spit-up and washing breast pumps and bottles that Liv and I barely have time to climb under the covers before we're asleep. It's all so fucking precious to me.

So it's with a smile that I lean down and lick the drop of milk off Liv's breast. She shivers. "Tell me we'll finish this," she says, looking up at me with needy eyes.

"We'll finish this," I promise in a husky voice, giving her tit one last lick. "Do you want me to uncuff you first?"

She sighs and shakes her head. "Angie's too hungry to wait. Put her in bed with me so she can start eating while you get me untied."

We both groan as I slide out of her, and then I go find a pair of pajama pants. "Be right back, babe."

Angie's worked herself up to a five-alarm fire by the time I walk into the nursery. She's just gotten the knack of sitting up on her own, and right now she's sitting in the middle of crib, chubby fists clenched in fury, screaming. I flick on a light and heft the chunk up into my arms, where her screaming abates—a little. She knows I'm transportation to Mommy and therefore extends me the grace of lowering her bellows the tiniest bit.

I can't resist giving her a little squeeze—she's like a stuffed sausage in her footie pajamas—and giving the blonde curls on her head a big kiss. Then with the ease born of lots and lots and lots (did I mention lots?) of practice, I carry her over to the other crib and scoop Dylan out with one hand, so that I've got both babies tucked into my elbows.

Dark-haired Dylan Emmett—named after my father and Pop—snuggles in tight to my chest and makes a sleepy fuss of protest at his sister's continued wailing. And Angela Marie—

named after my mother and my gran—shoves a chunky fist into her mouth and starts noisily sucking on it, alternating her screams with fist-sucks, as if to say, *see? See what you've reduced me to by starving me so cruelly?*

I croon to her wordlessly as I hitch Dylan up a little higher and we go to find Mommy. Once Angie sees her, she starts kicking frantically in my arms, reaching for Livia like Livia is the only thing in the world that matters. And hey, I know the feeling— aside from these two squishes, Livia is my entire world too.

I set Dylan down in a bouncy chair, turn the vibrations and songs on with the edge of my foot against the switch, and then set Angie on the bed facing Livia, who's got enough give in her restraints that she can mostly lie on her side.

Angie's screams turn into angry grunts as she roots for Liv's nipple and latches on. A pudgy hand comes up and starts flexing possessively over Livia's breast, and Angie looks up at me with narrowed eyes as she starts nursing in earnest, as if I'm to blame for the delay in her getting fed.

Which I kind of am.

"Sorry, girly," I tell her as I start uncuffing Liv. "Daddy really needed to fuck Mommy."

"Chase," Liv scolds, but she's smiling. I rub her wrists where the cuffs have turned them red and then move to her ankles. Soon, I've got her completely free and covered up with a soft blanket, Angie tucked into her arms and still nursing with the occasional grunt.

Now I rescue Dylan from his bouncy chair. He's wide awake now but totally calm, and he stares at me with deep blue eyes as I change his diaper and then sit with him in the glider, cuddling him close. He's just as squishy as his sister but less demanding, happy to wait his turn in my arms.

Liv looks across the room at me, her eyes warm. "You're so sexy when you're holding a baby. Especially all shirtless like that."

I grin at her. "You're so sexy all the fucking time. No matter what."

She rolls her eyes and drops her gaze to our daughter, who is finally starting to slow down on the milk. "Liar."

But it's true. She was a bombshell wearing leggings and a T-shirt when we first met. Even more of a bombshell on our wedding day, five months pregnant and glowing in a tight lace gown that showed off every gorgeous curve. She was even more beautiful on the day the twins were born, sweet and nervous and stubborn on the operating table, dark tendrils of hair escaping her puffy blue cap.

And now she's the sexiest of all to me. I know she doesn't believe me when I tell her that, but I've never gotten harder for her than I do now, never been as obsessed with her body, never needed to have her so close to me and never needed so much to lavish her with kisses and caresses. She's softer now, her belly streaked with stretch marks and carved with a low dark scar, and even though she's shy about her tummy, I'm in awe of her every time I see it. In awe of her strength, of her body growing and carrying *two* entire lives inside it. And okay, yes, there's some fucked up male pride involved. She carried *my* babies, and every reminder of that makes me want to tackle her and get her pregnant again.

It's not all that abstract, though. She smells different, intoxicating. Her skin itself is addictingly soft. Her tits are full and ripe and spill over my hands when I try to hold them. Seeing her curled around one of our babies as she nurses sends bolts of pure elemental lust through me. It's all caveman, the urge to protect her and our babies and also to plant more babies inside her.

Add to that the fact that I'm totally fucking in love with her, and it's a heady mix.

I can tell by the deep baby snores coming from the bed that Angie has finally filled her little belly, and I stand up and help Liv swap out babies. She rolls over to give Dylan a fresh breast and snorts at the Angie lump in my arms, who is now passed out harder than any drunk I've ever seen.

"Oh, I forgot to ask," Liv says as I change the sleeping Angie's diaper. "Wasn't today the first day with the body cameras on the streets?"

I smile. Our plan from last year had worked, and we had almost a thousand signatures on the petition, almost double what we needed to convince the chief. The money took a little longer to scare up, but with a couple of federal grants and a bulk discount from the local supplier, it finally happened. "Yeah. It was totally uneventful and therefore perfect."

Liv smiles back at me. "Good. The fair worked."

"The fair worked for more than that," I say, shooting her a hot look. She flushes, and I don't have to be a mind-reader to know she's thinking of our heated rendezvous in the stacks…the rendezvous that triggered so much. Heartbreak and honesty and need.

When I think of that day, the way my chest had been filled with what felt like a mixture of broken glass and hope as I picked out an engagement ring, I can't help but think that I wouldn't change any of it. And I don't mean just that day—I mean all of it: the contract and the longing and the uncertainty. How could I want to change even the tiniest thing when it led to this? Two fat, adorable babies and a smart sexy woman in my bed?

"Chase," Liv whispers softly. "I think Dylan might be asleep too."

Thank you, patron saint of hungry twins and also the patron saint of alone time for Mommy and Daddy.

Within a few moments, I've got both babies snoozing in their cribs, and I'm back in bed with my wife, pajama pants off and long forgotten.

"You know…" I tease, as I run a hand over Liv's body. "You turned thirty a couple of months ago, and I haven't heard you once talk about how you're turning into a living zombie. I think you might have gotten over your fear of dying."

Liv arches underneath my touch, a naughty smile on her face as she reaches down for my cock and pumps it until it's stone-hard again. "I found the cure for my fear."

I grab her hips and pull her on top of me, jabbing into her soft cunt and savoring her gentle moan as she sinks down to the hilt. "Is the cure my dick? Or my super, Captain America sperm that gives you squishy soon-to-be avengers for justice?"

She laughs, leaning down to kiss me. "No, Mr. Officer Blue Eyes. The cure for fear of dying is *living*. You taught me that."

Her words cut me in the best of ways, warm me until I think my entire body might melt from loving this woman.

"Fuck, I love you, Livia," I breathe, my eyes pinned on hers.

"I love you, hot cop. And I swear to God if you don't finish what you started earlier tonight, I'm going to die for real." She scratches her nails down my abs to underscore her point.

And then I'm out of jokes, out of playfulness.

And there's only sweat and kisses and adoration as we *live* late, late, late into the night.

Want more Chase and Livia? Sign up at
http://www.subscribepage.com/HotCopback
for our newsletters and get a bonus wedding night scene
sent straight to your inbox. If you're already signed up
for our lists, please sign up again! It's the only way to
get the Hot Cop bonus scene!

ACKNOWLEDGEMENTS

Hot Cop was a fun, delightful romp to write, but it still wouldn't be possible without lots of love and support from our community.

First of all, giant hugs and kisses to our agent, Rebecca Friedman, who is there to hold our hands when we're wailing, dispense wisdom when we're stumped, and just overall be our writing guardian angel.

Also, our foreign agents, Flavia Viotti and Meire Dias of Bookcase Literary, for being our champions across the world!

Second, our publicist Jenn Watson of Social Butterfly PR. Somehow you manage to coax us, soothe us, advise us, and all while keeping a thousand plates spinning. You're the bee's knees, baby! And all the other gorgeous faces at Social Butterfly—Candi Kane, Nina Grinstead, Kathy Snead Williams, and Autumn Davis—we would not be able to do this without your constant dedication to promotion, scheduling, networking and inventiveness. Thank you!

Thirdly, to Sara Eirew for another brilliant, sexy cover, and to Nancy Smay of Evident Ink for being our sharp eye, our voice of reason, and the ever-constant cheerleader.

Fourthly, to our team—Ashley Lindemann, Candi Kane, Melissa Gaston, and Serena McDonald. Ladies. You are the only reason we have time and energy to write. Thank you for eternity for working hard to keep the real world at bay while we disappear to write.

Fifthly, our CPs and betas and people who listen to us fuss and whine and pat us on the head. Kayti McGee and Melanie Harlow—you two are always there for our every squall and every minor victory. Soon we will be at the lake squalling together! C.D. Reiss, Lauren Blakely, TG, NCP, and JM—you all are in the front lines of our messiest, neediest selves. Thank you for all the advice, hard words, and encouragement.

Sixthly, to our beta readers who met Chase and Liv early on and guided and cheerleaded us: Roxie Madar, Liz Berry, JM, and Melanie Harlow, your enthusiasm made these characters so much fun to write. Who knew writing didn't have to be miserable?

And to our readers—all the people in Laurelin's Sky Launch, Sierra Simone's Lambs and to all the blogs who continue to support us (we see you!) and countless others. Without your cheering, fangirling and fantastic gifs, we'd be lost. Thank you!

And also to our husbands and families! To Sierra's husband, an actual hot cop (who only rolled his eyes a little at being constantly inundated with trivial questions) and to Laurelin's husband, a constant source of encouragement and nurturing. To our kids, who forgive their mommies for disappearing to write books. We love and adore you, and we do it all for you!

And finally, to our God. We thrive under your greening power, and we're constantly in awe of the lives of wonder and joy you've given us. Thanks and worship and peace. We can't wait to see your viriditas at work in the future. Amen.

MORE FROM LAURELIN PAIGE

With over 1 million books sold, Laurelin Paige is the *NY Times*, *Wall Street Journal*, and *USA Today* Bestselling Author of the Fixed Trilogy. She's a sucker for a good romance and gets giddy anytime there's kissing, much to the embarrassment of her three daughters. Her husband doesn't seem to complain, however. When she isn't reading or writing sexy stories, she's probably singing, watching *Game of Thrones* and *The Walking Dead*, or dreaming of Michael Fassbender. She's also a proud member of Mensa International though she doesn't do anything with the organization except use it as material for her bio. Find her at **laurelinpaige.com** or on Facebook in Laurelin Paige's Sky Launch.

The Dirty Universe
Dirty Filthy Rich Men (Dirty Duet #1) (March 27, 2017)
Dirty Filthy Rich Love (Dirty Duet #2) (September 11, 2017)
Dirty Filthy Fix (a spinoff novella) (November 7, 2017)
Dirty Wild Player (a spinoff novel) (2018)

The Fixed Universe
Fixed on You (Fixed #1)
Found in You (Fixed #2)
Forever with You (Fixed #3)
Fixed Trilogy Bundle (all three Fixed books in one bundle)
Hudson (a companion novel)
Free Me (Found duet #1)
Find Me (Found duet #2)
Chandler (a spinoff novel)
Falling Under You (a spinoff novella)

First and Last
First Touch
Last Kiss

Written with Kayti McGee under the name Laurelin McGee
Hot Alphas
Miss Match
Love Struck

Written with Sierra Simone
Porn Star
Hot Cop

MORE FROM SIERRA SIMONE

Sierra Simone is a *USA Today* Bestselling former librarian (who spent too much time reading romance novels at the information desk.) She lives with her husband and family in Kansas City. Find her at **authorsierrasimone.com** or on Facebook in Sierra Simone's Lambs.

The American Queen Trilogy:
American Queen
American Prince
American King (coming this fall)

The Priest Series:
Priest
Midnight Mass: A Priest Novella
Sinner (2017)

Co-Written with Laurelin Paige
Porn Star
Hot Cop

The Markham Hall Series:
The Awakening of Ivy Leavold
The Education of Ivy Leavold
The Punishment of Ivy Leavold
The Reclaiming of Ivy Leavold

The London Lovers:
The Seduction of Molly O'Flaherty
The Persuasion of Molly O'Flaherty
The Wedding of Molly O'Flaherty

CPSIA information can be obtained
at www.ICGtesting.com
Printed in the USA
LVHW021808131118
596990LV00001B/119/P